A Lissa Power Series

———

TRAVELING
A SLANT
RHYME

1973–1974

A Lissa Power Series

TRAVELING A SLANT RHYME

1973–1974

Christine Davis Merriman

GREEN WRITERS PRESS
Brattleboro, Vermont

Traveling a Slant Rhyme: 1973–1974 is a work of fiction. Apart from the actual historic figures, events, and locales that provide background for the narrative, all names, characters, places, and incidents are products of the author's imagination or are used fictitiously.

Printed in the United States

10 9 8 7 6 5 4 3 2 1

Green Writers Press is a Vermont-based publisher whose mission is to spread a message of hope and renewal through the words and images we publish. Throughout we will adhere to our commitment to preserving and protecting the natural resources of the earth. To that end, a percentage of our proceeds will be donated to environmental and social-activist groups. Green Writers Press gratefully acknowledges support from individual donors, friends, and readers to help support the environment and our publishing initiative. Green Place Books curates books that tell literary and compelling stories with a focus on writing about place—these books are more personal stories/memoir and biographies.

Giving Voice to Writers & Artists Who Will Make the World a Better Place
Green Writers Press | Brattleboro, Vermont
www.greenwriterspress.com

ISBN: 979-8-9870707-5-8

COVER PHOTO: URBAZON MEDIA/ISTOCKPHOTO

PRINTED ON PAPER WITH PULP THAT COMES FROM FSC-CERTIFIED FORESTS, MANAGED FORESTS
THAT GUARANTEE RESPONSIBLE ENVIRONMENTAL, SOCIAL, AND ECONOMIC PRACTICES.

For Richard, my brother

Who believed

that I could fly,

and gave me wings

so I could try

TRAVELING
A SLANT
RHYME

1973–1974

CHAPTER ONE

\ ſ

Arrival

*Upon reflection, I have found that truth makes its way to us, like
light through the many planes and angles of a prism—often fragmented, fractured, distorted by a multitude of human perspectives.
—Lissa's notebook*

C LERMONT-FERRAND, FRANCE, home of Michelin tires,
reposes in the bosom of the Massif Central, as if deposited, spewed out long ago by volcanoes that have gone
impotent. Puy-de-Dôme, an ancient lump of dead lava, broods
over the surrounding countryside, and tourists like officious ants
with cameras toil up a winding path for a view.

So, here I am in Clermont, in 1973. Having deposited me at
my destination, the Place de Regensburg, the taxi driver pulled
away, leaving me to stand alone, on my own two feet. I am
young, strong, and free. And I am American—a privilege I'm
just beginning to fathom. Twenty-two years old, I've survived
the death of both my parents—just recently that of my nine-
ty-four-year-old father—and am embarking on my junior year
abroad, as a French major, in a foreign student program at the
University's Faculty of Letters.

Lugging a solitary suitcase and wearing a vintage 1940s British fireman's jacket—coarse blue wool, NFS (for National Fire Service) embossed on its double-breasted silver buttons, I cross the square, posing as a brunette version of Jean Seberg in *Breathless*. I approach the dormitory—two looming concrete towers joined by a lobby on the *rez-de-chaussée*—press the entrance button, and the concierge buzzes me in through large glass doors. As I cross this foreign threshold, a curious vibration rises up my spine and explodes out the top of my head. A new door flies open, and through it shines a pure, white light—so very bright, and yet it doesn't hurt my eyes. I soar beyond the sheltered, once-upon-a-time upbringing bestowed by my elderly father (he was seventy-two years old when I was born!) to here, to now, where everything begins. Later, many years later, I will come to know this sensation as the *Shakti*, but for now, it is just a most beautiful manifestation of positive energy, a flight toward freedom.

From the time my mother died of breast cancer when I was just twelve years old, I have been my elderly father's closest companion and caregiver. Now he is gone, and thanks to my brother's generous funding, I have left the old Maryland farmhouse and have begun—with equal shares of exhilaration and trepidation—the journey to individuate, to find myself, to become.

From behind the barrier of a reception counter—after scrutinizing me, and then my passport, with exaggerated seriousness—a compact young woman introduces herself as Ghislaine. She greets me with a jovial smile and a jaunty Auvergnat "*bong-jour.*" Her twanging vowels and consonants catch me off guard—so different are they from the suave French I heard in Paris earlier today that I almost laugh. For "yes," she whistles what sounds like "*whheee*" or "*ouway*," instead of the simple "*oui*" my American professors taught me. Soon, I learn that Ghislaine grew up on a small poultry farm near the village of Mourjou. She has a penchant for teasing foreign students with puns. If we tell her, "*L'ascenseur ne marche pas*," meaning the elevator isn't working, she is likely to laugh at us and say, "*Mettez-lui des bottes!*" Put some boots on it!

Le Foyer, the dormitory, comprises two distinctly separated nine-story towers. These towers are home away from home to young workers from the surrounding countryside who've landed jobs in Clermont. I'm one of just a handful of foreign student residents here. The front desk staff in the lobby closely monitor, round the clock, the gender-designated stairwells and elevators. Only males may enter the stairwell or the elevator on the right. Only females are permitted in the stairwell or the elevator on the left.

My room, on the sixth floor of the girls' tower, is equipped with a sink and something that looks like a toilet without a lid, which I mistakenly pee in just after I arrive. Later, I learn from one of the French girls down the hall that, in France, it's customary to have a bidet in the bathroom. I look up bidet in the dictionary and learn that, traditionally, women use bidets to wash their private parts. After that, I notice that some girls keep their bidets covered—almost as if to disguise the intended purpose. A flat, custom-fitted sheet of plywood placed on top of the bidet transforms it into a practical platform where they can set miscellaneous toiletries. I don't have easy access to a washing machine—appliances seem to be in scarce supply here in France. So, I wind up using my bidet as a convenient place to soak my dirty laundry. The shower (*la douche*) and the toilet (*WC*) are down the hall.

Soon after I've settled in, I hear a knock at my door.

"*Toc, toc.*"

A full-figured blonde girl with cornflower blue eyes (very pretty) has come to welcome me.

"Hello, I'm Beatrix. I saw the nameplate, Lissa Power, on your door, and thought you must be English." Beatrix, I learn, comes from England's Lake District, and is enrolled in a four-month program to learn about conducting business in France. I guess, in an attempt to be helpful, the staff placed me in a room next to another English-speaking student.

The room rent comes with breakfast, fresh weekly linens for our cots, and maid service. Next morning over breakfast, Beatrix introduces me to her fellow student, Dorothy, a dark-haired, determinedly proper girl from a good family that owns a hotel in Bath.

For breakfast we serve ourselves on trays, choosing between a large bowl of *café au lait* or hot chocolate along with croissants, jam, and butter.

"So, this is the charming French cuisine everyone natters on about." Dorothy wrinkles her nose in disdain.

"Dorothy is posh, you know," Beatrix teases. "Speaks only the Queen's English. Don't you, old girl?"

Dorothy purses her lips, busies herself reviewing the selection of jams, apparently choosing not to dignify Beatrix's comment with a response, and finally, with an air of resignation, chooses the *confiture de myrtilles*.

We sequester ourselves at the far end of the dining hall. Seated together at a small table, we observe the young French residents.

"Blimey!" says Beatrix. "Leave it to the Frenchies to slurp their coffee from a bowl. Look, they even smear jam on the bread first, then dip it. What a slimy concoction that is."

I don't say anything. I don't do the jam dipping thing, but I do like sipping my *café au lait* from a bowl and savoring bites of crusty French bread. An enchanting change from the bowl of bland oatmeal back home.

Always an early riser, I get into the habit of waking my two British friends in time for breakfast, which is served from six to nine A.M. I'm usually out of the *douche* by six thirty. I dress quickly in corduroy pants and sweater, run up three flights of stairs to the ninth floor, and rap on Dorothy's door. She usually responds right away. Then I run back down to the sixth floor and knock on Beatrix's door. It can take a bit of knocking and calling to elicit a response from Beatrix, especially if she's been out drinking with her mates the night before. Sometimes she's annoyed with me for waking her, but later she thanks me; she appreciates not missing breakfast.

~~~

During my second week in Clermont, I venture outside the dorm to take care of some business and do some shopping. I walk everywhere. First, to Crédit Lyonnais to set up the checking account where my brother, Spence, will be sending monthly deposits. The staff here are very friendly, and it bolsters my confidence to discover that my French is good enough to get me through these basic financial transactions.

Next, I head out to Place de Jaude. I need to buy a hair dryer (didn't think to pack one). My self-styled, intentionally boyish haircut is beginning to grow out. Anyway, the voltage is different here, and it will be good to get something not American-made. Along the way, I pass Jardin Lecoq, a park right in the middle of the city, and glimpse a pavilion restaurant rising above a pond. Ducks swim in the pond and waddle around the edges in search of dropped crumbs. Two graceful swans float by, performing an effortless *pas de deux*.

In passing, I salute—discreetly, mind you—the statue of Vercingétorix. In my head, I call him "Big V" because he dominates Clermont's major shopping square. According to my Michelin guide, he's carved in bronze by the same sculptor who created America's Statue of Liberty. Mounted on his valiant steed, waving a mighty sword, he goes on defending Gaul, the ancient French nation, from Julius Caesar's encroaching armies.

I head over to the Galeries de Jaude, the iconic department store Ghislaine recommended for me this morning. It's hard to miss: white stone façade sprawling along the square's eastern flank, crammed into limited space. Impressive architecture, yet something challenges the eye's logic. Aha! I see it now. The grand tower that rises to circumscribe the building's left perimeter has no twin sister on the right. It leaves me feeling off balance somehow.

Even so, once inside, I do find what I need—a small portable hair dryer in a compact black vinyl case with a snap closure. Wired for local outlets. Easy to pack. Yes, I will buy it!

I exit the store, carrying my small but significant purchase with an inordinate sense of accomplishment. In the past, I would have consulted with Daddy or my brother, asking permission to buy something for myself. But now, here in France, I make my own choices and take full responsibility for my actions. Sartre himself would be proud of me! Or should I say, instead, I'm proud of *myself*?

The purchase is one small step for this latently intrepid young woman. A minor enough transaction, trivial perhaps—nothing as grand as that first step Neil Armstrong took on the moon—but important to me. A symbol, I hope, of many giant leaps to come. Daddy insisted the moon landing was a hoax, but my fashionable new dress boots—a last-minute parting gift Spence stuffed into my carry-on bag at the airport departure gate—resonate here on foreign soil, confirming each new step I take in Clermont.

Finally, I walk along boulevard Gergovia to the *Faculté de Lettres* to register for my courses. The foreign student registrar—attractive and welcoming—is in touch with Dr. Albert, the French professor I have back home, and my paperwork goes smoothly.

As I turn to leave, I find myself face to face with the next person in line, a tall man. Ginger hair and mustache. Rheumy sea gray eyes struggle to swim into focus behind thick horn-rimmed glasses. Everything about him is awkward, all elbows and knees in a three-piece tweed suit with brown suede elbow patches.

His French, it seems, is very limited. When the registrar hands him the forms and asks for his information, he pulls a small dictionary from his pocket and attempts to form a response.

"*Je . . . je . . . j'ai . . . besoin. . . .*" I . . . I . . . I have . . . need . . . His French pronunciation is atrocious.

The registrar exchanges a comical look with me.

In desperation, he thrusts his passport at her, slapping it down on the desk in front of her. He's a Danish citizen.

The registrar pages through the passport and exchanges another look with me—still humorous but now gentle.

"*Peut-être il parle anglais?*" Maybe he speaks English?

I give it a go.

"Hello, do you speak English?"

"Ah! Yes!" With a release of pent-up breath and a grateful smile, the Danish man extends a confirming handshake.

"Maybe I can assist you," I say.

"Yes! Yes!" he replies, and a clarity of shared communication surfaces in his watery eyes.

The entire exchange is conducted in the most rudimentary English and French, tripping over grammar, and teetering around keywords like registration, tuition, schedule, and receipt. But I do manage to help this man—one Oscar Andersen, a kipper salesman from Copenhagen—complete his registration for beginning-level French courses. We part with ample smiles, a flourish of thank yous and *mercis*. A smallish leap, perhaps, for mankind?

In October, after my first two weeks in Clermont, I walk to the *fac* for the first day of classes, take a seat at the desk next to a dark-haired woman, and size up the other students. I'm one of fifteen registrants in this semester's international French letters program—intermediate level.

When called on in class, we speak French with varying accents—Greek, Turkish, Italian, Spanish, Polish, Danish, Scottish, English, and American—and with varying degrees of proficiency. I'm more comfortable writing French than speaking it, and—out of shyness and laziness—make the mistake of forming too many friendships with English-speaking students. Besides my English friends at the dorm, I hang out with American and Scottish classmates from the *fac*—Trudy, whose husband works for Michelin, and Clare, a red-headed spitfire from Dalgety Bay.

As the week passes, I rotate through the foreign student classes—French literature, conversation, civilization, language lab, and grammar—conducted in various buildings on the center-city campus.

For French lit, we read passages from classic French writers and engage in excruciating, paragraph-by-paragraph analysis of the text, *explication de texte,* with a pleasantly condescending French professor, Madame Vachon, a plump woman of a certain age. Our conversation classes are, thankfully, more informal, relaxed discussions of current newspaper articles, conducted by M. Bonhomme, a friendly, balding man with a trim mustache and an encouraging demeanor.

Our civilization professor, Monsieur Rossignol (Mr. Nightingale) enters in a flurry, chest puffed out under a green woolen vest, full head of hair combed back, and fluffy beard—I can't help thinking how much he resembles his namesake, the nightingale. During his lecture, M. Rossignol flits back and forth in front of us—bouncing lightly, toe to heel, and tapping, ever so delicately with a long, tapered pointer, at a series of pictures projected from slides. He shows us maps, graphs, and photos of new architecture surging up throughout the city—sturdy offices, solid apartment buildings (modern, utilitarian, concrete)—bragging about the city's amazing spurt of economic growth since World War II. Occasionally, he alights, gripping a wooden podium with tight, curled fingers, to summarize key points of his lecture.

Later my American classmate, Trudy, will point out to me the absurdity of his claims. "Of course, there's been a huge growth in the building industry! Had to replace all the old stuff that got destroyed during the war. Reconstruction! Clear out the rubble! Rebuild with ugly gray concrete!"

Language lab is scheduled, unfortunately, after lunch. Here I sit in a booth, plugged into a headset and microphone among the other foreign students, listening to and repeating French phrases, practicing phonetics. I'm half asleep from my lunch (this is before I learn to take advantage of the midday break to tank up on espresso at the student café) when the linguistics professor listens in to my exercise. "You're speaking in a monotone," his disembodied voice reprimands me through my headset. I stir myself from my stupor and try to speak more clearly.

Grammar class is held in an ancient-looking stone building,

overheated by bursts of whistling steam, yet damp and musty as a dungeon around the ankles. The grandfatherly professor drones on about the appropriate usages of varying forms of the past tense: *passé compose, imparfait, passé simple, plus-que-parfait*. He intersperses his lecture with grammar jokes and plays on words, most of which are lost on me. When he smiles and pauses at what he intends to be a punchline, I force myself to laugh, all the while imagining myself chained to the dank wall of a medieval *oubliette*, rotting away, as centuries seem to pass before the class is over.

Lunches and dinners are at the Resto, the student cafeteria, a massive building that serves crowds of hungry students. An impatient horde, they gather pulsing at the entrance, wait for the doors to open, then surge through, pushing, all at once. When I run into Beatrix there, she complains, "Bloomin' Frenchies. Don't even know how to queue up, now do they?"

Here food is served on larger trays than those we use for break-fast at the dorm. Here you can take as many chunks of bread as you want from tall bins at the end of the counter. Some Arab students are so poor they take extra bread back with them to hoard in their dorm rooms. There's water, but you can also buy a small bottle of wine to go with your meal if you like. That surprises me. I grew up in a household where alcohol was forbidden.

When the Resto is open, twice a day, at midday and evening, I slide into a spot at one of the long tables. Over the weeks, I watch and learn. French students wash their cherries by swirling them in small glasses of water. Apples are peeled and sliced before eating. The only Resto food I don't like is beef liver and tripe, but I've learned I can always give those to Zytka, one of my Polish classmates. She is a big-boned blonde chemistry student who eats whatever she's offered. Guess I'm a spoiled American.

Whenever I enter or exit the Resto, I pass a large café that opens onto the lobby. Each time I pass, I take a quick glance inside. The menu board behind the counter offers substantially cheaper coffee than what's on tap at other more intimate cafés I've visited in Clermont and the patrons here are more diverse.

Cafés, I'm learning, often attract, promote, and cater to an identity-driven clientele—locals or expats or students or businessmen—familiars. Cafés collect regulars who gather to relax over an espresso, tacitly in the company of their own kind. The Resto café resonates with international student life.

But what intrigues me most is the group of Arab students, gathered around a table at the café's far reaches, always apart from the other university students. All male, these Arabs exude a differentness that draws me to them. But, for now, I pass by, resisting the Arab table's pull, not ready yet to cross a certain boundary, to rupture a certain barrier. And certainly, I'm too shy to introduce myself to these strangers. No Arabs attend my international classes at the *fac*.

Over the first few weeks, I continue to hang out, after class and on weekends, primarily with an English-speaking group. We gather at a student-friendly café—about halfway between the Resto and the dorm—that's run by a middle-aged French couple. It has a table large enough to accommodate our group and a wonderful old jukebox offers an eclectic selection—Louis Armstrong, David Bowie, Jacques Brel. Besides my British dorm friends, Beatrix and Dorothy, there's a guy from Leeds. His real name is Arthur, but the locals have dubbed him Parapluie because he wears his long, frizzy hair combed out in all directions from the center. It hovers over his head like a quirky brown umbrella. Coupled with his bizarre hairdo, Parapluie's sallow skin, severe acne, and awkward behavior make him the butt of most of the group's jokes.

Then there's Danny from Manchester: compact, muscular, cocky, proud. Although all the Brits in this group are working class, it's only Beatrix and Danny who seem to embrace their upbringing. Beneath the shadow of his wide-ranging hair, Parapluie hangs his head, mutters, mumbles, and seems ashamed of everything about himself. Dorothy, it's clear, would like to be associating with a more refined social group.

Sometimes, Clare, my Scottish classmate at the *fac*, joins us at the café. Her hair is bright orange, her pale skin freckled, her eyes a glacial gray. Clare's rapid-fire Scot's burr is so thick the other Brits can't understand her half the time. I've gotten used to Clare's accent and have to translate. When Clare gets revved up, she talks so fast that saliva fizzes out around her lips. "Growing up, they used to call me Fizzy," she tells us.

Sometimes, if the Resto's closed on a weekend, Beatrix, Dorothy, and I join Clare for lunch or dinner in her third-floor walk-up a few blocks from the dorm. We all chip in for a round loaf of dark French country bread, local cheese (aged in barns outside the city, some with the straw still sticking to the rind), and wine.

If it's dark when we leave Clare's place, we press a button outside her door to illuminate the stairwell, then rush down narrow steps to push the button at the next landing before the light automatically clicks off.

On weekends when Clare's not available, we fall back on small plastic containers of Yoplait. We keep them chilled on the dorm's wide, concrete window ledges.

~~~

On weekends, Beatrix is always on the lookout for a party, which she calls a *do*. According to her, the French are far too serious; they don't know how to have fun. As we leave the Resto on a Friday afternoon, Beatrix notes a hand-drawn sign advertising something called *la boum* in large, bright letters.

"Oh, so that's what they call a *do* here, a *boum*! We should go, have a good time, improve our French. As they say, '*Il faut faire un effort,*' right, Dots . . . Dorothy? What say you, Lissa?"

Of course, we can't figure out how to find the *boum*. The sign includes no contact information. So, instead, on a blustery Friday night, I find myself pub hopping with my English friends. Clare joins us. She lives the way she talks, going at life a mile a minute, determined to seize any adventure that presents itself. As for me, I'm not much of a drinker, can barely finish off one tall mug of beer. But with nothing else to do for the evening, I tag along like a gullible puppy. Beatrix decides it would be fun to teach me some German. Says she knows more German than French.

"Lissa, just repeat this after me, *Ich bin blau*."

"*Ich bin blau*," I say. I have no idea what I just said, but Danny seems to think it's pretty funny. He's already downed quite a few pints of beer, and now pounds the table in our wooden booth, shakes his head, and laughs so hard that tears course down his cheeks.

"What's so funny?" I ask him. What did I say?"

"You just announced to the world that you're drunk as a skunk, me darlin'."

"Means 'pissed out of your mind' in German," Clare chimes in.

Dorothy adds a dignified nod to confirm and continues to sip politely at her beer. But then, in an uncharacteristic burst of spontaneity, perhaps brought on by the alcohol, Dorothy raises her mug and offers a toast, "I dub us the Oxies. That's short for Oxymorons. Undoubtedly, we would *never* have had anything to do with one another if circumstances and a common mother tongue had not forced us together. We are joined in our mutual struggle to survive the galling—no pun intended—Frenchness of Clermont."

Danny grins as he raises his glass. "More like the Oxford morons, I'd say." But the name Oxies sticks.

When we get up from our booth to move on to the next bar, Clare finishes off her beer and stuffs the empty ceramic stein into my leather shoulder bag. "I've taken a fancy to it," she says. You'll pinch it for me, won't you?" And so, I find myself slipping out into an unaccustomed night air, shamefully lugging stolen merchandise—something I never thought I would do. Here, in Clermont, I feel myself transforming into something foreign, entering previously forbidden territory. A phantasmagoric face, the image of my father, angered and disapproving, rises before me. But on I trudge, defiant, led on by new friendships. I follow blindly along the foreign city's landscape. Danny leads the

Oxies down a narrow alleyway toward an older bar that seems to crouch like a primal urge poised to unleash itself. We enter.

Beatrix finds a table and I look for a place to pee. Here, behind a narrow door, I find myself inside a smelly chamber. A dim ceiling light reveals two large, dirty white ceramic footprints above a darkened pool of water. I stand on them to relieve myself. My urine, frothy from the beer, flows between my legs and enters uncharted waters below. When I am finished, I pull the cord that dangles from the ceiling. I watch as waters roil like Charybdis beneath my straddled feet and are swallowed into an unseen abyss below.

～

The next night Beatrix and Dorothy invite me to go with them to a local dance hall. They hope to make some new friends, improve their French, and learn some new dances. Beatrix is looking for some fresh entertainment to keep her mind off Dave, the boyfriend back home she's been pining away for.

"I'm keeping my eye out for a good-looking French bloke who can give me a more intimate introduction to French culture, if you catch my meaning," she says and gives me a knowing wink. "Why not come with us, Lissa? You know what they say, *'Il faut faire un effort.'*"

But I'm still feeling raw and exposed from yesterday evening's adventures. So, I yield to the shyness that characterizes me better than the daring persona I've been experimenting with. Taking a more scholarly—and admittedly cowardly—approach to learning French, I hole up in my dorm room and read some Guy de Maupassant and Balzac. After a while, I pull out a notebook and try to sketch out my future. But what I come up with is a chaotic scrawling of lines intersecting, crossing, opposing, going every which way. I add labels to signify goals and possible directions. I scribble a riot of words followed by question marks: Greatness? Failure? Everywhere? Nowhere? Anything? Everything? Nothing? Famous writer? Rich? Alive? Unknown? Alone?

Officially, this is my junior year abroad and my coursework in Clermont goes toward my French major back home in the States. But, to be honest, I'm here—far away from home, removed from my native culture, wonderfully anonymous—to travel, see the world, and write about it. I aspire to become the next great American expatriate writer. I'm determined to take off the narrow blinders I've grown up with, and maybe shed some inhibitions. And yes, I have to admit it, I've come here to lose my virginity.

CHAPTER TWO

❧ ❧

Virginity Lost

"She had come to France for this." —Lissa's short story

O N A FRIDAY EVENING in October, heading back to the
dorm after dinner at the Resto, I spot a man who is
young, but not quite so young as I am. He stands on
the corner, just outside a popular café. Handsome, feral. With
wisps of fine black hair caught and displaced by gusts of a rising breeze. Tight pants, a fitted leather jacket, collar turned up
against invasive huffs of wind. He is decidedly foreign, decidedly
attractive, and I find myself staring at him. He stares back at me.
But his eyes are fathomless, revealing nothing of himself, only an
enigmatic reflection of myself.

I continue walking, intending to go past this man, cross the
street, and continue on to the dorm. But my eyes are locked
on his.

"*Est-ce qu'on veut du café?*" Does one want coffee? That's all
he says.

"*Oui.*" That's all I say. Then, drawn to this complete stranger, I
follow him down several steps to a terrace beneath a red awning.

We take seats at a small round table. He orders two coffees, and I study his face. Its perfect proportions overwhelm me, and I find it difficult to speak. At first I just listen to him while I sip my coffee, savoring his long, thick eyelashes.

He tells me his French name is Georges. He tells me his Arabic name, too, but I don't quite catch it. He says he's from Beirut and that he's in Clermont studying to be a doctor.

I don't tell him much about myself, just that I'm American, a student at the university.

When we get up to leave, Georges asks me where I live. I tell him, and he walks me back to the dorm. He invites me to take a drive with him tomorrow, to see the countryside. He kisses me goodnight, a French kiss, his tongue exploring deep inside my mouth. I break away, startled at the sensations this arouses, and hurry back inside to the safety of the dorm in the girls' tower.

On Saturday afternoon, I meet Georges, as we agreed. He is waiting downstairs for me, in the lobby of the *rez-de-chausée*. I find him playing chess with Junjei, a fellow student in my international student classes at the *fac*. Junjei is from Hong Kong.

George and Junjei sit opposite each other, heads bent over a chessboard. Georges's hair forms a dark cirrus cloud around his face. He has a creamy brown complexion, strong cheekbones, and a thick black mustache above a determined mouth. His hands move quickly, with discipline and precision.

Junjei's skin is pale. He has a round face, smooth features, full lips. His straight black hair is parted in the middle and cascades to his shoulders. With its absence of facial hair, Junjei's face appears innocent, open. His expression remains passive, divulging nothing. His hand movements are gentle and flowing.

Sunlight projects through tall windows, casting a soft blue sheen on Junjei's hair, making Georges's skin glow like polished mahogany, and clarifying the positions of the small black and white figures poised mid-battle on the chessboard.

"Checkmate," says Junjei quietly.

Georges notices me standing nearby, gets up abruptly, and greets me. "My car is parked just over there," he says in French, pointing toward a beat-up Citroën parked at the curb outside.

He drives us into the mountains surrounding Clermont, toward Mont-Dore. The day is unseasonably warm. We stop beside a sailboat lake and gaze out, our eyes not meeting. I don't know the lake's name. It, like me, remains aloof, anonymous. A solitary sailboat scuds past, its white sails piercing the deep blue sky. The lake water sparkles, waves lap at a grassy embankment. We take only a step or two from the car before heading back to Georges's room in the medical student residence. I pass the rest of the day dissociating, watching, as if in a dream, a young woman opening her body willingly to a man she scarcely knows.

～～～

In the evening, Georges drives me back to my dorm. A song comes on his car radio, the Rolling Stones' *Angie*. He sings it to me, imitating the English lyrics. Hearing him use English is sweet to me. It makes me want to love him. But it also makes me sad because, even though we have been intimate, he is still a stranger to me. I feel no closeness. He drops me off. No kiss this time. We agree to meet here next weekend.

Later that night, alone in my dorm room, I try to process what just happened. I imagine Daddy standing over me, furious that his daughter had sex out of wedlock—and with a foreigner! My father's old-fashioned values assault me. Feeling ashamed and repentant, I try to cope by scribbling my thoughts and feelings. I write in one of those odd French notebooks, the pages delineated not with lines but with small squares, like graph paper. But then, again, so much is odd to me here. My scribbling becomes a disturbing fantasy. It goes like this:

Arabian Night–Fall 1973

She dreamed a white-robed stranger guiding in single file a caravan, a shimmering procession approaching, forming a right angle beneath a vertical blade of sun; the connection between herself and the sun-point a projected and logical hypotenuse. She had come to France for this.

So now she walked a dark French night's sidewalk with a strange man who spoke in spartan French and rolled his "r's" too roundly. They walked. He offered. Her lips formed vague protestations, but she continued walking in step with him, away from both their previous destinations.

The afternoon of the next day, this stranger, whose name is Georges, waited for her downstairs, playing chess with Junjei, a student from Hong Kong. Georges's hair, very fine and wispy, formed a cloud around his brown face. He had a mustache and smoked a Gauloise.

The stranger's hands were strong and square, their movements sure and swift over the chessboard and to and from the ash can. The fingers of the right hand gripped securely the pawns, the queen; those of the left hand pinched hard on the cigarette, from time to time flicking sharply at its tip, cutting off the ashes.

Junjei won the chess game quietly.

She followed Georges to his car, a battered "voiture d'étudiant," a student's car. He drove a winding road, mounting a rocky plateau of Auvergne. He stopped for gas. She watched from the passenger seat. He stood by the gas pump unfolding his wallet. He looked very foreign.

She dreamed a Hollywood dream of robed and turbaned oil sheiks, with kohl-lined eyes set in sun-baked faces.

This strange man wore a soiled white shirt, a cheap and sweat-filled tweed suitcoat, and rumpled gray trousers stained at the crotch.

They continued farther up into the mountains, toward Mont-Dore. He parked beside a sailboat lake. The stranger made advances—curiously universal these advances. She accepted, clumsily. He was, after all, still a stranger.

"Trop de monde ici," said Georges, too many people here, and he drove back down the mountain to his room in the medical complex.

Panicking on the voyage down to the narrow student cot, she babbled a crippled French phrase, attempting to connect with his medical background.

"J'aime les génétiques!" I like genetics!" She was afraid, and she felt stupid.

Her reason raced to form the first-time foreign words, to make him understand. "Je suis vierge! Tu comprends? Je ne veux pas devenir . . . enceinte, pregnant. Tu comprends?"

Georges got a condom.

"Ne pousses pas," he said.

Stalemate.

Georges poured himself some whiskey and offered some to her. She did not accept. He drank.

She asked, "Are you disappointed?"

"In me?"

"No, in me."

He finished the whiskey. "No. Do you want to play chess?"

"No. Not now."

"Do you want a cigarette?"

"No."

"You don't smoke? That's very good for the health."

"No. I don't do anything."

He told her he wanted to be a surgeon or a psychiatrist. She told him she wanted to be a writer.

They spoke of war—the Middle-East War. She said she hated war, not knowing what war was. He said he hated war to answer her expectations—a painless, detached gift. He said he wanted to become a doctor so he could save lives, not destroy them—a Trojan gift. She accepted.

"Do you want something to eat?"

"Yes."

"Do you like poulet?"

"What?"

"Poulet."

She shook her head. I don't understand.

"I don't know how to explain. Poulet." He flapped his arms and cackled.

"Oh, chicken. Yes, I like chicken."

"Moitié-moitié. Ten francs each."

"Oh . . ." She gave him the ten francs. "Is that enough?"

"Yes."

The stranger left and she explored his room, explored her first lover. On the desk was a copy of Le Monde *with headlines about Arab-Israeli flare-ups and US intervention. On the shelf by the sink an elastic arm-muscle exerciser and a pair of soiled bright-colored bikini jockey shorts; above the bed a stack of dusty notebooks—piled high. She took the top one down, sat* cross-legged on the bed—she was still naked—and stared at a red-ink diagram of the human pancreas.

Georges came back and saw her on the bed. He smiled.

He cooked for her—not chicken—but spiced, fried sausage. He handed her four tomatoes, told her to wash them. She washed them, one by one, quite carefully, and laid them in a row. The Arab did not have a knife. He used the handle of a spoon to open the baguette.

She called him "le chirugien."

He made a sausage sandwich, broke the bread, wrapped each half in a page of Le Monde, and gave her half. The sausage grease dripped onto the floor. They sat opposite, each taking huge dripping bites over the wastebasket. They ate the tomatoes whole and swallowed mouthfuls of cheap red wine.

Georges pointed to the nearly empty bottle.

"Do you want more wine?"

"No. That's for you. Do you want this?" She offered him the remainder of her sandwich.

"No. Do you want to lie down?"

"Yes."

She dreamed sand beaches and cobalt waters lapping, bright sun-stabbed colors, striped caravan tents, brown skins mingling, and then a timeless burial beneath shifting waves of sand-grit and piercing sun. . . .

She sat up sweating, feeling moist and sticky in unaccustomed places.

Georges sat at the window, straddling a backward-facing chair, smoking, striking a formidable pose.

She dreamed deep-cornered, mazed pyramids and cryptic alphabets curling thickly right to left.

Suddenly he broke the pose, said he would take her home now; he had to sleep.

And she obeyed, rising from the bed into the heavy air. She could see molecules fusing, splitting, and floating in independent globules. Behind and somewhat beneath her, the cot was stained red.

"You see," she said and raised her face to him, "I really was a virgin."

He drove her to her dorm and borrowed twenty francs for gas, said he would come back next Friday if she could lend him more.

Some later time she would laugh a hard, face-cracking laugh, would *laugh to see inscribed for an instant, chiseled on shifting, corroding sand walls, the magic lantern frieze of a deluded American in France, presenting money for gas to a hieroglyphic Arab. She would see in parodied panorama the oil-rich Middle East bleeding a dreaming America into a soiled, bed-sheeted France.*

But now she dreamed of distant nomads and camel caravans marching away—a wavering sunset mirage. And then an empty desert.

On the following weekend, late Friday afternoon, Georges comes to meet me, as we had agreed. Just before the appointed time, he arrives. I see him from my dorm window, six stories down, waiting on the terrace, hunched against the cold and smoking a cigarette, his back to me. From this elevation, he seems so distant, so foreign. I am afraid to go out with him again. As I watch, daylight wanes, streetlights go on, and Georges fades into an anonymous silhouette, a dark figure isolated in a pool of yellow lamplight. So, I close the blinds, crawl into my cot, and pull the sheet and blanket over my head.

The maid—looking like a Modigliani portrait I've seen somewhere before— arrives next morning to change the linen. She has a Mediterranean complexion, a black uniform with white collar, and a thin face carried at an angle above her long neck. She finds me still cocooned in bed.

I rouse myself and poke out my head. She drops her stack of clean sheets, stifles a scream, and clutches at her chest. I hear her say, quite distinctly, in English, "Junjei's dead!" But my mind misleads me, racing ahead of itself.

As the maid peers closely at my face, she speaks in French, as of course she would. "*Mon dieu, mademoiselle! Je pensais que vous étiez morte!*" I thought you were dead!

I leap out of bed and ask, "What day is it?" The cleaning woman stares back, mouth twisted across her face, unable to answer.

Desperate for fresh air, I rush from the confinement of my narrow student bed and leave the maid behind to do her cleanup.

⟩ ⸙

CHAPTER THREE

Delicate Illusions Shattered

"I'd be careful if I was you, Lissa." —*Danny's warning*

I N 1973, on the Jewish High Holy Day of Yom Kippur and during the Muslim holy month of Ramadan, an Arab coalition led by Egypt and Syria launches a surprise attack on Israeli positions. Through most of October 1973, the cafés buzz with news of this intense Arab-Israeli War.

The day of October 30, 1973, marks my father's birthday and less than one year since his death last December. In the evening, the clouds above Clermont lower and a sudden wind assaults me as I make my way to dinner, up the incline from dorm to student cafeteria. I clutch the single piece of mail that came for me today, the *Grangerville Chatter*, my rural hometown's community newsletter. Mail from back home is rare, typically just a letter or two each month.

"La poste, est-ce qu'elle est arrivée? Est-ce qu'il y a du poste pour moi, aujourd'hui?" That's what I ask Ghislaine at the front desk every day. Is there any mail for me today?

So now, afraid that an aggressive squall will wrest from me this precious news from home, I tuck the *Chatter* deep into my jacket's inner pocket.

A sudden pelting of heavy drops splatters on my head and shoulders. Then the vaults of heaven burst open, releasing buckets of rainwater on the city. The sidewalk, once a pale and solid gray, is darkened by rivulets that flow beneath my feet. It's as if the sharp twin towers of the Cathédrale Notre-Dame-de-l'Assomption have at last pierced the rain clouds, ruptured the sky, and released the tears of a thousand grieving angels.

I run the final block, head bent into the driving rain, take shelter inside the Resto, and wipe my eyes to clear my vision. The thick wool of my fireman's jacket, having sucked up as much water as it can hold, weighs heavy on my shoulders and now drips down my pantlegs. The fancy dress boots ooze diluted black polish, leaving a trail of footprints across the floor of the Resto lobby, an embarrassing reprise of an earlier pathway of shame. You see, in second grade, too timid to ask permission to use the restroom, I wet myself at my small wooden desk. And when the bell for recess forced me to get up and walk to the playground, my very own shoes betrayed me, tracing damp prints that followed me accusingly across the classroom's black and gray linoleum floor tiles.

Now I trudge through the propped-open double doors into the communal dining hall. At this hour, the immense institutional hall is keenly alive with the voices of hundreds of university students, the babel of many nations. I slide my metal tray along the railing and pause to reach across the countertop to accept the plate of beefsteak and *pommes frites* offered to me by a pink-faced, cheery food worker who wears a starched white uniform. As I hand my meal ticket over to the cashier, I spot my English friends at a table near the front, not far from the food line. Beatrix greets me with a shout of recognition and a merry wave and Dorothy grimaces disapprovingly at my dripping jacket.

I slide into a space next to Beatrix, inspect the newsletter from home, and am relieved to see that it's still legible, just a bit damp around the edges. Glad I had the foresight to tuck it inside my jacket before the downpour. But as soon as I set the *Grangerville Chatter* aside to eat my dinner, Beatrix giggles, snatches up the newsletter, and begins shuffling through its pages, which are roughly typed and crudely duplicated on coarse pale green paper. She reads aloud from the announcements section, trying to put on a folksy American accent, cracking up over the funny-sounding American names.

"Reba and Ernest Frack are proud new parents of a baby boy, Freddie."

Dorothy makes a face. "Oh, splendid! Growing up to be called Fred Frack! Can you imagine?"

Beatrix chuckles and continues. "Keep your eyes on the road and your hands on the wheel, neighbors. Viola Davenport just got her learner's permit.

"Otha Teasdale will be hosting the Grangerville Women's Sewing Circle at seven p.m. on Saturday, November 10. The ladies will be knitting and stuffing Christmas stockings for the orphans at Children's Village.

"Congratulations to Freed Mason. Freed will be replacing Rufus Dewey as Fire Chief at the Grangerville Volunteer Fire Department. Rufus will be taking a well-earned retirement after forty years of service to the community."

"Well, I say cheers to Old Rufus. No more singed britches for you, eh?" says Danny as he makes his way over to the institutional bread bins, stacked just past the cashier's station. Here seemingly limitless thick slices of *pain* wait to fill the stomachs of hungry students. I am reminded of the Arab students who routinely stop at these bins on their way out, stuff their pockets with wads of bread to hoard in their dorm rooms above the Resto. This bread will tide them over between meals and during weekends.

As I finish my meal, I see Georges for the first time in weeks. He's just exiting the food line, carrying a dinner tray. He follows close behind a fashionably dressed young woman, a redhead in high heels. He looks thinner, oddly meek and obedient as he trails just a few steps behind her. They sit five tables away. Heads together, intimate, they converse, seemingly aware only of each other.

As I sneak glances over at them, I feel jealous and regretful. I watch as this Frenchwoman whispers indecipherable phrases to Georges that seem to seduce and keep him under her sway. I imagine her as a voracious little red coquette, a female bird of prey, deceptively petite, who plucks at, rips open, and relentlessly consumes the exposed flesh of my first real lover. Losing him to another has made him dear to me. The narrow confines of my own social and moral inhibitions have kept me bound, causing me to deny myself a relationship with a man who attracts me so viscer- ally. At my first taste of a foreign and forbidden desire, I had shut the door. I had let this chance at freedom and adventure, the very things I had come to France to find, slip away. Seeing Georges so deeply engaged with another woman awakens my frustration. Why have I been so timid? I hate this polished Frenchwoman, this well-groomed redhead who takes for herself that which I have denied myself. She is my opposite, the opposing queen on my chessboard.

❧

After dinner, I stop in at the student café just off the Resto entry- way, purposely pulling away from my English friends. I'm trying to avoid the temptation to speak English, trying to immerse myself in the local student culture. This café, so convenient to the Resto, is frequented by Arab students, many of whom are home- sick, poor, and friendly. Over the weeks, I've begun to come here for a coffee, especially on those lonely afternoons and evenings when I find myself missing Georges, and have begun to gravitate more and more to the Arab table. It was Mohammed, I think, who first called me over to sit with them. And since then, they have all welcomed me.

Today, as I enter, their greeting rises like a chant from their table near the back. They pound the table, shout, *"Amérique, Amérique! Ça va, Amérique?"*

Three are from Syria, and two are from Lebanon. The Syrian brothers—Mohammed, with sparse light-brown hair and goatee, and blond Ibrahim—have sallow complexions. Mohammed is an aspiring artist with a sensitive demeanor. Extremely thin, his face a pale shade of gray like finely powdered ashes, he stays wired on back-to-back demitasses of heavily sugared espresso. Ibrahim chain smokes, jokes a lot, and coughs fitfully over his espresso. Their cousin, Yusuf, is darker, younger, healthier-looking, and actually a bit chubby. Paul, from Beirut, oversees young students at a boys' dormitory, sports a bushy beard and a beret, proclaims himself a Marxist, and waylays the conversation with unresolvable political and philosophical polemics. Latif, also from Beirut, has a gentle manner and seems serious about his future.

"So, *Amérique*, why does Israel drop bombs on us?" Ibrahim asks. "We are peaceful artisans. My father makes shoes. My mother weaves carpets."

"Yes, why, *Amérique*?" Yusuf chimes in. "My family was at dinner when the bombs fell. We hid under the kitchen table. We are farmers in a small village. We have no wish for violence. We just want to grow our wheat, raise our sheep, harvest our olives."

I have no answer to give them. I just sit with these friends, hoping that maybe Georges will stop in after dinner. But he doesn't come, and I torture myself with images of him, back in his dorm room in the medical complex, having sex with the redhead. In my mind, she becomes *la coquette rouge*. I christen her Coco Rouge.

~

On a sunny, brisk mid-afternoon, the first Saturday in November, I stroll along boulevard Lafayette with Beatrix and Dorothy, along the border of Jardin Lecoq, Clermont's mid-city park. The dark green hornbeam leaves have turned bright yellow. Prickly chestnut burrs, ripe and split open, litter the sidewalk beneath our feet. Ancient oaks drop acorns and shed leaves of such delicate and intricate patterns I imagine my father has cut them out on his jigsaw.

We stumble upon a street market. Rows of long wooden tables.

Beaming with pleasure, clapping her hands, unable to contain her excitement, Beatrix rushes over, calling back to us, "Oh, how exotic. I must have a look! Do come along." Dorothy and I follow close behind, lured by the striking assortment of goods.

Apparel is piled high. Stacks of Moroccan blouses trimmed with loops of white ribbon, corduroy pants, potted chrysanthe-mums—russet, gold, burgundy. A chestnut vendor, standing behind his parked wagon, roasts the smooth brown nuts and sells them in small paper cones. On an adjacent table, a pyramid of glass jars displays candied, glazed chestnuts—*marrons glacés* floating in thick syrup, looking for all the world like miniaturized brains preserved in formaldehyde solution by some mad scientist. A sturdy woman offers free samples of what looks to me like brown apple butter but turns out to be chestnut spread: delicate, sweet, nutty *crème de marrons*.

Beatrix, Dots, and I each buy ourselves a pair of black corduroy pants. I get myself a peacock blue Moroccan blouse and two tins of chestnut spread. I will keep one tin, and the other I will mail to Spence. Too late now to reach him by his birthday, which is just a few days away, but probably in time for Christmas. As an after-thought, I buy two bath mitts, white with burgundy lettering. One is labeled *moi*. The other says *toi*. Me and thee.

༄

On weekdays, I go faithfully to all my classes. On weekends, while the Oxies go out drinking or seeking new adventures, I stay in and study, get depressed, and obsess about Georges.

It's late on a Sunday afternoon when Beatrix taps at my door. I'm half asleep and don't respond immediately. So, she comes bursting in, her cheeks bright pink from the cold, and refreshes the stale air in my dorm room with a smell of the crisp outdoors.

"Well, you didn't miss much this time, Lissa. Dots and I went to a so-called *club de musique* across town. Ghislaine recommended it as a way to learn to play an instrument. And, you know, get to know some of the locals. Sounded like a great idea to me at the time. I've always fancied learning to play the flute or maybe a stringed instrument. Have a bit of fun. Improve my French. All in one go."

Beatrix heaves a dramatic sigh and throws herself down on a chair.

"But nothing of the sort. You'll never guess what they had us doing, Lissa. They had us playing the bloomin' spoons!" She pulls a pair of silver teaspoons from her coat pocket, grips them together in one hand, and in an awkward attempt, begins to tap them together to produce a tinny beat.

"So, Lissa, here's our Dots." Beatrix continues to tap the spoons while pursing her lips in a parody of Dorothy's most uptight and disdainful expression. "Can you imagine?"

As usual, Beatrix has a way of cutting through my seriousness, and I find myself laughing my way out of my depression.

So, I'm in good spirits that evening when I join the Oxies on the long walk to the Resto that's part of the medical school complex. We go there about one weekend a month when our usual Resto is closed.

Danny, Parapluie, Beatrix, Dots, and I sit together at one of the cafeteria tables. About halfway through dinner, I see Georges carry a tray to a table across the room. This time he sits alone. No redhead. I find myself staring at him, forgetting to eat. Danny, who's sitting across from me, looks over his shoulder to see what I'm gawking at, then turns back to study my face.

Georges's looks draw me to him. I find myself unable to resist going over to his table, saying hello.

Georges looks up, says *"Comment ça va?"* then resumes his meal.

I take a seat across from him. *"Comme çi, comme ça. Et vous? Comment allez-vous?"* I can't bring myself to *tutoyer* him, to address him using the familiar *tu*.

He looks at me, his expression unreadable. He tells me he is short on cash this month, and that his funds from home got held up. *"C'est à cause de la guerre,"* he tells me. Because of the war. He shoves his tray aside, looks away from me, places both hands flat on the table, spreading the fingers. He seems to express more with his hands than with his face. I remember those hands, competent, touching me in the most private of places.

"*On peut me prêter de l'argent?*" Could one lend me some money?

I stare at those hands, fingers splayed and pressing down so forcefully on the cafeteria table that the flesh around the tips of his brown fingertips becomes white.

"I'm sorry," I say, and shake my head.

In reaction to my words, Georges's hands retract into tight fists. I look away, and it's then I notice Danny watching intently from across the room.

When I return to the table, Danny seems concerned and asks me, "What was that all about, love? What'd that bloke want from you?"

"Oh, that's Georges. From Lebanon. His funds got held up because of the war. Having trouble getting by."

"I'd be careful if I was you, Lissa." Danny sounds gruff and hangs his head when he speaks to me. His lowered eyelids, I notice for the first time, are fringed with the prettiest long sandy lashes. He looks up at me intently, "Just sayin', love."

CHAPTER FOUR

≀ ƒ

Shenanigans and *Aérogrammes*

"You must not be afraid of life—I know, I have always been afraid." —Lissa's advice to Spence

O N A BLUSTERY Saturday afternoon in November, I take long strides along rue Jean Jaurès, finding myself drawn toward the cheerful yellow awning of an *épicerie* where I go in to buy some Yoplait. I haven't eaten for I don't know how long. I missed breakfast this morning while feeling sorry for myself and fantasizing about Georges making love to Coco Rouge in his cot in the medical student dorm. Or, alone with her somewhere around Clermont, probably in an affluent neighborhood, lying with Coco in her shell pink and gold rococo bedroom. Getting laid by Coco across her big brass bed. Floral swag rattling on the headboard, polished gold finials vibrating, reproducing the music of the spheres.

The weather has turned chilly and I shiver. Didn't think to wear my NFS jacket. Just my red pullover and jeans. I've done so much walking since coming to Clermont, my boots are giving out on me. The uppers are breaking away from the soles, letting in cold air, and the heels, worn down at an angle, misalign my gait, forming blisters on the sides of my feet that throb with every step. A wind has come up. Crisp chestnut leaves scud past along the sidewalk. I buy three yogurts in the grocery shop, then meander up and down both sides of the street to give the maid time to finish tidying my room.

Across the street from me, two men walk side by side, heads together, chatting, smoking. As they pass the doorway of a *rotisserie*, where plucked chickens turn slowly golden on spits behind the shop window, these men look me up and down. The guy farthest from me calls over to his companion, "*C'est une fille ou un garçon?*" The wind delivers his words to me. Is it a girl or a boy? The other guy takes a longer, second look, grins, and replies, "*Elle n'a pas de poitrine!*" She's flat-chested!

With that, I retreat back toward the dorm, watching for my reflection as I stride past shop windows. Yes. Short curly hair. Chest flat beneath the coarse wool of my sweater. No bra to give the illusion of a woman's bosom.

The *en panne*—out of order—sign is up on the girl's elevator. So, I mount the six flights to my room, resolutely counting to four over and over again to ensure personal safety—an old childhood ritual. I pull off the boots, massage my aching feet. Then I eat all the yogurt, undress, and go back to bed.

Toc, toc! I crawl out from under the covers and open the door. It's Beatrix. She's all smiles and dimples with a hint of concern. "We missed you at breakfast this morning. You all right?"

Ah, Beatrix, dear Beatrix! She's the oldest girl in a large family. "Mum always expected me to look out for the littluns," she once told me. So now, away from home, she's a mother hen in search of a brood of chicks to take under her wing.

I'm wearing just a t-shirt and undies, no bra. I see her glance down at my flat chest with a commiserating smile. In contrast, she wears a soft blue sweater, intentionally close fitting, cut low at the throat. Ah, Beatrix. How I envy you and the *panache* of your exceedingly ample bosom. I've seen you launch into a room, chest first, a Helen of Troy figurehead, capturing the attention of every male in the place.

"So sorry, Lissa. Didn't mean to catch you in your knickers."

Beatrix takes a seat on my desk chair. I sit facing her on the edge of my cot. She leans forward, squeezes my hand. Gives it a pat. She peers at me now, eyes bright like tiny blue searchlights, sizing me up with her periwinkle frankness.

"Shouldn't stay holed up in your room, you know, Lissa. Life is too short to be moping about. Six foot under and pushing up daisies soon enough. Need to be out and about. Seize the day! Isn't that what we Oxies are here for, when you really get down to it? To have a go. Savor a bit of the French life. *Ooh la la* and all that. Isn't it?" She gives her blonde head a whimsical toss. And there go the dimples again.

Beatrix can be charming and endearing. And she does make a good point. Have to give her that.

"Dots and I have been chatting up Ghislaine at the front desk, and she tells us we need to spend more time with the natives if we're really serious about improving our French. She has time off today. So, we're going to meet up with her in the lobby, walk with her to Place de Jaude, and she'll show us around. Come along with us, why don't you, Lissa. Do you good."

◡◡◡

Ghislaine gives us a guided tour of the Place de Jaude. She notes the row of fountains that gush along the square, pointing to a majestic geyser that heralds the shopping center. Toward the north, our footsteps echo along Jaude's grand basalt parvis. We continue on to an extensive granite esplanade and wind up at a fantastical pastry shop on rue des Vieillards.

"This is the place I was telling you about," says Ghislaine, and guides us past a gold-scripted sign and through the entryway.

The décor is posh, a *mélange* of once-upon-a-time and

Baroque. Everything is presented elegantly on delicate china with crisp linen napkins. I can see that Dorothy approves. A serene smile has replaced her usual dour demeanor. She scans the menu, gives it a nod of endorsement, and orders a cup of steaming hot chocolate. I order a *café au lait*. Beatrix does the same. Ghislaine orders a strawberry syrup, a particularly French concoction. I watch with my two Oxie friends as Ghislaine pours a viscous red liquid from a slim vented bottle and stirs it into her glass of water. Dorothy looks as though she's going to gag. The mixing of this drink reminds me of an experiment I might expect to see performed in a vial in high school chemistry lab.

I marvel when the waiter lifts two small silver pitchers, one in each hand, and pours—simultaneously and in equal measure—coffee and steamed milk into the waiting cup. Delicate streams of black and white converge to form an exquisite frothy blend. Perfection!

∿

In the second week of November, my birthday shower begins. By that I mean a shower of birthday cards sent to me by members of my Methodist church back home in Grangerville. I'm about to turn twenty-three, and each of my friends in the congregation mails me a card. So, every day now, for the past three days, Ghislaine, or whoever is manning the front desk, hands me a stack of envelopes, a rainbow of bright pastels. Beatrix, nosy as she is, cannot fail to notice this unusual occurrence in our fairly boring student lives here at the *Foyer*.

"Lissa, why ever didn't you tell us your birthday is coming up?" She's peering over my shoulder at the opened card I'm holding at breakfast. "Dots! Let's give Lissa a *do*! The *do* of all *dos*!"

So, on Saturday evening I find myself in Clare's cramped and sparsely furnished sitting room, surrounded by the Oxies and Ghislaine, plus a couple of French guys Danny has rounded up. I'm seated in the center on the lone hassock. The others sit on the floor on pillows forming a circle around me.

They've brought me a cake from the bakery, chocolate and cherry cream, which I slice and pass around. Beatrix, Clare, and Dorothy have signed a *Peanuts* card that displays a distressed Snoopy telling me he had a nice gift for me but doesn't remember where he buried it: "*J'avais un chouette cadeau pour toi!! ... Mais je ne sais plus où je l'ai enterré!!*"

Ghislaine presents me with an embossed birthday postcard, illustrated on the front with an elaborate floral bouquet and the words "*Heureux Anniversaire*" in gold script. On the back she's penned a gushing message, welcoming me to Clermont, wishing me a happy birthday, an excellent stay in France, success in my studies, and happiness in the future, signed off with "*Amitiés sincères, Grosses bises, Ghislaine.*"

We wash down the cake with cheap red wine. A curious rite of passage, directed by Beatrix, unfolds. One by one, each partygoer kneels in front of me at the circle's center, leans forward, and gives me twenty-three birthday *bises*, kisses, on alternating cheeks.

As the ritual unfolds, laughter and teasing mount. The group falls into a rhythm, counting each kiss: *un, deux, trois* . . . all the way up to *vingt et un, vingt-deux*. . . . On the last kiss, everyone chants an exuberant *vingt-trois*, clinking spoons on wine glasses and slapping palms against floorboards.

When Danny's turn arrives, he takes me by surprise. For his final kiss, kiss twenty-three, Danny swerves his face at the last moment and presses his lips firmly on my mouth! I find myself breathing in sharply, holding my breath, leaning so far away from him I start to topple over backward from hassock to floor. Danny grabs me around the waist, pulls me to him, engulfs me in a warm embrace that seems to go on forever. When Danny finally releases me, I gulp for air. The French guys cheer. Parapluie whistles.

The evening accelerates. Wine flows. Voices crescendo. Noisy stumbles reverberate on the floorboards until—*TOC, TOC!!!* A loud, insistent knock at the door.

Clare answers. It's the landlady complaining about the noise. Danny shoulders his way over to the door, yells at the landlady,

"*Va te faire foutre!*" Fuck you! He adds a few other expressions, which I never learned in school, but they sound pretty crude. In the short time he's been in Clermont, Danny seems to have mastered a variety of French obscenities. The landlady, shocked at his language, threatens to call the police. It takes all of Beatrix's charm and Dorothy's sophistication to defuse the situation. Beatrix rounds up Danny and his friends, shushes them, and escorts them out the door, all the while gushing to the landlady, "*Désolé, désolé, vraiment désolé.*" Sorry, sorry, truly sorry.

Dorothy uses her most refined schoolgirl French to condemn the young ruffians and placate the landlady, "*Ces jeunes hommes grossiers!*" Such rude young men!

And so, on a wave of turbulence, I cross the threshold to twenty-three.

On our walk back to the dorm Beatrix takes a sharp look at me and remarks on Danny's passionate kiss. "Well, well, now Lissa. That was quite a birthday performance. Still waters do run deep now, don't they? And I thought you were the shy one."

I'm still in a state of shock. All warm and tingly inside. But confused.

"Well, I didn't expect *that*," I say.

Beatrix gives me another look, sizing me up with those all-seeing periwinkle eyes. She half smiles, shaking her head. "As they say, Lissa, it takes two to tango." I'm starting to think maybe Beatrix knows me better than I know myself.

꙳

Somewhere in Beatrix's travels, I never learn quite where or how, but I'm guessing it was in a bar, she picks up a young Frenchman. He works, or so he tells Beatrix, at the Michelin factory as a driver on their tire testing track, *la piste* Michelin.

"His name's Jean-Claude. I'm dying to have you meet him and tell me what you think of him."

So, on a rainy November evening, Beatrix arranges to have Jean-Claude pick up the three of us—Dorothy, me, herself—at the Resto after dinner. A long, sleek red sports car comes roaring out of nowhere, and screeches to a stop in front of the Resto. A rainstorm has just ended, and the streets are slippery. I don't know much about sports cars, but this one looks expensive.

The driver, not bad looking—a sinewy guy, no fat, all nerves and muscle, small of stature by American standards—leans across and opens the passenger door. Beatrix folds the front seatback forward and holds it while Dorothy and I bend low and squeeze into the compressed back seat. Up front, Beatrix cuddles close to J-C. After a high-speed ride, zooming precariously around a traffic circle and charging through shiny night streets, we're at the dorm and Beatrix is enlisting us to help sneak Jean-Claude up to her room in the girls' tower. More accurately, Beatrix is enlisting me because her room is on the same floor as mine and Dorothy wants nothing to do with her compatriot's illicit scheme.

I push the buzzer, press my nose to the glass entrance, and wave to the attendant on duty at the front counter. He glances up from the newspaper he's reading, nods at me, presses the door release, and goes back to his newspaper. I signal to Beatrix. The coast is clear! She and Jean-Claude hurry in, both huddled inside Beatrix's duffel coat. Dorothy follows discreetly at a distance and then stays behind in the lobby, loitering at the front desk and watching as the three of us board the girls' elevator.

Fortunately, the elevator's empty—we're nearly home free. We stop at the sixth floor. I poke out my head. The hallway is empty. I whisper, "All clear," and run down the hall to unlock Beatrix's door. Behind me, a four-legged duffel coat, its two heads squeezed into a bulging hood, makes a running hobble down the hall and topples into Beatrix's room. I toss Beatrix's room key onto her cot and rush out of the lovers' lair, slamming the door shut behind me.

Back in my own room, I lie back, head propped against my pillow, take a deep breath, and try to figure out how I've so unwittingly, yet so willingly, taken part in these shenanigans.

Next morning, *toc, toc.* A rumpled Beatrix stands outside my door, yawning complacently, running her fingers through her tangled blonde hair.

"Would you be a love, Lissa, and bring us *le petit-déjeuner?*" And so, like a dupe, I go down to the dining area, eat my own breakfast in a hurry, and smuggle a tray back up the elevator for Beatrix and her overnight visitor.

A few days later, Beatrix gets a letter postmarked Ambleside. That's her hometown. Turns out the letter is from her boyfriend, Dave. Beatrix reacts by holing up in her dorm room. When I call her for breakfast next morning, she appears at the door wearing a long, flowing, low-cut Japanese robe with white lotus blossoms sprinkled over ice blue silk. Flourishing the opened letter and waving the gown's long draping sleeves, she looks like a dramatic Madame Butterfly while she sings along with a cassette tape recording of David Bowie's "Sorrow."

Emerging from her room, Beatrix sweeps up and down the length of the sixth-floor women's hallway, reminiscing about how her Dave used to sing these lyrics to her. How he teased her about always falling asleep halfway through every movie. The song, Dave had insisted, was about her, with her blue eyes and blonde hair. Like the girl in the song, Beatrix took his money, broke his heart, kept him awake at night. Beatrix allows herself a good cry, wiping the red rims of her purply-blue eyes on the kimono's billowing sleeves. "He misses me," she sighs and releases her breath in a deep shudder.

I help Beatrix sneak Jean-Claude up into her dorm room one more time. Then he disappears from her life forever, just as quickly as he appeared. Several weekends of heavy drinking in the company of Danny, Dots, and Parapluie are, apparently, enough to assuage Beatrix's guilt over her fling with J-C.

And what do I do while all this transpires? Well, for now, I choose to attend my classes dutifully during the day. At night, I cower alone in my dorm room, scribbling ideas for short stories. Or, I write long letters to Spence on flimsy blue paper.

Tuesday, December 4, 1973

Dear Spence,
There are some things I must tell you—I know you are my brother, that you love me, and that if I am honest, you will not judge me falsely.

I wrote to Jill about a month ago. I know you probably wouldn't want me to. I know you were really upset when she broke off your engagement right before I left for France. I know she thought your devotion to me was excessive, and I never really got a chance to talk with you about it. I still feel so very guilty about the whole thing.

But I really needed to get another woman's advice. You see, I am no longer a virgin. So, I wrote to Jill in New York. I told her I wished I had gotten an IUD before coming to France. She wrote back saying I should get one immediately, and sent me $50. After much hesitation and indecision, I have finally come to the conclusion that—for all practical and moral purposes—I should get one.

I must tell you that at this point there is no real danger, in fact, no chance of pregnancy. His French name is Georges. I slept with him only once. He is a medical student here. He is 26. Lebanese. He is the one I lent money to—20 francs for gas for his car. (Imagine an American in France supplying gasoline to someone from the Middle East!) At the time he asked to borrow more money, but I did not give him more and do not think it right that I should. (Please do not think me cheap or sordid for what I have done. I did what I did in good conscience and have no regrets.) I see Georges in passing, but have not been out with him since. But I do have feelings for him, which I believe are natural and good.

So, I have decided to get an IUD to simplify matters, if and when I need one. I am frightened at the idea of getting one here on my own. I have written to the American Embassy for a listing of American doctors near Clermont or in Paris. I mailed it yesterday. I'd like to try to make an appointment in January—after I return from Scotland. (I'll be going there for Christmas and Hogmanay/New Year's with Clare, my Scottish friend.) I suppose I could get an IUD in Scotland, but I hardly know Clare's family well enough to explain. If all goes well, I might be able to stop off in Paris on the way back from Scotland and save paying extra train fare to Paris later on.

I do hope you understand my reasoning and are not disgusted, or shocked, or hurt. You know that your respect is very important to me— you must write to me and tell me your true feelings.

As for the cost of an IUD, I have no idea, but I think I can manage it with the $50 from Jill. If not, I will let you know. I have also decided to try to get a room at the university dorm where the cost is only 134F/ month as compared to my present 200F/month here at the Foyer.

Also, you must not feel obligated to support me. I realize that this letter may change things.

I want you to be free to be honest with me about your emotions. You must not be afraid of life—I know, I have always been afraid. I can be very strong if necessary and maybe even give you support for a change.

Write to me soon.

Love, Lissa

When I fold the letter into an *aérogramme* and print the familiar home address on the front of the envelope, I am struck by how foreign and out of place Grangerville, USA, looks. Tricolor diagonal stripes—meant, I suppose, to represent the French blue, white, and red (not to be mistaken for the American red, white, and blue)—frame the envelope's perimeter like a flattened barber pole. Marked for delivery, *PAR AVION*, from the *république française*, the missive is clearly French in origin. And I feel my own origin slipping, inevitably, away.

Next morning, after breakfast, I leave the *aérogramme* with Ghislaine in the lobby for mailing and get detailed instructions from her on how to mail Spence a package in time for Christmas. The parcel contains the tin of *crème de marrons* tucked inside the bath mitt that says *toi*. I've kept the *moi* mitt for my own personal use.

❧ ❧

CHAPTER FIVE

Collaboration or Resistance?

"Imagine June 21, 1940, that infamous hot summer day, when Clermont-Ferrand became, for a little more than twenty-four hours, the capital of occupied France." —Dr. Albert's lecture

ALTHOUGH ABOVE CLERMONT volcanic mountains rise clear and sunny, here at the bottom of the valley, the city itself lies gray and freezing this December morning. Cold air, trapped beneath a heavy cloud cover, obscures the city's true face beneath a thick layer of frost.

Today, I'm sitting in on a class about the French Resistance presented by the mayor, a close friend, I'm told, of the late Albert Camus. I sit at the far-back, upper level of a cavernous lecture hall. Clermont's mayor speaks of Camus's philosophy, his literature, his role in the Resistance, his honesty, gentleness, and authenticity. I want to ask the mayor a question: Was Clermont's response to the Nazi invasion as much collaboration as it was resistance? But I'm too timid to raise my hand and pose the question in French.

I must be squirming in my seat—or maybe it's just my foreign appearance that attracts the mayor's attention. But now, the mayor pauses in his lecture, points in my direction. "Ah, I see we have a visitor today. And you are American?"

I manage to nod and confirm my nationality. "*Oui, je suis américaine.*"

"Ah, the land of the free and home of the brave," he says in English, and gives me a broad smile of welcome.

Again, I nod. Not sure how to take him. Not wanting to contradict this important man. Then, not knowing what else to say, I reply—stupidly, "*Oui, bien sûr.*"

Clermont's mayor continues, this time in French. "And so, miss, have you come to France in search of the truth? And do you know where to go to find this truth?"

I can think of nothing to say. So, I shrug. Sit in silence.

The mayor continues. He clears his throat and propels his answer into the far reaches of the lecture hall. "You must go too far, miss. As Camus himself has told us, you must go too far, always go too far. That's where you'll find the truth."

I continue to sit. Silent. Looking like an idiot, I suppose. But I'm remembering last year, before coming to France, when my French professor, Dr. Albert, told us about *The Sorrow and the Pity*, a documentary film about Clermont-Ferrand under Nazi occupation during the second world war. Dr. Albert had recently seen the film in New York, and because his junior-year-abroad students were bound for Clermont, he made a point of discussing the documentary in his Advanced Conversation class. He challenged us to examine the tensions at play in Clermont between collaboration and resistance during World War II. Anxiety, fear, upheaval, uncertainty. Desperation. The need for something solid to hold onto. Moral trade-offs proffered to achieve a sense of order and continuity. Uncertainties about the true meaning of patriotism.

"You must imagine those days in 1940. Paris fallen to the Nazis. Refugees fleeing, exhausted, pulling carts filled with random belongings. German soldiers arriving, commandeering the best rooms in hotels. The local police bullied and manipulated by the occupiers: 'First, surrender your weapons to us. Okay, now, cooperate with us, and we'll give them back to you.'

"Imagine June 21, 1940, that infamous hot summer day, when Clermont-Ferrand became, for a little more than twenty-four hours, the capital of occupied France. Imagine waiting, watching as a German Panzer division bore down on your city under the command of a German officer named Joseph Dietrich. Imagine hundreds of Nazi soldiers swarming into Clermont, occupying the Prefecture, taking over City Hall, moving into the Grand Hotel. Imagine catching a glimpse of Philippe Pétain, the Old Marshal, the once-venerable Lion of Verdun, now foggy, eighty-four years old, and sweating beneath his white mustache in a dark wool suit. As a young citizen of Clermont, how would you have felt? In those circumstances, how would you have comported yourself? Would you have collaborated or resisted?"

Dr. Albert hands us his copy of a sepia-tinted archival photo of the Place de Jaude in the center of downtown Clermont. As naïve young American college students, we are more affected by the Vietnam War—which wounded and killed many of our peers, young guys right out of high school—than World War II, that tired old war our elders still brag about. The war in Vietnam just "formally" ended earlier this year with the signing of the Paris Peace Accords and American troop withdrawal.

So, we simply pass the World War II photo around our seminar table, study the uniformed men, and try to make sense of it. Who is French? Who is German? Distinctions of nationality seem blurred in this old picture. A crowd of faded soldiers look on as a separate flank of helmeted soldiers stand guard—sharp-pointed bayonets positioned on their right shoulders, left elbows jutting out at right angles, left arms held across their chests, fists pressed in tight salute over their hearts.

Safe and distanced by thirty years and the vast Atlantic Ocean, Dr. Albert discussed with his American students how the Vichy government under Marshal Pétain turned 180 degrees, validating this new French State's integrity, conflating its aims with those of the nation's ancient Gaulish chieftain. The Vichy regime portrayed its collaboration—not as spineless—but instead, as a noble act. Pétain, like Vercingétorix, was a unifier, preserving French culture, claiming the German invasion in 1940 as an opportunity to assert French nationhood once again. This new French regime, established in Vichy, just 28 miles from Clermont-Ferrand as the crow flies, resurrected two ancient symbols—the baton and the *labrys* (double-headed hatchet), which some say were Gallic/Celtic in origin—arranged them to resemble the *fasces*, the Italian Fascist symbol, and displayed them on the new French State's flag as the *franchisque*.

On my way back from the mayor's lecture, I return to Place de Jaude to reflect before the bronze statue of Vercingétorix that still commands the square—pointed helmet, flowing mustache, raised sword, slain Roman soldier under his horse. I imagine him watching Nazi soldiers parading in the Place de Jaude.

How would big V have reacted to the German invasion? Would the formidable chieftain strain in his saddle, roll his eyes in fury and derision, and wave his sword, eager to come alive and thwart these new invaders—albeit, this time, Germans under Adolf Hitler, instead of Romans under Julius Caesar? Or would he foresee that, ultimately, he'd be compelled to throw his arms at the feet of this new invading Caesar, surrendering Gaul as he had done those many centuries ago?

In the end, what would Vercingétorix have done? Now here in France as in the United States, I am confronted with the polarities of good and evil, of black and white. And once again, I learn that truth is not so simple. It hides beneath the grayness of rain shadow, buried under layers of black lava. However, there were those, like Albert Camus (a.k.a. Albert Mathé)—along with countless French men and women, who found ways to resist. It is those who resisted who give me hope. Perhaps *they* will help me find *my* truth.

Although I love and respect my father's memory, I am determined to grow. I want to move beyond the misconceptions he taught me. Daddy was born in 1878, and he carried with him some harmful nineteenth-century beliefs: people with different skin colors were meant to live in separate worlds, sexuality was taboo and should not be openly acknowledged or discussed, intercourse was not to be indulged until marriage.

I was not a normal teenager. When my mother died, I went directly from preteen to family housekeeper and meal maker. I wasn't allowed to date or go to boy/girl parties. I seem to have skipped adolescence. Now I hover somewhere between childhood and old age, trying to find my footing.

~

On a Thursday, Clare invites me to spend the weekend with her in Boudes. Clare has somehow struck up an acquaintance with Mme Beauchêne, a young woman who teaches English at the *fac*. She's not one of our instructors. Apparently, she teaches English literature to the regular French students at the university. Anyway, this professor is married to the mayor of Boudes, and Clare has somehow obtained an invitation to their home for the weekend.

"Madame Beauchêne said, if it suits me, I can bring along a friend. She and her husband like to meet the international students—especially the English-speaking ones."

So, after classes on Friday, I find myself squeezed into the back seat of this professor's small car, next to Clare, heading south toward the village of Boudes.

The woman up front driving her car seems unusually fit for a professor of English—lean, athletic-looking. Her hair is the color of straw, straight, cropped in a short, practical style. She has an air of self-confidence that reminds me of some of the gym teachers I had in high school and college back home. She drives with an air of authority, shifting the gears efficiently, and maneuvering the car expertly through Clermont's rush-hour traffic.

It's getting dark by the time we reach the outskirts of the city. So, I can't make out much of the countryside as it slips by the car window. But, after a while, I notice that the roads are narrower and twisty as we pass through a heavily wooded stretch.

"We'll be there very soon," our driver announces. The commute from Boudes to Clermont takes me about forty-five minutes, more or less." Another few minutes and we're pulling up to a large stone house set among numerous outbuildings. Lights come on. A dog—a shaggy, russet beast—comes rushing up to greet us.

"Eh, Flâneur, you silly hound! Don't jump up on her like that." Mme Beauchêne humorously scolds the big mutt. "Make the acquaintance of Flâneur. He's totally useless, but entirely loveable."

"It's okay," I say. "I grew up on a farm. I've had lots of dogs. I'm used to it." Flâneur licks my hand and I smooth his silky head.

Mme Beauchêne flashes me a wide grin as she swings open a heavy door into a huge rustic-looking sitting room—yellow lamplight, logs crackling in a black stone and mortar fireplace. The thickness of the walls and the massiveness of the furnishings make my Depression-era farmhouse in Maryland seem flimsy and underbuilt. This French country house must be at least a century old. It exudes stability and a proud heritage.

A robustly handsome and genial man emerges from the shadows of another room, and Madame introduces her husband, Monsieur le Maire. Madame rushes off somewhere, Flâneur bounding along beside her, his tail wagging furiously. M. le Maire greets each of us with a hearty handshake. "Would you like to sample some of my new wine?" he asks. But rather than pulling out a bottle, he gives a facetious wink and leads us back out into the night, toward one of the outbuildings. I notice my hair getting wet. It has begun to sprinkle rain.

We follow him down a steep wooden ladder into a cavernous room, carved underground out of the region's ubiquitous black volcanic stone. "This is my wine cellar," M. le Maire says. He holds a lantern up to a large wooden cask, beaming with pride. The lantern's light seems magical down here. Warm and golden, it causes shadows to dance on the stone walls and plays with the smile on the mayor's ruddy face.

M. le Maire turns a wooden tap on the barrel and starts dispensing the wine freely, filling glass after glass. Halfway through my third glass. the roof of the cave seems to skew a bit to the right. Clare seems to have receded somewhere, back into the cave's hidden depths. Just her hand emerges, slipping me her glass, nearly full. Her voice is barely audible when it reaches me. "Finish this for me," she says. "Be a shame to waste the mayor's wine." Is this my friend Clare, the daring young Scotswoman who brags among the Oxies about how often she's been "p'd out of her mind" in Dalgety Bay? My big American shadow stretches itself against the cave's wall, dwarfing Clare's pintsize reflection. So, hoping for a greater capacity to absorb the alcohol, I oblige Clare and drink the rest of her wine.

Next thing I know, we've been escorted back into the house, to an immense kitchen. My hair is drying in front of a stone hearth. It sends off woodsmoke, the snapping and popping of kindling, and an orange glow that comes hot on the face. Fantastic shadow puppets are performing against a backdrop of thick plaster walls. Plates have been placed before us on a rough-hewn oak table. Clare and I seem to be eating something small, black, and crunchy. Tiny bones splinter between my teeth, and I hear myself laughing uncontrollably, saying, "What the heck is this? Some kind of wild bird?" Clare is laughing, too. Her face has gone dark pink, and her Scot's burr is more slurred than ever. Everything we say seems riotously funny.

"Yes, poor thing. Likely some luckless bird's been shot for your supper. And another one gave up his feathers for me," says Clare, wiping tears from her eyes. And at that, we both laugh harder than ever. Next thing I remember, M. le Maire is talking with someone, chuckling. A woman's voice weaves in and out of the conversation. Then I hear someone—must be our hostess—saying, "Let's get them off to bed."

I wake up in a twin bed. Clare is propped on an elbow in the other bed, observing me. "So, you're awake now, are you? Have you come through?"

I rub my eyes. Massage my forehead. "Still a little groggy. No worse for wear. How about you?"

"Had a head full of mince last night. Right as rain now."

The bedroom door opens a crack and a young girl, dainty and blonde, peeks in at us. Flâneur pushes past her and dashes from bed to bed. Sniffs at Clare. Sniffs at me. Plants his big front paws on my chest. Licks my face. Rousts me from bed.

～

By late morning, the weather has cleared and become mild. So, after a hasty breakfast—croissants and lots of strong coffee—Madame takes us for a brisk walk, between low stone walls, along a dirt and gravel road. Up ahead, a gray draft horse pulls a wobbly old wagon on large spindly wheels, away from a church. The wagon transports a coffin. A small crowd of mourners is walking behind it, carrying flowers.

"It's a traditional funeral procession," Madame explains. "The graveyard is just down the road." We follow along at a distance, headed toward the village to explore the local market. A noxious odor hangs in the air above an embankment on the left. As we approach, we can see a buzzard plucking meat from the carcass of a small animal at the side of the road. Intent on gorging itself on the dead flesh, it waits until we are quite close before it lifts its heavy wings and takes to the air.

When we pass the graveyard, I see the mourners gathered around the gravesite. A priest is making the sign of the cross over the casket as it's lowered into the grave. A young woman, wearing a black veil, holds the hand of a frail girl who tosses flowers into the grave. I hear crows cawing from the distant woods.

The marketplace is chaotic with vendors, large crates of produce, potted flowers, handmade baskets for sale, and villagers milling about. Madame fills several mesh bags with potatoes, cabbage, carrots, leeks, endive, apples, pears, and rounds of cheese. We help her lug them all home and leave them in the kitchen with the cook.

～

On Sunday at noon, we feast on *lièvre*. A large hare, skinned and roasted dark brown, reposes on a magnificent dining table. The wild creature rests now on an elaborate platter, centerpiece to an entourage of seasonal vegetables, a variety of potato dishes, and multiple loaves of bread—some dark, some golden. An array of sauces, creams, butters, jams, vinegar cruets, and gravy boats line up on a field of starched white linen. On the buffet, a sumptuous cake awaits—circled by a set of fine china dessert plates, cups, and saucers—next to an elaborate silver coffee machine and a selection of local cheeses and fruit.

In the afternoon, Mme Beauchêne shows me the stables. She sits on top of a wood-slat fence. Clare and I climb up next to her. As we watch, two young girls emerge on horseback, posting, secure in their saddles, backs held straight as ramrods. The girls wear identical riding outfits. The only distinguishing feature is the ponytail—one blonde, one brunette—that pokes out from under each of their black riding hats. The smaller girl, the blonde, is mounted on a docile-looking pony; the older girl rides a well-be-haved chestnut filly.

Madame waves to them. "My daughters," she says. "The mayor and I are looking for a governess for them, someone who can help them with their English." She looks at me. "Preferably, someone who knows American English. These days, you know, American English is considered an advantage. What I believe one calls a 'perk.'"

Just then, a stable hand steps out into the paddock, leading a large black horse. The horse is beautiful, but fierce-looking. It strains against its tether, tosses its head, kicks, and tries to rear up, away from the old man's restraint. The old man's fingers, short and thick as sausages, grip at the bridle of this proud and defiant steed. I study the man's face. Beneath a peasant's cap, the skin is deeply wrinkled, and the cheeks chapped. From a lifetime's expo-sure to wind and weather? His nose is purple-veined. Too much heavy drinking?

Madame calls out to her stable hand, "Bring him closer if you can." And turning to me, she says, "That's Bonaparte. Exquisite, isn't he? An Anglo-Arab, a mixture of the Arab's elegance and endurance and the Anglo thoroughbred's height and speed. You know, Napoleon favored pure-bred Arabians. It's said they made excellent warhorses."

The stable hand manages to coax Bonaparte close enough to the fence for Madame to feed the horse a carrot. Bonaparte calms a bit and Madame strokes his sleek nose, croons to him, "Ah, my big black brute." She turns to me again, "Bonaparte could be your mount, Lissa, if you come to stay with us as the girls' governess."

I stay quiet, surprised at Madame's offer. What an idea! Maybe a good opportunity for me? Staying on in France, living with this well-connected family. But I just say, "Hmmm," and give no immediate answer. I don't want to shatter Madame's images of me as the athletic American horsewoman. I'm not sure I want her to know what a greenhorn I really am.

I decide, for now anyway, not to tell her I've only been on a horse once in my entire life—that time I sat briefly on a young filly's back at my friend Paloma's farm. Paloma was my best friend in high school. Her father told me he got a good deal on this thoroughbred because her unpredictable performances had banned her at an early age from the racetrack. I could imagine how that might have played out given her edginess, her fear of the cheering crowds, her erratic behavior in the starting gate, and her terror when the bell went off and the gates released. Fortunately, there's no opportunity during this short visit for me to do any horseback riding, no time to demonstrate my ineptitude as an equestrian.

In the evening, Clare and I fill up on a buffet of leftovers from our noon feast. After a couple of drinks, I find myself relaxed by the fire on a comfortable sofa, becoming more and more fluent, discussing a flurry of topics with M. le Maire and his wife—politics, philosophy, literature. Sleepy and relaxed, Clare and I return to our twin beds for the night. Feeling sequestered and secure, I confide to Clare about Georges and my decision to get an IUD, maybe in Paris.

Clare sits up in bed, suddenly alert. "Lissa, have you gone totally *doo-lally*? You'd do better to look for an IUD in Scotland. We have the national health service there, and I could always ask my sister for advice. Abbie. She's studying to be a nurse."

I doze off wondering how I would even get to Scotland.

Early on Monday, the mayor drives us back to Clermont, drops me back at the dorm, and drives on to leave Clare at her walk-up. I take a hasty shower and review some of Guy de Maupassant's stories we'll be going over this afternoon in Madame Vachon's French lit course.

One day that week after class, Clare comes up to me, excited as usual, fizzing on about a ski trip to Mont-Dore she's planned for this weekend, and winds up asking me, "Do you think I could use your shower at the dorm? Can only stand at the sink and take sponge baths at my place. I can feel the dirt building up on the back of my neck. Starting to grow some kind of crust back there. Could you smuggle me in, do you think?"

Clare scratches at the nape of her neck and continues, "Oh, and *by th'wey*, I just got a letter from me mum and dad. I've been going on about you, no end. How I'm friends with an orphaned American here in France. And so, they've invited you to come home with me for the holidays. Better than staying here alone in the dorm, don't you think? And while you're there, we could chat up me big sister about getting you that IUD. Murder two birds with one stone, so to speak."

Then, fairly bursting with glee, Clare gives me a smug grin, pokes me with her elbow, and adds, "So, Lissa, you will smuggle me up to your tower for a shower, won't *ye*?" It's more an assumption than a request.

Oh, no, here we go again, I think to myself, recalling the near-fiasco we had sneaking Beatrix's French beau up the girl's tower and into her dorm room. But me being me, I just tell her, "Okay," and promise to help her out the next afternoon.

The next day, after grammar class, I escort Clare back with me to the dorm, through the lobby and over to the girls' elevator. She's toting a change of clothes and her toilet articles, but has taken the precaution of stuffing these items into a large pillowcase, which, she hopes, is not as obvious as an overnight suitcase might be. And, after all, we girl residents are allowed to entertain female friends in our rooms. Ghislaine glances up from the front desk, and gives me a nod. She doesn't seem to notice Clare's bath towel sticking out the top of the pillowcase. At least she's brought her own instead of borrowing my towel and leaving it soggy on the bed as I'd imagined she might.

Clare's actions are swift and cunning. When the coast is clear, she speeds down the hallway, takes her shower, and returns unobserved to my room in what seems like no time at all. Here, she pulls her hair—still wet and dripping—off her neck, and asks me to look at how clean the skin is there now.

She's scrubbed her skin so hard back there, it glows. "Yep," I tell her. "All pink, and shiny."

Clare dances around my cot, jumps up and down, and parrots every slang expression she can think of to announce her cleanliness: "Squeaky clean! Clean as a whistle! Spic and span! Fresh as a daisy!"

"Enough!" I say and escort her out through the lobby, without arousing suspicion.

When I go back to my room, I do find a hairbrush Clare has left behind on my bed. But no big deal. I can return it to her tomorrow at the *fac*.

I fall asleep that night, feeling proud of myself. Another secret mission accomplished!

~

On a dreary weekday afternoon, I return from the *fac* to find Ghislaine smiling at me from behind the reception counter. She pulls a letter from its pigeonhole and hands it over to me. It's an airmail from Spence. I go to my room to open it..

Spence is angry that I took money from his ex-fiancée. He has sent me a check for seventy-five dollars, saying he hopes this will cover my needs, and instructs me to pay the fifty dollars back to Jill. Immediately,

I sit reading Spence's letter, over and over, feeling crippled and weak and insignificant. I want to cry or scream, but I can't. I put my head down on the desk and whisper, "I won't *always* be dependent on Spence. I won't!"

In mid-December, just after our evening meal at the Resto, Clare and I stop at an African crafters' table. It's set up temporarily in the cafeteria lobby, offering colorful gifts for the coming holidays—bright scarves, soapstone hippos, ebony elephants, thorn tree giraffes. A necklace of bright wooden beads, shiny red as polished ripe cherries, catches my eye. At the crafters' carved wood frame mirror, I hold the beads up against my throat, pleased at how they look on me. Reluctantly, I hang the choker back on its rack—not ready to indulge myself. Clare rushes up beside me, grabs the same necklace, hastily tries it on, buys it for herself on the spot, then heads back to her flat, leaving me standing alone, flabbergasted.

On my way out, I pass the Resto café and spot Georges sitting way in the back, at the Arab table. No Coco Rouge. He's chatting with Mohammed and Ibrahim and Yusuf. As always, seeing Georges has a visceral effect. I take a deep breath to steady myself, make my way over to the table and take the empty seat next to him.

I tell Georges I'm going to Scotland with my friend Clare for the holidays.

"Ah, *l'Écosse*," he says and smiles, as if approving. He *is* handsome. And I find myself caught up in an unreasonable desire for him—something undeniable that defies my better judgment.

Mohammed, Ibrahim, and Yusuf follow our conversation and exchange glances, but they say nothing to me. I feel shut out somehow. So, I get up abruptly and leave the café, confused but determined to get some birth control in Scotland.

CHAPTER SIX

゛ヾ ʃ

Emerging from the Fog

"I do believe I heard a groaning of the arch." —Clare's dad as we pass through the West Port gate

OUR PLANE LANDS in a heavy fog at the Edinburgh airport. I tag along behind Clare, and when we pass through customs, I'm relieved that no one opens and inspects my suitcase because, at Clare's insistence, I'm carrying two bottles of French wine for her family. We wheel our luggage past a gift shop that's crammed with stuffed Loch Nessie monsters sporting tartan tam o'shanters and head toward the passenger pickup area.

Just as I reach into the luggage cart to remove my suitcase, a heavyset man grabs it away from me and lifts the large case as if it's light as a feather. I freeze, paralyzed with a sense of fear that runs through me like an electric shock. Is this man a Scottish customs agent tailing me for smuggling contraband into the country? Will he pry open my suitcase, and find the undeclared bottles of wine? Seize the wine? Fine me? Arrest me? I begin to tremble all over.

But no! This strange man seizes my right hand and begins pumping my arm in a vigorous handshake. His face, unrestrained and craggy, is a dead ringer for the granite carving of Teddy Roosevelt on Mount Rushmore—without Teddy's spectacles and mustache. Clare suppresses a smile at my stunned look, exchanges a bear hug with the man, and introduces him to me as her father.

"Lissa, meet me dear old Da." A huge upturned crevice emerges on the rugged Scotsman's face, like a rock smiling, and my fears melt.

"Clare has told us all about you in her letters home," he tells me. "It's grand to have you here in Scotland. Clare tells me you're an orphan. I know what that's like. Never knew me own mum and dad. Raised by an *auld* widowed auntie."

I imagined that Clare might live with her family in a stone and thatch cottage, nestled at the bottom of a misty glen, with smoke curling whimsically from its chimney. But instead, Clare's dad drives us just outside Edinburgh to a coastal town called Dalgety Bay. He swings through a well-kept neighborhood and comes to a halt in front of a tidy modern suburban house that reminds me of Beaver Cleaver's home in *Leave It to Beaver*.

Clare's mother greets us at the door. Trim and pretty with neatly coiffed auburn hair, she seems to hop about the house, active as a tiny russet bird. "You must be tuckered out, Lissa." We've heated water for your bath in the tub upstairs."

"Well, I'm completely shattered," Clare says. "Night, night. Lissa. I'm straight off to bed now."

My first night in Scotland, I dream vague dreams of Georges. Someone wearing a surgeon's mask—Georges?—is trying to insert a hideous-looking IUD in me. It looks like an oversized mousetrap wrapped in barbed wire. My mouth forms a large black hole, shaped like an "O." I am screaming, but there is no sound.

∼

The next morning, I awake like a pupa maturing, cushioning herself within the seemingly perpetual fog that subdues the Scottish landscape outside the window. I find myself swaddled in a down comforter, a hot water bottle cooling at my feet, my senses blurred and softened.

"You sleep so quietly," Clare's sister, Abbie, informs me as we breakfast on fried eggs, square sausage, porridge, and tea. "When I looked in on you last night. I thought you had stopped breathing. Reckoned you were dead!"

"I guess I am pretty quiet. My father was always working on watches. I wasn't allowed to make a lot of noise."

"Well, you gave me quite a scare, until I grabbed your wrist and felt a pulse."

"Don't mind Abbie," Clare tells me. "She's in training to become a nurse. Always on the lookout for an emergency."

"My mother was a nurse," I say, then add, "Guess I must be a very quiet sleeper. The maid at the dorm in Clermont once thought I was dead in my cot."

I remember my father used to tell me how I nearly died when I was not much more than four years old. On a hot summer's afternoon, Daddy found me in a deep sleep in the back seat of our Oldsmobile. My mother had left me there, sealed up in the parked car while she stopped in to check on the old lady across the back alley. When Daddy found me, he had trouble waking me. He said I could have suffocated.

Other memories surface. My draconian Grandma Magda punished my four-year-old self for throwing a tantrum. She made my mother lock me in a hot black car. My grandma made my mother leave me there even though I was gasping for breath, fearful of suffocating.

To this day, I'm claustrophobic and ever wary of the narrow threshold through which my soul will pass from sleep into death—a slender passageway, hovering close by, just a few short breaths away. At times death seems sealed in blackness, and I fear it; at other times, I see a pure white light beckoning to me from the farthest reaches.

True to form, Clare packs my first few days in Scotland with hours of frantic activity. I follow along, desperately trying to keep up. On the first day, Clare decides to immerse me in a bit of Scottish history. We take a short walk to the old village to have a look at St. Bridget's Kirk. It's in ruins now, just the shell of a medieval church that dates back to the 1100s. There's still a loft, the piscina (the shallow basin once used to wash Communion vessels), a few gravestones, and a guard post built into the church-yard wall where beadles could keep watch for potential body snatchers. Clare points out a burial vault that houses the remains of Scottish earls.

On his day off, Clare's dad drives us to the north bank of the Firth of Forth where Longannet power station monopolizes the skyline. Clare's dad, who works in this immense coal-fired power bastion, gives us a personal tour of the facility, relishing every detail of the plant's operation. He brags about its 2,400-megawatt generating capacity, the highest of any power station in Scotland, its 183-meter (600-foot) chimney stack, its four boilers, its eight pulverizing units able to process 40 tons of coal each in an hour, the fans—two draft and two induced—on each boiler, its ability to produce 1,800 tons of steam per hour at an intense pressure and an extreme heat, and its two turbo generators. By the end of the tour, I'm still not sure exactly what job Clare's dad performs here, but it's clear he takes pride in knowing exactly how every-thing works.

The pace doesn't ease up. On the next afternoon, Clare takes me ice skating at the town rink where I'm forced to rent a pair of well-worn skates that give me no ankle support. Not a strong skater anyway, I find myself groping along the walls, trying not to get in the way of the other skaters. Another day we go bowling, and Clare easily beats me at every round.

On the way home she insists on stopping at a chip shop for some authentic fish and chips. We walk away munching on batter-coated haddock filets and chunky potato wedges. All this has been deep-fried to a crunchy perfection, sprinkled with salt and vinegar, and wrapped in layers of greaseproof paper and newspaper. So good!

~~~

On one of Scotland's rare sunny days, Clare's dad drives us to St. Andrews to see the sights. We stop along the way for lunch at the Crusoe hotel.

"Some say," Clare's dad tells me as we pull up chairs in the hotel restaurant, "this is the birthplace of Alexander Selkirk. Some say he was the model for Daniel Defoe's Robinson Crusoe character. Have you read the book, Lissa?"

"Well, my brother, Spence, did when he was a kid. I remember him reading some parts of it out loud to me."

Clare's dad leans back in his chair. His whole body seems to expand as he signals the waiter. "You know, I'm quite the reader me self. Try to read at least one novel a week. Go through it the first time to pick up on the story and the characters. Then I go back and read it a second time to soak up the setting. And if it's an especially thought-provoking book, I'll have a third go to ponder the ideas or the philosophy the author is putting forth."

At the end of lunch, Clare's dad orders me a shot of Dram Buie. "This'll put a smooth ending on your meal." I sip the drink. It does take the chill off and seems to have a mellowing effect. I'm not surprised they drink it here where wind and water can be such cold and rough playfellows.

As we finish our drinks, Clare's dad leans toward me, pats my hand, and says, "You know, you Yanks saved us during the war. My uncle's family settled in Canada. A pilot in the Canadian military, he was."

We drive on to the old coastal town and pass through the West Port gate. "Legend has it," says Clare's dad, "if a genius passes under this archway, it's sure to collapse."

So, Clare and I huddle together in the back seat, pretending to cringe and hold our breath. But no, not a single stone falls.

"I do believe," says Clare's dad as we drive along South Street, "I heard a groaning of the arch. Maybe a wee straining against the keystone."

We pass over cobbled streets through the heart of the old city, past cafés and pubs, catching glimpses here and there of St. Andrews University. Its buildings are an architectural conundrum—modern abutting medieval.

Clare's dad insists that we stop just outside the wall of the Old Course. We stand near the entry as, with a grand sweeping gesture, the proud Scotsman holds forth: "Aye, it's a grand old course. A course of legend. The Scots it was who invented the sport, don't you know? Sometime in the 1400s. *Ah dinnae ken* exact when. Invented by shepherds, so they say. Bored out of their minds with walking their sheep across the fields. Apparently, one of the herders cooked up the idea of using a stick to knock a rock into a hole." He stops a moment to reflect, pulling at his chin. "Might very well have used their own crooks as the first golf clubs."

He glances over at me then and gives me a hearty clap on the shoulder. "Does that brother of yours play golf? Bring him over then; I'll take him on the tour." This, it occurs to me, is a very kind gesture, even though my brother, Spence, has never—to my knowledge—shown any real interest in actually playing the game. But Spence is surely acquainted with golf. He did, after all, during that long, lean summer after finishing high school, hire himself out as a caddie. Earned enough money to buy his first car, a cheap old Plymouth coupe.

Just outside the Old Course, we go for a stroll on a long stretch of beach that's backed by sand dunes. In the distance, we can see ruins overlooking choppy gray water. Clare breaks into a run and I sprint along beside her, my boots pounding the wet sand. Clare's face is pinkening with wind and salt mist, and the sting on my own skin tells me my own face must also be glowing. I have never felt more alive!

We race for a time, neck and neck, then pause to let Clare's dad catch up. A bit out of puff when he reaches us, he pauses to catch his breath and points far out over the water, "Lissa, we're looking out from St. Andrews Bay across the North Sea. You can sail all the way to Norway from here, did you know that?"

Just before leaving St. Andrews, we visit a discount woolen mill. I buy myself a Fair Isle sweater—the color of deep purple heather. For Spence, I select a warm pullover, handmade of Scottish blue-faced Leicester wool.

As Christmas Day approaches, we take a train into town to do some Christmas shopping. Once off the commuter train, I try to keep up with Clare as she rushes through Edinburgh's busy city streets, but my senses are challenged by the reverse traffic patterns, cars and buses all barreling down on me from the side I'm not expecting. When crossing Edinburgh's busy thoroughfares, I habitually look the "wrong" way and nearly get hit a couple of times.

Clare advises me that, as the family guest, I'm expected to buy a gift for her mother. Also, her two maiden aunties, who are sure to dine with us on Christmas, will each bring me a gift. So, I must be sure to have a gift for each of them as well. We plan to shop at Jenners department store on Princes Street.

To get there, we take a double-decker bus. I follow Clare, hop on quickly, and scramble up steep twisting stairs to the top deck. This is my first time riding a bus that has two storeys. The view up here is fantastic—winding cobbled streets, historic buildings, and shops of every kind! Like Clare, who dashes through life at an accelerated and madcap pace, the bus plunges recklessly forward, making swift starts, sudden turns, and abrupt stops. At the last moment, just as we reach the stop for Jenners, Clare launches herself from her seat, races down the steps, and leaps off. I trail close behind, feeling the bus pull away just as my back foot leaves the bottom step. We draw near an imposing five-storey building. Solid Victorian architecture. Female figures on the exterior appear to support the edifice. Clare explains that these caryatids (statues), were placed at the insistence of the founder, Charles Jenner, to show that it is women who support the house.

Inside, the store exhibits impressive displays of expensive perfumes, clothing, homewares, and furnishings. Clare guides me over to the Dior counter where I buy Clare's mom a large bottle of her favorite perfume. I use the American Express card Spence gave me before leaving home and enjoy bragging to Clare that my brother is rich, though that is an exaggeration. His income makes our family newly—and barely—middle class. But I'm finding the average American's standard of living is very good compared to what I'm seeing in France and now in Scotland.

We stop for lunch in the store's restaurant. In the States, I have to ask for milk or it's assumed I want black coffee. Here, when I order, it's presumed that I want coffee brewed with milk. By the time we leave Jenners, it's late afternoon. As we exit the building, Clare points across the Princes Street Gardens toward a massive fortress that rises on a rocky promontory.

"That's Edinburgh Castle. You're not to leave Scotland without a visit there," says Clare.

♨

At the end of the first week, life takes on a more comforting rhythm. Errands are run early in the day. By late afternoon the family gathers in the living room to chat, play cards or board games. I find a wanderer's solace in the mundane household activities: water heating all day in an electric pot plugged in at the back of the kitchen stove, continuous brewing of a full-bodied black tea, endless cups of this Highland blend poured and passed around. Stodgy meals consumed to stave off cold and damp: mince and tatties or thrifty concoctions—hefty main courses called stovies—that use up leftover meat, potatoes, onions, vegetables, fat, and gravy.

Here, in Scotland, the practical mingles seamlessly with the sublime. In the evenings Clare's younger brother, Andrew, sets kindling ablaze in the fireplace and the family gathers around to hear Clare's older sister, Abbie, play folk music on the guitar. Abbie has a penchant for sucking on hard candies when she plays, and her teeth are not in the best condition. But she shrugs philosophically and tells me, "I'm not worried about my teeth. Going to have them all pulled when I'm about thirty. By then, I'll qualify for free dentures with the national health service."

With that she launches into a medley of Scottish folk tunes: "Annie Laurie," "Roamin' in the Gloamin'," and the enchanting "Skye Boat Song." Andrew feeds the fire. And finally, by popular request, Abbie strums "Loch Lomond." Behind the grate, embers smolder like an ancient dragon's teeth, and the evening draws to a close with father, mother, and siblings all singing, and me joining in as best I can on the chorus.

After the singing, Clare's parents and her brother go off to bed. And, for the first time, Clare and I are alone with Abbie. Clare seizes the moment, nudges me, revives the fire, and pushes me to consult with her older sister about my stymied relationship with Georges. When my story is told, Abbie informs me, in no uncertain terms, "Well, if you plan on resuming sexual relations with Georges—or with any man for that matter—you really ought to get yourself some protection." She suggests a diaphragm. And so, late on a frozen evening in December, beside flickering firelight in Dalgety Bay, plans are made and my destiny shifts toward independence.

CHAPTER SEVEN

A Scottish Christmas

"I leave the clinic feeling very adult." —Lissa's notebook

O N CHRISTMAS DAY, Clare's family gathers at the snug little house in Dalgety Bay. Clare's two spinster aunties drive out from Edinburgh. Just as Clare predicted, the aunts give me wrapped presents. From Auntie Fiona, a Cadbury Milk Tray of assorted milk chocolates. From Auntie Elspeth, a carton of After Eight mint chocolate thins. Fiona, the younger of the two, who works for a downtown legal firm, is pretty and lively and quick-witted. And she does all the driving. Elspeth, who keeps house for the two of them, is very sweet, but reserved and plain, with a face as wrinkled as a prune.

As a holiday treat for Clare and me, Auntie Fiona has bought tickets for an evening performance of *The Nutcracker* at the Royal Lyceum. So, on Christmas night, we pile into the back seat of Auntie Fiona's Hillman sedan—an economy car the color of faded brown mustard with the personality of an anxious middle-aged spinster—and ride home with the aunts to their flat in Edinburgh. Auntie Elspeth tucks us in twin beds under thick blankets, placing hot water bottles at our feet. In the morning, to take off the chill, she serves us a hearty breakfast: instant coffee made with milk instead of water and steaming oat porridge topped with a pat of butter, brown sugar, golden raisins, and a splash of milk.

We spend the day after Christmas doing 1,000-piece jigsaw puzzles, assembling a challenging assortment of barely distinguishable pieces to reveal Scottish castles, rugged landscapes, and churning seas.

In the evening, Auntie Fiona takes us to the Royal Lyceum, a grand old theater that rises just west of the Princes Street Gardens. As we approach, its impressive cream-colored facade glows in the lamplight like a beacon of culture. In the auditorium, we mount carpeted stairs, locate our places among the rows of tiered red seating. As we wait for the ballet to begin, Auntie Fiona gives us a brief lecture.

"The Royal Lyceum has been around since 1883." She points out the theater's features as she speaks, "A brilliant example of late Victorian theater architecture. Magnificent crystal chandelier."

Clare nudges her aunt, and whispers dramatically, "Tell Lissa about the ghosts."

"Ah, Clare loves the ghost stories." Fiona gives her niece an indulgent look.

"Can you believe it, Lissa? This place is haunted!" Clare says, leaning in close to my face, flashing me a gleeful and menacing grimace.

"Aye," says Fiona. "Theater patrons have reported sightings of a blue lady. Thought to be a famous English actress who performed at the Lyceum's first show."

"Auntie, tell Lissa about the shadow."

"Ah, well. There's also a mysterious shadow-like figure that's been sighted way up high, above the stage, among the lighting fixtures. It's appeared many times along with a kind of ringing sound."

"Oh, I hope the blue lady appears tonight," says Clare, clapping her hands, as excited as a little girl.

The orchestra begins to play. Then, with a majestic sweep, thick velvet curtains part to reveal a magnificent backdrop. Exquisitely costumed dancers emerge, and scene after scene unfolds behind the broad proscenium arch. All thoughts of phantoms fade and are replaced by a story more fascinating to me than any rumored ghost.

We are transported to a family parlor where a Christmas tree stands brilliantly decorated. Awestruck children—among them a brother and sister—gather, a holiday party begins, and a march resounds. The toymaker enters to work his magic. Dolls dance. A nutcracker is conjured. Ignored by the other children and broken by the brother, this marvelous wooden man claims the little girl's heart, unleashes a dreamlike adventure, and calls forth a wonder I haven't experienced since I was a child myself. Music, dancers, and colorful outfits captivate me. The Snow Queen makes her appearance by the side of the Snow King and performs a willowy dance, surrounded by her Snowflakes.

Then suddenly it's intermission, and Auntie Fiona is saying, "A magical world, isn't it?" She buys ice cream for us in the lobby, studies me for a moment at the counter, then pays me an unexpected compliment. "Lissa, you remind me of the Snow Queen. So tall and slim and statuesque."

Clare is quick to protest. "But what about me, auntie!"

Fiona hurries to placate her niece. "Why, you're the Sugar Plum Fairy, dearie. Bonnie and sprightly. Watch out for her in the next act." Clare seems satisfied with that appraisal, especially at the end when the animated Fairy receives a series of curtain calls for her fancy footwork.

❧

Clare insists on helping me do the practical thing. And so, two days past Christmas—exactly one year, I realize, since my father passed away at age ninety-four—Clare takes me to a women's health clinic in Edinburgh. I'm guessing it's all part of the national health system, which seems to cover just about every part of the human body. The clinic is downtown, just a few blocks past the Walter Scott monument, which rises above the Princes Street Gardens. On impulse, Clare grabs me by the arm and insists that we climb the monument's tower before going on to the clinic.

"The exercise will relax you for your exam." Unable to formulate an objection, I follow a step or two behind Clare, up the tower's 287 steps. We take a series of spiraling staircases and stop at the various viewing platforms along the ascent to gaze out over the city's center and surroundings. Clare reads from a brochure she's grabbed, "The tower is Victorian gothic, 61.11 meters high, built from Binny sandstone extracted from a quarry in West Lothian."

We pause in the center space inside the tower's four columns to contemplate the statue of the great Scottish author himself, seated beside his dog, at rest from his writing, quill pen in hand. Clare resumes her reading. "The statue was carved from a single piece of white Carrara marble weighing 30 tons . . . Took the sculptor six years to complete. . . ." She hands me the brochure. "Here, Lissa, keep this as a souvenir, inspiration for that great American novel you're going to write someday."

Before we leave, I look up, trying to glimpse from the ground some of the characters in Scott's novels. The brochure says the monument displays sixty-four of them, carved by Scottish sculptors. It dawns on me that Sir Walter must have been pretty prolific, even though I know only one of his stories, and that's *Ivanhoe*. My brother's class read it in high school, and I remember seeing the film based on it at a high school May Day event back home. More and more I'm realizing just how much great literature I haven't read. Increasingly, my ignorance astounds me.

I don't have long to reflect, though, because as always, Clare is on the go. She rushes on toward the clinic, and I hurry to keep up. The family-planning suite on the second floor seems very clean and welcoming, almost homey compared to the institutional, self-consciously sterile, settings I've encountered in American hospital clinics. I'm feeling a little sweaty from my climb up the Walter Scott monument and my dash to the clinic. But the nurse who attends me is very kind and not at all judgmental when I explain why I'm here. I fill out a standard form. Then the nurse does a routine vaginal exam and fits me for a diaphragm. I leave the clinic feeling very adult, carrying my brand-new protective device in its discreet blue plastic case. The clinic has provided a small tube of spermicidal jelly along with an inserter, but Clare insists we stop at a Boots pharmacy to pick up an extra-large tube of vaginal gel. "Don't want to run out," she cautions me, and I laugh to myself at the thought of using all that jelly.

꙳

CHAPTER EIGHT

Hogmanay in Dalgety Bay, Then on to a New Year

"Success in my second-level exams at the fac, a second chance with Georges, and the freedom of birth control." —Lissa's silent New Year's wish

THE LAST DAY OF THE YEAR, what we Americans call New Year's Eve, is Hogmanay in Scotland—a day of visiting door to door and sampling each household's personal Scotch. Clare's dad sits me down in his favorite lounge chair and pours me a sampling of his special malt blend. I sip the golden liquid slowly. I don't like the taste. It burns all the way down. But when he pours me a second shot, I take it, not wanting to insult him, and nurse it, feeling an unfamiliar warmth spreading through me. Then time seems to collapse, and suddenly I'm wearing a party dress borrowed from Abbie, black velvet and lace. I didn't bring any dresses with me to France.

"You can't wear those," I hear Abbie shout, as she snatches Clare's red African beads off her sister's neck and fastens them on me. "That color doesn't suit you. Clashes with your orange hair. See. They look so much better next to Lissa's dark curls."

Next thing I know, I'm boarding a crowded bus, riding with Clare's family on my way to the community hall for a dinner and dance.

"Everyone takes a bus to the Hogmanay Dance," Clare informs me. "We all know we'll be p'd out of our minds before the night's over."

✧

In the hall, the liquor flows, talk grows louder, and laughter intensifies. Although I drink sparingly, the alcohol blurs my mind so that I'm hardly aware of what I'm eating. Clare is shouting in my ear and tugging me out on the dance floor. "You're about to learn to dance the *Dashing White Sergeant*."

Before I have time to object, the band—comprising a guitar, fiddle, drum, and accordion—strikes up a lively folk tune, and I find myself part of a set of three couples. Similar sets have formed all across the hall. Women wear a variety of dresses— some formal, some folksy. Most of the men wear ordinary dress shirts and pants, but a few have donned traditional Scottish garb—long-sleeved white shirts, ties, vests, tartan kilts, sporrans (waist pouches), knee-high hose held up by garters, and brogues. The pace is fast and exhilarating with moves that remind me of an American square dance. I follow along with my set of dancers—circling, jumping and kicking, lifting an arm on occasion, weaving, stamping, clapping—until the last chord sounds and we bow or curtsy to one another. I finish flushed and out of breath, but very pleased with myself for catching on so quickly.

As I sit out the next dance, Clare takes a seat next to me. She points across the dance floor to where a dignified-looking man in traditional attire escorts an obese woman whose dark thick hair is piled high on her head.

Clare elbows me and shouts in my ear above the din. "That's our neighbor Ian and his wife, Maisie. She's an amazing dancer."

Maisie wears an elegant low-cut, river-green gown. Its skirt cascades in a graceful waterfall from her enormous bosom, pools around her girth, then comes to an abrupt halt just below her knees to reveal a pair of incongruously slender legs and delicately tapered ankles that flow into high heels. Ian stands proud and tall, gallantly leading his lady, as Maisie glides above the smooth wooden floorboards, so light on her feet she appears to be floating.

"Incredible, wouldn't you say, Lissa?"

I can only nod in admiration and wish I could dance so well. The hours float by on Scottish guitar melodies, folk songs, and dancing. When the band begins to play an American country tune, Ian crosses over to me, extends his hand, and says, "I hear you're an American lass. Won't you join me? Surely you can show us how to dance to this one."

I shake my head. "Sorry, but I don't really know the steps." Ian looks surprised and disappointed. He rejoins Maisie, and together they put together some pretty credible strutting.

The music, drinking, and dancing go on and on and the festivities end with the singing of "Auld Lang Syne."

It's well into the wee hours when the revelers board the bus for home. I nod off during the ride, my head on Clare's shoulder, and eventually wind up back in bed, with no recollection of how I got there.

～

On New Year's Day at Clare's, the first guest to cross the threshold after midnight turns out to be Auntie Fiona, followed closely by Auntie Elspeth. Elspeth is carrying a Scottish black bun—a homemade loaf cake completely covered with pastry—as a token of luck for the coming year. Clare's mom slices through the gold-brown crust, revealing a dark fruit cake within. She passes the slices around, and I take my first taste of this holiday treat—a complex blend rich with raisins, currants, candied orange peel, and almonds.

"It's Auntie El's special recipe," Clare explains. "She laces it with a tad more brandy than most and lets it soak for a full seven weeks before Hogmanay."

Clare's mom holds up her slice of black bun and asks, "And so what luck do we hope to receive from the bounty of Auntie Elspeth's glorious cake?"

Clare's dad takes a huge bite from his thick chunk of cake and pronounces, "For 1974, I foresee a year of prosperity, good health, and more than a wee bit of fun."

Silently, for myself, I wish for success in my second-level exams at the *fac*—they're coming up soon after the holidays—a second chance with Georges, and the freedom of birth control.

<center>~~~</center>

On my last day in Scotland, Clare and I make a final trip to the capital city and dash over to Edinburgh Castle in time for the last tour of the day. We enter through the Portcullis Gate, and I race along behind Clare as we make a whirlwind circuit. Clare is disappointed that we've missed the firing of the one o'clock gun. "It's the last working canon, and I did want you to hear it go off," she laments. But from Castle Rock, we get a fantastic view of the city. The tour guide provides explanations of Scottish symbology and goes on to recount—in a Scot's burr even thicker and swifter than Clare's—an amazing assortment of tales featuring genera-tions of Scottish kings, a famous knight, and the rise and fall of Mary, Queen of Scots. At the end of our tour, I buy a king-size postcard of Edinburgh Castle for my brother. Later that evening, snuggled in bed beneath a pile of blankets, I write to Spence on the postcard, outlining my adventures in Scotland, purposely leaving out the part about the diaphragm. I don't think he really needs or wants to hear all that.

Dear Spence,

It's Wednesday evening, 10:33 p.m. Scottish time, and I'm all packed to return to Paris tomorrow. Have seen lots of sights here and enjoyed my stay, but am homesick for France. I plan to have an evening in Paris with Clare, Dorothy, and Beatrix. I'm going to treat them to dinner on my American Express card.

I go on to tell Spence about all the adventures I've had in Scotland and end with:

Visited the sale at the woolen mills and bought some jumpers (sweaters). I mailed you one. So, let me know when you get it and if it fits and you like it, etc.

I wish you a Happy Hogmanay (New Year's Eve) and a Happy 1974. Hope you weren't lonely or unhappy. I'm reading Antonia Fraser's history of Mary, Queen of Scots.

I'll write to you from Clermont. Hope to find a letter from you waiting. I feel very selfish for doing all these things while you stay at home and work. Can you come? Tell me what you've been doing.

Love, Lissa

PS: Also visited Longannet electrical power station.
How's the gas situation hitting you?

On Thursday morning, just as I'm at the front door—suitcase in hand, ready to follow Clare to the car where her dad is warming up the engine, preparing to drive us to the airport—Clare's mom pulls me aside. "Lissa, you seem a sensible lass. You'll look over our Clare for us, won't you? She's easily kittled up, worried she's too fat." I try to nod reassuringly, all the while startled at two novel ideas: one, that I come across as being the sensible one, and two, that Clare has weight issues. She's always seemed slim and athletic to me. Not a trace of fat. Living at a pace that wouldn't give a single extra calorie a chance to accumulate.

Feeling the winter holidays drawing to a close, I fly back with Clare from Scotland to Paris. On the outskirts of the French capital, at Le Bourget Airport, the Oxies reunite. Danny, looking scruffy from travel, takes jaunty strides to join us. He gives me a big grin and says, "I guess you know what happened at Le Bourget back in 1927."

When I tell him I don't know, he wags a finger at me and says, "Shame on you, Miss Yankee Doodle. Don't you know your American history? This is where Charles Lindbergh finished his famous transatlantic flight, landed his Spirit of Saint Louis right here."

Beatrix rushes up, warm, pink, and well fed from her visit with family in the Lake District. She waves, calls out cheerful greetings, and forever the mother hen, rounds us up at the luggage terminal. Dorothy emerges from her flight, subdued and wary. She walks stiffly, neck craned, searching frantically for her suitcase.

Danny spots her bag, grabs it for her, and gives her long dark hair a tug. "You've not been sentenced to the guillotine then, have you?" Dorothy allows herself a restrained smile. Parapluie lags behind, keeping his distance, his wide mushroom of hair looking even more unruly than usual.

Together, we wait outside the airport, huddled for warmth against the chill of an intermittent night drizzle. Danny hails the first cab and Beatrix gives the driver an address.

"*Passage Molière, numéro douze, Le Restaurant des Poètes,*" she says, speaking slowly, enunciating to be clear, putting an English emphasis on the French syllables. The cab carries us across Les Halles, along streets that are shiny with rain.

"The guidebook says it's a good spot for students," Beatrix reassures us. "Prices are reasonable." The driver drops us off at the entrance to a narrow passageway. We find a door numbered twelve, but the restaurant's name is nowhere in sight. Guided by dim pools of light, spilled from cast-iron lanterns set high on the walls, we pass through a mysterious gauntlet and head for a slate blackboard that's propped on the sidewalk by a side entrance. We pause for a moment, doing a quick read of the menu, trying to decipher this evening's dinner offerings, which are enumerated in the customary white chalk squiggle of French lettering. Then we duck inside, eager for food and warmth.

The decor is no-frills, but the waiter is friendly. He approaches with a brief smile, gives a droll wink, then performs a whimsical mime of exquisite French formality. He bows from the waist, tilting his head, and recommends a specific wine to accompany each dish. Speaking to us in clear and careful French, he appears unperturbed by our odd mishmash of English accents, accepting our tortured French phrases with aplomb. This dear fellow, untainted by the Parisian snobbery I anticipated, frees me, for the moment, from the narrowness of my own vision, and I look forward to taking the train back to Clermont and embarking on my life's next chapter there.

CHAPTER NINE

\ (

Out of the Dorm,
Toward Independence

*"Don't shut yourself off in that dark old house of ours." —Lissa's
advice to Spence*

O N A DULL SATURDAY AFTERNOON in mid-January, the
Oxies regroup in Clermont-Ferrand, just off the Place
de Regensburg, in the dorm's central lobby. Beatrix has
mustered us, an unlikely squadron, to move me out of the dorm.

But why are the Oxies moving me out of the dorm today? Well,
Beatrix, Dorothy, Danny, and Parapluie are just finishing up their
business courses in Clermont and will soon return to England.
So, rather than staying on alone at the student dorm, I'm moving
into a one-room apartment that's recently been vacated by Clare's
Irish friend, Bridget, who's gone home to finish her studies in
Dublin. Bridget was *assistante d'anglais* at a girls' high school here
in Clermont.

Ghislaine is on duty today at the front desk. As I turn in my
dorm room key, she rushes around from behind the counter and
seizes me in a dramatic embrace.

"*A bientôt, ma chère, Leeza!*" she gushes, and proceeds to plant multiple wet kisses on alternating cheeks. Eventually, she releases me and I notice my acquaintance, Junjei, across the lobby. He is very much alive despite that fantastical voice intoning the words "Junjei's dead" that I imagined coming from the Spanish maid all those weeks ago in my dorm room. Since then, I've come to know him vaguely as a classmate in my intermediate French classes at the *fac*. He is always polite, but formal and reserved.

Now he is playing chess with a guy named Jules. Jules looks to be in his mid-twenties. I've heard from Ghislaine that Jules works at Michelin and stays half-drunk most of the time. Today's chess game takes me back to those early days in Clermont and my rendezvous with Georges. Junjei was playing chess with Georges that day, in the same corner of this lobby. Now, unexpectedly, Junjei looks up and waves. I wave back, and he calls over to me in English.

"So. Are you moving out? Going home?" Junjei's English is excellent, better than his French. So, whenever we talk, we both tend to lapse into our Anglo comfort zone.

"Moving out. Not far. Just across town."

"Ah. Yes. So, I will see you again?"

"Yes. At the *fac*. I'm getting ready for exams."

"Ah. Good. I also am preparing for the exams."

"Good. So, see you soon?"

"Yes. Soon." And with that, Junjei turns his attention back to the chessboard.

I take a seat near the lobby's entrance and wait while Beatrix rounds up the other Oxies who will help me move across town. Just then, the entrance buzzer sounds, and Ghislaine opens the large glass front doors to a young girl I've never seen before. She has long blonde hair, totes her belongings in a small backpack, and wears a leather jacket and jeans. She looks like a hippie.

She walks over to the reception counter and seems to be trying to register. After a moment, Ghislaine calls over to me. She sounds a bit frantic. "*Mademoiselle Leeza! Pouvez-vous m'aider ici. Cette jeune fille ne parle pas francais.*" Ghislaine needs my help. Apparently, the new girl doesn't speak French.

I rush over, introduce myself to the girl, chat with her, and provide Ghislaine with the basic check-in information she needs. The girl's name is Serena, she's Canadian, from Toronto. As we talk, I'm struck by the calmness of Serena's voice and the clarity of her eyes. She appears to be very young, barely out of her teens. She speaks slowly, conveying both innocence and wisdom. Ghislaine assigns her a dorm room, and I offer to escort Serena. But just then the Oxies arrive and start grabbing my packed boxes. I only have time to point out the girl's elevator, wave goodbye, and join the moving squad.

It's about 1400 hours when I depart the dorm with the Oxies. Together, we form a ragtag band of expatriates transporting all my belongings across town. Surely, we must raise the eyebrows of the locals as we parade through the city streets, impromptu allies, hand carrying a single suitcase and five awkwardly packed boxes. But then again, this is Clermont and its citizens have witnessed far more startling scenes in their streets.

I may have the option, I'm told, of taking on some of Bridget's duties, beginning with a stint teaching English to French girls ages twelve to seventeen, four hours a week at the *lycée Jeanne d'Arc*. Starting out, it would be a voluntary position. I wouldn't get paid, but it would be good experience, and I could eat lunch at the *lycée* if I wanted and use their library. It's worth considering.

A few days after first hearing about this opportunity, I visit the school, spend some time checking out the library, paging through a huge bound volume of Van Gogh sketches and paintings. Even in these glossy reproductions of his artwork, I find an ineffable appeal, a vibrancy of color and texture, a sense of urgency, and the intimacy of an artist who signs with just his first name.

At 250 francs per month, this new room is more expensive than the dorm, but it's close to the *fac* and *the lycée*. And apparently, American English is in demand in Clermont. Based on what the mayor's wife told me, I may be able to get paid for some private tutoring. Besides, in my new room, I'll be more independent. I can do some light cooking and have unrestricted visitors. No concierge to check me in and out and keep an eye on me. It feels as though I'm embarking on a brand-new adventure.

So now, as a farewell gesture of friendship and solidarity, Beatrix has organized the Oxies to help me move. With Danny in the lead and Parapluie bringing up the rear, we zigzag our way across town. Danny and Parapluie each tote a large cardboard box of my jumbled belongings, hurriedly packed. Beatrix and Dorothy each carry a smaller packing box. Clare pedals alongside on her *velo*, the little motorized bike she's bought to get around on in Clermont. She's transporting my personal library—a stack of French novels and my *Grand Larousse* dictionary—in the wire basket attached to the bicycle's handlebars. I lug my stuffed suitcase. We wind our way from Place de Regensburg to a modern apartment complex, a bland mass of concrete that occupies most of a block on avenue Léon Blum.

We find my room, number 36, and hurry to free ourselves of my belongings. We set everything down on the nearest surface that will accommodate—floor, writing table, ladder-back chair, or bed—in the room's constricted space.

Beatrix surveys the room. "Blimey, it's dark in here!" There's a single small window above the bed, and it's shuttered.

Danny tries to open the metal shutters. He tugs and pries, and gives a mighty heave. "Can't get 'em to budge! Must be painted over or summat!"

Finally, he gives up. And we go out to a nearby bar to raise a glass or two and exchange goodbyes. Clare will be staying on in Clermont, but the other Brits will be traveling home in February.

Hours later, we exit the bar and breathe in moist chill air that hovers just around the freezing point and signals the arrival of snow. Parapluie splits away from our group, heading God only knows where. He's a bit odd like that, I tell myself, a bit of a loner. I stop myself from going deeper, remembering how my mother used to chide me for dwelling on negative thoughts.

Clare wheels her bike along the sidewalk next to me. The others are bunched together, walking behind. "So, Lissa. I'm heading out for a ski trip this weekend. Would you be keen on babysitting my *vélo* for me while I'm gone? It even has a wee bit of a motor when you really need to zip along. Here, give it a go!" Clare turns the handlebars over to me.

"Sure," I say, remembering the fun I had as a kid, riding my bike. It was blue, a girl's bike—carefully designed, I had heard other kids say, not to break a young virgin's hymen. In those days I rode close behind Spence, along winding, hilly country roads. He on his sturdy red boy's bike with its strong central support rod running horizontally in front of the rider's saddle.

Pressure of feet against pedals, pushing. Leg muscles straining, propelling me forward and up, slowly up, the long, tedious incline from home to the Methodist church for Vacation Bible School. Then later, loving the long coast down that same curving hill, feet lifted from spinning pedals, effortlessly accelerating, face slapping hard against air solid enough to swoosh back my hair, rush at my ears, press my blouse flat against my chest. Racing past horses that grazed in a lush green blur of field, past flashes of whitewashed fence, riding free down the long, curved hill. Then a brief flat stretch of road beneath me, pedaling normally again. Then home.

So, now I mount Clare's *vélo*. It's smaller, shorter than my American bike, and I find myself standing up as I pedal, accelerating easily along the deserted city street. After a block or so, I look back, press the brakes, step off, and wait for the others to catch up. I'm standing beneath a street lantern, in a pool of yellow light. My face turns up to watch large snowflakes twirl gently down. I stick out my tongue, just as I did as a child to welcome the snow and taste its pure coolness melting here inside my mouth.

Danny comes running up behind me, wraps his arm around my shoulders, and pulls me in close for a hug. "You're doin' it, me darlin'!" he shouts and waits beside me, grinning, as the others catch up. Clare approaches on quick, confident steps, retrieves her *vélo*, and pushes it along the street. Beatrix and Dorothy move more slowly, side by side, at a saunter. "Still waters!" Beatrix taunts as she pushes between Danny and me. But this time, she's not smiling.

Dorothy pulls me aside. "I'd back off Danny if I were you, Lissa. Over the holidays, Beatrix spent some time with Danny in Manchester. Apparently, they're an item."

"But what about Beatrix's Dave?"

"Oh, sure. Dave's her steady. But, as you may have noticed, Beatrix has a healthy appetite for men. Just a warning, Lissa, my ingenuous American friend."

At the intersection, we go our separate ways—Dorothy, Beatrix, and Danny back toward the dorm, Clare riding her *vélo* back to her walk-up. I make my way alone toward my new home on avenue Léon Blum. But, impulsively, for a quick moment, I glance back and see Beatrix snuggling up to Danny, pulling his arm around her. And in that moment, Danny glances back at me, shrugs, and sends me a wink. I know these English friends will be leaving Clermont soon. But I'm going to hold onto that wink. It'll be mine now, forever and a day.

I arrive at the mass of concrete that's to be my new home. At night, the building's walls seem to stretch beneath the darkened sky, threatening to stifle anyone who dares to enter. The silent snow has dissipated as secretly as it began and the stars have shrouded themselves in primordial mists. Relying on the imagined light of Danny's wink to guide me, I cross the lobby, and make my way through unfamiliar corridors, past the locked doors of other residents. It's almost like being inside a morgue. At last, I find and unlock the heavy door to my tiny room, a monk's cell buried in the belly of a modern-day catacomb. I have a feeling I'm going to need the love from that wink to warm me for a while.

When I return from the *fac* on a dreary afternoon near the end of January, a pale blue airmail envelope awaits me on the floor of my room, just inside the door. The unexpected letter from the

United States breaks through my winter doldrums. It must have been dropped through the mail slot while I was out. It's from Dr. Albert, my French professor back home, the one in charge of my French study-abroad program. And to be honest, it's because of him I came to Clermont.

The fall before last, I found myself itching to get out of the house, away from caring for my old father. I resumed college part-time, taking French and English lit classes in the evenings. Spence kept an eye on Daddy while I was gone. So, while I was distancing myself from my father, I became acquainted with Dr. Albert, my attractive, new French professor. I guess Dr. Albert became some kind of transitional object. Although I knew very little about him personally, my imagination transfigured Dr. Albert into some sort of French Byronic hero—a slightly older man but still quite virile, alluringly foreign in his Frenchness, originally from Paris and, in my mind, far more worldly and experienced than guys my own age. A man with a mysterious past, troubled, brooding over some unspeakable personal secret, and apparently as enamored of literature as I was. The rumor among my fellow French majors was that he'd recently gone through a turbulent divorce and was painfully separated from a young daughter who still lived with her mother in Paris.

And then, right after Christmas, my father died. When I went back to school for the second semester my heart was empty and ripe—and there was Dr. Albert, presumably lonely and harboring tortured memories of lost love. He fascinated me, and I clung to every word of his lectures. Often, he favored us by reading aloud passages from great French authors. I savored his dramatic renditions of compelling French heroes: the beautiful ugliness of Victor Hugo's hunchback, Quasimodo, and the disillusionment of Alexander Dumas's Count of Monte Cristo.

When he read to us at the front of the lecture hall, Dr. Albert would step away from the lectern, strike a courtly pose, his right profile turned toward the students. With his head bent slightly forward over the open book, a long fringe of his parted hair would tumble over his brow, and I would have the urge to rise from my seat, dash to his side, run my fingers through that unruly fringe, caress his pensive brow, and . . .

And once during a lecture, when a student—whose French was painfully limited—persisted in chewing gum while asking pointless questions in the most alarmingly bad French accent, Dr. Albert's customary veneer of genteel self-control dissolved. His mouth contorted; he mimicked a scornful parody of the student's fractured, gum-chewing French. Then he gave the chagrined young man an ultimatum: either dispose of the gum and refrain from asking any more absurd questions, or leave the lecture hall forthwith.

The intensity of Dr. Albert's scorn and the violence of his anger added shadows and depth to the sketch I was mentally composing of my beloved French professor. From that moment, my fascination with this man was sealed. For me, his eyes shone with a deep sadness, despairing at human imperfection, longing for a more beautiful life that only I could give him. With the passion of emerging womanhood, I spun a fantasy of fated love. With the innocence of a schoolgirl, I assumed Dr. Albert would love me in return. With the shyness of a virgin, I spoke none of this to Dr. Albert.

And so, longing for any kind of closeness I could share with him, and at the same time yearning for the adventure and romance of travel, I seized upon the idea of enrolling in Dr. Albert's study-abroad program in Clermont. Spence, admonished by my father over the years to "always take care of your little sister" agreed to foot the bill, not knowing how else to get me out of his hair.

So now, alone in my room here in Clermont, Dr. Albert's letter reaches out to me across the Atlantic. He encourages me to do my best on my second-level exams, which are coming up in less than two weeks. His words animate me, and of course, I want to make him proud of me. He also wants me to try for the third-level exams later in the year. He's certain I have the ability. So, yes, I tell myself, I must really buckle down to my studies.

Dr. Albert goes on to mention that the other students, who were supposed to come to Clermont in February as part of the exchange program, are not coming after all. He regrets that I will be on my own for the rest of the year. But he will be coming to Paris during the month of February, and if I can make it, would like to meet up with me there. He gives me the address of an apartment in the eleventh arrondissement, on boulevard Jules Ferry, where he will be staying, and asks me to respond regarding my availability.

A wave of excitement rouses me from my lethargy. A rendezvous in Paris with my treasured Dr. Albert! Of course, I will meet him in Paris! I sit down at my writing table and draft a response. Later that same evening, I rush over to the dorm. Fortunately, Ghislaine is on duty. She is happy to look over my letter. I want it to sound just right. I make the changes she suggests, seal the *aérogramme*, have Ghislaine drop it in the outgoing mail slot, and rush back to avenue Léon Blum, realizing I have lots of reading to do, plus a full schedule of classes. I sit at my writing table, drink mug after mug of coffee, finish reading Giono's *Les Grands Chemins*, and move on with eagerness to the next assignment.

~

Inexorably, the second-level examinations for international students are upon me. On Monday, I find myself seated at my desk in the usual classroom at the *fac*, surrounded by my fellow students, waiting for the first part of the written exams—a two-hour session of translation from French into English. I'm not at all sure of passing the exams, but I tell myself to do my best for Spence and for Dr. Albert and for anybody else who may care.

The next day, I sit at the same desk, in the same classroom, and take the second and third parts of the written exams. A sheath of printed pages, placed on each student's desk, poses six essay questions on the French literature we have studied; we are instructed to choose and respond to four of these questions. Next, we are given a printed text to read, and asked to write a *compte rendu* (sort of a resume) and a *commentaire* (commentary) based on our reading of the text. The essay questions and text are written in French, and all our responses must be in French.

On Friday, I gather with the rest of the intermediate students in the second-floor hallway. We have been told the results of the written exams will be posted on the wall across from our classroom sometime this afternoon. We wait here for several hours until, in late afternoon, a teaching assistant affixes a single sheet of paper to the wall. The sheet lists the names of only ten of the fifteen students in my class. To my relief, my name is among them. This means I am eligible for the oral exams, which will be held next week.

After an anxious weekend, on the following Wednesday morning, I trek back along avenue Gergovia to sit my orals. The orals are administered to one student at a time. So, I wait in the hallway with the other students as one by one our names are called. The orals consist of two parts, and it is mid-morning when I hear Professeur Bonhomme calling my name. "*Mille Power.*"

With a good bit of trepidation, I follow him into the classroom. He gives me a text, an article in the local newspaper, *La Montagne*, and tells me I have fifteen minutes to read and prepare for his questions. I pore over the article. It's about current traffic conditions in the surrounding mountains. Snow and strong northerly winds blowing at more than 100 kilometers per hour have formed snowdrifts. Travel there is now extremely difficult if not impossible.

When I finish reading and look up, Professeur Bonhomme takes a seat beside me and asks me to explain what I have read. Speaking French is not my strong suit, but I do the best I can and am relieved when he nods and follows up with a few simple questions about the article's vocabulary and grammar.

The second part of the orals, French civilization conducted by Professeur Rossignol, is scheduled to begin at two thirty that afternoon. All the students break for lunch, but I am too nervous to eat a solid meal. I escape back to my room where I have coffee and soup.

At the scheduled hour, the orals resume, and I wait nervously in the hallway, along with the other foreign students, to be called into the classroom. The final results will not be posted until next week, after the professors have time to consult and determine a final grade. One-by-one, each student is called in, completes part two of the orals, and files past me to leave for the day. It is getting late, nearly six p.m., when the ninth student, Junjei, is called. I wait anxiously for my turn, and nibble on some chocolate to keep my strength up. When Junjei finally emerges from the classroom, looking even more pale than usual, it is seven p.m. As he passes me on his way out, Junjei hangs his head, refusing to make eye contact. A perturbed and disheveled Professeur Rosignol emerges shortly after Junjei, checks his watch, and asks me to come back tomorrow, at *quatorze heures* to complete my orals. As he hurries away, the professor resembles an agitated bird with ruffled feathers. I am shaken. Everybody else has finished their orals, but I must endure another sleepless night.

On Thursday afternoon, I return to the *fac* and take a seat across from Professeur Rosignol for part two: French civilization. The professor asks me to talk about differences between state and federal government in the US. I manage to say something about the need for regulations at the local as well as at the national level. In response, this funny man speaks at length, giving me what feels like a mini-lecture that extols the efficiency of centralization in the contemporary French government, keeping me there for a full hour.

On my way back to my room, I replay the civilization exam. I don't think I did very well on the topic M. Rosignol asked me to discuss. The results should be posted by tomorrow evening, and I find myself hoping Dr. Albert and Spence won't be too disappointed if I've failed. I did pass the written, though. At least there's that. But, anyway, I'm really glad to have the exams over with.

Agitated, I sit at my writing table and begin to scribble the beginnings of a short story. I pause to make myself another mug of soup, brew a fresh pot of coffee, and reread my most recent letter from Spence, which arrived about a week ago in a battered shipping box. The letter was tucked inside a brand-new pair of blue leather hiking shoes:

Dear Lissa,
Merry Christmas! You told me you do a lot of walking these days. So, I thought you could use these hiking shoes. New coders at work are making my life difficult. These dark days are depressing. At home with the flu today, reading Poe's "The Fall of the House of Usher," then moving on to read about astronomy. One of the cats gave birth in my lap this afternoon. Just one kitten. I'm calling it Baby Fuzz.

Spence

I pull out a blank *aérogramme* and begin a letter to Spence:

Dear Spence,
Your Christmas package arrived a week or so ago. Sorry to take so long to write back and thank you. The hiking shoes are a lifesaver! I've been wearing them ever since they arrived. The dress boots you gave me have just about given out on me.
And wow, a new kitten born right in your lap!
I'm really sorry to hear about your difficulties at work, your depression, and, on top of all that, the flu! Hope you're staying warm in that drafty old farmhouse. Don't read too much Poe. You don't want to get sucked into that miasma! Looking up at the stars sounds like a better path. Don't shut yourself off in that dark old house of ours. I know what that's like.
But finally, I am finished with this round of exams—passed the written, waiting for result of orals. Uncertain how I did. Hope I don't let you down.
I am at work just now on a short story. After many false starts and feeble ramblings, I've settled on my subject matter. As is necessary, it is drawn from my own life, from my emotions, passions, my life blood. Writing is like giving birth, and as is the case with any sort of

creation, I will only succeed when I have completely drained myself of all life energy. It must be like a blood transfusion from me to my work—type O—universal donor—nothing of itself yet perfect in its geometry.

If it's not too much trouble, I wonder if you could send me a couple of my favorite books—my collection of Katherine Mansfield stories and my leather Byron collection? I think they should still be on the desk in my bedroom. Also, would love if you could send some American mixes for pancakes, devil's food cake, fudge brownies, and seasoned popcorn.

Thanks again for the hiking shoes! I'm wearing them right now. All the postal strikes in France apparently held up the mailings. When Aunt Essie's Christmas package finally arrived, the homemade Christmas bread she sent me was green with mold and completely inedible.

I hope you got the sweater I sent you from Scotland.

I'm sending you some Scottish recipes (see below) to pass along to Aunt Essie.

Would be wonderful if you could plan to spend your three-week summer vacation traveling with me. I'd really like to see Copenhagen with you—the Tivoli, the little Mermaid, but especially Elsinore Castle. Or really, I'd just like you to get some traveling in—get some perspective. Is it feasible? Desirable?

What do you think?

Love, Lissa

CHAPTER TEN

❧ ❧

In the Darkness of Black Lava

"Mea culpa, mea culpa, mea maxima culpa" —*Order of the Roman Catholic Mass*

IN CLERMONT'S HISTORIC SECTION, twin towers project from the roof of the Cathédrale Notre-Dame-de-l'Assomption, aspiring, with delicate strength, to pierce the heavens. For support, the tandem spires rely upon thick earthbound Gothic cathedral walls, cut centuries ago from local black *pierre de volvic*, volcanic stone. Our Lady has endured the Hundred Years' War, during which five generations of rival French and English dynasties fought to dominate Western Europe, forging two strong national identities in the process.

Our Lady went on to survive centuries more of disturbing human history. And to this day, the staunch lady persists, projecting mystical black magma phantasms onto musty cobblestone streets, dominating her surroundings, and manifesting her presence far beyond the city's limits.

Here, on a Saturday night in February, I find myself trivialized, an insignificant marionette performing at the whim of the

TRAVELING A SLANT RHYME

Master Puppeteer in the shade of the cathedral's dark lava walls. I am at the Crêperie, an expatriate hotspot in Clermont's medieval quarter, seated at a long plank-top trestle table, surrounded by the Oxies and an assortment of aimless expatriates—temporary students, dilettantes—drifting through Europe, funded by Daddy's money or inherited largesse. I sit with Beatrix, Dorothy, and Parapluie. This is their last night in Clermont. No Clare tonight. She must be off somewhere with French friends, and Danny has gone home early to Manchester. His dad, Beatrix explains, is in hospital. I feel a pang, as if something important is missing without Danny.

We're joined this evening by an artsy couple from London, a young woman who appears to be anorexic and a young man who sports an elaborate three-piece herringbone tweed suit in the Edwardian style. They are passing through Clermont as they gad about Europe for no apparent practical purpose. "Just idling about, sampling life," says the young woman from under a theatrical red felt hat. Its wide brim droops dramatically around her ghoulishly powdered white face and deep black curls. Her words emerge through a gash of crimson lipstick. A tight black velvet jumpsuit highlights her skeletal physique.

A young American couple, Jim and Carla, sit across from me. We recognize each other as Americans. I wave. Say hi. I've run into them a few times at the university's English film club. We sat together during a bunch of films: *Easy Rider, Bob & Carol & Ted & Alice, Midnight Cowboy, Alice's Restaurant*. Sometimes we chat during intermission.

Jim and Carla are upper-middle class, button-down preppies who are wintering in Clermont, holed up in a small apartment until spring when they plan a Mediterranean cruise in Jim's small two-person sailboat. Jim spreads his napkin on the table before him and sketches, in red ink, with a great deal of exuberance, their anticipated itinerary—in France, from La Seyne sur Mer to Nice, then down along the west coast of Italy, then west to Barcelona and back to France. Carla—an athletic-looking, perennially tanned blonde—looks on in a state of coiled yet relaxed contentment. She exudes a characteristically American optimism, an inbred self-confidence that has always eluded me.

Jim and Carla are auditing beginning French classes at the *fac*, where I often pass them in the hallways. They are part of the wave of United States college-age kids who have fled the country, disillusioned with what The Establishment is doing there these days. Just a few years back, my best friend Paloma dropped out, did drugs, joined a commune, and took off to Canada with her husband, Gary, to dodge the Vietnam draft. And now, Nixon's rumored involvement in the Watergate scandal has emitted, from the bowels of the American presidency, a stench so foul it can no longer be ignored, and the political scene seems nowhere near a return to normal.

In light of the state of affairs back home, Jim and Carla seem impressed by my intentionality. Once, during *Fritz the Cat*, Jim leaned over to me and whispered, "You know, Lissa, you're the only serious student I know here in France. You actually have a specific goal, and you're doing what you came here to do."

It's true, I *am* serious. Yet sometimes I feel completely out of touch, like an indeterminant fragment of debris, mired midstream. I watch passively as a stream of drifters, adventurers, and malingerers bum around for a while in Clermont and then move on.

But I've also met a few students who are far more serious and dedicated than I am. For example, my Polish acquaintance, Zytka. And Junjei. Compared to them, I'm a spoiled American, a pretender dreaming of becoming the next great American author but lacking the requisite intellectual power, drive, and dedication. Sometimes I despair, but the misery is not strong enough to push through the inertia.

Just then, a young blonde girl ambles over to our table. It's Serena, the Canadian girl who checked into the dorm when I was moving out. She seems to be wearing the same clothing she wore then, a leather jacket and faded jeans. Serena greets Jim and

Carla, who seem to know her from the *fac*. They invite her to join us, and she sits next to them, across the table from me.

Serena notices me right away and says, "Hey! It's Lissa, right?" I nod and say, "Hi, Serena." She gives me a big smile.

Tonight the anorexic young woman is celebrating her birthday. Twenty-five years old. The waiter brings her a birthday crêpe alight with sparklers. We all join in to sing her "Happy Birthday" and partake in a round of crêpes and ice cream. Parapluie gobbles his crêpe, wipes his mouth with the back of his hand, mutters something about meeting some of his French friends, and slips out abruptly.

"What's he about, anyway?" says Beatrix, her eyes following him like deep blue searchlights. "Strange bloke. Always wandering off somewhere. Never has a girl. Though I'm not surprised. Daft hairdo. Ruddy spots all over his face. What would any girl want with him?"

∼

After the birthday festivities, I leave the Crêperie with the other Oxies, who head out to a favorite bar. Beatrix invites me to tag along, but I'm not up for drinking tonight.

I start back to my room alone, wandering along labyrinthine cobbled streets, and pass a narrow alleyway that runs along the back side of the Cathedral. And there, in the shadows, I see a very young man, splayed against the cathedral, facing the massive stone wall, naked, almost as dark as the black lava itself. His feet spread in a wide stance, he balances on the pavers, hands reaching out and up, fingers curled tight like claws trying to grip the wall. A taller man seizes the young black man from behind, around the waist, enters him, begins to thrust. Atop the taller man, a wide bush of wavy hair lifts and falls with each thrust like a flimsy umbrella surging against gusts of wind. Parapluie! I watch in horror until he emits a final spasmic groan and begins to pull away. Afraid he might see me, I turn and run away as quickly as I can.

Shaken, I move my lips to petition the Deity for forgiveness of my trespasses. For yes, in this moment, I believe I have trespassed, crossed onto unholy ground, and have witnessed an act I am not supposed to see.

I try to focus on something else, anything else. But the image will not leave me. Parapluie with a young black guy. White on black, male on male, thrusting against a dark cathedral wall. And my mind—unprepared to accept, dismiss, or assimilate the image—represses it, shoves it down deep, stores it in a sealed compartment where it will fester among other memories and visions I have been taught to classify as taboo—unless or until I am equipped to examine and make peace with it.

So, I run, retreat. My new blue hiking shoes carry me swiftly along the basalt parvis, each footfall delivering me from some vaguely detected, unfathomable evil. I suck in draughts of cold night air that sting like razors in my chest. But the pain, to me, is strangely purifying and explains something of the saints' self-flagellation.

I rush beneath the gaping mouths of gargoyles, push open heavy wooden doors, find refuge inside the black cathedral. I pass a side chapel where the red sanctuary lamp is burning. My father once told me this means that Jesus is present in the tabernacle. I genuflect, as Daddy taught me, as a sign of adoration.

I take a seat in a pew near the back. Somewhere above me I hear the chiming of a clock, and looking up, see two mechanized Roman gods—Mars and the horned Faunus—beating the head of Saturn, ancient deity of time. I feel the presence of my father—mechanical wizard, horologist extraordinaire, perfect regulator of time.

I must do penance. I feel myself going down on my knees, and feverishly, fervently, begin to pray, "My Father, who art in heaven, forgive me my sin!" A voice replies, reverberating now inside my head. It is the voice of my own deceased father, telling me as he did before, such a long time ago, "Pray, always pray to the Blessed Virgin Mother whenever you're in trouble, Lissa." And so, as always in the past, I obey my father's words.

I fall into a deep state, what I will come to know as meditation. And in that state a woman, glorified in a pure white light,
appears before me. She speaks to me, and her voice is that of my
own mother, Jimmie, lost to me when I was only twelve, on the
threshold of womanhood myself. As she was leaving this world, I
asked, "Mommy, if I talk to you after you die, and if you can hear
me, will you answer me back?" And she said, "Yes, I will." But
those were the last words I heard her say.

Until now. Now her answer comes to me in this holy space.
She whispers, "Lissa," and my heart leaps, opening to receive the
joy. But then, oh then, her long-awaited answer merely echoes her
response when I am seven, lucky seven, and think the hired boy
Lonny may have stolen my virginity. When I confess to her, tell
her what Lonny did to me on that rainy afternoon in a darkened
corner of our barn's hayloft, my mother tells me, "We won't worry
your father with this, will we? He'd be hurt for life."

But this time I find myself standing up tall, so much taller
than before, no longer that fragile little girl. For the first time, I
hear myself speaking in a strong woman's voice. *I* am the mother
now, holding that damaged girl child in my arms, comforting her,
cherishing her. "You have done no wrong," I tell the girl. "Love
yourself, my little one."

And carrying that young self with me, I leave the pew. On my
way out of the cathedral, I pass a shrine to the Holy Mother in
an alcove near the main entrance. I pause, approach the Virgin's
statue, gaze up at Her. I light a candle, place it on the altar at
the feet of this feminine principle, the now-elevated Mary, risen
equal to the three masculine figures of the church. I offer the light
to Her and to myself and to all the women in this universe so that
they too may be lifted up. Unsteady on my feet, I make my way
back through night streets to my room and cry myself to sleep.

꒰ ꒱

CHAPTER ELEVEN

Enter the K Girls

"I dub them the Kalamazoo Girls, this favored breed ... who carry with them the unmistakable cachet of America's upper middle class." —Lissa's notebook

FEBRUARY PLODS ON. Days of endless gray. Nights of ceaseless dream. Flowing on and on—signifying nothing. That's until, into the bleakness of winter, the well-heeled American girls arrive, a bevy of them. They strut through the streets of Clermont, spreading a gloss of affluence and self-satisfied prosperity. They are junior-year students from Kalamazoo College in Michigan who—having just completed two weeks of total French immersion in Grenoble—descend on Clermont-Ferrand like an ostentation of peahens for a few weeks of French Studies at the university.

I dub them the Kalamazoo Girls, this favored breed, these daughters of physicians and dentists, attorneys and corporate executives, who carry with them the unmistakable cachet of America's upper middle class. As such, they move primarily in privileged social circles. During their sojourn in Clermont, they take up residence in the homes of well-to-do French families and attend special seminars at the university. However, when the K Girls audit some of our international student classes at the *fac*, they mingle with a more diverse and representative sampling of this town's inhabitants.

The K Girls are easy to spot in their trendy clothes and hairstyles, their fine leather designer handbags and boots, their exuberance for all that is local and "quaint," their fondness for fine food, art, and culture. They esteem French nobility and, at the same time, exhibit—toward the poor and downtrodden—an exaggerated sympathy, which they mistake for empathy. They make a show of their support for good causes and charitable giving.

During time shared in the language lab, I make a passing acquaintance with one of these girls, Marilee. We've just completed a grueling session of phonetics exercises, and I'm experiencing my usual post-lunch linguistics doldrums. I feel sleepy and half-drugged. So, I'm startled when Marilee—who has never before spoken one-on-one with me—approaches my booth with her customary K Girl *panache*.

I drag the headset off my ears, leap up from my desk, and stand at attention. The sound of Marilee's voice comes at me as if through water. ". . . only American English will do for Martine. So, it would be lovely—and a wonderful opportunity for you—if you could take over for me when I leave Clermont."

I pause a moment to clear my head and to be certain I heard correctly. Then I blurt out, "Sure."

Marilee goes on to explain that speaking English with an American accent is quite fashionable, practically a requirement, in affluent social circles. "In fact, it's *de rigueur* among most of my French friends here." Marilee tells me that she has been giving English lessons to a certain Martine, daughter of a prominent local politician.

Marilee digs around in her oversized handbag and continues, "My student, Martine, is making good progress. Great gal! Knows all the right people. But, you know, I'll be leaving Clermont in just a few short weeks. So, Martine will be desperate for a replacement tutor . . . Ah, here it is!"

Marilee draws out a large address book/engagement calendar, its front cover embossed with her initials, bold in gilt lettering. She unfolds the buttery leather and withdraws an inserted Cross pen from its sheath. "So here, before I forget, let me give you Martine's address. And her phone number." She inscribes her prized pupil's contact information across a page designated "Notes," tears the notepaper along its perforation, hands it to me, and hurries off with her K Girl friends to their next commitment. Marilee's large, flourishing script loops across and fills the entire page.

Marilee strives to be beautiful, seeming always in urgent need of attention. She wears a lot of makeup, especially around her dark brown eyes, which makes them look extra-large and expressive. Someone must have told her they are her best feature—even though one eye is noticeably larger than the other. Her skin is coarse, with large pores, and her mouth is curiously lop-sided.

Her voice, dramatic and resonant, can frequently be overheard—before and after class in the language lab—regaling the other K Girls with idylls of her budding romance. Apparently, Marilee has fallen suddenly and overwhelmingly in love with a cousin of the family she's been boarding with.

A few days later, when I'm eating lunch at the Resto, just before class, Marilee catches my eye and waves. The cafeteria is crowded today, and Marilee calls out to me a strident greeting, "Hi there! Can you save me a seat?" She asserts her way across the room, conspicuously self-aware, clearly American, and grabs the space across from me. Usually, she eats with the other K Girls, but today she's alone, in need of a place to sit, and apparently has some important news she urgently needs to broadcast.

Today, her eagerness to chit-chat comes across as oddly vulnerable, almost endearing. She barely touches the food on her tray as she waves her left hand around, showing off a huge engagement ring. She talks incessantly about her fiancé, her young Frenchman, who just yesterday evening "popped the question." Throughout lunch Marilee chatters about her deepening relationship with her new beau. "Who could have known I would find my love in Clermont! Never in a million years could I have dreamed it!"

After lunch, we walk to the language lab together. The others in her K-hive are noticeably absent, apparently occupied elsewhere. "Isn't it awful the girls aren't here today? I'd love for them to meet him. I can't help myself. I just want to show him off to everyone! I can't wait to visit him after class."

As we leave class, a light rain begins to fall. "Too wet and too far to walk," says Marilee. "My fiancé rents a *maisonette* in Chamalières," she tells me and hails a cab, hops in, and gives the driver an address. As the cab pulls away, Marilee gives me a funny little wave with her palm turned toward herself. It's a good imitation of the Queen of England's royal wave.

⁓

Next weekend, when I'm walking around Place de Jaude, gazing into shop windows just to amuse myself and clear my head, I run into Marilee as she exits the main entrance of the magnificent white stone opera house on boulevard Desaix. She rushes over and invites me to take tea with her at a nearby café and tea salon.

We sit in a corner, in warm shadows, near the languor of a large white masonry woodstove. Marilee sits across from me at a polished wooden table. "This is one of my favorite spots in Clermont," she says.

The woman who waits on us is tall, silver-haired. She wears a long black dress, a high collar of white lace clasped with an ornate brooch. Marilee orders Sochi tea and recommends the Viennese cocoa for me. The waitress rustles off to fill our order.

Marilee leans in close to talk—elbows on table, chin resting on folded hands. "The proprietors are Soviet immigrants. The Saltykovs. Sweet couple."

Marilee tilts her head toward the kitchen where our waitress has disappeared. "The lady who just took our order—that's Mrs. Saltykov. She rarely speaks. But occasionally, I hear her say something to her husband in what sounds like Russian. At first, I thought her French must be very limited. But one time I overheard her slipping into French—a very formal and old-fashioned sort of French."

Marilee points across the room to the elderly gentleman who held the door, bowed, and greeted us when we came in. "Over there. That's Mr. Saltykov, the owner. Debonair, isn't he? Claims to be descended from an eighteenth-century Russian nobleman, Sergei Saltykov, Catherine the Great's first lover."

"Wow!" I say. As I ponder the credibility of this claim, the fire in the Russian stove's hearth seems to puff out a rainbow-hued bubble that rises trembling in the stove light, defying any disbelief. Inside this fantastical bubble, a miniature Russian royal court materializes, a tableau resurrected from an earlier century, captured in a snow globe. Suspended on my imagination within this bubble, impossibly elegant courtiers assemble before a splendid throne, ingratiating themselves, jockeying to be acknowledged by their ruler, the storied Catherine, Empress of All the Russias.

Mrs. Saltykov has returned with our beverages and is gently placing the tea and cocoa before us. Her eyes are very large, dove gray, shaded with a profound sadness. When she catches me studying her, the old woman averts her eyes. She turns her attention to the next table where her husband is seating two new customers. Pivoting away—slightly unsteady on her feet, but still supple as an aging ballerina—Mrs. Saltykov moves on to serve the next customers.

Marilee savors a tall glass of steaming black tea, pauses in her sipping, and blows on her tea to cool it. Then lifting her glass to the stove's firelight, she says, "And this is my favorite tea." The dark tea glows like melted ebony. I glance over at the top of the white monster stove, half expecting to see a character from Russian literature sleeping up there.

"I adore the way they sweeten their tea with jam and how they serve it in these traditional glasses. And see the tea holder." Marilee grasps her glass by its holder, rubs her thumb along its decorated surface. "It's silver-plated," she says. "Stamped with the

Russian double eagle crest. Mr. Saltykov tells me they import their tea from Sochi. It's grown on the slopes of a plantation near the Black Sea."

Marilee points out an immense urn—more work of art than mundane brew pot—that's making simmering noises on a sideboard near the entrance to the kitchen. "Did you notice the samovar over there?"

"Wow!" is all I manage to say. But to myself I think: blue and white ceramic, exquisite.

"That's where they heat the water for their tea. See the teapot on top?"

"Oh, wow," I say again, and realize how *not* exquisite I must sound.

By this time, practically swooning over my mug of hot cocoa, moving my feet in three-four time under the table, I'm transported back to a time when nobility held sway, emperors waltzed in grand ballrooms, and bloodlines determined fortunes. Romantic? A time to be yearned for? Maybe. I reflect over my cocoa.

Or maybe not. Maybe a shameful time. A time when prejudice and deprivation were doled out freely to those with ancestors of the "wrong kind." A time that echoes forward even now, sustaining—if only figuratively—the treacherous moats and impenetrable walls that bar entry into the age-old castles of privilege.

Marilee is watching me. "Like it? Viennese cocoa. The perfect drink to fend off the cold or the blues. As much dessert as beverage. The Saltykovs gave me their recipe. Milk, cocoa, sugar, raspberry brandy . . . and egg yolk. The secret lies in the egg yolk. How you control the heat. Too hot and you'll scramble the egg. And, always, always, that dollop of whipped cream goes on top."

I learn of Marilee's infatuation with French music and art as she regales me with an inventory of the many events and showings she's attended since coming to Auvergne—everything from classic opera, to ballet, to symphony concerts, to *avant garde* theater presented by troupes of actors touring central France. She's even set herself the goal of browsing through every museum and art gallery in the city. I find myself admiring Marilee's cultural itinerary, even though it makes me feel like a sloth. I promise myself to get out more, be more social.

"They have wonderful opera right here in Clermont," she tells me. "I'd just bought tickets for this weekend's performance when we bumped into each other. Oh, and by the way, there's an abundance of the most scrumptious cuisine around here. Have time for another cocoa?"

I agree, and we savor a second round of hot drinks. Wood crackles in the Russian stove. Shadows dance in our corner. Time seems to pause, floating above us like a held breath, as Marilee reels off an inventory of the many fine dishes she's sampled in Clermont and its environs. The foods she describes sound so delightful I want to capture them. I take out a pen and listen intently, trying to jot down the list of names and ingredients as she recites them. The list is long.

"I adore *patranque*," Marilee says. "It's an amazing scramble of local ingredients." She counts them off on her fingers. "Bread from home-grown grains, half rye, half wheat. Cantal cheese. Chopped garlic." As she speaks, Marilee's face is flushed with enthusiasm. "At the university, I met a girl from Salers who invited me home with her one weekend. Her mom let me watch as she prepared *patranque* in the kitchen.

"The *maman* soaked the sliced bread in water until it got soft. Then she squeezed out the bread and sauteed it in butter until it turned into a thick soup. That's when she added in slices of cheese and chopped garlic. When the cheese started to melt, she whipped it all up in the pan until it got smooth and stretchy when she pulled on it with the wooden spoon."

I flip to a new page in my notebook, struggling to keep up with Marilee's discourse. "The girl's mother cooked this *mélange* until it was gooey, then cooked it some more, until the bottom was crispy. She seasoned the whole thing with salt and lots of pepper. Really hit the spot! Warm and chewy and crunchy. The perfect food for damp, chilly weather."

Marilee licks her lips, rubs her tummy, and moves on to describe the next dish. "*Cassolette de cèpes, escargots et noix.* That's a casserole. Earthy mushrooms, shallots, and snails sauteed in butter with double cream and walnuts. Doused in local dry white wine, flavored with an aniseed apéritif, freshly grated nutmeg, salt, and an abundance of pepper." I continue scribbling as fast as I can, trying to get all this down in my notebook.

Marilee continues, not skipping a beat. "Then there's *omelette au boudin*. Eggs mixed with black pudding, cooked in butter. Now that's potent stuff! A little goes a long way." She pauses, drinks some tea as if to clear her palate, and resumes.

"But my all-time favorite," Marilee says, "is *gourmand de truite*. Has a much longer name on the menu. It's a specialty of the master chef at a darling little country restaurant. A culinary masterpiece!" Marilee kisses her fingertips and spreads them wide.

"The chef was kind enough to give me his recipe. Layers of trout fried in olive oil, spread with a creamy chestnut puree, and tucked into a blanket of cabbage leaves. The whole thing gets baked. When it comes out of the oven, it's topped with crispy thin slices of fried salt pork belly. The trout is served with an accompaniment of vegetables—carrots, leeks, celery—that have been fried in olive oil, seasoned with herbs and garlic, and simmered in a mysterious sauce. The chef won't disclose all the sauce's ingredients—except to say that it's scented with a bouquet of good white wine."

At the end, Marilee puffs out her cheeks, pats her expanded belly, jokes about all the weight she's been gaining in France, and confesses with a wink and a chuckle, "Food is my hobby." Actually, Marilee has a really good figure; I don't think she's at all fat. I guess I should tell her that. But for some reason I don't. I just listen, relax, and enjoy her company.

As we leave the Saltykovs' establishment, I browse my pages of notes. The words are scrawled in such a disorderly jumble, I'm not sure I'll be able to decipher them later. But I am beginning to make sense of Marilee, to see beyond the gloss of privilege. She's passionate about local culture: art, music, and cuisine. Maybe we can become good friends and explore Auvergne together.

꧂ ꧁

CHAPTER TWELVE

In the Grip of Depression and Self-Doubt

"I cannot see a way forward." —Lissa's notebook

LTHOUGH ALL THE OTHER K GIRLS have moved on to study in Paris, Marilee marries her young Frenchman and remains in Clermont, apparently spellbound by matrimony. I haven't seen her since we went to the Saltykovs' for tea and cocoa. The band of Oxies has dispersed. The English have gone home and my Scottish friend, Clare, is moving in broader circles with new French friends. She has dropped out of the university courses, taken up skiing, and has little time for me. Feeling abandoned by my friends, I recede into a gray Clermont winter.

Alone at 36 avenue Léon Blum, I pin my intermediate-level certificate on the wall above my square wooden writing table. *Lettres français deuxième degré, Université de Clermont-Ferrand*—printed in large, incontrovertible script on oversized heavyweight vellum—validates my time here. The smaller lettering below relegates my level of achievement to a mediocre *Passable*.

I'm losing track of time. How long ago did I sit taking second-level exams—conversation, writing, grammar, French civilization? And how long after that did I assemble with the other international students at the *fac*'s main building, anxious as we strained to view our rankings posted on the wall? How many days have passed since Clare ran up to me in the hallway, waving her certificate under my nose and crowing, "I got a *Bien!*" How long since I watched as Junjei searched the list of second-level certificate rankings, saw that his name was missing, and disappeared silently down the long hallway.

I'm disappointed in myself. My father—such a perfectionist—would have expected more from his little girl. But *quand même*, even so, I tell myself, at least I didn't fail the exams. I'll be moving on now to the more challenging third-level courses. But the conviction of not being good enough persists.

My friend Trudy from New York City tries to cheer me up, inviting me to her apartment for hot chocolate. Although she tries to come across as big-city, tough-as-nails, Trudy is really a softy underneath. With me, she's like a big sister.

"Nothing to be ashamed of," she reassures me, passing me a steaming mug. "I got a *Passable*, too. So what? We passed, didn't we? And that's all that really matters. With everything that's going on these days with Nixon and those Watergate tapes, nobody back home gives a crap about this small stuff."

I blow on the tall white ceramic mug, take a sip, look up at Trudy, give her what feels like a pathetic smile, and say, "But Clare got a *Bien*."

My words and expressions seem to set Trudy off. Leaping to my defense, she goes on to say, "Seems Clare has impressed the professors, despite that annoying Scot's burr of hers."

Trudy's on a roll now. "If, as the French would say, if *one* were to ask my opinion, which *one* probably wouldn't, I'd say that our Scottish acquaintance muddles every French 'r' that passes through her lips. Sounds like she's got a piece of thick Highlands wool pulled over her mouth." Trudy's voice has taken on a tone of superiority—national superiority. In this case, American superiority, but I don't think Trudy's aware of it.

~~~

I attend the third-level international student courses, at first with enthusiasm. But then, on an especially frigid afternoon, I return from the *fac* to my room to find a slim blue envelope from the US, handwritten in Dr. Albert's familiar French scrawl. I am thrilled—until I read the brief note inside. Dr. Albert informs me, with sincere regrets, that he will not be coming to Paris in February and hopes I have not suffered any inconvenience.

I find the message unnecessarily terse, formal, distant. I had vaguely imagined sipping wine opposite Dr. Albert in some private location, discussing, at first, my classes in Clermont, then moving on to our love of literature more generally. Finally, we would speak—hesitantly, at first—about our personal lives, drifting effortlessly into addressing each other by our first names—Lissa, François—and inevitably lapsing into *tu* instead of *vous*. So now, disappointment overwhelms me, plunges me into a stunning darkness that seems to settle like a dense vapor around me.

When last I spoke with Trudy, she told me she'd decided not to pursue the advanced degree in French letters. "I'm not all that interested in French literature," she said. I force myself to continue with my classes. But after a few weeks, I lose interest in spending hours in lifeless classrooms, poring over tedious French texts. No disrespect to Stendhal, but analyzing every paragraph in *Le Rouge et Le Noir*, this chronicle of France's nineteenth century, is not how I want to spend my time right now.

So, without the K Girls and the Oxies, with Trudy no longer attending classes at the university, and now without a rendezvous with Dr. Albert in Paris to motivate me, I begin to skip classes. I hole up alone in my small room, in limbo, contemplating becoming an *assistante d'anglais* at the *lycée*.

My room is dark and stuffy. Just the one small shuttered window. I have set out my essentials on the small writing table: a copy of the *Grand Larousse* French-English dictionary, notebook, pens, a stack of letters from home, bright yellow ceramic drip coffee maker newly purchased from Les Galleries, a plug-in cooking pot—a cast-off from Clare—for heating water for coffee and tea. I have stocked up on infusions and packets of dried onion soup from the local shops. So, I only need to venture out once or twice a day for meals at the Resto. All the familiar faces in Clermont seem to have vanished. Day by day, the loneliness builds. I open the notebook to the next blank page and try to resume my journal, jotting down ideas for stories. I find myself writing, "I cannot see a way forward."

For Christmas, Clare gave me a small secondhand tape recorder. So, sometimes, I try to narrate and record my stories. Also, for Christmas, Clare's dad gave me two large bottles of his personal Scotch whiskey blend, which I smuggled back from Scotland. Now, I discover that narration is more appealing after a glass or two of whiskey.

One afternoon, I skip lunch at the Resto and return to my room alone. As I approach my building, my attention is drawn to a tattered old man on the opposite side of avenue Léon Blum, trudging along slowly, pulling a small grocery cart behind him. On impulse, I call out to him, "*Comment ca va?*" How's it going?

He glances over at me, mumbles something unintelligible, stops walking, and begins to rummage through the cart, pulling out rags. For some reason, this old man fascinates me. I stop for a moment to observe him.

He feels around inside the pocket of his shabby overcoat, eventually pulling out a large needle and a spool of thread. Then he sits, just there, at the edge of the sidewalk, under a naked chestnut tree, with rags gathered in his lap. As I watch, he threads the needle and begins to stitch his rags together. Completely engaged in this task, he seems to have forgotten I am still there, watching.

But after a while, he stands and stretches out his rags. They are all assembled now, sewn into a single sheet, and he waves it like a rumpled flag. Over and over, he cries out, *"Allons enfants! Allons enfants! Allons enfants de la patrie!"*

At last, he folds his flag, and with great respect, salutes it. He pulls a large burlap sack from his cart, tucks the folded flag inside it. Then, using the filled sack as a pillow, he curls up beneath the bare chestnut tree, on a pile of dead leaves and debris.

I continue to watch this man, mesmerized. After a few minutes, he seems to doze off. On impulse, I cross the street and stuff a crumpled franc note into his overcoat pocket. He must be asleep because he doesn't stir. It's then I realize I've become quite cold, and head back to my room.

I spend the afternoon there sipping at Scotch, Clare's dad's personal blend. After the first glass, I start to commiserate with myself, *poor me, poor me,* then pour myself a second shot. As the whiskey softens the edges of the room, the muse is summoned, and I feel a story coming on. I get the tape recorder going, and with speech slowed and slurred, narrate the following words: *"There is a ragman here, a weathered patriot, stitching together the remnants of his nation...."* Here I fall asleep.

I wake up hungry and with a fierce thirst. I drink some bottled water, splash cold water on my face at the sink, run my fingers through my hair, button on my fireman's jacket, and trudge up the hill to the Resto for dinner. Whiskey on an empty stomach has left me groggy and light-headed.

Tonight, they're serving beef liver. I force myself to eat a few bites and fill up on mashed potatoes and bread.

On the way out, I glance into the Resto café and am surprised to see Georges in there, sitting alone at the coffee bar, apart from my other Arab friends. I'm still feeling the effects of the Scotch. My inhibitions are down, and I'm not held back by my customary shyness. In fact, Georges seems to be watching for me. He nods when I come into the room. And I find myself going over to the bar, sitting on the stool next to him.

"How was *l'Écosse?*" he asks. How was Scotland?

But I'm lost again in the molten liquid of his eyes, and for the moment, Scotland seems irrelevant aside from the fact that I've come back armed with birth control.

"I've moved out of the dorm," I tell him. "I have a room now on avenue Léon Blum. Not far."

He drives me back there. I usher him in, excuse myself, rush down the hall to the WC, and insert my new diaphragm. We try to have sex, but seem to be at cross purposes. I am wanting something romantic. A kiss. An embrace. But Georges pushes me down on the cot, climbs on top of me. I'm feeling hesitant and shy. That first time we were together seems so long ago.

Georges tries to find his way inside me, goes limp. He rolls me over, tries bumping me from the rear, but can't get aroused. He gets up abruptly, pulling on his pants, and prepares to leave.

"*Je t'aime! Je t'aime!*" I find myself declaring to him. I feel desperate and foolish.

Georges doesn't respond. He looks annoyed and turns away, staring at a board game of four twenty-one on my writing table. This game is ubiquitous in local cafés, kept for the amusement of the clientele. Just last week, in a wave of homesickness, I bought one as a souvenir I can take home to play with my brother.

Georges picks up the three dice from the gameboard's green baize surface, cups them loosely in his palm, and caresses each one, several times, with his thumb. "I am not in love with you," he says softly, not looking at me, staring instead at the dice in his hand. "We are *copains*." We are buddies.

Georges places the dice, one by one, not touching, back onto the board. He adjusts each one, precisely, with a surgeon's touch, to form a perfectly straight line. Then he exits the room, closing the door firmly in my face.

CHAPTER THIRTEEN

Love at First Sight and the "Arab Head"

"To be called the 'Arab head' is an insult inflicted on our people by prejudiced little white men." —Lissa's friend, Mohammed

NOW WHENEVER I GO to and from the Resto, I find myself peering into the student café, hoping to get a glimpse of Georges. Days go by, but Georges is never there. I can't bring myself to cross that threshold and join my other Arab friends.

But finally, on a dreary Friday evening, Mohammed catches my eye as I pass and waves frantically at me, calling me over. He is alone today.

"*Amérique, Amérique!*" He pulls out a chair for me. "Are you okay, *Amérique*?" he says in English, his voice plaintive.

"*Qu'est-ce qu'il y a?*" What's the matter? I ask him.

Mohammed's response startles me. Returning to his customary French, he begins by posing an intriguing question: "So, *Amérique*, do you believe in love at first sight?"

As I consider Mohammed's question, an image pops into my head. I see Georges, standing outside on a sidewalk not far from here, alone, buffeted by a strong wind. Desire, powerful and irrational, surges inside me, unresolved, that same yearning I felt the first time I saw him. And, it occurs to me that my love at first sight—if that's what it was—could not be trusted.

"I don't know," I say to Mohammed. "What is love? I haven't figured it out yet."

He looks concerned for me and says, "*Amérique*, you owe it to yourself to figure out what love is. True love reveals itself, comes knocking at your heart, refuses to be ignored." And with that, Mohammed finishes off his demitasse of strong black coffee and goes over to the counter to order a refill. He returns with a cup in each hand, sets one in front of me, and resumes our conversation.

"*Amérique*, you see before you a man who suffers from love and yet rejoices in it." Mohammed thumps his chest and says, "This man rejoices, even though others condemn him." As he speaks, Mohammed strips the paper wrappers from three cubes of sugar, dropping them one by one into the opaque black brew. "In this country, men denounce my bloodlines and prevent me from marrying the woman I love.

"For as far back as my memory goes, I have been aware of light and color and the beauty of things." Mohammed pauses to stir the sugar in his coffee.

"But, in my country, in Syria, turmoil has become a way of life. This has kept me from attending any school long enough to earn a formal degree. And yet I have learned priceless lessons outside the shelter of classroom walls. I carry these lessons with me, here and here." Mohammed taps his head and then his heart.

"I grew up running from violence," he says.

Mohammed tells me that for more than two decades he lived through military coups and uprisings. He witnessed bloody riots in the streets and fled from them, journeying from west to east through Syria's mountain passes, crossing vast steppes and blistering desert.

"Seeking peace, I was pursued by violence. Seeking connection, I found only alienation," Mohammed says as he adds another cube of sugar to his coffee and stirs it.

As I listen to Mohammed, I reflect on how hard growing up in Syria must have been–so different from growing up in the United States. The hardest part for me was losing my mother. "You must have missed your family," I say. "Did you ever get in touch with your family?"

"I longed to see my mother again. I returned to my birthplace in Aleppo, but she wasn't there. I searched for her everywhere— from north to south, from Aleppo to Damascus."

As he speaks, Mohammed's hands begin to tremble. He pauses to light a cigarette, then continues. He recalls traveling by foot along narrow coastline, unpaved roadways, damaged footpaths. His memories are vivid, his voice becomes strained, and I can see anguish in his eyes.

"In the end," says Mohammed, it was fear that drove me." He describes passing under ancient archways, through the twisting alleyways of *souks*. "These *souks*," he says, "are what we call our marketplaces." He speaks of his homelessness, of seeking temporary shelter among distant relatives and friends—sometimes even among sympathetic strangers.

"Eventually, I made my way to France to find refuge, and then here to Clermont." He peels another sugar, dips it in his coffee, and then sucks on the brownish cube.

Mohammed explains that his struggles have reinforced his sensitivity to his surroundings. He has learned to appreciate fine architecture—palaces and mosques and temples and churches alike—knowing that they are not immutable, that their beauty is most fragile in times of conflict.

Mohammed's voice has become calmer, more resigned now. He leans back from the table and crosses his legs. "And yes, I have also learned to pay close attention to the people I encounter, for they too are impermanent." He tells me he has witnessed how easily legs and arms are blown off, bodies disfigured, faces scarred beyond recognition, and innocence violated.

So now, when he comes in contact with an object of particular charm, his instinct is to capture it with pencil, ink, or charcoal—whatever comes to hand—to preserve that which is lovely before illness or old age or war comes to destroy it.

"When did you come to Clermont," I ask.

"It is five years since I first arrived in Clermont. I hoped to pursue a degree in art, but I had no steady income. I found a job at a small photography and frame shop, not far from the train station. At first, I worked there sweeping floors, earning just enough to sustain myself. Later, I learned to assemble frames and was paid a slightly higher wage. I work there still.

"Now, I assist the owner with his photography. I earn enough to buy art supplies and take coffee here with my friends." He moves his hand in a circling gesture to indicate the Arab table where we sit. "Since settling in Clermont, it has been my good fortune to reconnect with my brother, Ibrahim. You have met him. He has found housing nearby."

I glance down at my coffee, sitting there on the table, untouched. I take a sip. It's cold. Mohammed notes the shift in my attention. "Have I spoken too long?" he asks.

"No, no. Please go on," I urge him.

"You see, *Amérique*, the shop owner, my boss, is a kind man, an immigrant himself, a Russian Jew." Mohammed explains that his boss worked as a photographer for a Soviet newspaper when Khrushchev was in power, at a time when people thought censorship had eased up. So, this Russian photographer was surprised when—at the height of his career—the newspaper began censuring his work. Officials claimed that certain of his photos presented Party members in a 'less than favorable light'—no further explanation was given. He was fired, summarily, his photos banned. He fled his country, with only the clothes on his back, the bare essentials in his wallet—and his camera. Later, he was denounced as a Soviet dissident.

As he speaks of his boss, Mohammed becomes pensive and frequently strokes his goatee. His voice takes on a solemn tone.

"My boss has taught me many things. Authoritarianism feeds on prejudice, and in Russia, Jews are convenient scapegoats."

Mohammed's mention of Khrushchev reminds me of my own childhood, of growing up with routine air raid drills, the fear of Russians dropping bombs on us. I remember President Kennedy urging Americans to build bomb shelters. I remember Daddy saying, "The Cold War is heating up."

Mohammed continues to stroke his scant goatee. "I don't know my boss's real name. I don't think he wants it known. He calls himself, quite simply, Monsieur Moïse. And it is through him that I have come to know what love really is."

Mohammed's eyes grow misty. "Two years ago, I fell, as they say, in love at first sight, with a lovely young French girl. The moment I first saw her, when she walked through the door of the shop, our eyes fixed on each other. She came with her father, her mother, and her little brother to pose for a series of family portraits. Monsieur Moïse tasked me with adjusting the lighting and changing the backdrops as he directed the family to take different seating arrangements and assume a variety of poses. The session continued for more than two hours. And for the entire time, the girl and I could scarcely take our eyes off one another. During the course of the session, I learned her name—Juliette, an apt name for a star-crossed lover, as it turns out."

Mohammed's voice intensifies. "I became obsessed with Juliette—for how many days and nights, I do not know. But for a time, I scarcely knew who or where I was. Around me, I saw nothing but Juliette. No matter how I occupied the hours—emptying garbage, stacking frames—my thoughts dwelled always on Juliette. At night, my dreams filled with Juliette, my dear, dear Juliette."

Mohammed shifts in his chair, leans in closer, assures himself of my attention.

"As I said before, Monsieur Moïse is a kind man. He has no use for enmity between Arab and Jew. In me, he sees not an adversary, but a fellow human being, an immigrant who, like himself, has fled his country, has suffered for being descended from a different tribe—the wrong tribe. He saw me not as a foreigner, not as a stranger, but as a frightened young man who needed understanding. And so, he took me into his business and mentored me."

Mohammad sits back a bit, squeezes his lips into a tight smile. "To me, it is ironic that some who follow the teachings of the Prophet Jesus, as disseminated by their Saint Paul, might even describe the behavior of this Jew, this Moïse, as Christian. And it fascinates me that this Saint Paul—this Hebrew, Saul—found his Christian faith on the road to Damascus in my own country."

Mohammed leans in toward me again, pierces me with his eyes, and draws me further into his space. The intensity of his voice increases. "Fate," he says. "*Amérique*, do you believe in fate?" As if compelled, I nod in affirmation as Mohammed reaches across the table to squeeze my hand.

"You see, *Amérique*, as fate would have it, Juliette and I crossed paths again. As you must know, Clermont is not so big a town. So, one day, as I walked home from work, taking my customary route, I passed Juliette on rue Pascal. She carried a bookbag on her shoulder. I carried the sketchpad that travels with me everywhere. We were both startled and, for a while, just stared at each other. Then, as if in a trance, we held hands and strolled together to the Fontaine d'Amboise. This fountain is very old and made of black stone. It is topped by the statue of a wild-looking man, bearded, with a mustache, perhaps some ancient ancestor of this region. He is dressed in an animal pelt. He wields a club and defends himself with a shield." Mohammed flexes his muscles, strikes a fierce pose.

"The water in this fountain flows in three tiers. Juliette took a seat on the lip of the lower basin, half facing me, and let the water play over her hand. Her posture entranced me. I wanted to imbibe her, capture her in this instant. My fingers flew across my drawing pad, sketching her in charcoal—the flow of long hair coursing down her back, the contours of her body, so alive and sensuous against the backdrop of antiquated European fountain.

I sketched until the light faded. And then she let me walk her to the front door of her home, to a stone townhouse in an exclusive neighborhood.

"We climbed the front steps and embraced at the entrance, under a small portico. Just then, a light went on above us, came at us through the hammered glass of an antique bronze fixture suspended from the interior of the porch roof. The light exposed us, pooled around us, and spilled at our feet and on the marble steps below. As I turned to leave, Juliette made me promise to return next evening, at this same time, to meet her parents. I promised, and with that, I ran—literally ran—home, eager to put the final touches on my drawing." Mohammed pauses, taking a sip of coffee.

"Next evening, a manservant opened the door. He ushered me in, to a corner near the front door, told me to wait there, and went to announce my arrival. He failed to ask my name. I was simply left to stand alone beside a tall clock and listen to the long strokes of its brass pendulum.

"Soon, Juliette and her father came walking toward me, through the long front hallway. Her father is a short man, balding; Juliette is a full head taller. She had linked her arm in his, was smiling across at him, pulling him along to meet me. I waited in my corner, obscured against a backdrop of dark wood paneling.

"As father and daughter drew near, Juliette seemed so very happy to see me. She broke away from her father and rushed up to greet me. I stepped forward to meet her, away from the wall. As I did so, light from an elaborate ceiling fixture washed over me.

"It was then Juliette's father saw my face and recognized me. Juliette must not previously have identified me or said my name—perhaps she has never heard my name; I don't believe I ever spoke it to her. In any case, the father stopped there in the hallway, seeming to be startled.

"At first, I thought he was reaching out to shake my hand. But no. He thrust both hands into the pockets of his suitcoat. The look in his eyes became one of horror. He seemed disgusted to see me in his house. He turned on his daughter, yelled at her. 'What is this?' His voice was ugly. 'Is this the man you want to go out with? This *tête d'Arabe?*'"

Mohammed touches my sleeve and asks me, "Do you know this expression, *Amérique*, this *tête d'Arabe*? Do you know what it means to be called the *Arab head*?"

I have no idea. "*Pas d'idée,*" I say, shaking my head.

"It is an insult inflicted on our people by prejudiced little white men. French-born men who need constantly to convince themselves of their superiority. Men like this define themselves by their possessions, their social status. Their pockets are filled, but their souls are empty."

Shocked by what Mohammed says, I turn my face away, feeling embarrassed for my race.

Mohammed tugs at my sleeve, and for a moment I think he is going to weep. "*Amérique*, I cannot describe the pain I felt—and feel even now—hearing these words come from her father's mouth." I feel an intense mix of sadness and anger erupting from Mohammed as he speaks.

"Juliette's smile collapsed. She put her hands over her ears and began to cry. I wanted to go to her, to speak out in her defense. But the father's look was forbidding, and he blocked my way. Though short, he is compact and the stance he took against me there in his hallway was imposing. Legs spread wide, the alpha dog defending his territory. I felt badly beaten, and so, like a mangy cur from an inferior pack, I hung my head and slunk away. Though my mind swirled with schemes of vengeance, my heart went limp." Mohammed takes a final sip of his coffee and pushes the empty cup aside.

"When Moïse saw me moping, performing my tasks like a man more dead than alive, he asked me what was wrong. I told him of my love at first sight for Juliette and how it is forbidden here in France. As he listened to my story, many of his own sad memories rushed in to confront him. He spoke to me of being a Jew in Russia. As a schoolboy, he had felt the sting of antisemitic slurs, had overheard his parents whispering at night about this or that family member who had vanished. He grew up in fear of Stalin's pogroms, had nightmares involving his own exile, imprisonment, torture—even murder. And so then, he understood me. Perhaps better than I understood myself."

"And what happened after that?" I ask Mohammed. "With you and Juliette?"

"I have not seen her since. I hear that she has married a prosperous lawyer and is living elsewhere."

ﮩﮩﮩ

Depression settles in. A miasma worthy of Edgar Allen Poe. A classic French *ennui*. Chronic boredom. More and more homesick, I spend days and nights alone—how many I don't know; I lose track of time—sleeping, dreaming, crying in front of the full-length wardrobe mirror. I drink whiskey and bottled Vichy water until the yellow roses blur on the wallpaper, until the birds and lions waltz together on the Persian rug, until the edges of my desires are blunted and the pain is dulled, until the noble French lady on the tapestried wall hanging assumes a coy smile as she begins to couple with the rampant white unicorn.

Then, slowly, from the mists of dreams, an apple tree emerges, ripe red fruit bursting—so unlike the fruit that grows, deformed now, withering and falling, uneaten, from the blighted tree behind our farmhouse back home.

These red dream apples call to me like the forbidden fruit that tempted Eve. I long to disobey the patriarchal God, eat the apple, and understand the difference between good and evil so that I can make my own choices. These red apples lure me from depressed inertia, make naivety seem claustrophobic, and compel me to resume my quest.

In other words, I kick myself out of that sealed and suffocating room, my self-inflicted scholar's Eden—not exactly the Paradise I'd imagined it would be—and resume my wanderings, ready to take another bite from the world's Garden of Earthly Delights.

I take a long, hot shower in the *douche* down the hall. Then, dressed in fresh jeans, t-shirt, red crewneck sweater, my trusty wool fireman's jacket, and hiking shoes, I plunge outdoors determined to face the real world. But none of the hoped-for sunlight welcomes me this afternoon. A fog has descended across the city. Avenue Léon Blum, withdrawn behind a vaporous wall of thick gray mist, is aloof and unfriendly. I crisscross a maze of side streets, making my way to Clare's walkup. The familiar neighborhood hides from me now—blurred, tenebrous, fearsomely impermeable. I mount dark stairs to Clare's walkup, neglecting to hit light buttons along the way. I knock on her door. No answer.

I run down two flights, tap on the door of Clare's friend Nicole. "*Toc. Toc.*" Clare's friendship with Nicole is blossoming. She and Clare play card games, belote and tarot, and Clare gets a kick out of the fact that Nicole, who hails from a rural village in Auvergne, plays a French version of the bagpipe, a bellows-blown *cabreta*.

Nicole tells me my Scottish friend has taken off on a skiing trip to Mont-Dore. So, I jot down a note for Clare and leave it with Nicole. My note says: "Hey, Clare, can I tag along on your next trip to Mont-Dore? I'm determined to learn how to ski."

CHAPTER FOURTEEN

Mont-Dore

"Just how long I wallow on the French mountain's haunch I cannot say." —Lissa's notebook

PUY-DE-DÔME, a dormant black lava mountain, a crouching prehistoric beast, dominates the Clermont-Ferrand skyline, silently surveying the city's inhabitants—students, professors, priests, nuns, and factory workers—as they dart about like unsuspecting prey below, carrying out their diminutive human affairs on the plain of Limagne. Is this beast aware of me, scurrying to and from the *fac* less and less frequently, with diminishing enthusiasm? Can it sniff me out, this foreign student, playing hooky from my classes, hunched for hours alone at a small writing table in a rented room at 36 avenue Léon Blum, poring over books, touching pen to paper, scribbling English words in French notebooks. Maybe. Maybe not.

By late February, something deep inside urges me to jettison my self-imposed cocoon, to take to the mountains to ski. But echoes of my father's words hold me captive. He raised me to be cautious, to protect myself from all physical danger. I must confront the fact that I am afraid to try skiing. I hear my father warning me that I might fall and injure myself in some way. I spend countless days alone in my room, imagining myself a serious scholar dedicated to the lonely, yet exhilarating pursuit of great ideas and the mastery of a foreign language. I fill my time reading portions of Stendhal, Flaubert, Gide, and Giono for school, poring over my hefty French-English dictionary, scribbling notebooks full of vocabulary lists to memorize. I delude myself in this way until one Saturday in February, *en route* to the WC at the end of the corridor, I hear a couple making love behind one of the darkened hallway's locked doors. Suddenly, my room no longer seems a scholar's haven, but a nun's cell, a young woman's denial.

I think of Georges, remote and unapproachable somewhere in the med students' dorm at the other end of town. I can't return to my rigid schedule, hole up in my room any longer. I begin to pace. My cheeks burn. I pull on the heavy wool fireman's jacket my brother bought me at the military surplus store back home. Although the rush of cold air on my face feels like a physical assault, it soothes the burn on my cheeks and the heat of my emotions as I march with singular resolve toward Place de Jaude to do some targeted shopping. I pass the major stores and sleek cafés that form the square, guarded at each end by a statue—one of General Desaix, one of Vercingétorix. Here I wander in and out of shops, confused by the unfamiliar sizes of clothing, not knowing exactly what I'm looking for, but refusing to go back to my cloistered room empty-handed.

Finally, in the Galeries Lafayette, I decide on a colorful pair of men's socks that I guess will fit my large American feet. As an afterthought, I buy a new notebook, and carrying my purchases, I cross the esplanade. The catalpas are leafless now. Their long pods hang, forlorn, until a sudden gust of wind stirs them and they rattle like a harbinger of death itself.

By the time I turn down rue Georges Clémenceau, the sky has begun to lower like a lead weight over the city. I am hurrying home along boulevard Lafayette when the glossy cover of a book catches my eye. The glittering gold of its title seems to wink and beckon from behind the bookstore window. On impulse, I buy the book, without opening the cover, and hike back to avenue Léon Blum.

The volume proves to be a collection of mysterious local legends. For the remainder of the weekend, I immerse myself in magical tales that unfold in the nearby Auvergne mountains, that chaotic mass of extinct volcanoes, healing mineral springs, and bizarre rock formations upon whose ragged slopes Clare skis. With the artistry of dreams, these stories confound the real with the legendary, time present with time past, the natural with the supernatural. All become equally credible to me: wolves and werewolves, thrushes and water fairies, feudal lords and sorcerers, foxes and dragons, hermits and ogres, pious virgins and enchanted temptresses. The Evil One in his many guises—a goateed *bourgeois*, dressed in blue serge, a *seigneur* in velvet mantle and plumed hat, a black rider astride a black horse, a rag picker—seems no less real to me than the medieval monks who roam the isolated heights.

On Monday, after half-heartedly participating in vowel exercises at the language lab, I run into Clare on the way back to my room. We grab a table at the nearest café, and over cups of espresso, I relate to her some of the Auvergne tales I've been reading. My Scottish friend produces a wry grin and tells me, in a rush and a burr, "You're daft, Lissa. Ought to get out more. You need exercise. I saw the note you left with Nicole. You said you were determined to learn how to ski. Why not come skiing with me this weekend? Great way to meet the French."

So, on that weekend, determined to overcome my fear of tumbling down a mountain and ending up at the bottom buried at the core of a mammoth snowball, I travel southwest from Clermont toward Mont-Dore. I ride alongside Clare in a rusting red bus that seems to bulge with French university students and their ski gear.

From time to time, as the bus grinds its gears and climbs the twisting mountain road, I catch my reflection in the window beside me—features nondescript, hair beginning to grow out, sprouting a mass of curls. I'm reminded of how I chopped off that hair, short as a boy's, the day after Daddy died. Why did I do something so drastic? I still don't understand. But I remember placing those two long ribboned braids, coiled like sightless reddish-brown snakes in the small cedar chest where Daddy always kept his dead sister's auburn hair.

Beside me on the bus, Clare chats easily with a shock-haired French schoolboy. I wish I could be as fluent as Clare. But the university classes are mostly lecture. So, I speak French rarely, only when I need to ask for something in a store or when I exchange brief greetings with other students. Clare, on the other hand, has been working since her arrival in Clermont as an *assistante d'anglais* at the *lycée Jeanne d'Arc*. She gets to practice her French daily with faculty members, one or two of whom have actually invited Clare home for dinner.

As if she's been following my train of thought, Clare turns abruptly to me and says, "They happen to be looking just now for someone to fill my position at the *lycée* next year. If you're keen on teaching, I could put in a good word for you. You'd have to stay on in Clermont another year, then. They'd pay you enough to live on and then some. Think it over. Let me know what you decide."

Should I pursue this? Another whole year in France and I figure I'd be much more fluent. If I stay in Clermont, could I, maybe, rekindle my relationship with Georges? Occasionally, I see him in the student restaurant, but he seems to be avoiding me. Once we had, by accident, met face to face in the Resto lobby. Embarrassed, we had exchanged *bonjours* and continued on our separate ways. Several times I've seen him from a distance, walking arm in arm with the auburn-haired French girl, *la coquette rouge*, Coco Rouge. On those occasions a bitterness flooded my mouth as if I had bitten into a bad piece of fruit. But once or twice since then, as I sat at one of the long dining tables, listening to the banter of

French students all around me and feeling like an outsider, I caught Georges watching me from across the room. I wanted to go to him but feared another rejection.

The red bus halts now at a wooden shed, a way station where those who have no skiing equipment can rent skis, poles, and boots for the day. The shed squats at one corner of a crossroad. According to my book of legends, the mountain crossroads of this region are the meeting places of phantoms, werewolves, and sprites who are personally guided by Satan. Here, on the first Friday of every month, a soul market is held. Any mortals wanting to sell their souls have only to present themselves, at the crossroad, bearing a black chicken and repeat, *"De l'argent pour mon poulet s'il vous plaît."* Money for my chicken, please.

A half dozen or more students line up inside the shed. A mustached Auvergnat of sturdy peasant stock dispenses the equipment, swinging it down from storage racks with gusto, palavering with his customers in a twangy mountain dialect. In my turn, I mount the steps onto an elevated platform. The Auvergnat runs his eyes up and down my foreigner's silhouette, sizes me up, and gives a cry, *"Ah, vous êtes américaine! La grande américaine."* He gives me a rundown of all his opinions about America, and fits me—the big American—with very long skis and poles. I dismount the platform, feeling oafish and gawky, and lug my ski apparatus onto the waiting bus.

In the United States I never felt clumsy. There I'd been considered average in height, slim, a graceful enough dance partner; there I had even been called pretty. But after five months in France, I've come to think of myself as hulking, awkward, almost masculine. My feet are sizes larger than any of the shoes the French stores carry for women. My bone structure seems massive compared to the petite frame of French women. My wrists and ankles seem too thick, my hands too big, my shoulders too wide, my facial features too coarsely defined.

In contrast to the studied femininity of many of the French girls, my manner seems almost brusque. Etched upon my memory is a conversation I heard one afternoon last fall when I left the dorm to buy some yogurt. I was wearing my usual loose sweater and jeans, my hair cut short, taking long strides past two men walking shoulder to shoulder on the opposite side of the street. These men stared at me, and one man asked. "*C'est une fille ou un garçon?*" Is it a girl or a boy? Grinning, the other guy replied, "*Elle n'a pas de poitrine!*" She's flat-chested! Again and again, I have replayed that dialog in my mind; the words will not fade; even now they make me angry and ashamed.

The red bus strains up a steep incline. The route has become more winding, constricted, and tortuous. Deciduous woodland gives way to forests of fir and scrubby juniper. We pass along the outskirts of Mont-Dore, a health spa town of bleached pastel colors and orange tile roofs that seem to bake in the rising sun. The Dordogne River glitters as it flows through the town. At last, the bus disgorges its passengers. A chairlift waits to carry skiers up to their field of winter combat.

I share the ride up with the shock-haired boy, introduced by Clare as the athletic club's ski instructor. My feet, encumbered by their ungainly appendages, swing helplessly in the open air, uncontrollably banging into each other. The instructor cautions me to hold the skis straight and, by straining my ankles, I gain intermittent control.

Slowly, between walls of jagged rock, the *télésiège* ascends. At times these walls encroach on either side, forcing the flimsy chair to pass narrowly through crevices. At times, the rock falls back into shelves, baring a gaping chasm and allowing a glimpse of vertiginous depths from which faint gurglings of mountain streams rise, muffled by shrouds by mist.

The grandeur of this mountain scene passing slowly beneath me has a hypnotic effect. Creatures from the book of legends seem always near at hand, yet forever beyond my reach. My eyes catch the merest flutter of a water fairy's translucent wings behind the precipitous veil of a waterfall. The vision of a mountain woman, large and beautiful, dressed in a hooded cloak and wooden shoes, emerges from between the crystal branches of a fir tree. I recognize her as the Grande-Fade, the fairy of fairies, who appears in the book of legends. The Grande-Fade, so the book says, is the keeper of all the mountain's secrets, guardian of the fire in the mountain, nurturer of the farmer and his harvest, of the shepherd and his sheep. Each year, it is the Grand-Fade who chases winter from the land, who, with her breath, thaws the earth and warms the tender shoots of grain.

"*Vous êtes américaine, une étudiante à l'université? Vous êtes ici depuis combien de temps?*" The ski instructor's voice recalls me from the mountain's spell, asking me the typical questions: Are you an American, a student at the university? How long have you been here?

I recite my pat answers, and for a moment, the boy casts a sidelong glance in my direction. "*Vous êtes sportive?*" he says hopefully. Are you a sportswoman?

"*Pas tellement.*" Not so much, I say, feeling I'm letting him down. I would like to believe I'm a daring sportswoman. Lissa the Intrepid. It might compensate for the femininity I now seem to lack.

As we near the end of the ascent, the instructor tells me I will have to push off from the chair and ski down a ramp onto the field of snow. I am to ski off to the right, he to the left. I am to watch out for the chair as it continues past us. I am to get out of the way as quickly as possible to leave the ramp clear for the next pair of skiers.

I listen to these last-minute instructions with growing apprehension. I had assumed I would ease myself off the chair, then step cautiously onto the snow. But suddenly, the ramp is directly beneath me. Into my ear comes the instructor's command, "*Pousser hors!*" Push off!

I obey and ski down the ramp before I have time to panic. Only after the fact do I panic, topple to the ground, and find myself locked in fierce combat with the too-long skis, forced to flounder in the snow until the instructor skis over to tug me upright.

I go with the instructor to join a group of novice skiers practicing on the beginner's slope. The instructor teaches me how to keep my balance here, down the slight decline. He demonstrates how to turn on my skis and how to stop.

I fall down a lot at first and find picking myself up increasingly difficult as my muscles tire and my clothing grows heavier and soggier with melted snow. Soon I begin to feel sorry for the bushy-haired young instructor. His glances furtively at the upper slope, preoccupied with the activities there. So, when after a half-hour of practice, he suggests I come with him to try the faster slope, the *pente rapide*, I don't have the heart to detain him any longer on the nursery slope.

The sun is now a swollen yellow presence as it arches toward its zenith, gilding rock and causing a blinding glare to reflect off the field of snow.

Fatigued by the unaccustomed exercise, numbed by the cold, and mentally exhausted from speaking French, I dog along behind my tutor, tracing an insignificant trail among the many crisscrosses already carved on the mountain's insensible flank. I ignore my father's voice, telling me to be careful. I ignore my own voice telling me I might very well stay behind and practice while the instructor ventures farther up the mountain.

Words of warning pass among the skiers. The snow crust that developed overnight, though hard and crisp this morning, is expected to become soft and heavy by noon. The transition will soon be reached, creating breakable crust, the skier's bane.

I take my place in the line of skiers who wait to mount one of a series of disks. Each disk is attached to the end of a bar suspended from a moving cable overhead. Far ahead of me in the line, I see Clare's orange hair flaring like flame beneath her ski cap. She calls back to me, "They call this contraption the *tire-fesses* because it pulls your bum up the hill."

"Yeah? Well, how do I ride this thing?"

"Hold your ski poles in your right hand, away from the operator. When he hands you the lift, you grab hold of the bar. The trick is to keep your arms straight and your knees bent a wee bit. Your body should be relaxed, but not limp. When you're ready, you tell the man and he starts the lift. The contraption will extend when it starts to move. That's when you push the bar between your legs so you feel the disk in the back of your thighs and behind your bum. Just watch the others. You'll learn. But mind you don't sit down! The moment you put any weight on the disk, you've had it."

I watch Clare, and shortly thereafter my instructor, mount the *tire-fesses*. It looks simple enough. The skiers seem to glide effortlessly up the mountain, gaily-colored ski caps bobbing against a backdrop of brilliant blue sky. I feel my heart palpitate in anticipation. My senses heighten as my turn arrives. A wind blows in my face and cold air stings my nostrils. The moving cable creaks, metal claps metal. The operator's hand looms large before me— black hairs on cracked red skin.

I will myself to be tall, strong, genuinely *sportive*. The operator shouts, "*Preparez-vous!*" In a wave of trepidation, my body tightens, senses dim. I seem to be clasping a stick of cold metal when the operator's voice comes to me from a great distance, "*Partez!*"

A blurred sequence of events follows, and I merely react. The lift begins to move, pauses an instant as it extends. I am aware of the disk's presence between my legs—hard, demanding—and realize I must have, somehow or other, tucked it in place. The cable moves above me, and I find myself being pulled slowly up the mountain. Clare's instructions tumble through my mind. Clare had said to relax. I try to relax. But I let my weight down onto the disk. It gives me no support! Instantly, I fall.

Not knowing what to do and fearing I will fall off the mountain if I let go, I clutch the bar and let the lift drag me up the slope. I slide on my buttocks, skis scrambling in the snow. Excited shouts rise from the bottom of the slope, but the French words cannot reach me; they surrender their meaning to the wind. Yards of snow pass beneath me. On my right, a fiery patch of orange hair descends, rousing me from my stupor.

"Let go of the bar and roll out of the way!" Clare shouts as she skis past.

I release my grip, jolt against the ground, roll over, and crawl awkwardly on hands and skis to one side of the trail. When I try to push myself up, the crusted snow breaks away from under my palms.

Just how long I wallow on the French mountain's haunch I cannot say. On one side skiers swoop downhill, shooting narrowly past me. My floundering causes one man to swerve. He yells belligerently at me. Although the French words outrange my schoolgirl vocabulary, their meaning is clear: I am a menace who has no right to be here, blocking the route. But no matter how hard I try I cannot stand on my skis.

By the time the instructor skis down to me, my legs are as insubstantial as the breakfast of bread and *confiture* I swallowed hastily this morning. Public shame breaks my spirit. When the instructor helps me to stand and my skis begin to slide forward down the slope, I let myself collapse at once. Fear makes me stubborn, and though I'm certain all the people below must either be laughing or cursing at me, I am past caring. Better to sit down on this mountain and look just plain silly than to ski down and break legs or ankles or who knows what.

As I sit, I see, or think I see, a figure gliding down toward me from a distant stand of firs, which rise like a row of abrasive scrub brushes along the western horizon. As the apparition draws nearer, I can just distinguish from the terrible whiteness a woman wearing ancient peasant garb. She seems to hover an inch or so above the ground, her *sabots* never quite touching the snow. Her face, rimmed by an antique bonnet, is fleshless, its features skeletal.

"Try again," the instructor urges me as, once more, he sets me upright on my skis. Again, I collapse. All the while the skeleton-woman comes nearer, stretching her bone fingers out to me, mouthing words with her horrible gaping mouth, which seems to grow until it has eclipsed all the world, swallowing me up in a black void.

I recover from the snow blindness as the instructor helps me up again and instructs me this time to clasp him around the waist from behind, to wedge the front ends of my skis between the backs of his own, and to ski down in tandem with him.

Leadenly, I obey, causing us both to topple over twice on the voyage down. After depositing me at the bottom, he skis off, hurriedly I think, as if he were fleeing a shameful connection.

Still on skis, I make my way slowly to the chairlift. A slender girl, dressed in professional-looking red ski togs, is just taking her seat in the waiting chair. She gives me a wave and greets me in a cheery twitter of English, "You are American?"

"Yes. Are you riding down?"

"Yes. You will like to come with me?" Her English comes to me like birdsong.

I accept, readily succumbing to the temptation to speak my own language, and climb in beside the girl in red. I ride down the back of the mountain, my indifferent ravisher, descend past waters that burble inanely over a half-frozen cascade, through hardened lava passages, beside this sleek French girl. She introduces herself as Marie Claire, then goes on to chatter endlessly about the English exams she is planning to take in the spring. Pert in her red cap and jacket, perched daintily here in mid-air, Marie Claire reminds me of an indigenous red bird, naively chirping in the face of my distress.

At the bottom, I step off the chairlift—no need, thank God, to jump this time—ready to kiss the flatness of the ground, and hobble toward the parked red bus. Not until I glimpse Marie Claire, slipping out of her ski boots, do I remember that my own boots and skis are indeed removable. I pry the two ski poles from the grip of my right hand and fling them aside with immense relief as a miraculously cured cripple might cast off crutches. I free myself from skis and ski boots and stuff my feet back into the blue hiking shoes.

When the bus makes its stop at the way station, I return the rented ski equipment, re-board the bus, and take a seat by the window. The bus's heater makes me drowsy and I begin to doze off. But Marie Claire, eager to practice her English with an American, takes the seat next to me and forces me awake, posing question after question about American music, movie stars, and universities.

At dusk, the red bus empties in front of the athletic club. A blustery wind stirs papers in the gutters and disperses the skiers like so many flecks of colorful debris along the sooty gray Clermont sidewalks.

CHAPTER FIFTEEN

\ ((

Après Ski

"She is my lover, not my friend." —Georges to Lissa

AFTER THE SKI TRIP, I walk toward my room, alone. But I'm too agitated to go straight to bed. Instead, I make my way up an incline, past the student Resto, which stands aloofly closed for the weekend. I find myself continuing along the street, turning at the corner onto a side street, and pausing in front of a popular café that crouches a few steps below street level, hooded behind a red awning. More than four months ago, I ducked beneath this awning, following an unknown man who wore tight pants and a fitted leather jacket. The awning was flimsy, the round table small. We huddled close on our chairs to take shelter from the wind.

Inadvertently, our hands brushed and I stared, fascinated by his incredibly beautiful brown skin touching my own—which was morbidly pale and unattractively freckled. He wore his shirt open at the throat, the collar turned up. That was my introduction to Georges.

Now, I enter the café knowing he comes here from time to time to drink hot tea, hoping and fearing he might be here. Red globe lamps distend over the black sheen of polished tables, distinguishing from smoke and shadow the faces of tarot cards, ivory chessmen, dark-skinned faces. Out of the darkness a visage emerges and seems to float, round and white and full-lipped as the man in the moon. Junjei? No, someone else. In one tenebrous corner stands a jukebox, glowing yellow from within, giving voice to doleful American blues.

I sit at a vacant table near the bar, toward the front of the café where a few patrons sit. The tables in back are filled. A French waiter, dressed in red jacket, white shirt, black bow tie, and tapered black pants breaks off a conversation with the bartender and makes his way, agile as a cat, to take my order, "*Un café crème.*"

When the waiter sets the demitasse before me, I sip cautiously. I'm grateful for its warmth today when I am chilled to the bone. Someone casts a winning combination of dice on the baize interior of a round four twenty-one board, and triumphant shouts swell above the music in the rear alcove. After my exposure to the mountain's frigid expanses, I welcome the noise and the sensation of anonymous human closeness the café offers.

Adjacent to me stands a young man speaking Arabic at the pinball machine, legs spread, thrusting his pelvis forward each time he presses the buttons on the sides of the machine. Like some technological beast, the machine flashes its electronic eyes, squawking at the young man. Several times, in rapid succession, the man thrusts violently until the machine falls dead. With a franc piece, he revives it. The combat resumes.

Watching this, I am for some reason reminded of the skeleton-woman on the slopes, and wonder what inspired that vision. I hadn't read about such a woman in the book of legends. But had these supernatural tales been prodding my own imagination to create my own ghost? Or, did the vision materialize spontaneously from some other source? Had I been so afraid of life, so afraid of the pain and embarrassment and rejection that come with living that, today on the mountain, I was ready to let it all slip away without a fight? I made it back this time, but only because of others, only because Clare and the ski instructor took the responsibility that I refused to take for myself. Surely, Jean-Paul Sartre would scold me for living in bad faith!

I finish my cup of coffee, but hesitate, fingering the cup, unwilling to face my empty room and the hobgoblin of loneliness that lurks there behind the locked door. I have just ordered a second cup of coffee when Georges comes in, dressed in a black suit I have never seen before. It makes him look older, more distinguished than I had known him to be. He passes my table without stopping or looking up, takes a seat at an empty table by the window, unfolds a newspaper. I notice patches of white in his wispy black hair and want him more than ever. When he puts his paper aside, he catches me watching him. He stares back intently, seems to be deciding something, then gets up and strides across the room to me.

He shakes my hand. "*Ça va?*" he says softly. How's it going?

"*Ça va,*" I say solemnly, studying him closely, scarcely able to breathe.

"*Tu es toute seule, Lissa?*" Are you alone, Lissa? He pulls up a chair and sits facing me.

I look down at his hands that are spread on the table before me—square, brown, competent-looking—and remember how I had always been able to speak French freely with him, without the self-consciousness I felt with the French. And it's now I realize we are both foreigners here.

"Lissa, Lissa," he tugs at my elbow, trying to engage with me. "Why do you always look so sad?"

"Because I miss you." I look up and see both impatience and pity in his face, but I do not regret my words.

"I'm not in love with you," he tells me, a defensive harshness in his voice, and his words cut me with the depth and precision of a surgeon's scalpel. Then Georges continues, more gently, "*Nous sommes copains.* Okay, Lissa?"

I smile at the sound of the American "okay" coming from Georges, and nod. Yes, okay. We are pals. Just pals.

The waiter, the elaborately discreet *garçon*, arrives at the table with my coffee, takes Georges's order of tea, whisks away my empty first cup, and scurries off, melting into the shadows behind the bar. It's then I say to Georges what I have to say. "I've seen you with another girl." Not knowing the French word for auburn, I add, "Her hair is a sort of red."

His answer comes quickly, matter-of-factly, without hesitation. "Yes. I know her. I have sex with her from time to time."

I lower my eyes.

"I'm not in love with *her*, either."

"But I don't understand."

"She is my lover, not my friend."

"But how can she be one and not the other?"

"It's often the case."

We sit, without a word. Time seems to have stopped.

Then Georges's tea arrives and ordinary sounds—the click of the saucer as it's set on the table, the clink of Georges's spoon stirring sugar in his tea—break the silence, restart the universal clock, and prompt me to resume the conversation.

"Have you ever thought of coming to the United States? To study medicine there?"

"No. I will finish my studies here, then return to Lebanon. They need doctors there." Georges sips his tea.

"I think I can get a job as an *assistante d'anglais* in Clermont next year."

"You are going to stay in France?"

"I haven't decided yet."

Georges glances at his watch. "I have to work at the hospital tonight." He finishes his tea, shakes my hand firmly, and bids me "*au revoir.*"

That night I lie on my narrow cot, the book of legends spread open on my chest. From the floor I pick up the bottle of whiskey from Clare's dad, hold it toward the light. Its contents, half empty by now, sparkle a warm amber. The book of legends tells of magic potions, concocted at the base of the Auvergne mountains, *philtres* of forgetfulness for use on mortals. I put the bottle aside, stare at the sealed shutters, switch off the light, and close my eyes to dream of masses of ripe apples weighing down the boughs of trees. The dead tree in my orchard back home appears; it has miraculously revived and is fruitful once again.

I wake eighteen hours later, head throbbing, debating what I will do when the school year is up. Will I go home to the United States, finish my bachelor's degree and move on to follow the conventional timeline? Will I return to the old farmhouse and the apple tree?

Or, will I stay on in France for a while? Become governess for the mayor's daughters in Boudes? Maybe I can reach out to Marilee's Martine, see if she's still looking for an American English tutor. Martine could open the door for me to Clermont's high society. I'm still carrying her contact information in my leather bag, but have never reached out to her. Will I stay on in Europe and open myself to more foreign adventures? Explore exotic new worlds? I'm still not ready to decide.

\) (

CHAPTER SIXTEEN

Back to High School

"But, Mlle Power, the politicians—are they not all corrupt?"
—French high school student

IRONICALLY, MY QUEST FOR INDEPENDENCE and adulthood takes me back to high school. But this time I find I am not a shy student, lost and trying to fit it at an American public school, sequestered among rolling green farmland in northern Maryland. At the end of February, I volunteer to be an *assistante d'anglais,* an English assistant, at a private French secondary school for girls, Clermont's venerable *lycée Jeanne d'Arc.*

Excited about this new venture, I visit Trudy's apartment. As I tell her my news, she brews fresh coffee, serves us each a cup, and plops down beside me on the sofa. "Congrats, Lissa. Good for you to get out more instead of being cooped up in that claustrophobic room of yours."

"You know, Trudy, besides coming over to boast about my new position, I wanted to get your take on what's happening in the US these days. This morning I was given a briefing by an administrator at the *lycée.* The school wants me to discuss current events in America."

"Well, you gotta say something about Watergate and the Nixon administration." Trudy lights a cigarette, takes a puff, and releases a long stream of pent-up smoke. "I am so tired of Richard Nixon! Last November he went on TV and told the country, 'I am not a crook.' And now he's just started his second term. Jeez!" Trudy looks around for an ashtray, grabs the nearest one, drops her used match into it, and resumes her diatribe. "Watergate keeps grinding on and on, and the President's character flaws keep getting more and more obvious."

"What do you mean, Trudy? I don't keep tabs on what's going on in the US the way you do."

"What I mean is, Nixon's been cutting himself off from people more and more, losing his temper, and getting vindictive. And Nixon has this weird way of smiling while he's saying the most terrible stuff." Trudy pretends to shake her jowls and does a comical imitation of Nixon's smile.

"You remember seeing him on TV when you were still in the States, don't you? He's just a puffed-up phony. And so freaking paranoid! Nixon should either resign or Congress should remove him." Trudy finishes her cigarette and grinds it in the ashtray. "Anyway, congrats on your new job. Sounds like a good opportunity for you."

My first day lands me at the head of a classroom, facing a small group of teenage girls. As a result of some inquiries and intercessions from Clare, I've been asked to work with Mme Angelique Arlette, a dynamic young English instructor. At the moment, her class is studying twentieth-century American literature and culture.

Mme Arlette is a brilliant teacher. She conducts her class with disciplined informality. Her youthful energy—alert and always attuned to her students' reactions—keeps the spirited adolescent girls on track. With an impish humor, she maintains a relaxed atmosphere that puts everyone at ease and makes learning relatively painless.

Mme A. asks me to stand in front of the class. As she introduces me as Mlle Power, I take off my wool fireman's jacket and hang it on the back of a chair. Today, I'm wearing jeans and my Minnie Mouse t-shirt, under a green Shetland cardigan I bought in Scotland.

In slow and what I hope is clear English, I say, "Hello. I am from the state of Maryland." The girls give blank looks. Like most people I've come across in Clermont, the students don't seem to know where Maryland is. So, I give my usual explanation. "It's on the east coast, not far from Washington, DC." Spotting some nods of recognition, I continue. "Back home, we are worried about the Vietnam War, the Middle-East War, about Watergate and potentially corrupt politicians."

Here in Clermont, I don't usually read the newspapers. But news about what's going on in the US reaches me intermittently, second hand: random comments made in my brother's correspondence, an occasional news article Spence clips from the *Baltimore Sun* and tucks inside the mailing envelope, my Arab friends' reactions to America's role in the Middle East, and my friend Trudy's grim observations about the goings-on in American politics.

So, today, I try to explain to these young French students why American citizens are becoming disillusioned with their President, how the Watergate break-in led to our distrust of Nixon and his administration.

When I finish speaking, a girl's hand shoots up. "But, Mlle Power, the politicians—are they not all corrupt?" She sits in the first row. Her voice is bold, challenging. Her question startles me, and I don't know how to respond.

I see myself as a kid, watching Superman on TV, cheering him on as he fights for "truth, justice, and the American way." I guess I'd still like to believe that America and the majority of her politicians are honest—or at least intend to be. But I can't quite shut out the image of Vice-President Spiro Agnew, Maryland's former governor, pleading no contest to a felony charge of tax evasion and resigning from office. That happened just this past October. Now, back home, Agnew's name is synonymous with "crooked politician."

My mind confounds itself, balks at the attempt to reconcile the unreconcilable. So, to avoid an awkward silence and keep the conversation flowing, I retreat to a simpler space and ask, "What do you think of Americans? How would you describe the typical American?"

The same girl raises her hand again. "A tall man with a big cowboy hat, riding a horse and smoking a cigarette," she says, and gives a jolly, pink-cheeked laugh. I smile at her caricature. It reminds me of the Marlboro Man, the handsome, rugged cowboy who promotes American cigarettes on TV.

"Well, for many Americans, a typical Frenchman wears a beret and drinks wine," I say. Then I laugh at my own stereotype, and the class laughs right along with me. I pause for a moment and, trying to be sincere, add, "We don't really know very much about each other, do we? Mostly just what we see in the movies." The girls seem to take everything in. They look thoughtful.

Mme A., who has been observing attentively, smiles approvingly. She hands me a textbook, opened to a marked excerpt. "Would you read this passage aloud for us? It's from the work of your notable American author Sinclair Lewis. We are studying his novel *It Can't Happen Here*."

I read Lewis's description of a fictional US Senator, one Berzelius Windrip, who is running for President in 1936. Windrip is crude, can scarcely read, and regales the public with obvious lies and so-called ideas that verge on the ridiculous. I'm just a few phrases into the text when a titter erupts from the bold girl in the front row, followed by a wave of laughter that, contagious as a common cold, ripples through the class. I look up, puzzled. I know Lewis's work is partly satirical, but these words are getting at something pretty serious, something that seems pretty relevant to what's going on with President Nixon. "What's so funny?" I ask. "Why are you laughing?"

Once again, the bold girl up front thrusts her hand in the air and proclaims, "You speak with a drawl!"

Me? A drawl? I don't think of myself as having a drawl. Isn't it just hillbillies and folks from the Deep South who talk that way? Hmmm. Guess I need to examine my own biases about Americans.

I smile at myself as I continue to read Lewis's sardonic portrait of a pious American politician who resembles an itinerant peddler of church furniture and is known for his wry homespun sarcasm. Somehow this Windrip draws large crowds of supporters and wields a mesmerizing power over them, even though his speeches are based on a feeble point of view spun from flimsy policies. The perverse political maneuvering that Lewis describes in his imagined Great-Depression-era America seems to foreshadow what could actually happen in the US some day. Is Sinclair Lewis some kind of prophet? Has he contrived an unthinkable American history that somehow echoes forward, becomes real? His storytelling makes me think twice about what's going on with President Nixon and Watergate and the Congress, right now, in 1974. I remember Trudy fuming—not long after I met her last October—about what the papers started calling the Saturday Night Massacre, saying, "So how can we trust a President who sets in motion a chain-reaction of firings and resignations. He's just about destroyed his own Justice Department!" I've finished reading the marked text. So, I close the book and hand it back to Mme Arlette.

"We are very fortunate to have Mlle Power here with us so we can hear the author's words in an authentic American voice. Aren't we girls?" The girls smile, nod in agreement, and led by Mme Arlette, they give me a polite smattering of applause.

When the class is dismissed, I button up my NFS jacket and prepare to leave the schoolroom. Mme A. gently pulls me aside. "We are used to hearing English read and spoken by assistants from the United Kingdom. They say their words quickly, pronounce them with an accent that is clipped. Your voice is slower, more relaxed. It's a wonderful voice! I'm sure my husband would love to meet you. Won't you come to dinner at our apartment? Friday evening?" She pulls a sheet of the school's stationery from the desk drawer, jots down her home address, and hands it to me.

"That's very nice of you," I say, grateful to escape an empty weekend.

~~~

The much-anticipated Friday evening arrives, and I find myself walking north on avenue Léon Blum toward rue Dr. Chibret, turning left onto rue Philippe Lebon. The Arlette family lives in an upscale modern apartment building on the left. I take the elevator to the second floor. Mme Arlette opens the door. A buoyant little girl is chattering, pirouetting around the bottom of Mme A's. skirt, eager to get a look at this tall American guest.

"*Bonjour, Madame,*" I say, and present a bunch of potted paperwhites, purchased—almost as an afterthought—at a flower stall I passed along the way. I bend down to greet the little girl, "*Bonjour!*"

Mme Arlette smiles, makes a fuss over the inexpensive bouquet, and introduces me to her daughter, Mimi, who beams at me, holds up four fingers, and announces in no uncertain terms, "*J'ai quatre ans!*" I'm four years old!

A pleasant-looking man, wearing a slightly rumpled business suit—jacket removed, tie loosened, shirt sleeves rolled—puts aside his newspaper, rises from an armchair, and comes to shake my hand. He introduces himself, "Guillaume Arlette." Mimi tugs at his pantleg. He scoops her up; she covers his face with kisses. He tickles her; she squeals in delight, shouting, "Papa, Papa, Papa!" He totes her out of the room, gently scolding, "*Tu devrais déjà être au lit.*" It's past your bedtime.

While M. Arlette is putting Mimi to bed, Mme Arlette seats me on a sofa in the tastefully decorated living room.

"Guillaume always reads Mimi a bedtime story," says Mme Arlette. She offers *l'apéritif*, an array of small snacks—mushroom canapés, peanuts, olives—arranged in small dishes on a Japanese lacquer tray and serves me a sparkling amber drink in a champagne flute.

I take a sip. "Oh, this is very good! What is it?"

"Kir Royale, Guillaume's favorite, champagne with a splash of *crème de cassis*."

When her husband returns, Mme A. ushers us into a small formal dining room. The table is elaborately set: gold-rimmed porcelain dinnerware, a complex array of sparkling silverware, and multiple crystal glasses at each place.

My hostess sets the pot of paperwhites on a polished walnut side table beside an exquisite brass lamp. The soft golden glow filtering through the pleated silk shade reveals discoloration and withering at the tips of the otherwise pure-white blossoms. I am embarrassed at the shabbiness of my gift. But Mme Arlette seems not to notice.

"Oh, and by the way," she says, "we are very informal here. Now that we are friends, you must call us by our first names, Guillaume and Angelique. And may I call you Lissa?"

"*Bien sûr,*" I say, as she seats me at the table. "Angelique," I say softly, savoring the first-name casualness as my new friend rushes off to the kitchen.

M. Arlette, Guillaume, takes his seat at the head of the table. Angelique returns with an ornate tureen, lifts the lid, ladles soup into three bowls, and stirs into each a dollop of *crème fraiche*.

Wine is poured, bread is passed, and course follows course— after soup, chicken breasts with herbs, mushrooms, grape tomatoes, and tender asparagus. More bread and wine. Then a lime sorbet to cleanse the palate. And just when I finish the last of my dessert, a tantalizing *tarte aux pommes*, sip my freshly brewed demitasse of coffee, and think the long meal has ended, Mme Arlette brings out platters laden with fresh fruit and pungent local cheeses from farms nearby.

After dinner, I walk back to my room feeling well-fed, content, and hopeful. The Arlettes have welcomed me into their home and accepted me as a friend. I admire Angelique and Guillaume because they combine intelligence and sophistication with play-fulness and informality. They are traditional but also modern. To me, the Arletette family is a rare and precious one, a refreshing contrast to the eccentric and cloistered family I grew up in. The Arlettes represent a model of stability I can aspire to.

It's cold today as I walk to the *lycée*. So cold, I leave my fireman's jacket on when I reach Mme Arlette's classroom and take my seat. I run my fingers through the short curls on my head—now that my hair has begun to grow out, I've developed this nervous habit—and wait for her to call me up front. Today, I'm supposed to talk about busing in the United States. I've had a few days to prepare, but I'm still not sure how I'm going to explain something as complicated and controversial as race-integration busing to a bunch of teenage French girls.

When Mme Arlette beckons me forward, I'm slow to take off my coat, reluctant to shed its protection. But I grit my teeth, make my way to the front of the classroom, and march into uncertain territory.

Mme A. is announcing, "Today, Mlle Power will share her thoughts with us about a practice called 'busing' in the United States."

I launch into the mini-lecture I rehearsed last night in my room. I begin with a brief mention of the 1971 Supreme Court decision, how it ruled that federal courts could use busing as another way of achieving something called racial balance. I try to explain how lots of people in the United States—white people *and* black people—complained and found it a hardship, having to uproot their kids and send them on long bus rides to strange schools across town.

The girls are listening. A couple of them are taking notes. But then I stop speaking. My explanation falls short. What altered bus route, what detour can possibly carry American schoolkids across the racial divide, through neighborhoods where skin color still determines who gets to own a home? This ugly black-white racial gash that's cut through America's heart since our country was founded—even before it was founded—still pierces deep. Can buses, transporting our children across the boundaries of persistently segregated populations, really solve anything?

I stumble on, talking about how parents with more money can get around this by putting their kids in private schools, Catholic schools, or schools affiliated with other religions. I get into how white people in America have been running away from racial integration for a very long time now. I explain how, back in 1954, the Supreme Court ruled that racial segregation in our public schools was unconstitutional. How, after that, when schools were integrated, white families—lots of them—started moving out of the big cities to live in white suburbs and in rural places. I tell these French girls how, when I was a little girl, our family moved from our row house in Baltimore City out to our grandparents' farm in a rural community where white landowners had, for generations, established themselves on the largest and best plots of land. "It's called white flight," I say, and notice that one girl—the bold girl up front—is printing WHITE FLIGHT in large letters across the top of her notes.

"So," I say, and shrug. "I don't see how busing is going to solve the problem."

"Are there any questions for Mlle Power?" Mme Arlette asks. This time the girls are silent, heads down. Some shuffle papers or play with their pens. Even the bold girl makes no comment. She surveys the classroom, trying to look nonchalant. She seems to be assessing the other girls' behavior. She purses her lips, then shrugs and yawns. I go back to my seat.

When I leave Mme Arlette's class that day, I feel somehow defeated. As I walk back to my room, Mohammed's words *"la tête d'Arabe"* vibrate in my ears, and I imagine an insistent, militant rapping coming from the direction of Place de Jaude. The echo of Nazi boots on pavers, marking time, replaying recent history, approaching, ever forward, darkness encroaching. And suddenly, bullets of rain have arrived, pelting the sidewalk and strafing my feet.

~~~

One day, after class, I chat with Mme Arlette in her small, crowded office at the far end of a school corridor. The walls are lined, floor to ceiling, with book-laden shelves; her desk is piled with tests and assignments waiting to be graded.

Out of the blue, I say to Mme A., "*Les philanthropes sont en fait des misanthropes.*" This thought—philanthropists are actually misanthropes—has just come floating weightless into my head. Ah, the joy of cognates! They make it so much easier for me to share my ideas in French.

Mme A. seizes on my words, repeats them. She laughs, seeming delighted with them, and takes up an unlit pipe from a shelf behind her. "A souvenir of my father," she says. Then smiling wryly, she puffs her cheeks, pretends to smoke the pipe, and leans toward me across the desk, jabbing in my direction with the end of the pipe stem, "You must discuss your theory with my father. By profession, he is a corporate lawyer. But at heart, he is a philosopher."

A week later, I find myself seated at an ornate mahogany dining table in an affluent Clermont neighborhood, having a meal with Angelique's parents, M. and Mme Legris. Here, I learn the art, or more precisely, the ceremony of eating an artichoke.

Steamed artichoke, served as an appetizer, precedes the main course. At each place setting, a single green globe poises grandly on a small Limoges serving plate. I stare at this odd vegetable—rows of daunting, intimidating petals, tops clipped.

Monsieur instructs me to remove the tiny thorns because, "*Il est, après tout, un chardon.*" It is, after all, a thistle.

Madame surveys the table to ensure that each of us has access to an individual cut-glass dipping bowl, half-filled with a golden liquid. With a subtle nod, she signals her husband to begin. M. Legris extends his hand, removes a single petal at the base of his artichoke, and demonstrates for me how to flourish it in the melted butter sauce. How to hold the leaf delicately to the mouth, drawing the base of the leaf through the teeth to scrape away the soft pale flesh. He savors its delicacy before swallowing, then discards what remains in a small dish, set for this purpose at the side of his plate. He nods to me and I follow suit, trying to duplicate his technique. Once again, he favors me with a nod, and I assume that my attempt has passed muster. Following his lead, I continue to pull off and eat the leaves of my artichoke, one at a time, progressing upward and inward from the base.

"You will notice, mademoiselle, as you work your way up—and in—the petals will become more tender, the edible portions more generous." And finally, with a sigh of anticipation, M. Legris reaches for the fuzzy, hairy, rather ugly flower at the center of his artichoke.

"*Voilà, le chaut!*" And cradling a stringy clump, the choke, in the palm of his hand, he scrapes away the hairy part with a spoon and scoops out the soft tender core, calling it, "*Le coeur d'artichaut.*" M. Legris relishes this heart within his puckered lips, and pronounces it, "*la pièce de résistance!*" I sample the heart of my own artichoke, and he's right! It is exquisite.

Between courses, M. Legris leans in toward me, across the table, and says, "My daughter tells me you have an interesting theory regarding philanthropists."

By now, having consumed two glasses of wine, I find the courage to present my theory. "*À mon avis les philanthropes sont en fait des misanthropes.*" As usual, the wine has improved my French speaking skills, and now the words flow more smoothly.

"And why is that, mademoiselle?" M. Legris queries. Despite the wine, I squirm under his probing gray eyes. They are alarmingly magnified behind his thick round glasses. The pupils close in on me, pointing toward me like tails of inky tadpoles protruding from murky waters. His intensity recalls book jacket photos I've seen of Jean-Paul Sartre.

But the wine I have drunk propels my awkward response.

"Because," I say, "to devote large sums of one's own fortunes to mankind's betterment, one must first recognize and accept human nature's fallibility and its innate inability to improve itself."

"*Ah, très interessant,*" he says. He seems to reflect, begins to respond, but winds up merely heaving a heavy sigh to conceal a belch.

By now, Mme Legris is serving pork tenderloin. The cutlets, she explains, are seasoned with tarragon, and bathed in a creamy wine and Dijon mustard sauce.

M. Legris slices aggressively into his tenderloin, impales the cloven meat with his fork, grinds the delicately cooked flesh between long feral teeth, and swallows with great intention.

Mme Legris pours more wine all around. My attempt at philosophical discourse, it seems, has fallen flat, and on we move to the next course.

But in the end, has not philosophy actually risen to the occasion here? Our egos engaged in theoretical abstractions, we have managed to skirt those ugly little everyday realities—like the *n* word and the *tête d'Arabe* and not-too-distant remembrances of Nazi occupation—and keep them off the table, at a safe social distance.

CHAPTER SEVENTEEN

A Delicate Bond

"Il faut faire un effort." —*advice from Lissa's friend Beatrix*

N OW THAT THE OXIES HAVE ALL LEFT FRANCE—with
the exception of Clare, who occupies herself these days
with a new set of French friends—I strike up a friendship with Junjei. He's from Hong Kong and is fluent in English
as well as Cantonese and Mandarin. So, when I feel the need to
lapse into the ease of speaking English, I invite him for tea in
my room at avenue Léon Blum. I convert my writing table into
a small dining area, a chair pulled up at either end. I lay out the
package of shortbread brought back from Scotland and pour cups
of steaming oolong tea into two large, mismatched cups. I learn
that he's the second son of a wealthy, influential diplomat. His
elder brother runs a successful trading business out of London.
Junjei's father wants his younger son to follow in his footsteps
and become a diplomat. So, to honor his father's wishes, Junjei
is here in Clermont to increase his foreign relations assets by
becoming fluent in French.

Initially, Junjei is very reserved, but the enchantment of tea and shortbread puts him at his ease. As tranquil hours pass, he reveals himself to me in the way a sealed morning glory opens to warm sunlight.

"I wish to honor my father, but by nature I am not equipped for diplomacy. I am not a social person, as you can tell. I prefer to read and contemplate in my own company. Though I do make an exception for chess."

"Yes. I remember watching you play chess in the lobby of the dorm."

Junjei tilts his head slightly and releases a delicate sigh. "Yes," he says, his eyes glowing with pleasure. "Do you play, Lissa?"

"My brother taught me how each chess piece moves. But I'm not really very good at playing the game."

"Perhaps I shall teach you to play." His eyelids flutter, and again, a trace of light plays across his eyes.

"Well, maybe. But right now, I'm trying to force myself to get out more. I'm like you. Shy. But I'm here in France, after all, to seize life—not hide in my room with my books. My dream is to be a great writer. But, in order to write, I need to find out more about the world and the people in it. About all kinds of people."

"That is a worthy goal, my friend. May I call you my friend, Lissa? I could use a good friend. Someone I can trust. Someone who can trust me."

"Yes, of course we can be friends, Junjei. You remind me of my brother, Spence. Spence says he is unclubbable. He's not comfortable at parties or in groups. He actually refused to have his picture taken for the high school yearbook, and although he got his diploma, he didn't go to the graduation ceremony, didn't want to graduate on stage with the rest of his class. He's very smart, but he couldn't manage the social pressures of college."

I'm beginning to understand that Junjei, like Spence, needs to be approached slowly and gently. I recall a favorite scene in Saint-Exupéry's *The Little Prince*, an encounter between a fox and a little boy who is searching for a friend. The fox says, "Please tame me," and tells the boy how to do it. The boy learns that by being very patient, day by day, he can get closer and gradually tame the fox. In this way, the fox and boy come to need each other. They form a unique bond, a special relationship unlike any other in the world. Maybe, little by little, Junjei will let me tame him.

☙

February has given way to March and Clermont's winter days creep past, enfolding me in a sustained grayness, an unaccustomed atmosphere that chafes me like a stranger's blanket, its unfamiliar fabric threatening to smother me in a terrifying loneliness. At this critical time, Junjei's friendship visits my solitary room, drapes itself around me, becoming a familiar comforter.

Junjei visits me frequently now, two or three times a week. On his fifth visit, although initially reluctant to speak, he becomes more relaxed and talkative with each cup of oolong tea. This afternoon, for the first time, he speaks of his mother.

"I don't have my mother's musical talent, but like her, I feel the world's vibrations too strongly. She is quite beautiful. But very frail. She is a gifted musician, trained as a concert pianist in Italy. She excelled at the music academy. So much so that her instructors were in awe of her. They said the music flowed directly from her heart—through her blood vessels, coursing down her arms and wrists until it emerged through her fingertips onto the keyboard. She was said to caress the piano keys and call forth the composer's intended feeling.

I pour more tea for Junjei. "Does she perform?"

Junjei accepts the tea, and his long fingers move gracefully, like pale butterflies, to enfold the cup—so delicately. He peers into the cup as if seeking a response from within its depths.

When at last Junjei responds, it is a whispered, "No."

I lean forward across the small table to catch his words.

"She does not perform. She cannot perform."

"Why ever not?" I find myself saying, and get up to pour myself another cup of tea. I notice shadows beginning to lengthen across the floor.

Junjei waits until I sit back down with my tea, then continues. "She cannot play on a stage, before an audience."

"No?" I'm eager to understand her odd behavior.

"No. She is like me that way. Her nervous system cannot tolerate the eyes and ears of a group of strangers. At the academy, she was able to perform perfectly before a few trusted professors. However, whenever she was forced to play on stage before an audience, her concentration would be shattered, she would lose her place, and her fingers would betray her."

I try to picture Junjei's mother, in a cluttered music classroom, performing confidently before a small group of senior musicians, her mentors. Then I envision this same beautiful woman—Junjei's mother must be quite beautiful—freezing up onstage as she tries to meet the expectations of a large audience of strangers gathered in an elegant concert hall.

"Upon missing a single note, my dear mother would freeze in the spotlight, terrified like a small animal in a hunter's searchlight."

Junjei looks distraught, and runs his fingers repeatedly through his long black hair as he speaks. "I can relate to my mother's situation because I experienced a similar inability to perform just recently when taking my second-level oral exams. I was able to converse in French with Professeur Bonhomme; he is truly a gentle man. But when confronted with Professeur Rossignol's rigid questions about French civilization, I grew flustered. And sensing that proud man's disapproval of me, I froze and could not complete a sentence coherently. And so, I failed to be awarded a certificate."

"I remember how upset you looked that day after your orals. You walked right past without looking at me."

"Yes, I was shaken. And when I confessed my failure to my father, he became disgusted with my ineptness. He has insisted I repeat the second-level classes and try once again to earn the certificate. I must not fail a second time."

"When I didn't see you anymore at the university, I wondered what had happened to you. I thought maybe you had just dropped out of classes. Maybe returned to China. My friend Trudy dropped out, and my Scottish friend, Clare, spends most of her time skiing. I've been skipping classes lately. Don't think I'll try for the level three exam. But I'm trying to hang in there. Learn as much as I can whenever I can. So glad I finally ran into you. Glad we're both still at the university. Just on different schedules."

"You and I are alike, Lissa, in that we are the steadfast ones."

Visit after visit, I repeat to Junjei the advice Beatrix, my British friend from the dorm, used to give me about the need to make an effort to take full advantage of the experience of living abroad. "*Il faut faire un effort.*" One must make an effort. I seem to be trying to motivate myself as much as Junjei.

To my surprise, Junjei takes this advice seriously. One day when he comes for our usual afternoon tea in my room, he is uncustomarily excited, an exuberant smile playing over his lips. Usually during his visits, Junjei savors several cups of oolong tea, chatting languidly for several hours. But today, he rushes to finish his first cup of tea, rises abruptly, says to me, "Come outside with me, Lissa. Come and see!"

He walks me to a shiny blue Citroën DS, parked at the curb. "I've rented a car."

"Wow, Junjei! I didn't even know you could drive."

"Yes, I have my own car in Hong Kong. My father bought it for me when I completed my A levels there. He called my achievement a rite of passage and urged me to use the car as a resource to win friends and influence people. He even gave me a book by an American telling me how to do that, but I have not read it. Being gregarious doesn't come naturally to me. But now I have rented a car and will try anew here in Clermont to win friends and influence people. You are right, Lissa, when you say *il faut faire un effort!*"

Junjei takes me for a short ride. His driving is a bit erratic. I find myself bracing my feet, gripping at the dashboard. But he manages to make his way around the block, drops me off in front of my building. "Don't worry, Lissa. My driving will improve. In Hong Kong we drive on the left, like the British. So, here, driving on the right is new to me."

"Well . . . Yes." I search for the right words. "I guess practice makes perfect, as they say." I frame my statement in what I hope is an encouraging voice, even though I'm feeling a little shaken by the uneven stops, starts, and unpredictable swerves I just experienced in Junjei's passenger seat. I watch as the compact blue car pulls away, speeds to the intersection, then brakes suddenly, just in time to allow a stout elderly lady, dressed all in black— probably one of the many local war widows—to cross in front. I see her raise her cane at Junjei, hear her mutter something, her words muffled by the black scarf drawn closely around her face and knotted tightly beneath her chin.

~~~

True to his word, Junjei makes an effort to become more social. He has seen flyers posted in the dorm, inviting people to join a local Bahá'í group. Next Wednesday, they are hosting a recruitment and planning meeting at a home on the outskirts of Clermont.

"Please accompany me, Lissa. Your presence will make it so much easier for me."

I don't know much about Bahá'í, just that it's a religion that embraces many other religions. Evidently, it's currently popular with young people. So, I agree to go.

~~~

On the following Wednesday evening, I find myself seated in a circle of folding chairs next to Junjei at my first Bahá'í meeting. Local meetings are usually held at Bill and Mindy's place, a ground-floor *maisonette* in Chamalières, just a few minutes' drive from Clermont. Bill, the local Bahá'í group leader, sits across from us, handing around pamphlets that describe, in French, some basics about the Bahá'í Faith. Bill is thin and wiry, and his gingery Caucasian Afro reminds me of Art Garfunkel.

Bill introduces himself as being from the American Midwest and informs us he's taking a year off between college and law school to "find himself." His wife, Mindy, circulates pouring steaming cups of black herbal tea for the handful of attendees. She circles for a second time, offering a platter of raw vegetables, dried bread, dried fruit, and hummus. When everyone is served, she takes a seat next to Bill and explains, in a manner that exudes sincerity and wholesomeness, that she is from Minnesota, is a student of social justice, is contemplating becoming a Peace Corps volunteer in West Africa (hence her need to improve her spoken French), and that she and Bill are vegetarian. She wears her brown hair long and straight, parted in the middle. With soulful eyes, a benign smile, and incredibly white teeth—despite the black tea— Mindy circulates among us, making sure our needs are met.

"The Bahá'í Faith," Bill tells us, "teaches that throughout history all religions have come to man in an orderly progression, revealed by one God in a series of dispensations. Each dispensation is delivered by a Manifestation of God who supplies a text, scripture that carries within it a broader, more advanced revelation, appropriate for the current era. Manifestations of God have appeared over the generations—most recently, Buddha, Jesus, Muhammad. Then, in 1863, Bahá'u'lláh announced himself as the next manifestation of God and founded the Bahá'í Faith. Bahá'í teachings focus on prayer, reflection, and service to others as a means of fulfilling human purpose."

At the end of the meeting, Bill announces a Bahá'í fellowship outing this coming Saturday, a winter picnic at a campground not far from Mont-Dore. Maybe this time I'll be able to enjoy the snow without having to embarrass myself on a pair of skis.

Bill outlines the logistics. "We will take a small convoy of cars—two, maybe three—to the parking area. Then we'll hike to the picnic ground. I'll need one or two volunteers for the drive."

Junjei's hand shoots up, fingers fluttering, playing silent arpeggios in the air at the end of his long slender arm. "I will be honored to drive. I have a rental car."

So, on a sunny Saturday morning in March, Junjei's luxury Citroën takes its place, second in line, between two more modest European cars. I sit up front next to Junjei. Three passengers fill the back seat—two bearded Turkish guys and a vivacious Spanish girl, who sits sandwiched between them. Her upper torso sways suggestively as she sings a Rolling Stones hit over and over, declaring that, no matter how hard she tries, she can't get the satisfaction she yearns for.

Large flakes of snow pirouette around the automobile's fringes. Some land gracefully on the windshield, only to be pinned and swept aside by the wiper blades. Like miniature white swans they self-immolate, melting, forming streaks of water like tears on the heated glass.

A little before noon, we reach the car park and hike along wooded pathways to our destination, a large clearing flanked by a multitude of tall, pointed firs. We descend a thousand cuts of earth. The soggy marshland, half-frozen at this time of year, sighs beneath our tread. The swamp grasses, bent and coated with gems of ice, crackle against the brush of our pantlegs—our destination, a meadow at the very bottom where the soil is more stable.

Suddenly the summit of a peak, shaped like a pointed monk's hat reveals itself above the treetops, an apogee of black lava imposed upon a clear blue sky. The snow has stopped for now, but the meadow is covered with a thick white carpet, hardened at the base but topped with a moist layer that's perfect for packing snowballs.

Soon I am at the center of a battlefield, dodging icy spheres flying in all directions. I run to higher ground at the far edge of the melee, let myself drop flat on my back, and move my long arms and legs to carve the wings and skirt of a snow angel. Junjei has followed me, apparently concerned. But when he sees me smiling, he laughs, bends over me, extends his gloved hands, and pulls me up. I step forward gingerly, careful not to disturb the intaglio seraph I have left behind.

"What is that?" he asks. "I have not seen that before."

"I've made a guardian snow angel to look after you."

"Oh, yes. I see. An angel. Yes, that's a good thing."

"Yes, good thing," I repeat.

By now, Bill has cleared snow from the tops of two wooden picnic tables, and Mindy is serving up sandwiches from a knapsack, pouring cups of steaming chocolate from a thermos. Bill is saying a Bahá'í grace. Everyone gets quiet, demonstrating reverence. So, I stare at my lap, trying to think grateful thoughts. Then we all scarf down the food like a pack of wolves with ferocious appetites.

Soon heavy shadows, opaque as indelible ink, spill down the walls of the hardened lava summit, threatening to drown us in our meadow. We hurry to ascend the long, irregular trail back to the car park before darkness can engulf us. As I strain to climb quickly, a primal fear chews at my tendons. I am grateful that my legs are strong, their strides long, well trained by all those years of tagging along, keeping up with my brother.

Our small motorcade reforms, makes its way back to town—a disciplined convoy, same order of cars, same seating of passengers. I get cold easily, so I relax and revel in the flow of hot air as my feet begin to thaw. The warmth makes me sleepy. Gradually, the backseat passengers cease their chattering and jostling and settle down. I turn around to check on them. The two Turkish guys slump inward, slumbering heavily on the Spanish girl's tiny shoulders. She sits still, eyes closed, satisfied, for the moment anyway. I turn back around, face front, and watch the sky darken around Junjei's car like a stage curtain dropping at the end of a scene. Before long, I nod off.

A sudden thud, then a jolt, and I am awake, staring at an icy tree trunk smashed into the right front of Junjei's hood. The front bumper on the driver's side is dug into the rear bumper of Bill's car, which has now stopped in front of us.

"So sorry! So sorry!" The motorcade has halted. Junjei stands outside his car, fluttering his hands, apologizing at the same time to everyone and no one in particular. Bill gets out of his car, comes back to Junjei's car to examine the damage. The fellow driving the third car, a good-natured Swiss, joins Bill in the assessment.

"Nothing major," says Bill. The Swiss fellow agrees. The passengers whisper among themselves, more groggy than alarmed.

"I have followed too closely on the icy road. I am so sorry!" Junjei murmurs, bestows a short bow from the neck, keeps his face down until Bill gives him a reassuring pat on the shoulder.

Bill and Junjei exchange insurance information, then all drivers hop back into their respective cars. This behavior—this quick exchange of insurance cards—I have learned, is customary in France, where fender benders seem to be a common and unremarkable occurrence. The motorcade resumes. Junjei drops the other students off at the dorm, then drives me to my room on avenue Léon Blum.

"I am so sorry, Lissa. So sorry," Junjei repeats as I get out of the car. "My father will be very angry." He drives away, abruptly, before I'm able to respond.

I watch the car creep very slowly down the avenue. I give a desperate little wave, an ineffectual effort to offer comfort, wishing Junjei to see it, to feel the company of his guardian snow angel, but knowing he does not. With dread, I apprehend a great and inevitable loss to come. I am reminded of the clairvoyance I shared with my father, that uncanny ability, on occasion, to see clearly, to perceive that which is beyond the normal range of the senses. Those dreaded words echo once again, as in a hollow cavern buried somewhere deep in my mind. "Junjei's dead!" I shake my head as if to deny the thought, toss it off into hostile night air, and retreat to my empty room, seeking some comfort in numbness.

CHAPTER EIGHTEEN

⸙ ⸙

À Poile!

"Collectively, we escape the tedium of a poor student's life. . . .
Together, we conjure a hazy vision of something great to come upon
us, somewhere in Italy. . . ." —Lissa's notebook

O N THE PENULTIMATE SUNDAY IN MARCH, jostling among
fellow students, I board a crowded bus. Toward the back,
I find a seat that's not taken, next to a very ordinary-
looking French girl in a beige trench coat who seems intentionally
unadorned, and surprisingly complacent about her own plainness.
She reminds me of the brown laboratory mouse my best friend in
high school gave me as a pet.

"Est-ce que je peux m'asseoir ici?" I ask her. Is it okay for me to
sit here?

Her bland face issues a vague smile as she slides a beige handbag and collapsed beige umbrella out of my way. She observes me
closely as I settle in beside her, and when I return her gaze, she
bestows a polite nod of approval.

Rumbling its engine, the tour bus pulls away from the
curb in front of the main entrance to the *Faculté de Lettres,*

embarking on a weeklong spring tour of Italy—Milan, Verona, Venice, Bologna, Pisa, Genoa—organized by the university. Last month, when a glossy brochure tacked to a bulletin board at the *fac* caught my eye, I was seized by an urge to escape the grayness of Clermont's winter, to seek a new adventure. What was it that made my hand quiver as I signed up for this trip and paid for it with a check from my own personal account at the *Crédit Lyonnais*? A sense of newfound independence? Of disregarding the precautions of safety and self-preservation my father had instilled in me as I grew up? "Be careful, Lissa," he would caution. "I don't want my little girl to hurt herself." And always, I obeyed. Or tried to obey.

This time, I've struck out on my own, without any of my usual Clermont friends or companions. Today, my fellow travelers are all strangers, and I wonder what, over the course of this journey, we will reveal about ourselves to each other.

At the Italian border, our bus halts. Uniformed guards board the bus, check each passport, nod, and move on down the aisle. My American passport seems to elicit a certain deference from the guard—or do I imagine it? His voice sounds almost respectful as he looks up at me and says, "Ah, *americana*." The pace slows when the guards reach the back of the bus where the Arab students are seated. Without a word of explanation, the officials collect all their passports and exit the bus. A couple of the students complain loudly at having their passports confiscated, gesticulating and shouting in Arabic. But nothing deters the guards. Eventually, all the passports are returned to their owners, the bus engine growls to a start, and on we roll into Italy.

محمد

It's dark when we arrive in Milan and our group gathers for its first evening meal. I'm seated among fellow voyagers at a long dining table in an ornate but shabby restaurant. We are served multiple courses, not the best food—pasta served without sauce, small unidentifiable fish, bottles of vinegary red wine. With each glass drunk, the volume of voices increases, until a roar of boisterous excitement crescendos all around—a dizzying chorus of French and Arabic with ribbons of Italian flowing through. Here and there, a snippet of something Germanic, or is it Scandinavian? We are all so young, or so recently young. Spirits burgeoning, verging on raucous. Out for a change of scene, in search of something new or unanticipated. Collectively, we escape the tedium of a poor student's life—broke, with no secure future in sight. Together, we conjure a hazy vision of something great to come upon us, somewhere in Italy—will it be in Milan or Venice? Or in Verona, that city of "star-crossed lovers"?

The next day, in Milan, we roam the shopping district and search for something inexpensive, but authentic, to bring back to France. I know very little Italian. So, in a *pasticceria,* I point to the shelves and, making up some words, ask the shopkeeper for "pasta longie," all the while gesturing dramatically with my hands held far apart. The shopkeeper is good-natured, indulges my made-up Italian, smiles, nods enthusiastically, and fetches me a packet of what appears to be a nest of very thin noodles. "*Capelli d'angelo!* Is how you say, in English, angel hair," he tells me.

On our way to Venice, we stop in Verona to have lunch and see Juliet's tomb. Her sarcophagus is a red marble shell, open and worn. It resembles a bathtub, and tourists are allowed to sit inside it. So, one of my fellow voyagers, from Tunisia, a student of architecture and engineering, teases and challenges me to get into the coffin beside him to seal our fate together. I laugh, take the dare, and crawl in with him. Later, I stop at a kiosk to buy a postcard of the tomb.

In Venice, our group disperses at night, consigned to a variety of lodgings. I am assigned to a convent guest house—six guest rooms, three beds per chamber, where I share a room with two other young women. The three beds are identical, plain, with narrow frames. Formerly nuns' beds. A vaguely fetid odor, incense and mildew, rises from the tiled floor. As I hesitate, the other girls claim the outer beds, and I'm left with the one in the middle. My cot is sandwiched between the other two in a space so tight I have to turn sideways to squeeze into bed each night. On the first night, when I try to rest my head on the pillow, I find it to be flat and hard—more like a rock than a pillow. The mattress is thin and rigid. The large crucifix that hangs on the wall above my bed keeps me vigilant, and I have trouble sleeping.

On my right, the bland French girl, the one I sat with on the bus, is sleeping placidly. On my left, a very quiet, very serious French girl lies awake, staring straight up at the bedchamber's high ceiling. Her fingers and thumb move fretfully over the worn beads of a rosary that, apparently, travels with her everywhere. Her lips move, hailing Mary, who seems to hover—full of grace— somewhere above the pious girl's bed.

Stale vapors assail me. Where do they come from? Do they rise from the floor? Or seep from the damp walls? This room is small, unventilated. The odor threatens to smother me. I find myself struggling to catch my breath, and as I watch, a dewy mist slowly accumulates and, hypnotically, begins to swirl around the dutiful girl. It encircles her body and, almost gently, engulfs the human form beside me, possesses it. This mist is otherworldly—I imagine it to be, perhaps, the spirit of a devout novitiate who, centuries before, wrestled for the salvation of her very soul, while lying on this same stringent bed.

I shut my eyes, craving respite, longing for sleep. Behind my closed lids, a fathomless void stretches. Then a searchlight appears, sweeping the emptiness; its vivid russet beam pierces the darkness. And on this searchlight's beam, a red marble urn floats toward me, rotating, revealing itself to me as the vessel of story. Timeless, it speaks of the universal truths it holds, how it carries these truths forward, imparting them to generation after generation of writers.

Tonight, the red stone urn tips toward me, pouring from its lip the tale of Romeo and his ill-fated love for Juliet, then rights itself. The vessel tips a second time, spilling out again the very same story. But this time, it is my friend Mohammed's voice that narrates the grim testimony of *his* ill-fated love for *his* Juliette. As the story echoes forward—though transformed by centuries of telling, embellished by the teller—its truth remains, immutable.

I wake next morning, stiff in the narrow bed. The placid girl on my right still sleeps, the pious girl on my left has disappeared—gone off somewhere? She's left her bed fastidiously made, its coarse sheets tightly tucked, its thin blanket neatly folded. I seize this quiet moment to write a note to Spence on the back of the postcard I bought yesterday in Verona:

Spence,
Stopped in Verona yesterday (Tuesday) for lunch and to see Juliet's tomb (pictured). People have carved hearts with names all around and on the stone tomb. There's a garden and a well—I threw a coin in and that means I'll return some day.

Arrived in Venice in late afternoon and took boat to city—it's lovely. This city is sustained by tourism—mainly American, it seems. American Express good everywhere. Am afraid of something here—American power, influence, corruption.

Lissa

On Wednesday, our first full day in Venice, I explore the city in the company of three young Arabs from North Africa. As we scope out the landscape, the Arabs boast of their region, the Maghreb, and regale me with achievements of the Arab World in general. The one from Tunisia, the guy who shared Juliet's tomb with me—his name is Aziz—is animated, arrogant, sure of his male attractiveness. "In mathematics," he says, "we Arabs excel. We created the numbering system you use today." The others join in the boastful chorus. One of them says, "We created an alphabet." The other one says, "We invented algebra." I don't know enough to agree or disagree with these claims; so, I just tag along, letting these guys brag away.

As we wander the streets, my senses are assaulted—the

screeching of sea birds, the gliding of boats and gondolas on the canals, the snapping of small colorful flags, and a vague smell of rot emanating from suspicious-looking waters.

"What is that smell?" I ask my Arab buddies. "Is it fish? Garbage?"

"Maybe it's dead bodies," says Aziz, laughing. He pinches his nose closed and gives me a lurid grin.

And so, on we ramble through a maze of walkways and bridges. I follow the Arabs, lost and reeling, until I stumble on an uneven paver. I take a seat on the nearest stone staircase and signal that I need to stop and rest. My companions humor me, but also talk among themselves, seeming to joke in Arabic. Finally, I call over to them and suggest, *"Peut-être qu'il est temps de rejoindre notre groupe."* Maybe it's time to rejoin our group. I admit to having no sense of direction, and leave it to the Arabs to plot the fastest route back to the designated meeting place.

After lunch, we visit San Marco Square and buy paper cones filled with shelled corn that we toss to the pigeons. We have our pictures taken with these birds, dozens of them, scrabbling for their food at our feet, more birds flying at our faces, perching on our arms and heads, pecking at the cones for more corn.

In the evening, after consuming another disappointing dinner—cheap, mediocre, part of the package deal—we return to the square, and navigate a sea of small round tables anchored under white starched linen cloths. Waiters, white-coated, dart from table to table, taking orders, carrying oversized trays, serving drinks. The waitstaff are dwarfed, like busy ants, within the square's imposing perimeter of massive stone archways. Under one arch, an orchestra plays romantic dance music beneath a voluptuous white cloth canopy that undulates whenever there's a breeze.

I listen, enchanted by the fullness of strings—violin and viola, cello and harp expanding the piano's melody. Captivated by the grandness of the square's proportions, I watch as graceful couples begin to stroll out from under the pilasters, spill out onto the magnificent floor of the open square. Here, they assume—leisurely, as if by second nature—the formal positions of ballroom dancers, and glide across the smooth tiles. I continue to watch, then stand, then begin to sway lightly to the music.

As the opening strains of a familiar waltz rise from the orchestra, the moon makes her appearance and I find myself rushing out into the square, twirling, stepping—one, two, three—in time to the music. My arms float out from my sides, white stars blurring overhead.

One of the older members of our group, an elegant man from Finland, moves effortlessly toward me, offers his hand, invites me to waltz with him across San Marco Square. The floor's vast expanse is alluring, but the pavement's geometric patterning is complicated. A wave of shyness washes over me, and I confess that I don't really know how to waltz, that I just make up steps. The man smiles and continues to extend his hand to me. But overwhelmed by his refined good looks and his gallant demeanor, I become self-conscious and rush off to take a seat.

The next night, we visit a nightclub where loud contemporary music throbs, strobe lights pulsate, and shards of color flash and rotate overhead. The band plays hit tunes. No words. Just instrumentals. I recognize some of them: "Stuck in the Middle with You," "Crocodile Rock," "Love Train." The room is packed, alive with young couples abandoning themselves to frenzied dancing. They seem so free!

When the band launches into Jim Croce's "Bad, Bad Leroy Brown," cocky Aziz urges me to join him on the dance floor. The wood floor is even and polished. The beat is fast and strong. No predetermined steps. This kind of music liberates my feet, encourages me to improvise; it invites my arms to flow, my hips to move. My partner leers at me and tries to imitate my movements. As the song speeds up, Aziz raises an arm and jabs a finger repeatedly at the ceiling, yelling, "*À poile, à poile!*" Before I know what's happening, he's peeling off his shirt, loosening his belt, pulling down his slacks, encouraging me to do the same with my clothes, shouting over and over, "*À poile, à poile!*" I continue to dance, and realize— too late—that Aziz is preparing to do a full strip. Right here. In the middle of the dance floor. A nightclub employee comes rushing over, signals for a bouncer, and with my overstimulated partner protesting all the way, Aziz and I are unceremoniously escorted out of the building. Such a stern rebuke for trying to discard my inhibitions.

꙳

After departing Venice, the bus makes quick stops in Bologna and Pisa where I witness the folly of architects who built on weak foundations. I get the two leaning towers in Bologna confused with the one I'm expecting—and later see—in Pisa. After another quick stop, in Genoa, we head back to Clermont-Ferrand via Avignon.

With one exception—no, make that two—the remainder of the trip is relatively uneventful. Both incidents occur on the road from Genoa to Avignon. From what I can make out from the road markers we pass as the bus leaves Genoa, we are heading north toward the Piedmont Region. The flat coastal landscape becomes more and more hilly, and after bumping along kilometer after kilometer of highway through Italian countryside, I begin to feel my bladder nagging at me. I hadn't realized how long we'd be on the road this time, hadn't used a toilet before boarding, and our bus is not equipped with one. But I'm young. I have good muscle control down there. So, I put my bladder on hold, stare past my bland seatmate out the bus window, and try to concentrate on the scenery. Hillside after hillside slowly passes by. The terrain is steeper now, rockier. A few more kilometers and the need to pee becomes more urgent. I clench my muscles so hard my face hurts. The bland girl in the seat beside me is wiggling back and forth, shifting her weight from buttock to buttock. She covers her mouth with her hand, whispers to me through the fingers, "*Je dois aller aux toilettes,*" I have to go to the bathroom.

"*Moi aussi.*" Me too, I admit, glad to have a companion to share my desperation. Together, we take action. The bland girl, more animated now and using an authoritative French, convinces the driver to pull off the road and wait for us while we scramble down a bank to relieve ourselves.

There we huddle side by side, keeping our backs to the bus, doing our best to minimize our visibility and maximize our privacy. But the bland girl, who is wearing a dress, fares better than I. She is able to spread her skirt out around her as she squats and pulls down her underwear. The full skirt conceals most of what is going on down there.

I'm not so lucky. To avoid soiling my clothes, I have to crouch and pull my jeans and underpants down around my ankles. I know my butt is exposed when I do this, and I cringe at the thought of scores of eyes on the bus, peering through the windows, straining to catch a glimpse. But when I finally release the urine, let it spill down the hill over rocks and dried grass, the immediate relief is so great that the embarrassment becomes meaningless—at least temporarily.

Our heads lowered, the bland girl and I trudge up the hill and climb back onto the bus. I half expect a rude comment from Aziz. No comment. But as we thread the bus's narrow aisle, a ripple of laughter pursues us, transforming our passageway into a gauntlet of shame so strong it keeps our eyes fixed on the floorboards until we reach the shelter of our seat.

The second event occurs just as we cross the border into France. At the very moment we pass through the invisible wall that arbitrarily separates one nation from another, the pious French girl appears in her seat on the bus, mysteriously reconstituted, apparently returned to the world of the living from the vaporous state she had assumed while in the nun's bed in Venice. Did I imagine the pious girl's disappearance and reappearance? Or have I witnessed an authentic Catholic miracle?

Our stop in Avignon is brief. But here I convince my bland bus mate, along with the pious one, to join me on the fabled Avignon bridge. Together—though the pious one still looks like death warmed over—we dance. And joyfully, we sing *"sur le pont d'Avignon!"* Then we board the bus for the final lap of our journey. I collapse on the seat, worn out, and glad to be heading "home" to Clermont.

CHAPTER NINETEEN

‏❧ ❧‎

Lonely Easter in Clermont

"I don't think you realize just how strong a woman you are."
—Trudy to Lissa

O N A GENTLE EVENING IN APRIL, I sit bent over my
writing table, notebook open to a page half-filled with
scribbled words and crossed-out phrases that meander
all over the paper. I am struggling to compose a short story.

When I become vaguely aware of a dimming of the daylight,
of twilight descending in my shuttered room, I look up from my
work, pull the gold chain to switch on the barrister's desk lamp—
it came with the room. I admire the lamp's polished brass finish,
adjust the thick green glass of the shade. It is then that I hear the
faint tap at the door and get up to answer it.

"Junjei, you look awful. What's wrong?" His face is distressed,
more sallow than usual.

"I have received this telegram." His hands tremble as he passes
me the teletyped message. I try reading the typing on the sheet,
but what I see is a string of intricate characters I can't decipher.

Junjei takes the message back. Slips it into his pocket. "I for-
got. It is written in Cantonese."

I pull up a chair for him. He sits, covers his face with his hands. Then, very quietly, he begins to weep.

"What is it, Junjei? Let me make you a cup of tea."

Junjei's breathing becomes spasmodic, transforms into a low moan like the slow scraping of waves on a grainy beach. Gradually, the sobbing stills and he is able to take a few sips of tea. And finally, the oolong calms him enough that he can look up at me and speak.

"My mother has fallen ill. She is asking for me."

For a brief moment, he takes my hand, turns it palm up, and touches the very center of it with the index finger of his other hand.

"Tomorrow," Junjei whispers, "I will take a plane from Paris to Hong Kong." Pressing with his fingertip, he traces his journey across my palm—from center to edge, a long, slow arc toward the east. "I must fly to her and take my place by her side." Then, as if embarrassed, he releases my hand, gets up abruptly, and begins to leave.

I touch Junjei's shoulder, and he turns to face me. He seems so lost, so devastated. I take his delicate moon face between my palms, lean in, and give him a gentle kiss on his full lips. They are as dry as parchment. He doesn't return the kiss, but looks down as if concealing something he's ashamed of, turns slowly away, and exits my room.

～

The next Sunday, April 14, is Easter. My neighborhood is deserted, and I find myself wandering aimlessly along the empty sidewalks, winding up at a nearby playground where mothers or nannies often take their children. Today, no one is here. I sit on one of the benches—for I don't know how long— looking up at a limpid blue sky, watching fleecy white clouds, imagining them as spring lambs gamboling. Half-formed thoughts come and go—something to do with joy and the loss of it—until the pealing of church bells cracks through the thin shell of my musings, like the piping of an Easter egg. I count twelve strokes; it is noon.

I remember Easter from my childhood, wearing that special outfit to Sunday School and church—the hat, the pastel dress with its full skirt billowing out from a scratchy petticoat. White patent leather shoes, white cotton socks, white gloves. Being forbidden to change into more casual clothes until the traditional family photos are taken. Me, smirking at the camera; Spence, looking miserable, a miniature version of a man in a small suit and bowtie. Then donning play clothes and dashing off with Spence across the lawns in search of Easter eggs. Later in the afternoon, thinking about the preacher's Easter sermon, watching Easter shows on TV, and feeling so tingly and spiritual about the crucifixion and resurrection that I give all the candy in my Easter basket to Spence. But today is very different for me, this first Easter alone and far from home.

Back in my room, I tear a blank page from my writing notebook, and fold it into a card. From a zippered case, I select some of the colored pencils I generally use for editing my stories, and draw a fat bunny on the front of the card. Inside, I print, "Happy Easter, Mimi!" I draw tulips and a pink heart underneath, and sign it "Lissa."

I fold another blank page into a makeshift envelope, seal the edges with tape, address it simply "Mimi." Then I trek over to the apartment building at 40 rue Philippe Lebon, and drop the Easter card into the Arlettes' mailbox.

A few days later, I receive a card from my friend Mme Arlette—Angelique. She senses my loneliness and invites me to the family's small home in the country. She drives me, along with her little girl, Mimi, to the outskirts of Clermont. I spend the afternoon with mother and daughter, digging in the dirt of a small orchard, clearing away brush from beneath plum, peach, and apricot trees just beginning to bud.

Later in the day, Mimi fetches one of her books, a story about a monkey and peanuts and an elephant. She climbs onto my lap, plops down, hands me the book, and in the commanding tone of a confident toddler, demands that I read it to her.

I'm doing pretty well, until I stumble over the French word for peanut. I'm familiar with the term *arachide*, but the story I'm reading uses the word *cacahuète*. Mimi erupts in laughter at my mispronunciation; Angelique looking amused, corrects me—but her voice is gentle, patient.

That night, alone in my room, homesickness hits me full force. I dream of our old barn and the gnarled apple tree behind it. Over time, a crack in the tree's trunk has expanded; the wood has begun to decay. Some limbs are brittle, leafless, barren. But a portion of the tree remains vital, thick with leaves, branches so heavy with ripening fruit they touch the ground. What was it Voltaire said in *Candide*, something about the need to cultivate our garden? My garden, I realize, needs plenty of work.

〰

On the day Junjei returns from Hong Kong, the local newspaper reports a train derailment between Vichy and Clermont. Lives, as well as train cars are derailed, with several passengers injured, one woman killed, and the engineer under investigation.

That afternoon as Junjei and I stroll through Jardin Lecoq, I am thinking about the train accident and life's impermanence. The spring air is tentative, still tinged with remnants of winter. Junjei turns up his jacket collar, circumspect, as he begins to disclose the circumstances of his mother's death.

"She was left in the care of a private nurse. My father stayed away, preoccupied with his work. My brother remained in London until the funeral date was determined. I spent those final days alone with her, by her bedside," he murmurs. "I believe she was in great pain near the end, and heavily sedated. But she knew me, and said my name."

I walk beside him, leaning in close to catch his words. He

walks quickly, but my own long strides easily match his along the paved pathway. I learned early on how to keep up with my older brother.

As I listen to Junjei speak of his devotion to his mother, I am reminded of my own mother's death. Breast cancer. I was only twelve, still a child. I begin to realize that, in many ways, Junjei, too, is still a child. For Junjei, as for me, maternal loss is a child's loss, innocent and pure.

In contrast, my father's death is an adult's loss. I was twenty-two. Innocence was tainted with guilt. I was my father's caregiver, the last person with him the night he died. But I couldn't bear to watch Daddy succumb to death, told him he would have to do this by himself, watched a tear flow down his cheek as I released his hand and fled the bedroom, leaving him to spend those final hours alone in the sick room. I abandoned my father at the hour of his death. I have suppressed this knowledge, but now it rises, threatening to engulf me.

I reach out, take Junjei's hand, and look deep into his eyes, seeking a way to channel our parallel grief, to join mine with his, and somehow, in confluence, attenuate both our sorrows. Right now, I have the urge to fall into Junjei's arms, summon our shared sadness, release heavy tears accumulated in deep internal wells. But something in Junjei's expression prevents me. I withdraw my hand and look away, denying myself the comfort of closeness. Am I punishing myself, atoning for abandoning my father as he lay dying? Or does Junjei not want that kind of closeness with me. Of course, this line of reasoning is unhealthy, perverse. And to what end?

We stop at the pavilion restaurant, sip an *Orangina* on the deck overlooking the large central pond and fountain—no ducks or swans out today.

"I am determined to pass the oral exams this time," Junjei says. "I must!" For a moment, he surveys the water as if looking for a solution there, the next move, the winning strategy. But, for now, the pond is empty.

He frowns, turns back to me, and leans in, studying my demeanor. "Your face," he tells me, "is complicated. Many planes and angles."

"And yours, my dear Junjei, is what many Westerners would describe as inscrutable."

He smiles and nods, conveying a wistful resignation to the stereotype. "I would not disappoint," he says, and there the conversation ends.

⁓

For a while, Junjei and I go our separate ways. He returns full-time to intermediate French classes at the *fac*. Slowly, quietly, I drop out of level-three classes at the *fac*. Instead, I continue to assist with Angelique's English classes and hang out with Trudy, who meets life head on and is a never-ending source of ideas for getting involved in politics, for taking part in the culture surrounding her.

In late April, Trudy, bursting with excitement, invites me to sign up with her for a series of cooking lessons, offered by Clermont's Chamber of Commerce. "I just heard about it from the wife of one of Buford's co-workers. The lessons are free. And the recipes are all collected in a cookbook that we can purchase at the end of the course if we want to. And we'll need to buy some measuring cups and spoons—everything's done in the metric system here, you know."

The cooking lessons are conducted by an attractive young woman at a local municipal building. The room's layout—a row of six kitchenettes with a view of some chalkboards up front—reminds me of my high school Home Economics cooking class.

Here, we are twelve students plus the cooking instructor. Trudy and I share a small kitchen near the back of the room. Our nearest neighbors are a Portuguese couple, a Muslim brother and sister, who refrain from using alcohol in any of their cooking—for religious reasons. That means they substitute some other liquid for the liquor in the recipes. Trudy, who views the couple's abstinence with cynicism, shakes her head and mutters over my shoulder, "Makes no sense to me, Lissa. The alcohol gets consumed when you cook it."

So, they don't *flambé*, which I think is a shame. My favorite cooking lesson, as it turns out, is making classic French *baba au rhum*. This recipe involves a yeasty dough, kneaded, risen, and baked in molds to produce a dozen small golden-brown cakes that are soaked in a hot syrup concocted with spices, dried fruit, and dark rum. The remaining rum is heated in a skillet, poured over the *babas*, then ignited with a long match—flambéed in the burst of a brief, but glorious fire.

At the final cooking class, we learn to make *beignets*. But Trudy isn't able to attend. She's devastated at missing this opportunity to practice making authentic homemade French doughnuts, but an ovarian cyst flares up, suddenly and painfully. She is forced into the hospital for a surgical procedure.

I find Trudy lying flat on her back in a hospital bed, shrieking in pain. She's attended by a strong, competent-looking nun dressed all in white. The nun gives Trudy a pill to swallow, then eases her patient's head back on an extra-large pillow that looks ethereally soft, like a fluffy white cloud. The nun bustles about, fixing the sheets, stroking Trudy's brow, making sure the convalescent is comfortable. After a moment or two, Trudy's pain seems to ease and her head sinks back into the pillow.

"Hi, Trudy. Are you okay now?" I say, in what I hope is a quiet, soothing voice. I'm still standing in the doorway to her room. Trudy turns her head in my direction, gestures for me to come in. Her face is much paler than usual.

"Liss! It's so good to see you," Trudy says in a half-whisper. She pats at a spot next to her, signaling me to sit down on the bed beside her. I hesitate, look around for a sign of permission from the nun. But the sturdy nurse has vanished, moved on, I suppose, to her next patient.

I sit there, feeling awkward, and ask again, "Are you okay, Trudy?"

She smiles a weak smile, says, "The sisters here are wonderful! So much less rigid and antiseptic than American hospitals."

I nod, to show Trudy I've taken in and accepted her assessment. Then I just sit for a while, holding Trudy's hand, not knowing what more to say.

It's Trudy who breaks the silence. "So, how's the cooking class going?" Her face is getting some of its color back.

"It's been good," I tell her. Trudy uses her elbows to push herself up, and I hop off the bed to give her room. "You missed the class on *beignets*, you know."

"I know," she says, and squiggles her face at me in mock disappointment.

Standing at the bedside, I help Trudy situate the pillow behind her back so she can sit, propped up. "I saved the recipe for you," I say, and Trudy smiles.

Just then, another nun—this one young, extremely thin, wide-eyed—comes in carrying Trudy's lunch on a tray. This lunch isn't at all like the insipid institutional food Daddy refused to eat when he spent time in the hospital back home—not long before he came home to die. Trudy's lunch actually looks appetizing. The bowl of thick, steaming soup smells good. And it's accompanied by slices of crisp bread, a serving of fresh strawberries.

The young nun pauses over Trudy's tray, an angel clothed in white, face radiant with innocence beneath her veil, she offers grace, asking the *Seigneur* to bless us, to bless this meal and those who prepared it, to provide bread to those who don't have any. And I remember myself as a little girl, hair in long braids, seated on Daddy's lap, saying grace, reciting similar words in English. And for the first time, I see Trudy with her head bowed.

"Well, guess I'd better go. Let you eat your lunch in peace."

Trudy looks at me, serious now. "I really appreciate you, Lissa. You know that. Don't you?" I shrug, not knowing what to say.

Trudy seems to be studying me. Then she says, "I don't think you realize just how strong a woman you are."

So then, Trudy and I say our goodbyes, and I head back to 36 Léon Blum, pondering what Trudy just said. I haven't really told Trudy much about myself, just that I'm here in Clermont for my junior year abroad. I've said very little to her about my family. Nothing about Georges or my aspirations as a writer.

Agitated, I walk quickly and dig my fingernails deep into the pockets of my NFS jacket, struggling to resolve the conflation of values, untangle the disparate threads—a nun's purity, a daughter's duty to her father, a young woman's emerging strength. This newfound desire for independence, is it a virtue or a vice?

Agitation stimulates my appetite. I pass a familiar bar, stop in for a ham sandwich, and continue along, munching on the crisp *baguette* and savoring the delicate thin slices of ham coated with butter. On impulse I turn toward Place de Regensburg and cross the square to enter *Le Foyer*. Ghislaine buzzes me in and gushes, "How are you, *Leeza*?

I tell her I'm well, and ask if Serena from Toronto is still living here.

"Oh, yes," Ghislaine replies. "Do you want to visit her? I can let her know you're here. She will be glad to see you. You know, she is still struggling to learn French,"

Serena does seem glad to see me when we meet in the lobby.

"Hey, Lissa," she says. "What's up? Me, I've mostly been hanging out here in the dorm, earning a little travel money. A guy here in Clermont pays me to address, seal, and put stamps on hundreds of letters that advertise his services. He runs his own real estate business. Speaks enough English for me to get the gist of what he's saying."

Serena stops talking for a moment, and seems to search my face for the reason I'm here.

I find myself saying, "Not sure why I came to visit. Guess I just want to get out more."

"Yep," she says. "I know what you mean." She laughs and adds, "But at least here I can keep myself clean. And I've learned the best way to wash jeans. I just wear them in the shower and give them a good scrubbing."

"More efficient than soaking them in the bidet, I guess," I say. We both laugh.

I look around the lobby. It's pretty quiet right now. A few residents come and go, but I don't see anyone I know.

Serena taps on my knee to interrupt my ruminations. "Hey, Lissa, I've got a great idea. You know the best way to get out and about without your own car? Hitchhiking! Ever hitchhiked?"

I shake my head.

"Well then," says Serena. "Let's get together and I'll teach you the art of hitchhiking."

CHAPTER TWENTY

✧

Learning to Flow

"How soft the early morning sun on just-mown grass, drying, giving up its sweetness as it dies. Mere grass, alas! Yet its soft surrender so close to grace." —Lissa's notebook

WE WALK AN UNDULATING RURAL ROADWAY. On one side, pale-green lentil seedlings tumble off into distant rugged foothills. On the road's opposite side, dark red cattle with gently arched horns interrupt their placid grazing, stare at us as we pass. The scent of sun-warmed manure, a struggle of sweet and acrid, rises to accost us. But when we reach the straightaway, a caressing wind blows on our faces and blesses us. It is springtime in Auvergne, and we are young, seeking adventure, yearning for expansion.

I am hitchhiking with my Canadian friend. Slender, blonde Serena. Vagabond hippie in skin-tight jeans, purposely laid-back, dreamy in speech. Her hair is straight, the color of ripe wheat. Parted in the middle, it falls well below her waist and moves as she walks—in cadence with the long brown fringes on the sleeves of her leather jacket. She ambles beside me, taking long, relaxed strides. I find myself adjusting my own pace to match hers, moving more slowly but covering more ground. I broaden my steps, letting go of tensions in my neck, my back, and swing my arms more loosely. As we walk, Serena shares her story with me.

"When I left Canada a year ago, I was at bottom's bottom." She doesn't say it in so many words, but I come to understand what bottom's bottom means for her. As a teen, she ran away from her parents' home in Toronto, hung out with other kids, who, like her, rejected their parents' values: the desire for security above all else, the addiction to material things. "I was totally bummed out." I have noticed the deep scars on both her wrists.

"I wanted to 'turn on, tune in, drop out,' as that famous dude says. And I went into this crazy, dark space where I could escape, let go of everything and everyone, just float in and out for a while—no ceiling, no floor. But that place got smaller and smaller. It started to contract, to squeeze the life out of me, until one day that whole world punctured like a circus balloon, smothering in around me. I couldn't breathe. That's when I hit bottom's bottom, became nobody's nobody. And since then—about a year ago—I have been trying to crawl my way back up and out."

Serena never goes anywhere without a small backpack—a day pack, she calls it—strapped across her shoulders, her omnipresent water bottle protruding from the pack's side pocket. And inside, along with a sandwich or a snack, she keeps a small notebook, a ballpoint pen tucked at-the-ready in the notepad's spiral backbone. From time to time, when we stop somewhere, she pulls out the pad and pen, and makes an entry in a childishly rounded script.

Today, as the afternoon heats up, we stop under a broad-leafed shade tree—Daddy would have known what kind of tree it is, but I don't. Serena takes a seat on the ground between two protruding roots, leans back against bark as coarse as an elephant's skin. I sit opposite her. She takes a sip from her water bottle, passes it over to me. While I sip and scan the road for any cars that might come along and maybe offer us a ride, Serena writes in her notebook with great intensity. Her skin is a pale white. Her glasses are oval with gold frames. She looks like a scholar, but her wisdom, I've observed—unlike mine—comes to her not so much from books, but from raw experience. I've never seen her reading a book, and she seems puzzled when I mention some of my favorite writers— Katherine Mansfield, Albert Camus, Leo Tolstoy. Her sentences are direct, blunt, not like the fancy words I've learned from my college courses. But, nonetheless, her words carry an unexpected depth of meaning.

She pauses in her writing, looking up at me. "I don't think I'm so un-understanding of things as much lately. I sort of got taught the lesson of listening more to what other people think and discussing gently, if you know what I mean. It was a painful lesson."

Serena gazes off into the distance. A bird lands in a puddle across the road, gulps the water, tips its head back to swallow, then lingers in the wetness ruffling its feathers. Serena resumes. "I still have my ideas and all that, but it seems more important to be and do what I sense is true than to make sure I say what I think all the time. That makes a big difference."

Serena studies me, a sadness in her gray eyes. "Just last weekend I learned another lesson. I went camping with a French guy. Said he gives all the women he sleeps with a grade from one to ten. Me, I was a six. That's a good lesson for me, right there." Before I can ask her what she means by that or how it made her feel, Serena gets up, brushes off her pants, shoulders her pack, and starts walking away along the road. I hurry to catch up and manage to fall into place beside her. I can hear a stream gurgling somewhere below the road bank. "Where are we headed?" I ask.

"You need to learn to flow in the present moment. Let yourself be carried along. Content with what comes your way. Moving from one beat of time to the next. No plans. No expectations. . . ." Serena turns to look directly at me. "So, no disappointments."

After a while, we come to a crossroad. Where the two roads meet, a crucifix rises and a road marker points its arrow toward "Montpeyroux." We follow the arrow's guidance, continuing straight toward a weathered fortress of white stone that weaves and shimmers on the horizon like an enchanted mirage. As we approach, a fortified village emerges, stone piled upon stone, rising just beyond the roadway, clinging to the side of a craggy bluff. We cross a parking lot beyond which no car is allowed. The smells of coffee and baking dough drift down, inviting us to mount the hill. We pass through a stone gateway, beneath a large mounted clock that has stopped. We follow our noses to a café that's cloistered within thick rock walls. Here, we sip fresh coffee and munch on fruit pastries still warm from the oven. And now, for this present moment, all our needs are satisfied.

After our breakfast, I wander with Serena through a maze of narrow alleys, high walls dotted with wooden doors, and shutters painted in shades of russet brown, cobalt blue, and periwinkle. We pass terra cotta pots bursting with red geraniums on low stone ledges. More flowers bloom above on balconies, spilling bright color from window boxes mounted atop forged iron railings. A woman emerges through a doorway at the end of a cul-de-sac; the door and frame are painted a beguiling shade of lavender. The woman wears a patterned headscarf and an apron the color of blue chicory flowers. She sloshes soapy water from a primitive wooden bucket into a ditch nearby. Applying a sturdy stick, a small boy propels a large hoop—it's taller than he is—down the slope of a cobblestone lane and past a skinny cat that arches its back, hisses, and escapes into a crevice between two watering cans as the boy approaches.

Walking alongside Serena, all worry falls away. With her, I float in a place that is removed from—yet somehow immersed in—the quotidian. In Serena's world, all things ordinary—an apron, a cat, watering cans—become celestial. All is right with the world, and I am divinely protected.

When the sun has long passed its zenith, we return to the highway and turn back in the direction of Clermont. Exhausted from all the walking, we find a seat in the shade, backs propped against the mossy side of a large rock, and Serena teaches me the gentle art of hitchhiking as we wait for a car to pass by, going in the right direction.

"It's perfectly safe to hitchhike in Europe. I do it all the time. You just need to remember that when someone stops to give you a ride, they do it out of loneliness . . . or boredom . . . or curiosity. They're looking for someone to talk with them, entertain them, tell them stories. That's the way you repay them. You don't need to give them money. You entertain them."

Serena stands up, stretches, then demonstrates her skills. She has mastered the crab-like art of walking sideways, looking back for cars while moving forward along the roadside. As the first car approaches, she stretches out her arm and signals, with a graceful pumping, that we want to hitch a ride. Her upturned thumb twists and points in the direction we want to go.

The car that's coming is big like an American car. A convertible, top down, its body painted a startling shade of watermelon pink. This is the first car that's passed in a while, and I'm surprised to see it slow and pull up beside us. The driver looks Mediterranean. Tanned skin, dark hair slicked back. He wears a silky shirt, open at the collar, and with garish purple pineapples printed on a neon green background. His car radio is blaring what I'm guessing is a popular local tune.

He twists in his seat, pops up the button to unlock the back door on the driver's side. "*Montez!*" he says, flashing a wide smile and gesturing for us to come around and hop in the back seat. Continuing to speak in French, the man asks us where we're from and where we're headed. I translate for Serena, and she replies, "Tell him we're from Canada, the United States, and wherever the road leads us." I relay this in French, adding that, actually, we live in Clermont-Ferrand and need to get back there at some point.

Serena laughs at me and launches into a story about her misadventures in Paris: washing dishes in an exclusive French restaurant to pay for the meal she'd eaten before realizing she couldn't afford to pay for it; being chased by an irate *gendarme* from a parked car where she'd taken shelter for the night; hanging out in a back street with prostitutes and narrowly escaping the clutches of their pimps; sitting in lotus position on the floor of an obscure meditation center, listening to the strains of a harmonium, joining in the Sanskrit call-and-response pattern of ancient Hindu chants, focusing on the compellingly luminous eyes of an orange-clad Indian guru in a picture placed up front on a chair, falling into a deep meditation and being transported beyond all time and space.

Serena's French is very limited. I wind up translating most of her story as best I can. It comes across as the tale of an inept young girl, alone and broke in the famed City of Light, cheerfully blundering her way through the vagaries of desperation. I don't know whether it's Serena's story itself or my bungling French translation of it, but something gets our driver laughing and crying at the same time. Soon we are singing along with him to a lively folk tune on the radio. By nightfall the man is dropping us off in Clermont and thanking us for the pleasure of our company. And so, I sleep soundly that night, in my own room, having successfully completed Serena's crash course in Hitchhiking 101.

When I mention my hitchhiking adventure, Angelique offers me the opportunity of taking day trips with her husband. As part of his job working for the Chamber of Commerce, Guillaume travels to meetings in surrounding cities. Eager for any excuse to travel and to stay away from the staid classes at the university, I leap at her offer. Guillaume picks me up in his efficient little French car and powers his way up and down hills and around curves, bragging about his car's capabilities and performance, his knowledge of the local terrain, and the excellence of his driving skills.

Traveling with M. Arlette, I get a glimpse of many rivers: the Yèvre, Auron, Rhône, Sâone, Cher, Vienne. When he reaches his destination, Guillaume drops me off at a central location and I am left to spend the day on my own, at my leisure, to wander through streets and parks and along riverbanks, take in the local sites in Lyon, Bourges, Dijon, and Montluçon.

At first, I love the sensation of freedom, this rootless drifting from place to place, left alone to daydream along the banks of the

Rhône or the Cher, to peer into countless museums and historic buildings. I begin to absorb a sense of history that shatters my American ideas of what is truly old. I am heralded by a fanfare of architectural styles, echoing forward through the ages. I see Gallo-Roman ruins and many churches—Romanesque, Gothic, High Gothic, Classical, Neo-Classical. For so very long they have endured, deep and dark, dank and musty.

As I sit in countless naves—empty or nearly empty—a chill always passes through me as I inhale pungent ribbons of scent, traces of incense burning through generations of sin and confession, penitence and salvation. I fancy odors and whispers coming from deep-buried crypts and sacred relics. The dark walls themselves seem to sorrow and sigh and lament. Their stones are damp to the touch as from cold tears, and they whisper to me of passages of time they have weathered, generations of war and peace and war. . ...

But I begin to tire of this, to grow lonely for companionship. On one bleak afternoon in Dijon, I seek the comfort of a movie house, whiling away the time, huddled for more than two hours at the back of a musty theater. The auditorium is empty except for an old man shrouded in a heavy black overcoat and a faded-looking middle-aged woman sitting up front, diminished beneath the giant movie screen.

I watch Steve McQueen in *Papillon*, portraying a French safecracker, wrongly convicted of murder, condemned to life imprisonment in a grizzly jungle labor camp in French Guiana. Larger-than-life images flash before me on the screen, portraying a harrowing cycle of harsh living conditions, attempted prison escapes, captures, solitary confinement, and final freedom for a graying old man.

I stagger out of the dark theater feeling disoriented and lonelier than ever under the full weight of life's futility. I fall silent during the drive back, scarcely listening to Guillaume's cheerful monologue about the efficiencies of French cars and roads and centralized railway systems. Forever the champion of the French way of life.

During my classes with Angelique, she senses my loneliness and one afternoon pulls me aside after class as I turn to go back to my room. I happen to mention my Canadian friend to her, and she brightens at the idea of inviting Serena to keep me company on the next day trip with Guillaume. So, on a bright morning, Serena rides along with us on the road to Limoges. This time, M. Arlette drives directly to the offices of the Limoges Chamber of Commerce. Here, a dashing man—in his early sixties I would guess—greets us from the sidewalk in front of the office building. For me, his dapper mustache, sideburns lightly sprinkled with gray, and crisp military bearing transform him into a French version of Ronald Coleman. M. Arlette introduces him as M. le Pilote.

"Currently, works for the Chamber of Commerce in Limoges. But before that he was an aviator in the French Air Force. He still keeps his own private plane at the local airport. And if you are nice to him, he may give you a ride in it."

Guillaume tilts his head toward M. le Pilote. With a debonair bow and a playful wink, M. le Pilot extends a hand, first to me and then to Serena. "*Enchanté mesdemoiselles,*" he intones in a voice that rivals the sexiness of the British actor himself.

Wide-eyed, Serena grabs my arm, squeezes it. "Wow! Ask him if he's ever flown a combat mission."

I'm surprised at Serena's apparent fascination with military combat. Based on her appearance, opinions, and lifestyle, I had assumed she was a hippie, a pacifist who wouldn't want anything to do with war. I pose Serena's question, in French. "*M. le Pilote, avez-vous déjà volé au combat?*"

When the retired aviator responds, my heart melts. Imagine Ronald Coleman's beautifully modulated voice speaking a French that throbs with the most exquisite Gallic accent. "Ah, this one speaks excellent French," he says to Guillaume, dips his head, ever so delicately, in my direction, and turns his full attention on me. I find myself drawn to him. His blue-gray eyes are like reflections of a cloudy sky. As I return his gaze, I am transported into a space that seems vast and decades deep.

The pilot pauses, seems to reflect, clears his throat, then replies, *"Oui, une fois, j'ai effectué une mission malheureux en Afrique du Nord."* Yes. I once flew an ill-fated mission in North Africa.

As the pilot continues, his countenance darkens as if unresolved emotions are moving in, gathering like agitated storm clouds, troubled by this wartime memory. Is it nostalgia? Melancholy? Regret?

The aging soldier closes his eyes, squeezes the lids under his thumbs as if trying to massage away a severe headache, and adds, *"Mais c'était il y a plus de trente ans. C'est un temps passé dont je ne veux plus me souvenir."* But that was more than thirty years ago. It's a time past that I no longer wish to recall.

Guillaume Arlette gives his friend a concerned look and changes the subject. "Limoges, you know, is famous for its porcelain manufacture. I've arranged a tour today for you two young ladies at one of our renowned Limoges porcelain factories." And with that he drives on to an address in the shopping district, where he deposits us at the front of a massive building. "I'll pick you up for lunch in two-and-a-half hours. That should give you ample time to take the tour and peruse the shop at your leisure. Amuse yourselves!"

As soon as we step inside the factory showroom, we are greeted by a sophisticated-looking Frenchwoman, impeccably dressed and coiffed. Her smile is well-schooled and charming. With a sweeping glance, she sizes up our clothes and demeanor, and bestows us with a welcoming smile that is as discerning as it is disarming. Even though she detects the limitations of our spending power, she treats us kindly. To each of us, she extends an elegantly manicured hand and says, "You must be Lissa and Serena, our visitors from the United States and Canada. Guillaume has told me you are to be treated as his special guests. So, come with me and I will start you on the grand tour."

She leads us into some rooms at the rear where pottery is being made and turns us over to a young man who guides us through a series of workstations, explaining each phase of the manufacturing process—crushing, cleaning and mixing, forming, bisque-firing, glazing, firing. Then we are left to browse through an elaborate showroom display—fine dinnerware stacked on shelves, floor to ceiling, or arranged in elegant settings on polished wood dining tables. We pass through aisles of decorative pieces—a gilt bronze hand-painted centerpiece tray, delicate mantlepiece figurines, and intricately detailed floral vase lamps. One aisle is devoted to soup tureens shaped like fish or fowl. One of these is a whimsical duck; many of the others are downright garish.

I desperately want a souvenir. So, I wind up buying myself the one item I find in my price range—a plain, unornamented, brown-glazed Limoges cup and saucer.

At the designated time, M. Arlette swings by in his eager little car. M. le Pilot leaps out of the passenger side, gallantly sweeps open the rear door, and ushers Serena and me into the back seat, then returns to his seat up front. As host, M. le Pilot insists on treating us all for lunch at his favorite restaurant, located on a quiet street near the train station, where he introduces Serena and me as his "honored" guests. We are given a personal welcome by the head chef, are fêted by the waitstaff, and feast on salad, escargot, and quiche. Lunch and wine seem to relax the former pilot and awaken a keen interest in our American and Canadian backgrounds. I follow Serena's lead and we entertain him with our usual patter.

Serena tells him—I translate for her—that although she grew up in Toronto, she considers herself a citizen of the world, not defining herself by cultural differences or separating herself by superficial borders. At this, the ex-pilot gives Serena what I interpret to be a gentle, fatherly smile from an older, world-weary man who treasures this young girl's innocence.

I give a more fact-based response, informing M. le Pilote that I come from the state of Maryland, near Washington, DC. Almost as an afterthought, I add that I live to the north of the city of Baltimore, where I was born. I don't usually mention my birthplace because most people I've met so far in France don't seem familiar with it. But this time, when I say "Maryland" and

"Baltimore," I'm startled to see the ex-pilot's eyebrows shoot up and his eyes spark with an ember of recognition.

"I once flew a Martin Model 167, a light bomber, American-designed. We called it the Martin Maryland. One of the first planes I flew, in fact. It was built at a factory called Glenn L. Martin. In your Maryland. Do you know of it?"

"Yes, of course. Everyone in Maryland knows Martin's. They have an aircraft factory in Middle River. But I've never actually visited the plant. Locally, it has a reputation for hiring a lot of people. But I never heard of the Martin Maryland."

"Yes. I believe Glenn Martin also manufactured a light attack bomber called the Martin Baltimore. That one was twin-engined."

Small world. "*Le monde est vraiment petit,*" I reply, for lack of anything better to say. I know next to nothing about military aircraft. So, in a clumsy attempt to connect with this dashing pilot in any way I can, I say "I used to want to be a commercial airline stewardess. Seemed like a good way to make a living and see the world at the same time."

M. le Pilote rewards me with an admiring smile. "*Ah, l'esprit d'aventure.*" The spirit of adventure. "I have known that spirit well. Even called it my friend." He looks directly into my eyes, then drops his head and looks away with a wistful smile.

We bond over a long discussion during which M. le Pilote reminisces about World War II, its wide variety of aircraft, Baltimore's reputation as a major manufacturing city, and how the US came in to rescue France from Hitler's clutches. He waxes sentimental now, seeming to have gotten past whatever horrific military memories he chose to suppress earlier in the day. His attitude reminds me of Clare's dad, who had gone all moist in the eyes musing about the Yanks in World War II. This attitude takes me by surprise. I have just come from a country that has taken to chastising itself for its involvement in the Vietnam War. I came of age viewing the evening news projected into my living room at home, seeing, night after night, horrific footage of American bombers destroying remote Southeastern jungles and learning of unspeakable atrocities performed on terrified women, children, and old men besieged in primitive-looking villages. And then, I saw Buddhist monks protesting, merging into clouds of flame as orange as the robes they wore.

Long and leisurely, our lunch spills over into the early afternoon—that magical time in France when businesses close so the populace can take a civilized break from work, unwind over coffee and conversation. M. le Pilote insists that we linger for coffee and dessert. He orders the house *tarte aux pommes*, which is about the size of a large American pizza, and we feast on the most scrumptious apple tart I've ever tasted.

As we prepare to leave, M. le Pilote escorts us back to M. Arlette's car, opens the back door for us. He ushers Serena in first, giving her a merry wave and a wink goodbye. Then he turns to me, bends slightly forward, eyes lowered. Very gently he grasps my hand, lifts the back of it to his lips, brushes it with a kiss as delicate and ephemeral as the quiver of butterfly wings, and murmurs, "One fine day, my dear, you and your friend must return to Limoges so that I can take you two young ladies high in the sky with me. The aerial view around here is a magnificent one." I'm not sure whether Serena takes in any of the pilot's parting words. The expression on her face is obscured from me now, her head bent over her notebook, long hair fallen forward. Her hand grips the ballpoint pen, laboriously entering the day's ponderings in her characteristic violet ink. So, though I am captivated by the pilot's charm, I keep these reflections to myself.

Filled with good food, snug in the back seat next to Serena, and soothed by the purring engine of M. Arlette's trusty little vehicle, I drift off to sleep. The next thing I know, we are pulled up in front of my building on avenue Léon Blum, and I am asking M. Arlette, "Where's Serena?"

He chuckles softly and says, "I just dropped her off at the dormitory. The two of you slept, side by side, all the way back to Clermont. Like two children."

CHAPTER TWENTY-ONE

Van Gogh Pilgrimage

*"I can see that you, my little lady . . . that you have strong feelings
for our dear Vincent." —Pyramus the Romani*

I N MAY, SERENA DECIDES IT'S TIME TO MOVE ON, hitch her
way to Spain, and find work as a grape picker. She's been
barely surviving these last few months in Clermont. Her job
addressing and mailing real estate materials for a local business-
man doesn't pay much, but it's the only job she can find. As a
parting gift, she gives me a copy of a collection of Van Gogh's
letters to his brother Theo.

"Here, Lissa. I think you're the one I'm supposed to pass this
along to." Serena hands me a battered paperback, its cover blem-
ished with age and hard use, its spine broken, its decomposing
pages coming loose. "When I left Toronto, before I came to
Clermont, I was staying at a youth hostel in Amsterdam, and
a guy I met there passed this book along to me. Said he was a
failing artist looking for a muse when this book caught his eye.
He bought it at one of those used book stalls in Paris. Said he was
still failing as an artist, but this book helped him a lot anyway and
I could have it for a while. But I had to promise him that—if ever

in my travels I came across somebody else who needed it more—I would pass it along to that person. I never really read the book, but it made me feel good, just carrying it around. And now, it's time to pass it along to you."

Back in my room on Léon Blum, late at night when I can't write and I can't sleep, I curl up in my cot with this book. I have long been drawn to Van Gogh's artwork, but now in my expatriate loneliness, I take to heart Vincent's struggles to express his love in a world forever alien to him, a world that cannot understand the depths of his senses and the intensity of his vision. Now, it's his writing that speaks to me. And even though his torments move and sadden me, I find comfort in his compassion and meaning in his yearnings for a broader truth. I bond with him now as a companion of the heart, a kindred spirit, a true believer in the innate goodness of mankind, a goodness that will, in the end, prevail despite all indications otherwise.

When I read the words that Van Gogh wrote from Arles to his brother in Paris, I find the courage I am seeking as a writer. Vincent speaks to Theo of a tremendous wind, the mistral, of how he knows that if he continues to work, he will, from time to time, create some things that will last.

Van Gogh's words tell me that he draws creative energy from the wind. The strong winds of the Midi empowered him, years ago, to paint masterpieces we still admire. I, too, feel the power of the wind. As a small girl I used to go outside to play with the wind. I would stand alone in our farm's wheat field, hold out my arms, and fall back into the wind, relishing its power to catch me and also buffet me this way and that.

I confess to my American friend Trudy the devotion I have begun to feel for Vincent Van Gogh. "I would love to go on a pilgrimage to see where Vincent lived and painted and passed his final years." Trudy's a good friend, and she's always up for an adventure. She persuades her husband, Buford, to take a few days off work at Michelin, enjoy the warm weather, and make a trip to Arles and Saint-Rémy. In exchange for what Trudy calls "kid-sitting" her young son, Raymond, she insists on paying for all my food, lodging, and incidentals during our *séjour*.

Trudy and Buford are an odd pair. Trudy is modern, energetic, opinionated, politically attuned, and a champion of liberal causes. She's only in Clermont because Buford has been hired to bring the Michelin tire factory up to speed with the latest in American computer software. Buford is obese and seems preoccupied with his work.

Trudy is concerned that her only child, Raymond, a pale and sensitive seven-year-old from a previous marriage, uprooted from his school in Queens, is having difficulty adjusting to life in France and to his new stepfather. She will go to great lengths to protect her young son from any harmful consequences.

The four of us ride south from Clermont. Buford and Trudy share the driving. I stay in the back seat next to Raymond. The air is sweet and gentle, *douce*. Springtime is joyous in the Midi. Our route is lined with cherry trees. Their pink and white blossoms have fallen and their fruit is ripening. We pass field after field of wildflowers. On the outskirts of Arles, we come across a caravan of gypsies camped on the steep bank of a rushing river. Their colorful wagons are pulled off the road, parked at precarious angles on the rocky embankment. Trudy tells me these folks are likely on their way to the Camargue to attend the Saintes-Maries-de-la-Mer Festival that's held each May. Buford slows the car as we drive by.

Dark women, black hair curling beneath bright head scarves, squat doing laundry, dipping clothing into the churning water, kneading the wet fabric, wringing it out, and spreading it to dry on the flat gray rocks. Vivid reds, purples, and golds of ruffled blouses and skirts catch the sun's late afternoon rays. The men gather in groups, smoking, swapping stories, polishing their leathers—shoes, saddles, harnesses. Their horses graze. A ragged assortment of children and dogs run and cavort freely among the painted wagons, unheeded by the adults. I am on the lookout for a dancing bear or two, but see none.

Trudy taps Buford's right elbow, "Oh, Bu, let's pull over. Let's get a picture." Buford eases the car off the road and we all spill out. Raymond walks close beside me, clutching at my hand.

"Raymond is really warming up to you, Lissa. I'm glad. He doesn't make friends easily."

Buford lumbers to the back of the car, pops open the trunk, pulls out an expensive-looking camera, and removes it from a leather case. He assembles the camera, then wears it—looped on a wide cord—around his beefy, perspiring neck.

As we approach, the nomadic children scatter like wild things. Raymond stares at them and grips my hand. The women on the rocks look up from their laundry, staring at us with suspicion. A man, tall and imposing, rises from the front steps of the nearest and most ornate of this band of gypsy wagons. He raises his hand in a silent signal to the women, who appear to relax as if reassured under this man's protection. They resume their work.

The man strides toward us and greets us in French, "I am Pyramus. Welcome to my *vardo*. *Vardos*, that's what we Romanis call our wagon homes." The man wears a fedora garnished with a tooled leather band, a buckle, and a nonchalant feather.

I cannot say how old he is. Somewhere between forty and eighty? Who knows? His coarse hair is black streaked with gray. His skin is swarthy, weathered by the sun, and wizened around the eyes.

"Your home is fantastic, a work of art!" Trudy is excited and seems to be trying to take in every detail of the encampment. "Could we get a picture of you and your home?"

"At this time . . ." says the man, keeping an eye on Buford, who is padding around the wagon, studying the intricate carvings on one of the large wheels, which are set wide outside the axles. "At this time, my *vardo* and my family and I do not pose for pictures." Pyramus has a full beard, which he strokes slowly, vertically as he speaks. The afternoon light catches in his beard an occasional strand of gold or a glint of copper much like the copper highlights my own father's hair retained even in old age.

Buford, who has been squinting into the camera, his bulk bent forward over a wagon wheel, snaps the cap back over the lens and steps away from the wagon. I'm surprised Trudy doesn't press for a picture or ask Pyramus to explain why he doesn't want us to take pictures. For once, Trudy remains silent, while the Romani man stands guard over his family. He appears to watch the four of us very closely, as if we are marauders invading his domain.

I look down at Raymond's head. It seems so innocent to me now, fragile somehow. In all this time, he has not once let go of my hand. Abruptly, an unpleasant smell scratches at the inner lining of my nose, something acrid and irritating. Is it sulfur? I look up to see Pyramus lifting a long matchstick to light a small pipe. He takes a few puffs, and I see him give a wink to Raymond, who clasps my hand even tighter and tugs at my arm.

"And so, you are Americans," says Pyramus, blowing out a stream of pipe smoke. Recognition, like steel striking flint, sparks in his deep-set gray eyes. The beguiling smell of cherry-scented tobacco wafts from his pipe and blossoms in the air around us.

Abruptly, Pyramus clamps his pipe between his teeth, and with a quick, light flourish, grasps his coat in front, just below the lapels. I hear a faint rustling at the tall man's feet and look down to see the hem of his black overcoat grazing the tops of his boots. The dark fabric parts dramatically, like a curtain, as Pyramus flings the garment open wide. Then, lifting both his arms like a large bird about to take flight, he displays row upon row of deep pockets, sewn into the lining. The tops of glossy postcards and trinkets poke out. "See anything you like?"

Trudy steps in closer and browses politely. Buford hovers somewhere in the background, imperturbable. I peel Raymond's fingers from my hand, kneel down next to him, put my arm around his small waist, and give him a squeeze. I can feel him trembling, so I stay close beside him.

Pyramus shoots me a benevolent smile and taps out his pipe against the sole of his boot. Setting the pipe aside, he pulls out a stack of postcards, fanning them like playing cards in his hand.

Two of the pictures catch my eye. In one, horses graze in a field of dried grasses beside the faded red and ripe gold and sun-washed teal of gypsy wagons; in the other, small boats sail in the distance beyond choppy sea waters.

"Are those Van Gogh paintings?" I ask.

"Yes, little lady." This expression strikes me as odd coming from him, but maybe because he says it in English. Again, he gives me the smile, and I find myself thinking of my father and feeling vulnerable, like a little girl. Pyramus hands me the two postcards, and goes back to speaking in French.

"And so, you have a great passion for Vincent, do you not?" he says. I turn the cards over, read the labels on the backs. Both pictures are copies of Van Gogh paintings. The one with the wagons is called "Gypsy Camp near Arles." The one with the sailboats is called "Seascape near Les Saintes-Maries-de-la-Mer."

Pyramus towers over me, and as he leans forward to tap at the postcard with the sailboats, he casts a long shadow across the picture. "Did you know that while living in Arles, Van Gogh struggled terribly and fell ill? So, in summer, he traveled the 38 kilometers, by stagecoach, to the little fishing village of Les-Sainte-Maries. He fled there to draw and paint, hoping that working beside the sea would restore his fragile health."

When I look up from the postcards, I can see that Pyramus is studying me closely. "I can see that you, my little lady . . . that you have strong feelings for our dear Vincent."

I stare back at him. It's as if he's read my mind in the way my father and I could read each other's mind. Pyramus nods down at me and says, "Yes. I have the Romani gift of reading people like a book."

Unnerved by this, I pass the postcards back to this strange man and step back from him. Pyramus takes the cards, smiles, and returns them to their pocket in his coat. He pats his coat and says, "A place for everything, and everything in its place." He surprises me by saying these words in English.

This aphorism was painted on a small cabinet that Daddy kept on his watchmaker's bench—just to the right of his lathe—for organizing and storing small watch parts. Daddy prized precision and order. And often, he would repeat these very words to me, "A place for everything, and everything in its place. That's my motto," he would say.

It's then I feel a tickle run up my spine, a sensation I used to feel sometimes as a child. And when I told my mother about it, she would always laugh and say, "A rabbit ran over your grave." I think she meant to reassure me, but the image that expression conjured for me was much more troubling than comforting.

Pyramus is speaking again, now in French. His bass voice, strongly accented, becomes dramatic, rich with vibrato. "As I said, I have the Romani gift of reading people like a book. And in you I recognize one who loves stories. Perhaps one day you will tell your own stories."

He bestows a knowing smile and, very much like my father, settles in to tell me a story. Sitting on the top step of his *vardo*—in much the same way that Daddy used to sit on the top marble step of our row house in Baltimore—Pyramus clears his throat and begins:

"We Romanis have our own patron saint, Sara e Kali, Sara the Black. Each year, at this time in May, my people make a pilgrimage to the sea, to a place not far from here where the three Saint Marys made their escape from Palestine. It was the forty-second year of Our Lord, and the Christ's early followers were being persecuted. Knowing that these three Marys had been very dear to Him, disciples sent these blessed women out to sea in a small skiff. And the faithful boat bore them across the waters of the Mediterranean all the way to the southern coast of Gaul. A dark woman appeared on the shore to welcome the Marys. She was of Romani ancestry and ruled a tribe on the banks of the Rhône. This noble woman was our Sara the Kali, a sacred vessel who held many secrets of our culture.

"Now, each year, we Romani travel from throughout Europe to pass through the Camargue swampland just south of Arles, where marsh grasses grow tall, where flamingoes preen pink feathers, and where black bulls and wild horses run free.

"And so, you find my family camped here, awaiting May 24, the day of our Festival, when we will convene in the small seaport town called Les Saintes-Maries-de-la-Mer. First, we will gather at a Romanesque church to pay homage to our own Saint Sara who lies buried there. We will light candles for our saint, pray to her, pass notes to her, ask her for all that we need. Then we will drape a sacred statue of our saint in fine linen robes and process with her from church to beach. A young Romani woman, chosen to portray Sara, will accompany us; this year that woman is my own granddaughter, the beautiful Rosa. Our pilgrims will march in a throng transporting our Black Madonna back to the sea.

"And all the while, a troupe of our most daring horsemen will speed along the beach. Many of them will ride bareback, straddling their mounts with bare feet bouncing precariously on either side. Beneath them, hoofs will pound the coastline, spattering pantlegs with clumps of hard, wet sand. It is only at the last moment, as Sara draws near, that these men will rein in their steeds and await Sara's arrival.

"At the shoreline, my Rosa will lift Sara's statue up to the foremost horseman. He will reach down, and lifting Sara's statue high above him, will plunge his white stallion deep into the foaming Mediterranean. The other riders will follow. Soon the blue waters will teem with celebrants—wading from the shore, arms waving, fragments of song swelling above the crash of waves—as they follow our Sara into the sea.

"Later, we will return Black Sara safely to her crypt. And as the evening shadows lengthen, strains of music—Catalan flamenco, Balkan brass, Hungarian violin, French accordion—will merge and rise to awaken the slumbering town. From dusk until dawn, we will fill the streets with story and song and dance, recounting the heartbreak of our diaspora. Hand-forged nails in the toes of our shoes will hammer out an intoxicating rhythm of raw emotion—melding love with betrayal, lust with fury, and enchantment with delusion. Together, we claim our space in this world."

Then, in a twinkling, as if waking from a timeless reverie, I see Pyramus standing in front of me, reaching deep into a pocket of his coat lining, drawing out a metal object that looks, to me, like some sort of trowel or putty knife.

"In effect," Pyramus says, flourishing the implement in the air like a dagger, "this mundane-looking instrument is an artist's palette knife. And you, my little lady," he points to me with the knife. "You are one who will find this artifact truly remarkable. Remarkable because it was wielded by a certain magnificent artist. Can you guess the artist I'm speaking of?" He points the tip of the knife at a signature in large red lettering, painted at the bottom left corner of the sailboat picture.

"Vincent," I whisper, and feel the breath whoosh out of me, emptying my lungs.

"Would you like to hold the great one's knife?" He starts to hand me the palette knife, then pauses while I stare at it. Then Pyramus draws my attention skyward, once again flourishing the blade in the air. I notice it is his left hand that wields the knife and I realize he's a lefty, just like me.

"In effect," Pyramus goes on to explain, "Vincent employed this very knife to smear thick layers of paint over some of his brushstrokes. He pulls out one of the Van Gogh postcards. For example, just here. In this very painting. Do you see it?"

Pyramus points, with the tip of the artist's knife, to choppy waves in the forefront of the sailboat painting. "Just here, you see, Vincent used the knife to create an effect of sunlight on the waves." Pyramus taps with the knife tip at a precise spot on the card. "It is with these touches that Vincent, as if by magic . . ." Again Pyramus, raises his arm, swirls the knife in the air. "As if by magic, Vincent made the painting come alive beneath his hands."

Almost in a trance, I reach out to touch the knife. But, with a cry, Pyramus pulls it back, warning, "Take care! As a rule, an artist's palette knife is blunt and smooth. But in this case, the edges have become abraded, perhaps by an impassioned and extended use of earth-toned pigments."

Still gripping the tool by its handle, Pyramus releases his left thumb, rubbing it gingerly in upward strokes along the knife's edge. Suddenly, he snaps thumb against forefinger, touches the knife to his other hand, and a small blaze leaps from the center of his right palm. I stare in amazement at the blossom of fire, burgeoning like some strange primordial flower in his hand.

Pyramus shimmies the palette knife up the long sleeve of his overcoat. Using the knifepoint as a hook, he draws out a bright red silk handkerchief, and with it, he smothers the flame in his hand. Then Pyramus wraps the silk many times around the knife's blade to sheathe its sharp edges, passes Vincent's palette knife to me, and gently closes the fingers of my left hand around its smooth black handle.

"This blade," he says, "is made of the finest steel, quite flexible. The handle is of polished ebony."

As I grasp the smooth wood, I feel an energy flowing up from it into my left hand, my writer's hand. And breath comes rushing back into my lungs.

In the end, desire and fascination outweigh common sense, and I wind up paying an extravagant amount of money for the palette knife. In fact, Pyramus himself seems almost apologetic as he takes the thick roll of francs from me. To sweeten the pot and maybe assuage his guilt, he tosses in the two Van Gogh postcards as part of the deal.

It's not until I've stuffed my purchases into the bottom of my big leather bag for safekeeping that I look around and notice how dark it's getting. I can see Raymond and his mother walking away from me toward the parked car. Trudy is looking around, calling out for Buford. From across the field, she waves at me, calls out. "Lissa. Over here! Have you seen Buford? We need to get a move on. Raymond's exhausted."

Fires have sprung up around the encampment, steam rises from iron pots and kettles, and the women stand over open flames stirring, tasting, and conjuring aromas of roasted coffee, spices, and boiled meat.

༼

Back in the car as we draw closer to our destination, Trudy goes over the arrangements she's made for food and lodging during our stay, and I realize how boastful, even insistent, she and Buford are about their expensive tastes. Trudy brags that she's booked rooms at a luxury hotel in Arles. And she's made dinner reservations at some of the finest Michelin-star restaurants in Provence.

"Here in France," Trudy explains, "Buford and I like to think of ourselves as gourmets in training." She beams over at her husband and adds, "Well, actually, Buford's a bit of a *gourmand*." He nods, lifts one corner of his mouth, and looks smug about having an appetite that is both lavish and excessive.

"Speaking of which," says Buford from the driver's seat. He's ensconced on his deep cushion, looking relaxed and intense at the same time. "You'll never guess what I saw one of those gypsies fixing for dinner while you two were busy shopping for souvenirs." He pulls a fragment of paper from his pocket, brandishes it in the air. "And *voilà*, a recipe for roast hedgehog!"

I cringe at the thought of a band of gypsies munching on dear Mrs. Tiggy Winkle's bones tonight. Beatrix Potter would be turning in her grave if she knew!

"How'd you get the recipe, Bu?" Trudy is bubbling over with excitement.

"Well, something smelled awfully good. So, I went over and asked the woman what it was. And she pointed at what looked like a lump of dirt there on the fire. Said she was baking *hochwiki*. Said that's a Romani word for what we call hedgehog. Apparently, it's a delicacy."

"Here, let me see that." Trudy grabs the slip of paper from her husband and reads from it out loud.

"It says you flavor the . . . *hochwiki?* ... with some herbs, like agrimony and sorrel, and whatever spices you like. You pack the small creature in clay and bake it in the fire. As the meat cooks, the clay hardens into a shell. When the flesh is tender enough to eat, you remove the shell, and the prickles come off with the clay. *Bon appétit!*"

I'm in the back seat with Raymond. He's fallen asleep with his head in my lap. I lean forward to get a glimpse over Trudy's shoulder at the recipe. It's written by hand in a flowing script, in indigo ink, with the smudges of a fountain pen.

"And she just gave this to you?" Trudy is looking at Buford. She seems impressed.

"Well for a price," says Buford, raising one hip slightly off the seat and patting at the pocket where he keeps his wallet. He seems quite pleased with his culinary acquisition. "You might say," and he tells us, chuckling, "that I had to cross her palm with silver quite a few times."

I wince. Old stereotypes do have a way of creeping in.

〜

At nightfall, we reach Arles, and I find myself checking into a lavish private room, decorated in tones of fawn and gold. Trudy has reserved it for me, just down the hall from her family's suite. My bed is immense. In the bathroom, my reflection darts out at me from a multitude of mirrors, and I am confronted on all sides by ovals and planes and angles of dazzling white porcelain. In the bidet, sink, and tub, water flows from the mouths of gold-toned dolphins. The plumbing, far more complex than anything we have at the farmhouse back home, is daunting. The network of spiraling pipes and hoses in the bathtub makes me think of Saturday-morning cartoons I saw on the TV as a kid, in which goofy hillbillies were brewing liquor through ludicrous twists and turns of tubing, filling jug after jug with moonshine whiskey.

But the plumbing here exhibits sheer sophistication—nothing crude about it. It takes me a while to figure out how to fill the tub, how to adjust the water temperature, how to manipulate the detachable faucet head so that I can shampoo and rinse my hair while soaking.

Afterward, pampered, perfumed, and softened with layer upon

layer of complimentary oils and ointments, and swaddled in a plush hotel bathrobe, I fold back the satin bedding, stretch out on the soft mattress, and pretend to be a reincarnation of Ninon de L'Enclos, the notorious French courtesan and author. After a moment of lying on the bed, with my damp hair twisted into a thick white towel, I pick up the American news magazine Trudy gave me for bedtime reading and am jarred by what's displayed on the front cover:

THE NIXON PAPERS, emblazoned in large red capital letters, is superimposed over a page of enlarged typewritten text that captures a disturbing fragment of conversation between the President and two of his men. I browse through the issue to locate articles discussing the Watergate Scandal. I scrunch around in bed, find a comfortable position, and settle in for a good read.

Along with a reporting of events, commentary, and some relevant photos, I find page after page of transcripts, extracted from the Nixon tapes, edited by the White House, and only recently released. What was Trudy thinking? Keeping me informed, I suppose.

But these news articles are hardly a soothing and reassuring nighttime read. Instead, journalists probe what Nixon knew, decry the White House for delaying and only grudgingly submitting edited transcripts to the House Judiciary Committee, and accuse the administration of "a desperate gamble for survival."

When I get to the pages of abridged excerpts from the Nixon tapes printed in this issue, I begin to read in earnest and am shocked by the words. The stench of corruption has crossed the broad Atlantic, unabated. Despite frequent interruptions of the narrative by slick full-page advertising, unscrupulous behavior rises from the printed pages, nauseates me, and makes me wonder what's happening to the USA I left behind.

Parenthetical breaks in the text, "(unintelligible)" and "(expletive deleted)" leap off the page at me. The crudeness of the President's language startles me. His conversations are brooding and riddled with hypotheticals that display a lack of decisiveness, a failure in leadership, and an absence of clarity. The President's personal involvement in breaking the law remains shrouded in ambiguity. And once again my moral reasoning is confronted by those infernal *maybes* and *maybe nots* that have tortured me since childhood.

I remember trying to express, during a lecture at Mme Arlette's class at the *lycée*, growing disillusionment in the sitting President. And I remember the assertive young French girl chiming in, "But, Mlle Power, the politicians—are they not all corrupt?"

I can imagine most of my French acquaintances shrugging off Watergate, saying, "*Pas une si grande affaire.*" Not such a big deal. Just another example of America's overblown sense of itself, its adolescent perspective on history. Nothing to be concerned about so long as the vast wheel of international relations continues to turn in favor of one's own country and personal fortunes.

I wouldn't even be thinking about President Nixon right now if Trudy hadn't given me this magazine. I don't remember ever discussing Watergate with any of my Arab friends—how insignificant compared to the problems they face in their world—persistent Arab-Israeli conflicts, delayed funds, homelands blown to rubble, family members gone missing, prejudice against their race. And on and on.

~

The next morning, we visit the Roman Amphitheater in Arles. "This place is ancient!" Trudy reads from a plaque and informs us that the arena was built in the first century A.D. and could hold 21,000 spectators. The towers were added in the Middle Ages.

Winded, Buford eases himself down on one of the stone seats. "Good Lord, these seats are hard," he says, and Trudy runs back to the car to fetch Buford's inflatable seat cushion. She calls back to me, "Raymond might like to walk around the top with you, Lissa. Would you mind taking him?"

Hand in hand, Raymond and I climb the stairs and make our way around the upper level of the oval, peering out from time to time through a series of archways, catching glimpses of the town below. When we return, Buford is ready to resume our outing.

Raymond looks more relaxed now. He smiles broadly at his mother, and she pulls me aside to whisper, "You have an amazing effect on Raymond. He's afraid of heights, you know. I'm surprised you guys made it all the way around the amphitheater. You are one special lady." She squeezes my hand, and we move on to follow the Van Gogh Trail and retrace the artist's steps.

The next day, we drive to the Saint-Paul de Mausolé Monastery to pay our respects at the mental hospital where Van Gogh committed himself as a patient after cutting off his ear. Here, the guide tells us, the troubled artist found comfort among the nurses and nuns, and inspired by the quality of the light and the beauty of the surrounding landscapes, painted many of his best-known works. We climb to the top of the stairs in the men's pavilion to view the wheat field that Vincent contemplated during his confinement. We walk the cloisters just as he must have done. And like Vincent, I experience a certain comfort here.

〉✔ ✔

CHAPTER TWENTY-TWO

Swallowed by the Moon

"They come to me, a murmuration of starlings. In the sky like a swarm of locusts. In the fields a coven of witches. All sixes and sevens. To plunder our deserted barn." —Lissa's midnight vision

O N SUNDAY EVENING, I return from my Van Gogh pilgrimage to find an expensive-looking envelope dropped through the mail slot at 36 avenue Léon Blum. Over a cup of tea, I break open the letter's seal, run my fingers over the single sheet of stationery. Trained as an apprentice in my father's home printing business, I can tell as I unfold the notepaper—just by the feel of it, the weight and texture and finish, the gracefulness of its deckled edges—that this is paper of the highest quality. Tucked inside, pressed between the folds, I find a small white blossom and read Junjei's message, written in fine sea green ink immediately below the elegant typeface of his embossed monogram:

My dear friend Lissa,
Often, as a child, I came home from school, shaken, sobbing, unnerved

by unkind epithets hurled at me by boys who seemed to derive their pleasure from my tears. My father, seeing my weeping as a sign of effeminacy in a son, chided me and threatened punishment for my weakness.

It was then that my mother, recognizing the similarity of my nature to hers, would take me by the hand and lead me away to her private music room. There, seated on the piano bench, she would lift me to her lap, encircle me with her arms, and allow her hands to glide across the keyboard, fingers touching down as lightly as feathered wingtips, playing the gentlest of melodies. At the end of particularly difficult days, after tucking me in for the night, she would sit at my bedside, interlace her fingers with mine, and recite her version of a favorite Chinese proverb.

Bending her face close to mine, she would whisper the words so my father could not overhear and reproach her for coddling her younger son. She sought to soothe the frayed nerves of a delicate boy child who, like herself, was perhaps too sensitive to weather the harshness of this world.

And so, as my mother lay dying, I held her hands and recited, from memory, the beloved proverb. I copy those words here, for you, my dear friend. May they guard you from all sadness and despair:

On the earth, we have entwined,
Frail trunks
Growing tender petals
On a single branch.
In the heavens, we shall fly,
Mighty birds, soaring,
Fearless riders
On a shared wing.

⁓

I have a restless night. I toss in my narrow cot and wake in the middle of a dream, sealed in the darkness of my room. What time is it? I have no idea.

Morning seems far away. I am disturbed by remnants of a dream in which, at nightfall, a swarm of fat black starlings takes possession of the hayloft in the old barn back home, battering through its sagging windows and pillaging bales of molding straw on the hayloft floor where, as a child, I took refuge to read my favorite books.

The vagrant birds, scores of them, screech messages in a code I do not understand. This must be what Mr. Clay, on our neighboring farm, had called a murmuration of starlings. He told me they communicate with each other in groups of six or seven, then hook up with like groups to form a murmuration, a massive formation of starlings that travel together.

Starlings, Mr. Clay warned us, are pests, a farmer's bane. Their hoards could take over a building, damage soffits, foul the vicinity with their filthy droppings, and ravage crops. This night my dream starlings roost in our old barn, taking shelter, weighing down already exhausted and warped ceiling beams that struggle to support a tar-coated, corrugated metal roof that is badly rusted and has begun to leak.

When morning arrives, I plod down the hall, like a sleepwalker on autopilot, toward the closet where the shower for my floor is housed. In the *douche*, I release a surge of hot water over my head and attempt to scrub away an unnamed taint and its residue of sadness. Afterward, I dress, have coffee at my writing desk, open my notebook to the next blank page, and scribble recollections of my dream.

It is mid-morning by the time I walk back to the dorm to visit Junjei, to thank him for the note and flower, tell him what I learned from my pilgrimage to Vincent's world, and present dear Junjei with the souvenir I brought back for him. I have it cloistered in the deep inner pocket of my fireman's jacket, wrapped in the red silk handkerchief. I am certain this treasure of a knife will surprise and delight my Chinese friend.

I can see myself giving it over to him, telling him its story, cautioning him about the roughness of its blade, and imploring him to take care, not to cut himself. He will turn the artist's instrument over and over in his hands while I observe in silence, anticipating the moment when Junjei's fingertips will acknowledge Vincent's lingering presence, and foreseeing that inevitable moment, when, through the grace of touch, two kindred spirits traverse the boundary of a century to reunite.

I cross the terrace to the dorm's large front doors, press the buzzer. Through the glass paneling I can see Ghislaine on duty in the lobby. Her back is turned to me; she is sorting mail, inserting envelopes into the wall of pigeonholes behind the front desk. When she pivots toward the door to answer the buzzer and sees me standing out there, she seems startled. I have come here rarely since my friends helped me move out in January.

I smile and wave as I cross the lobby. I'm surprised to see Ghislaine frown as I approach. Her demeanor is usually so easy-going. Laid-back as we would say in the States. But today she looks distressed.

"*Bonjour*," I say. "*Comment ça va, Ghislaine?*" Hello! How's it going, Ghislaine? I chatter on in French: "It's been a while since I was here. Just got back from a trip to the Midi. Came to see Junjei. Do you know if he's around?" She says nothing, stares so long at my moving lips that I begin to think my American accent has rendered my French incomprehensible to her.

Ghislaine's prolonged silence impinges on my speech, swells to fill the lobby, and is broken only by the faint, unidentifiable whirring of some essential mechanism. Perhaps the whisper of an elevator in its shaft, transporting an occupant up or down one of the dorm's twin towers?

At last, almost unwillingly, Ghislaine removes a folder from a drawer beneath the counter, hands me a clipping from a recent issue of *La Montagne*.

As I read the article, its small newsprint begins to swirl, becoming a meaningless whirlpool on the page. But inevitably, the jumbled letters bubble to the surface, and reassemble to form horrific phrases: *alcohol poisoning, choked on his own vomit, death by asphyxiation.* Unscrambled, the words impose on me a truth I am unwilling to accept. And once again that inner voice, that glimmer of clairvoyance that's mesmerized me since childhood, speaks to me, whispers insistently, informs me, "Junjei's dead!"

In a few breaths of time, the moon swallows everything, consuming the world. Lobby walls, pigeonholes, once-solid front desk—all self-immolate, flaring up, then melting, sacrificing themselves to become formless, a reflected softness of pale golden light. Paused within the space between two breaths, I imagine Junjei's death and am transported back in time to three days ago, just past midnight. Through the dorm window, the moon casts long shadows across Junjei's cot and onto his face.

Junjei lies on his back. His face is pale like the moon it's always reminded me of. His full lips, parted, form a deep crevice out of which hot liquid flows, as viscous as the molten lava that once erupted from the depths of Auvergne's volcanoes.

Stillness hangs heavy in the dorm room, weighs on Junjei's body, pulses in his ears. He struggles to breathe, to speak, to cry out, but cannot break through the muteness. Vomit pools in his throat, blocks his breath, stops his voice, defeats him.

Junjei's lungs collapse within his rib cage. His belly puffs out, contracts, heaves up more of the noxious fluid. Skin stretching taut over the hardness of bone, his body seizes, becomes a sweating rock. His face becomes clammy. With him, I experience a slowing of the breath, a numbness seeping through arms and legs. With him, I become aware of a wetness, of slender rivulets trickling from eyes to cheeks. Then the breath stops and I feel, he feels . . . nothing.

Finally, I am back in the lobby, peering at Ghislaine across the reception counter. She is whispering to me, "*Lissa, Junjei était différent. . . .*" Lissa, Junjei was different. . . . I recognize myself in Ghislaine, this unpretentious Auvergne farmgirl. She is, like me, a simple country bumpkin, uprooted, transplanted to urban soil, challenged to adjust and find sustenance in a strange city.

I find myself leaning against the counter for support. "What are you telling me, Ghislaine?"

Ghislaine leans in from her side of the counter, whispers, *"Junjei avait eu des relations sexuelles avec Jules. Mais cette nuit-là Jules avait quitté Junjei pour un autre homme."* Junjei had been having sexual relations with Jules. But that night, Jules left Junjei for another man.

At this moment, the whole world as I have known it is swallowed by the moon.

CHAPTER TWENTY-THREE

❧ ❧

Lessons from the Students and la Grande Dame's *Endorsement*

"This is my time to explore the world, see what's out there beyond hearth and home." —Lissa's notebook

I T'S EARLY JUNE when Angelique invites me to join her and her students on an annual field trip, a hike near Clermont among Auvergne's venerable chain of eight dormant volcanoes known as la Chaîne des Puys at the edge of the Massif Central. At mid-morning, we set out to walk the Puy de Pariou Trail. We hike under a clear blue sky that's dotted with tufts and wisps of benevolent clouds. The air is fresh, the breeze is tender, and the sun is bright with the promise of warmer days to come. I am strangely buoyed with a sense of hope and renewal. I feel inexplicably lighter, as if my shoulders have suddenly been released from a burden they didn't even know they were bearing. I sense, very strongly, the possibility of making my home here in Clermont.

Today we are a group of twelve—ten of the more intrepid schoolgirls, plus Mme Arlette and me. The bold girl, whose name I have learned is Hélène, falls in step beside me, reassures me that this trail is not a difficult one, that the incline is gentle, and that these are not really high mountains. She points out Pariou's neighbor, the Puy-de-Dôme, which, she tells me, is the highest volcano in the chain. It looms above and beyond us, beckoning and seductive as a lodestar on the horizon.

The wide dirt path leads us through a forest, still awakening. Although deciduous trees are budding and this year's alder leaves are emerging, dry brown leaves left over from last year cling to some of the massive oaks and crackle in gusts of wind. But the forest floor is carpeted with a multitude of white petals and fresh green foliage poking through, nourished by rotting leaves and dead branches, the fertile detritus of winter.

"*Comment s'appellent ces fleurs?*" I ask Hélène. What are those flowers called?

"Those are anemones. Let's speak in English, Mlle Power. It helps me to practice my pronunciation."

"Okay." I smile and she beams back at me. As always, she is confident, fervent to learn. At first, I had been somewhat intimidated by her assertive attitude and tough questions in class. My father conditioned me into believing that young girls should be quiet, respectful, and obedient, especially around their elders. But over the months I've come to admire Hélène's boldness, her willingness to speak up, to search for new meanings. And I'm also understanding, more and more, that outspokenness does not necessarily rule out kindness. Some things about Hélène's nature remind me of my two childhood heroes—my mother, Jimmie, and my high school best friend, Paloma.

Walking steadily, ascending gradually, and savoring the fresh scent of juniper, we reach the top of the trail in early afternoon. Here, we lunch on sandwiches, sip bottled water, and take in a closer view of the Puy-de-Dôme its rounded cinder summit protruding so abruptly from the flatness of the surrounding plateau. A large, majestic bird with golden brown feathers soars above it.

And then as I watch, a small plane appears in the distance on the horizon, crossing my field of vision from left to right. Almost imperceptibly at first, the plane seems to approach. As it passes, the aircraft comes near. Do I imagine it? The pilot appears to dip the right wing toward me, as if tipping his hat and delivering a courtly bow. I think of M. le Pilote, of his promise to take me up in his personal plane one day. I begin to envision the possibilities for me if I were to stay on in Clermont, in Europe, instead of hurrying back to my farmhouse, my apple tree, my brother, and to all that is familiar, all that I have always called home. Do I have the courage to open myself to new adventures, new challenges? Or, will I contract into my old self, go back to the shelter of Spence's protection, back to what is known and predictable and safe? As I watch, the plane becomes small in the distance and disappears behind Puy-de-Dôme.

"Mlle Power!" Hélène is tugging at my arm. "Mme Arlette says it's time to go home."

"Home?" I turn toward her. Startled and slightly confused, I follow mutely behind Hélène back down the Pariou trail.

✥

Near the end of the school year, Madame de la Rochette, patroness of *lycée Jeanne d'Arc*, invites me to her apartment for tea. According to Angelique, this is a great honor.

On the designated afternoon, I make my way to the medieval section of town, not far from Place de la Victoire, in the shadows of the black lava cathedral. I have not been here since last winter when I fled from the vision of Parapluie pinioning the male prostitute against one of the volcanic rock walls. But now I am reminded of my dear Junjei, and realize how very little I understand about homosexuality. My perceptions have been misguided and so very crude.

Madame's maid escorts me into a richly decorated salon—dark wood wainscoting capped with ornamental molding, gold flock on mushroom brown wallpaper, midnight blue velvet drapes. Seated regally in a lavish gold and silver brocade wingback armchair,

Madame de la Rochette greets me, pats the floral Aubusson tapestry on the antique sofa beside her, signaling me to take a seat in her proximity, and makes a ceremonious gesture toward an elaborate container of *langues de chats*.

"*Un chocolat, mademoiselle?*"

"*Merci, madame.*" Although I adore French candy, I find myself hesitating, repulsed by this offer. Here before me, laid out flat in a row, a dozen disembodied, life-size chocolate cat tongues repose in a small, coffin-like tin. These cleverly molded confections—top surfaces grooved for authenticity—are gruesome, severed reminders of the affection I received as a child from so many rough pink tongues on the skin of my hand, arm, or wrist—dozens of cats born in our barn, taken in, fed, played with, cuddled, taught to beg for bites of pancake tossed beneath the kitchen table. But they always departed, after such brief and vibrant lifetimes, flattened by car tires or done in by animal fights and falls and illnesses. We always gave each deceased pet a formal Christian funeral, burying them amid Jimmie's apricot and cherry and plum trees, to one side of the strawberry patch not far behind Daddy's woodworking shop. Their graves were ceremoniously marked by small wooden crosses Daddy made for them.

But, to be polite, I take a bite, and with its bitter sweetness, a childhood memory comes rushing in. I see my own small self, age four, hiding behind my mother's skirts, cringing from my new Sunday School teacher's smothering affection, her invasive voice. "What's the matter, Lissa, cat got your tongue?"

Madame de la Rochette, incredibly nearsighted, wears rimless half-glasses secured with a jeweled lanyard. The *grande dame* peers at me across a black lacquer Chinoiserie coffee table. The table's short legs are curved, ornately turned and gouged—evidence of a woodworker's painstaking craftsmanship that reminds me of my father and the hours of meticulous work he did, standing at the lathe in his workshop.

Madame's face hangs pendulous, mirroring this lady's descent from a long line of French nobility.

"Tell me a little about yourself." Madame speaks in deep and resonant tones, in a voice accustomed to making pronouncements that are obeyed without question or debate. I tell her the basics, that I'm from Maryland, grew up on a small farm, and am a student of French and English literature. I hesitate, on the verge of confessing to her my dream of becoming a great writer. But the grandeur of Madame's surroundings intimidates me, preventing me from speaking further. I feel a bit like a peasant girl, desperately seeking patronage, but cowering in the presence of a monarch. I fall silent.

The maid returns, carrying a sterling silver tea service. She sets the polished platter onto the black lacquer table and pours bright orange tea into elegant Limoges cups. She spreads a full tea before us—delicate sandwiches tempt the taste buds and iced petit fours, stacked to form a pyramid, seem too lovely, too perfect to consume.

Madame maneuvers the conversation, drawing me out, probing me with one question after another. "Did you keep chickens? What kinds of chickens did you keep? And what were their ages? What is the best method for plucking a chicken? Did your father breed the chickens? How many roosters were required? I find these questions odd, coming from such a privileged lady who, I imagine, has never plucked a chicken in her life. And what does chicken farming have to do with me now? I must really seem like a rube to this sophisticated lady.

But I try to respond as honestly as I can. "Yes, it was a chicken farm. I believe we had some Rhode Island Reds and some that were gray and speckled—I don't know what kind those were ... I think maybe my mother called them some kind of Rock. Oh, yes, Plymouth Rocks.

"We had chickens of all ages, starting with chicks that hatched from eggs in a big wire incubator under the cellar stairs. Outside, we had three chicken houses—small, medium, and large. And as the chickens grew, we moved them into bigger and bigger houses.

"Me. I never plucked a chicken in my life. My mother and aunt used to do that on Friday nights. I don't think they used a special method. Just held the dead chicken and pulled out all its feathers. Took a while. I didn't like watching. They got blood and gook all over themselves. They dropped the plucked chickens into a big tub of salt water, let them soak there.

"I think we only had one rooster. On Saturdays, I went with my mother on her chicken and egg route. She also grew and sold vegetables—tomatoes, corn, lima beans. . . .

"My father wanted nothing to do with chickens—especially killing them. He grew up on a tobacco farm in southern Maryland, but he left that a long time ago. Moved to Baltimore City. Became a watchmaker. Didn't like moving out to the country again. Lost a lot of his business that way."

Throughout our conversation, Madame seems fixated on chicken farming. She never once asks me what I'm doing in France, what I'm studying here in Clermont, what I want to do with my adult life. What my opinion is about literature or what's going on in American current events. She seems very different from Angelique. If I had to describe Madame de la Rochette in one word, I would say "staid."

~

Only after the fact do I learn that this tea was arranged as an informal job interview. After my next class with her English students, Mme Arlette pulls me aside. She smiles, her eyes sparkling with excitement, and tells me, "Madame de la Rochette was quite taken with you, Lissa. She's offering you a position at the *lycée* next year, with full compensation. You would work with me and the other English teachers. The girls in my class adore you. What shall I tell Madame?"

I'm a little taken aback at the *grande dame*'s endorsement. I hesitate, not wanting to disappoint. Finally, I say, "Sounds like a wonderful opportunity, but I'll need to think about it, discuss it with my brother." I've never mentioned my family situation to Angelique. She doesn't know my parents are both dead, that my brother, Spence, is my only close relative now.

"Oh, yes, of course," Angelique says. "Do think about it. Just let me know by the end of summer. We would love to keep you with us for a bit longer."

≈

I attend one last Bahá'í meeting—without Junjei this time. His absence is haunting, and it distresses me. This time, I have invited Clare. Out of curiosity as much as anything, she tags along, but she is skeptical of this group.

Clare and I have just taken seats near the back when group leader Bill swoops into the room, pauses briefly to greet me, grabs Clare's hand, and shakes it vigorously, shouting, "Welcome!" in a cheery voice. Before we have a chance to respond, he strides off to take his place at the front of the group. Giving a nod of his red-gold Afro in Clare's direction, he delivers his introductory speech, the one that's tailored for newcomers to the Bahá'í Faith. He follows this with a brief prayer.

As Bill prays, Clare pokes me with her elbow, asks me in an embarrassingly loud whisper, "What sort of daft cult is this?"

That's when Marilee shows up—noticeably pregnant and glowing. She wears a long, expansive peasant dress, lavishly embroidered, that drapes loosely over her expanding belly. She takes the empty seat beside me and begins her customary monologue, prattling on about herself. Secretly, I've come to call this Marilee's Soliloquy. This time it's about how excited she is to be expecting a child, what a wonderful *Papa* her husband will be, how she has found her true happiness right here in Clermont. All the while, she crochets away at an amorphous but growing blob of pink and blue yarn. After what seems like a mini-eternity, Marilee abruptly excuses herself, saying, "Oh, golly, I need to run to the bathroom. The doctor says the baby's head has started to press on my bladder. Oh, it's all so wonderful!"

Clare, having silently witnessed Marilee's performance, gives me a crooked little grin, and stage whispers, "Now what's she on about. You'd think she was the first woman ever to birth a *bairn*."

I smile and confirm to myself that, no, I'm nowhere near ready to settle down as a wife and mother. I've spent too many years already being a housekeeper for my brother and a caregiver for my father. I'm not ready to shut myself up in a house again. This is my time to explore the world, see what's out there beyond hearth and home. Staying on in France next year as *assistant d'anglais* at the *lycée* is starting to look like a good way for me to go. With Clermont as my base, I could travel around Europe while I'm still relatively young and unattached. Most of my girlfriends back home have already married and started families. But marriage is not for me, not now.

～

On the final day of the scholastic year at *lycée Jeanne d'Arc*, I stand in front of Mme Arlette's classroom to say goodbye to the class. I tell the girls I've probably learned as much from them as they have from me. "Well, I hope you've learned *something* from me," I tease. Some of the girls titter when I say this.

A pale, thin girl named Colette, who has always been very quiet in class, comes shyly forward from her desk at the back of the room and presents me with a gift. I tear open the wrapping paper to find a book with a glossy green cover, which I recognize immediately. I read the title, *Histoires et Legendes de l'Auvergne Mysterieuse*. Stories and Legends of the Mysterious Auvergne. It's the same book I discovered and purchased a few months ago, the book that inspired me to go skiing at Mont-Dore. I don't let on to the girls that I already own this book.

As I begin to page through it, I discover something that makes this copy unique—on a blank page before the title page, all the girls have signed their names. I hear hearty applause from the class and look up to see smiling faces, younger than mine, ready to learn, eager to grow.

"I will treasure this book, always," I say. These are my last words to this class, and I leave the *lycée* with a full heart, ready to embark on my summer vacation, vowing to be more like these young girls—ready to learn, eager to grow.

CHAPTER TWENTY-FOUR

An Awkward Goodbye

"Truth, Monsieur Moïse tells me, lies hidden all around us."
—Mohammed to Lissa

AS MY YEAR IN CLERMONT DRAWS TO A CLOSE and summer approaches, I stroll through Jardin Lecoq. Alone this time—no Brits, no Junjei. But now the presence of ducks, a swan gliding on smooth water. I circle the pond, look up at the pale orange and cream striped umbrellas unfurled above the pavilion's outdoor tables, and remember refreshments shared with new friends on that balcony.

A light breeze tiptoes across the miniature lake, rippling the cheerful umbrella canopies, and bringing a bittersweet nostalgia for friendship—with Beatrix, Dorothy, Danny, Parapluie, Clare, Ghislaine—that once felt essential, even permanent. But these have been little more than circumstantial relationships, expatriate alliances, unique bonds forged in a particular place, at a specific time, to meet a temporary need. These are once-in-a-lifetime relationships that can never be exactly replicated. The Oxies are dispersed now, gone far away, as irretrievable as childhood.

And Junjei. The senselessness of his death. Trying to pass through it fills me with trepidation, tugs at fading memories and revives them—Mr. Clay's cow pasture fence, my big brother, Spence, pulling apart two narrow rows of rusted barbed wire, urging me to crawl through, to join him on the other side so we can cross the meadow and continue our journey through the woods. I hesitate, imagine the metal spikes cutting deep slashes along my bare summer legs, snagging my t-shirt, snaring me like a rabbit in a trap.

I cannot reconcile Junjei's death. Unwarranted, pointless, it doesn't fit my sense of rightness. The cruelty of losing him runs deep, etches a scar that's impervious to healing. And also, I cannot forgive *myself* for Junjei's death. It seems I hardly knew him. Could I have been a better friend to this gentle soul? Could I have understood and accepted his homosexuality? Could I have reached out to him and, in some way, filled the void left by his mother's death. Could I have mitigated the father's power to destroy his younger son? Could I have found a way to nurture him and perhaps alleviate his hunger for the approval the father refused him? Instead, alone, misunderstood, Junjei turned to Jules for intimacy, and Jules abandoned him for another. But this train of thought unsettles me, and to escape it, I exit the park's stillness.

Quite unexpectedly, I find myself jonesing for American snack foods—peanut butter and Pepsi Cola. I'm sick of the local soft drinks—Pschitt! and Orangina. And I really don't like the flat, fruity drinks they make here—a splash of syrup whooshed around, dissolved in uncarbonated water.

And ice! Whatever happened to the ice you always get in cold drinks back home. I guess that's because refrigerators and freezers in Clermont are few and far between. Here, it's quite common to see women returning home each afternoon, toting, under an arm, a loaf or two of bread fresh from the *boulangerie*, stopping at specialty grocery shops along the way—*boucherie, magasin de fruits et légumes, patisserie*—buying meat, fruits and vegetables, pastries, filling a string bag with just what they need for the evening meal.

I stride along busy sidewalks among preoccupied pedestrians, most of them men and women shorter than I am. The insistent honking of small cars and the two-tone *nee-naw* of an ambulance siren remind me I'm not in America. I find myself hurrying toward a specialty store Trudy's told me about, a place called Goody-Goody that specializes in imported snacks. Inside, I am wrapped in smells of newness, plastic, packaging. Colors and lettering—bright, cheery, trendy—compete for my attention, announcing there's something here that I must have. I fill my own string grocery bag with a supply of Canada Dry ginger ale and two jars of American peanut butter.

At the checkout counter, I sort through the franc notes in my wallet, unfold the unfamiliar French bills, so large, so colorful. From a jumble of coins, I count out change—picking out the silver and gold francs from the few remaining US pennies, nickels, and dimes.

These goods are expensive here. But as I walk back to my room toting the shopping bag, hampered a bit by the bulk of my purchases, I feel happy, sheltered in a golden bubble of American privilege and optimistic consumerism that, for the moment at least, numbs all existential pain.

"Phooey on you, Jean-Paul Sartre!" I scold the evening's lengthening shadows, rail at the incrementally darkening French indigo sky.

For dinner, I head over to the Resto, knowing this will be my last meal here. I eat light—foregoing bread and dessert, determined—despite the soft drinks and peanut butter—to get in shape for a summer bikini on the French Riviera. I eat quickly and alone. No friends here this evening. On the way out, I stop in at the Resto café to bid a final goodbye to my Arab friends. Georges is there among them. I should be surprised, but somehow, I've been expecting him. He's wearing his black suit today, and I notice that it's rumpled, could use a good cleaning and pressing. I sit between Paul and Ibrahim. Across from me, Mohammed smiles gently and offers to get me a coffee.

But I tell him, *"Non, je suis pressée."* No. I'm in a hurry.

When he hears this, Ibrahim cannot suppress a grin. *"Pressée?"* he quips. *"Comme le citron?"* A common joke, a French play on words. Pressed? Like the lemon?

I return Ibrahim's grin, concede to his humor, and go on to explain, "I just came to say goodbye."

Mohammed, Ibrahim, and Paul wag their heads in feigned denial, purse their lips or click their tongues, looking sad, and reach across the table to clasp my hand. Young and slender Latif from Beirut, usually so quiet and reticent, chimes in unexpectedly. He blurts out in English, "I have a cousin in New York. I study English. Someday I come to America. You will give me your address there? I can maybe come see you there?" He pushes a notebook across the table toward me. Surprised at this shy one's sudden temerity, I smile, nod, and scribble out my home address and phone number.

Yusuf's chubby face scrunches into a pout. He looks like a disappointed little boy about to cry. Georges says nothing; does not make eye contact, staring instead into the murky black coffee in his demitasse.

Mohammed pulls his wallet from his pocket, slides out a photo, and passes it across the table to me. "I've been wanting to give this to you for some time, Lissa."

It's a black-and-white snapshot of me, standing balanced on the edge of a hilltop, smiling mid-spin, arms akimbo, face framed by mid-length curls, looking wild and windblown. As I study the photo, I discover something rare in it. This portrait goes beyond the basic skills of shading and composition.

"I have captured you, Lissa, in all your joy and freedom."

"Oh, Mohammed, it's wonderful." In Mohammed's photo of me I see a rare ability, the artist's gift to unveil the truth behind the façade. "When did you take this? Where?"

"Not too far from here. In a park. When you weren't looking. The best portraits are shot when the subject is unaware of the camera."

"Thank you, Mohammed." I hug the photo to me. "I love this! You've found the me I've been searching for."

"*Inshallah,*" Mohammed says. God willing. And lifting both his hands, palms up, he gazes heavenward. Then he reaches for a worn brown leather case, slung over the back of his chair, removes a sturdy little camera, and sets it on the table. As he shows off its complicated dials and knobs and its retractable lens, I'm reminded of the precise watch parts Daddy turned on his lathe, his love of fine mechanical engineering.

Mohammed touches the camera with reverence. "Isn't this beautiful? It is a vintage Zorki-3 Russian rangefinder, manufactured in the 1950s. This camera is the one treasure Monsieur Moise carried with him when he fled from Russia. It was his first professional camera, and over the years, he has cherished it and kept it in good condition." Mohammed runs a finger lightly over the camera's dials.

"And now, with his blessing, Moïse has passed it along to me, saying, 'We are all children of the same God. Muslim, Jew, and Christian alike descend from Abraham. Our God, may He be praised, has given each of us our talents. To you, he has bestowed the gift of creative vision. This camera, my son, will be your salvation.'" Mohammed lifts the camera, admiring it. "With this camera, Moïse is training me to be a photographer, to adjust exposure and shutter speed. He encourages me to take my own photos, and lets me use his darkroom to develop them."

Mohammed sets the camera down, leans in toward me. "Monsieur Moïse sees in me great promise. He finds me worthy." Mohammed taps the table in front of me, "Do you understand, *Amérique?*"

I nod. I think I understand.

Mohammed continues, "Truth, Monsieur Moïse tells me, lies hidden all around us. He used his camera to reveal that truth. Now that he is old he wants to teach me how to do that very thing."

As I listen to Mohammed, I realize I'm trying to do the same thing with my writing. I'm struggling to create characters who speak and act in ways that show who they really are. I want to write stories that probe false values and assumptions to retrieve whatever honesty and fragments of hope remain.

With great care, I slip the photo into a zippered compartment in my bag, where it will be safe. And in there, I come across an emergency assistance card I've been carrying around with me for months. I'd forgotten all about it. But now, with all the best intentions, I hand the card to Georges, and say, "You can use this if ever you need assistance." It's embossed, a card I picked up at the American Embassy in Paris the first time I passed through the capital, thinking the phone number and address might come in handy someday.

I hand this slick American card over to Georges, who was my lover once upon a time. The other Arabs look on, and I assume they are puzzled by my action. But then again, I have no idea how much they know about my relationship with Georges. Has he bragged to them about his sexual conquest or made fun of me? I will never know.

Georges examines the card, scowls at it, two parallel wrinkles etching more deeply between his eyes. I look away, embarrassed, realizing too late how patronizing this must seem to him. I half expect him to tear it in half or just hand it back to me in disgust. But no, he accepts the card, tucks it into the breast pocket of his crumpled suit jacket, and says nothing.

And with that, I get up and walk away, feeling awkward, defeated in my good intentions, realizing that Georges, my first lover, will be forever a stranger to me. I have failed to break through the otherness I have imposed on him. And it seems he prefers it this way.

As I leave the student café and begin to cross the lobby, Yusuf rushes up behind me. "Lissa! Lissa! Before you go, come to my dorm room. I have something special for you. Some homemade Syrian semolina and nut cake, my grandmother's recipe. From a cousin who is visiting from Damascus."

When I hesitate, he grabs me by the arm. "Come, come!" he urges, and I allow him to maneuver me to his dorm room upstairs. It's a grungy little room, dark, airless, stinking of male sweat.

Once I am across the threshold, he shoves the door shut behind me, backs me into the nearest wall, and tries to kiss me. Startled, I break away. He chases me across the room and around his rumpled bed. The sheets, I notice, are yellowed, in need of a good wash. He catches up, grabs me. Any sense of fear I have is replaced by my anger—anger at him for betraying my trust and at myself for my own gullibility.

He tries to push me down on the bed. "No, Yusuf! No!" I yell at him, pushing him away, running to the door.

But he beats me to the exit, blocks the door, grabs me, picks me up, carries me back to the bed, and starts to pull off my t-shirt.

When I scream, he pauses, looking hurt, and releases me. I run out of the room, back down to the Resto café, toward the Arab table where only Mohammed remains, sitting alone, smoking. Yusuf has followed me, but at a distance.

Mohammed, looks concerned for me, rises, and glares at Yusuf. Mohammed raises his voice, wags his finger, berates his fellow Syrian, yelling, "No! No!" followed by a string of Arabic. His voice transmits an anger, power, and authority I've not heard from him before. Yusuf looks down at his crotch, like a young boy who has soiled himself.

Grateful to Mohammed, but also humiliated, I escape back to the privacy of my room, feeling debilitated. I'm half asleep when I hear a sharp rap at the entrance. I peer through the peephole to be sure Yusuf hasn't followed me here. No, thank God! Not Yusuf. I open the door to a young man who wears what looks like an official uniform, gray with stripes in red piping that run the length of each pantleg.

"*Télégramme!*" he announces. Smiling broadly, he hands me the message. I sign for it. He tips his silly little flat-topped round hat, executes a brisk about-face, and speeds down the hallway, leaving me holding a note from my brother. The telegram details his scheduled flight number, the time and date of his arrival in Paris at the end of July. Spence is asking me to confirm receipt and advise ASAP whether I can meet him upon arrival at Orly.

Having no idea where or how to send a telegrammed response, I pad across the hall in stockinged feet, tap on the nearest door across from mine, number 37. I am about to knock a second time when a young woman pokes out a tousled head. A gaunt young man stands behind her, towering over her, scrutinizing me. It's then I realize it must be late at night. They look disheveled, like a couple just tumbled out of bed.

The woman stares down at her breasts, clutches at her bathrobe, and pulls the fabric tight around her, making sure nothing's exposed in the front.

"I'm so sorry to disturb you," I say and explain that I'm her neighbor from across the hall, that I need to know where to go to send a telegram.

"*Quel soulagement!*" she says, taking a deep breath. What a relief! "I thought it was my parents, coming to check up on me." She lets out a nervous giggle, presses both hands flat against her collarbone, looks over her shoulder, up at the young man. "This is my boyfriend, Robert." Robert gives a quick nod, flashes a tentative grin. She introduces herself as Celeste and instructs me on how to respond to my brother's telegram. I thank her and go back to my room, musing about twin vagaries: the elusiveness of Syrian semolina cake and the awkwardness of knocking on a neighbor's door late at night.

CHAPTER TWENTY-FIVE

Eurail Pass

"I'm ready to embark—solo—on my summer travels. —Lissa's notebook

IN JUNE, I BID FAREWELL TO CLERMONT and set off to explore Europe and expand my worldview. I've cashed in all my remaining bank funds and closed out my checking account at Crédit Lyonnais. Spence has thought to buy me a three-month Eurail pass, coach class. He's also supplemented my monthly school-year allowance with additional funds to carry me through the summer. So, flush with franc notes plus traveler's checks, an American Express card on Spence's account (for emergency expenses), and my pass for unlimited multi-country train travel, I'm ready to embark—solo—on my summer travels.

Trudy's invited me for a special send-off dinner. So, on my last day in Clermont, I pack in a single suitcase all the possessions that *won't* be boarding the train with me—the bulk of which are books, including my *Grand Larousse* dictionary and the book of Auvergne stories Mme Arlette's students gave me. I also cram in my Limoges cup, swaddled in my wool fireman's jacket. I lock up my dark little room one last time, deposit the room key in a designated drop box in the lobby, and head over to Trudy's where I stash the suitcase in a small hallway closet at the top of a steep flight of stairs one floor above Trudy's apartment. She's talked her landlady into letting me store my things there through August.

I've brought Trudy a colorful bouquet of mixed flowers. She arranges them in a vase on her dining table and proceeds to serve a simple, but elegant dinner—chilled soup, salad, bread, cheese, and a salmon-colored *rosé* with an aroma of cherries. Buford is working late tonight, but Raymond is here to say his goodbyes.

While Trudy is busy serving the soup, Raymond takes it upon himself to slice the crusty *baguette*. In a wave of youthful enthusiasm, he seizes a sharp knife and begins to cut. In the blink of an eye, the knife pierces his skin. Blood wells from his left hand. I grab the knife and call out to Trudy, "Raymond has cut himself," keeping my voice steady so as not to alarm Raymond unnecessarily.

With the uncanny speed of an attentive mom, Trudy grabs a dish towel, rushes over to her son, applies pressure to the wound, stops the flow, and pronounces, "It's okay. No harm done. Just a nick. A good lesson, though. Must be careful with sharp knives, son. Lissa, will you slice the bread for us this evening?"

After dinner, a sleepy Raymond gives me a kiss on each cheek and toddles off to bed. Then, with an air of mystery, Trudy hands me a package wrapped in bright tissue paper. "A gift for you, Lissa, as you embark on your new adventures." Trudy's eyes mirror my own excitement. "Here's something more romantic than those jeans and t-shirts you always wear. You're pretty, Lissa, and I think these will suit you."

I unwrap a bundle of clothes—a long, flowy bohemian skirt, a fitted blouse—and try them on. "You'll never guess where Buford got these, Lissa. Oh, wow, they look great on you! You remember when Buford got that hedgehog recipe from the gypsy woman near Arles? Well, he bought these clothes for me, too. They don't fit me. I'm too short and compact. But you! Slender. Statuesque. You do this outfit justice. Wear it with Romani blessings!"

Who is this intriguing woman posing in Trudy's full-length mirror? The gypsy outfit erases the boyish bravado I've wielded like a shield throughout this year abroad. A change of clothing dissolves the pseudo "masculine" image I've donned in an attempt to free myself from the terror, the vulnerability of being female while traveling alone in a male world.

"And the finishing touch!" Trudy has woven a garland from some of the flowers in the bouquet I brought her. She twines pale pink and white blooms around the edges of my hair to form a delicate crown.

As I turn to leave, I shoulder the large tan leather sack I've been using in France as a bookbag. I'm traveling light. So, this is to be my only luggage. It's stuffed with an extra pair of jeans, several t-shirts, a few changes of underpants, no bras (I don't really need a bra unless I'm concerned about keeping my breasts warm or giving myself the pretense of a bust), and a pocketbook French-English dictionary given to me by Clare—lots easier to carry than the hefty *Grand Larousse* I lugged with me to France. Also, as a talisman to safeguard my journey, I carry the palette knife I had intended to give to Junjei. The bag's front zipper pouch bulges when I jam in Trudy's final parting gifts—two large Belgian chocolate bars, a bottle of water, and two popular paperbacks—*The Exorcist* and *The Day of the Jackal*.

But Trudy intercedes, decides I'll need a suitcase to hold all these belongings, plus any souvenirs she says I'm sure to pick up along the way. "Here. Take this." From somewhere in the depths of the massive walnut armoire in her bedroom, Trudy pulls a battered vintage valise. It has reinforced corners and a faded pink sateen lining with pockets that are fraying. Trudy helps me pack this valise with my essentials, including the shoulder bag. Then she insists on driving me to the train station with a groggy Raymond bundled in his blanket in the back seat of the car.

At the station, I give Trudy a goodbye hug. She and Buford

and Raymond will be returning to the States in July. So, this may be the last time I'll ever see her—even though we've promised to stay in touch. The train station is deserted at this hour, and Trudy offers to wait with me until the night train for Nice arrives. But I tell her, "No, I'm okay." To Raymond, I say, "You need to get home and put Mommy to bed."

Just as I move away toward the tracks to wait for my train's arrival, Trudy surprises me. She rushes up behind, grabs me by the shoulders, pulls me around to face her, gives me a quick kiss on the cheek and blurts out, "*Bon voyage*, Lissa, my gutsy and fragile friend." I can see tears in her eyes, and I think to myself, *Trudy, I've always thought you were the gutsy one.* Keeping this to myself, I give her a quick hug, turn away, and continue toward the tracks.

For some unknown reason, after Trudy leaves, I walk onto the tracks themselves, grip the valise with both hands behind my back, square my shoulders, and face away from Clermont. For a moment, I have stepped into the darkening evening's solitude. Briefly, in this present moment, I stand alone, poised for my lone voyage into an unknown universe. And briefly, the vacant train station becomes suffused with a white light. A light so pure it doesn't hurt the eyes. And I realize that, once again, I am about to cross a new threshold.

❧

When the train arrives, I grab a seat by the window in a car that's nearly full. I haven't thought to reserve a sleeper. Just before we pull out of the station, a bulky-looking man enters and takes the seat beside me. His girth pins my right hip against the wall of the car, shoves my right shoulder into the window ledge. He wears a working man's attire—heavy gray cotton work shirt and matching pants, belt barely reaching around him, his vast paunch straining against the buckle.

Darkness comes and I fall asleep, the vintage valise tucked beneath my feet. I'm wading through dark, vaguely troubling waters when a strange sensation—coming from the seat beneath me—startles me awake. A large fist is groping, probing through the thin gauzy cotton of my gypsy skirt, feeling up my butt! My left hand strikes out, grabs the man's right arm, tugs his right fist out from under me, and shoves the offensive hand emphatically down onto the repugnant man's lap. Repulsed, I shout, "*Arrête!*" Stop it! I'm expecting some sort of protest, or resistance, or denial. But instead, my assailant restrains the offending hand within his other one, and merely nods silently. It's as if he takes my reaction as a simple, brokered "no." He seems to be telling me it's not a big deal and that I can't blame a man for trying.

Although this experience leaves me more disgusted than frightened, I'm not able to sleep or relax until this loathsome man deboards in Marseilles. I watch him lumbering away on the platform as the train accelerates, and I hold my breath until he disappears from view. Then I grab my valise and rush into the restroom at the front of the car. The flowers that Trudy wove so lovingly in my hair are crushed. A few petals have fallen to my shoulders, I pull off the garland, flush it down the toilet. Feeling soiled, I strip off the gypsy clothing, dress in my familiar jeans and t-shirt. I dump out the valise, transfer all my things to the trusty shoulder bag, shove the ill-fated blouse and skirt into the empty valise, and drag it back to the seat.

∞

At the train station in Nice, I spot a woman sitting at the end of a long wooden bench, muttering and rummaging through garbage. She stinks and the other travelers avoid her, sit apart. Her shoes are worn and coming apart. The soles have broken away from the uppers, exposing stockingless feet. Flies are crawling over crusted, broken blisters on her bare toes. The wrinkles on her face, filled with grime, look deep and harsh. Her teeth are rotting. I place the valise containing the Romani clothing at her feet.

"*Prenez ceci. Un cadeau pour vous. Bonne chance dans vos voyages.*" Take this. A gift for you. Good luck in your travels.

She looks up at me. Puzzled? Frightened? I'm hoping this Romani clothing will be more auspicious for her than it was for me. Maybe she will receive the blessing Trudy intended, instead of the curse that befell me.

~~~

I check into a modest hotel in Nice, and ask the slick, wiry young man at the front desk how to get to the beach. *"Pas loin."* Not far, he tells me and points me in the right direction. I head down a wide boulevard lined with palm trees. The air is balmy, and I breathe deeply, feeling light and free as a bright bird in a tropical paradise. I can't resist humming and thinking to myself, "Nice is nice! Nice is nice!"

The beach surprises me. Not gritty white sand, but smooth gray pebbles. I strip off the hiking shoes I've been wearing most of the winter in and around Clermont, pull off my thick socks, and walk barefoot. The flat stones are sun-warmed, and they soothe my feet.

When I see the Mediterranean for the first time, I nearly gasp out loud, it's so beautiful. Magnificent azure sea water rivals the clear blue of the sky. Beautiful people, tanned to perfection, stroll in pairs along the beach. Women in skimpy designer bikinis pass by, complacent in their physical perfection. Occasionally, the most dazzling of these women ambles alone on the beach, going topless, apparently unapproachable in her naked glory. I roll up my jeans to feel the sun on my pale winter skin; my legs are embarrassingly white.

Determined, I head back to a boutique I passed on the way, just a couple of blocks from the beach. On display in the shop window, beneath the lime-green awning, I spot a splash of blue and green fabric scantily splayed across a headless, armless, legless mannequin in the shop window. I go in, point to the mannequin. The salesgirl retrieves a matching swimsuit from a drawer, escorts me to a small curtained fitting room in the back. I try on this chic French bikini; it's skimpier than any bathing suit I've ever worn.

But its bright Mediterranean colors will play well here on the beach. My skin is a pallid white, but the strategic cut and drape of the fabric make my long, thin legs and thighs look good and somehow steer the eye away from the sad flatness of my chest—at least that's what I choose to think.

As the hours in Nice pass, I begin to notice posters—displayed in my hotel lobby and affixed on walls throughout the city—announcing the presence of the 21st Chess Olympiad right here, right now, in Nice, in June 1974. Wearing my new suit and a chic hooded beach jacket I couldn't resist, I head back to the beach, spread a towel, claim a spot on the smooth stones. Right now, the beach is not crowded.

At the edge of my sightline, on an outcropping of rocks about a hundred feet away, I spot a cluster of geeky-looking men—limp swimsuits, skinny bare chests, skin even paler than mine, virgin to strong sun. Huddled over unrolled vinyl chessboards, they are engrossed in the mutating positions of small plastic objects they push across green and white squares. Teams of feudal players face off, black pieces versus white. A cohort of pale, flaccid-muscled men move small shiny plastic figures strategically across chessboards. When not moving their own chess pieces, the men fixate on other boards, on multiple fields of play unfolding simultaneously on the craggy strip of beach. Their intense focus reminds me of beefy American men absorbed in a football game. But this is a different form of absorption, more powerful because there is no rowdy shouting or gesticulation. The chess players' passion expresses as a deeply concentrated silence.

~

I float through my remaining days in Nice as in a dream. I swim, buoyed and bobbing in tepid salt water, taking a long, relaxing soak cradled in an open sea. I am at peace here. Beneath this benevolent cerulean sky, I am guarded by a drift of angelic white clouds. The rhythm of limpid waves kissing the smooth-stoned beach lulls all anxieties. Swan-shaped paddle boats glide noiseless across my line of vision. I spend evenings just off the beach at what becomes my favorite outdoor restaurant. Here cool breezes charm me as *salade Niçoise,* fresh fish, and crisp white wine sate my appetite.

I take the obligatory bus tour to Monaco, pass along the Grand Corniche, peer out over the cliffs. The tour bus stops at the casino in Monte Carlo—so much smaller than I expected it to be. Wealthy patrons sit, dressed to the nines, intimate around a small dark wood table as if gathered for a formal family dinner. The roulette wheel spins. A croupier calls out, *"Les jeux sont faits. Rien ne va plus!"* The bets are placed. No more bets.

On the way back, we stop at the Hotel Regina in Cimiez, and I walk next door to the Matisse Museum to see the artist's vibrant work. His inspirations reflect the translucent sunlight, the blues of sea and sky. The guide explains that Nice was the love of Matisse's life, and I begin to understand why this city has such an impact on me and why it holds such a special place in my heart.

CHAPTER TWENTY-SIX

\~ ‛ ⸂

Vagabonding Through Europe

"And so, as if propelled by some primal wanderlust, I vagabond onward through Europe, hooking up with various fellow travelers along the way." —Lissa's notebook

I SOON FIND MYSELF TRAVELING among a throng of North American college students. Armed with Eurail passes, they crisscross the continent in economy train coaches, bearing water bottles and overstuffed backpacks. These ambitious pilgrims tote their bulky paperback "Bible," *Europe on $5 and $10 a Day,* which guides them to cheap eats and lodging and must-see tourist attractions, turning Europe into an affordable summer playground, the vacation of a lifetime. And so, as if propelled by some primal wanderlust, I vagabond onward through Europe, hooking up with various fellow travelers along the way. I join this band of wayfarers, and my own heady blur of days and nights begins. Hopping on and off trains, a new city every few days, sharpens my survival instincts.

From Nice I voyage on to Italy. On a night train to Rome, I manage to find an unoccupied lower bunk in the sleeping car.

Mid-voyage, I'm startled awake by a plump red cherry dropping onto my face from the upper berth. Then another cherry, and a fresh-faced young American guy leans down from his cot above, whispers, "Hey! You awake?" His hair is curly blond, his eyes a startlingly clear, pale blue. We exchange names, nothing more, at first. Then, from his backpack, he pulls a large bag of strawberry Twizzlers, my favorite American candy, and dangles the bag over the precipice that separates his berth from mine. He winks at me, reaches down. I reach back, and he pulls me up to his *couchette*. We lie together in the cramped sleeping unit. He feeds me cherries, and then extends to me one end of a Twizzler. We chew it from opposite ends until we reach the middle—and kiss. Then we roll around and giggle in the narrow upper bunk and fall asleep cuddled like two spoons in a drawer. We are awakened by stirrings of the mass exodus at Rome. So here, we part, passing acquaintances, any chance of lasting friendship lost, swept away in the vivacious urban bustle at the train station.

In Rome, I hook up with two Canadian nurses at the train station. As we chat, look around, and try to orient ourselves. A man greets us in English with a bouncy Italian accent. He asks if we are looking for a nice place to spend the night, holds out a glossy street map, and traces the route to a Catholic *pensione*. "Nice and quiet. Very clean," he assures us. "And not too far," he adds, taking note of my bulging leather bag. The bag is so heavy it pulls my shoulder down, causing me to walk with an awkward gait.

I tag along with the nurses. These women are smarter travelers than I am. While I struggle with my bag, they stride easily, bearing tall red backpacks—proudly adorned with Canadian maple leaf badges—supported on external metal frames. We make our way through crowded streets. The air shimmers in the heat, clinging to us. I am sweaty and relieved when we check into the *pensione*. I share a modest room with the nurses. Narrow beds, crucifixes. The room reminds me of the place I stayed last spring in Venice.

In the coolness of evening, we stroll the streets of Rome. I get pinched on the butt. I am surprised, but not freaked out, not affronted. I'd heard of this pinching that goes on in Rome, and I'm actually pleased that my butt is attractive enough to be rewarded with a Roman pinch. I realize that other women may not think this way. But my two nurse friends, ruggedly practical, don't seem to notice.

Next day, we venture into Vatican City. While the nurses roam throughout the Sistine Chapel, I remain staring up at the ceiling, directly beneath da Vinci's Creation of Adam, seeing the finger of God reaching out to touch the first man's fingertip, bringing human life into the world. I am still pondering the awesomeness of da Vinci's work as I resume my travel by train with the nurses. This time, we hop off in Venice. *Déjà vu* for me, then on to Florence. The art! The Uffizi. The Arno River. A student city. Home of the Brownings. My mind struggles to absorb it all, retains only flashes, colors, impressions, fragments like shards of colored glass. I feel feverishly excited, infected, overwhelmed, and confused. I develop what is known here as Stendhal Syndrome or Florence Syndrome, overstimulated by the city's breathtaking profusion of concentrated artistic beauty.

I continue on to Switzerland with my nurse companions. They invite me to sit with them in their roomy first-class compartment. Just as I put my head back on the cushy headrest and begin to savor the spaciousness of the seats, a punctilious uniformed conductor peers into the compartment, inspects all our passes, and shoos me down the aisle, toward the second-class section where I belong. I take a seat in a second-class coach squeezed next to a peasant in a beret and blue work smock. He reeks of garlic. He's helping himself to a meal from the large straw basket he's set on the floor between his feet. With a crude pocket knife, he cuts slices from a large sausage, trims the rind from a wedge of cheese, tears off a chunk of bread from a long, crusty loaf, and chugs red wine from a large glass bottle. I watch him for a while, wishing I had known to pack a lunch.

Eventually, I drift off to sleep, but suddenly am rudely awakened by a heavy clanking of metal, the unhitching of train cars.

I join a rush of passengers who are moving to vacate the south-ernmost cars. A conductor waves me forward just as my coach is about to be unhitched from the car in front of mine. Seems this back part of the train will not be crossing over the border from Italy into Switzerland. Halfway down the aisle in the forward car, I pause to look back and see a widening gap of empty track between the moving portion of the train car I've just entered and the tail-end remnant of unhitched cars that are left behind in Italy. With a jolt to my nervous system, I realize I have narrowly escaped being unceremoniously jettisoned in Italy! When one travels, I'm learning, one sleeps at one's own risk.

So, by the skin of my teeth, I continue on. I take a seat and marvel over the change in scenery. The sweltering Italian summer has given way to cool mountainsides dotted with sheep. The cows here actually wear cowbells. A scene from a picture postcard—clean, refreshing, green, and tidy. Spacious pastoral landscapes, backed by rocky slopes sprinkled with cleverly crafted, carved, and colorfully painted wooden chalets where masses of pink and purple flowers spill from window boxes.

One of the nurses comes back to my coach to find me. She tells me she and the other nurse are seated just two cars ahead. We agree to hop off at the next stop, at Interlaken. Here we stay at a chalet that serves as a youth hostel, boarding student tourists at affordable rates.

We purchase tickets to a summer performance of Friedrich Schiller's play *William Tell* at the eponymous open-air theater. The brochure tells us the play is a local tradition, performed annually in the Rugen Woods in Matten. Launched in 1912, its produc-tion was interrupted during the two world wars, but resumed in 1947 and hasn't missed a year since. I sit on the edge of my seat, wedged between the two nurses, awestruck as I watch actors of all ages—children through elderly—reenact the historic tale in this magnificent natural setting. The costumes are authentic; the cows and goats are live. I find myself catching my breath as actors come riding in on horseback. I gasp as Tell, legendary Swiss folk hero, symbol of resistance against aristocratic rule, expert with a crossbow, defies the House of Hapsburg's tyranny and redeems his young son's life by shooting an apple off the boy's head.

Another day, and I am hiking up a switchback somewhere in the Alps, plodding slowly upward, back and forth among thick trees, wondering where the mountain meadows with wildflowers and idyllic views are. Are we near Berne?

In Lucerne we explore wooden covered bridges—the Chapel Bridge, lined with paintings dating back to the 1600s, depicting events from Lucerne's history; the Spreuer Bridge, which is gruesomely decorated with medieval-style plague paintings.

We move on to Zurich, where we take in the Swiss National Museum. So much to look at—liturgical wooden sculptures, panel paintings, carved altars, the porcelain and faience collection, mannequins draped in linen embroidery and decorative textiles. The Armory's display of arms and armor from five hundred years of Swiss military history. I wonder out loud, "I thought Switzerland didn't fight in any wars, thought they were pacifists. So why all this armor?" The Canadian nurses don't respond; they just move on. Too late, I realize we should have sought out a tour guide. Too late, I discover I've made the mistake I often make— trying to focus on everything, take in the details of each exhibit, each display. By the end of the day, I'm left with nothing more than fuzzy images, a faded and jumbled memory of all I have viewed, no solid historical perspective, no solid timeline of events to hold onto.

The youth hostel in Zurich is a zoo, overcrowded, reeling with youthful tourist agitations. I spend a restless night pressed close to the ceiling in the top berth of a narrow bunk bed. I dream I am riding on a bright-painted merry-go-round that turns to a tinny carnival tune. My horse goes up and down, faster and faster, until it reaches a frantic pace, breaks free, escapes, leaping wild and unfettered into a moonless night sky.

Next morning, it's on to Austria with the Canadian nurses. We stop in Salzburg to visit the church where the wedding in the

Sound of Music was filmed. It's such a disappointment. So much smaller than it looks in the movie. The guide explains that the filmmakers used special camera lenses to make the sanctuary look larger, to extend the length of the aisle Maria walked.

A handsome young Austrian fellow with hair the color of spun gold offers to drive the three of us to a nearby lake for a swim. I put on the bikini I bought in Nice. The Austrian admires my broad shoulders. "Are you a swimmer?" he asks, running his fingers between my shoulder blades. "Come with me for a swim," he says. Before I can respond, he dives into the lake, swims across, then back. I watch, amazed that he swims so well, like an athlete. I join the nurses at the edge of the lake. We just play around, splashing each other. I swim a few awkward yards and back. The Austrian loses interest, drives us back to town, politely deposits us back at our youth hostel.

In Salzburg I part ways with the Canadian nurses. Their vacations over, they head back home to Edmonton. Early in the morning, we exchange addresses and recipes—I trade Auntie Elspeth's formulation for Scottish black bun for handwritten instructions from one of the nurses on how to make a poppyseed Bundt cake with peanut butter frosting. We wave goodbye and I watch the backs of their tall red backpacks bobbing away from me toward the train station. Suddenly, feeling lost and abandoned, I hurry across town toward a popular restaurant for breakfast.

CHAPTER TWENTY-SEVEN

Country Girl Meets Feminist

"I'm here this summer traveling as a liberated woman, exploring my sexuality. My husband, Ethan, is totally fine with it."
—Maggie, feminist from Chicago

"HELLO! Are you American?" I shout, struggling to be heard above the multilingual chatter, the bustle of waiters and waitresses, the clatter of plates and silverware. Three bright smiles open up to me, revealing strong white teeth. American friendliness. I appreciate this for perhaps the first time in my life, as if a missing piece of puzzle I've been looking for is finally falling into place. Something I didn't realize I was missing. Something I had taken for granted. Something under-valued, left behind. A mutual, unquestioning belonging, a stunning openness.

"Hi! Illinois here. Actually Chicago."

"Maryland," I reply. "Rural Maryland."

"So, Maryland, Country Girl, huh? You looking for a seat? Scooch over girls. I think we can make space for you here." I squeeze on the bench, at one end of the table, and over a scrumptious breakfast of chocolate pancakes, I gladly hook up with a three-some of American women. The one from Illinois describes herself as a feminist, a student at the University of Chicago. The pale red-headed woman is from Ohio; she's a cook at a chain restaurant in Youngstown. The third is an elementary school teacher, also from Maryland, the suburbs. Short, compact, a bundle of energy. Says she's a humanist, not affiliated with any specific religion.

Over the next few days, I travel with this trio of American women and fall into a safe haven of familiarity that soothes me after so many months living abroad as a foreigner. I indulge myself in a rollicking few days of adventure with my compatriots. With them, I take a cable car to a plateau above Hallein, Austria, to the entrance of a salt mine.

Here we are greeted by a guide—tall, movie-star handsome, quads and calves bursting beneath his leather Lederhosen. "*Guten tag*. Good day, ladies. My name is Johann, *und* I *vill* be your guide today." By now, the other American women and I are hanging on every word, swooning over this Austrian Adonis, sizing up the bulge of his leather-flap codpiece. "*Ve vill* move swiftly down the slide. This generates a lot of friction and heat. So, you must wear these to protect yourself during the ride." He passes out asbestos coveralls, puts on his own heat-proof garment, and demonstrates how to fasten ours in place. As we don our protective gear, Johann observes, assists as needed, all the while reciting his tour guide patter: a brief history of this place, anecdotes from ancient legends about dwarfs who once delved deep in Austrian mines, wielding hammer and chisel to uncover precious metals and gemstones, which they hoarded in caves deep beneath the earth.

According to Johann, "Dwarfs were generally short, ugly lit-tle creatures, old men with long beards. They wore strange knit hats—cone-shaped with tips that folded forward. A sort of pro-tective headgear. Like the hats *Valt* Disney's seven dwarfs wore in *Snow White*. But *Valt* Disney's dwarfs were pretty cute. Not like the dwarfs in some of our legends. Oh *ja*, some dwarfs were silly and child-like and some were maybe even friendly. A few female dwarfs appeared in some of the stories. But mostly, dwarfs were greedy and nasty. And they could be hostile to humans.

"It was the dwarfs who guarded the doorways in mountains, the passageways between worlds. And even though dwarfs were small, rarely taller than a grown man's knee, they were known to possess supernatural strength. They were very jealous of their hidden treasures, and used magical objects to play cruel tricks on any man who dared invade and plunder their secret storehouses. Dwarfs would wrap themselves in cloaks of invisibility, wreak havoc on mere mortals, and escape unscathed and with impunity."

As his stories unfold, Johann mounts the slide, sits, braces himself in place. I can imagine his well-developed leg muscles flexing beneath the protective suit as he braces the bottoms of his heavy-duty boots against the narrow walls to keep from slipping down the steep incline. Once he's securely propped himself in place, Johann instructs the rest of us to pile on—one at a time—behind him. We sit facing forward, feet first, each person locking arms and legs around the body ahead of her.

"This is the first of a series of wooden slides," Johann explains. "The miners rode these down to their work. To ease the tension and fatigue of their labor, alert the other workers of their arrival, and amuse themselves, the men would yodel on the way down."

So, swathed in asbestos, one guide and four American women locked together, we form a human chain. Johann glances back to check that we are all in place, then raises his right arm as if to signal whoever might be waiting below that our descent is about to begin.

"Keep your arms tucked in tight against your sides. At all times," Johann calls out. "These stone walls are closer than they appear, and they are unforgiving." Then, grasping the frame at the top of the slide, our stalwart guide gives a mighty backward pull, releases his boots from the rock walls, and expels an ululating yodel that precedes us into the gaping black void below.

Down we go, accelerating quickly. Encased at the center of a speeding human comet, I find myself zooming down a mine shaft. Johann uses his arms and legs to modulate our speed and position.

Down the first slide we zip. At the very end of the slide, Johann brakes abruptly. Then, staying in line, we follow him, walking a short distance to the next slide, and down we go again. My butt is beginning to feel heat through the asbestos. Then on to the next slide, and again, until we reach the mine's bottom level.

At the end of the ride, we board a small open train that transports us through a flat space at the base of the salt mine. Water drips on us from overhead. I'm riding just behind the feminist from Chicago, and I lean forward, say in her ear, "When it rains, it pours." She's smart, gets the Morton salt ad quip, and laughs with me. The train delivers us into open air, we climb off the mini-train, and Chicago whispers to me, "Did Johann say anything to you?"

"No."

Chicago gives me a quizzical look, says, "Well, he kissed me on the mouth."

I don't know what to say. So, I don't say anything, but I'm thinking, *When did that happen?*

That evening, I check into a youth hostel with my American companions. When we share the communal shower, I find myself gawking at Chicago. Her boobs! They dangle down her chest like two long sausages. I've never seen boobs like that before! More self-conscious than ever, I keep my flat chest strategically covered as much as I can with a towel until I can pull on a clean t-shirt. But not Chicago! Chicago, the proud feminist, trots around the room half naked, showing off her long appendages. She seems amused at my modesty.

Next morning at breakfast, Chicago leans in close, says to me in a stage whisper, "I met up with Johann last night. And we did it! Johann and I fucked!" She gives a languid stretch of her arms, runs sensuous fingers through her long straight hair, takes a big bite of pastry, and resumes, "It's all part of my European education. I'm here this summer traveling as a liberated woman, exploring my sexuality. My husband, Ethan, is totally fine with it. He's an anthropologist. Big fan of Margaret Mead. Ethan's a proponent of open marriage."

She takes a gulp of coffee and continues. "These are exciting times. The world is opening up for women. Now we have Roe v. Wade."

I give her a confused look. "I've heard of that," I say. "That was a Supreme Court decision, right?"

Chicago sizes me up, wags her head at me. "You are a naïve little Country Girl, aren't you, Lissa? Not so long ago, January 1973, the Court made abortion legal all across the US of A. Landmark decision. We've come a long way, my Country Cousin!" Chicago gives me a triumphant smile and a celebratory clap on the back.

It's going to take me a while to process all this. Over the years I've heard horror stories of desperate women trying to abort themselves with coat hangers and dying from botched, backstreet abortions. But I assumed women who had unplanned pregnancies were weak-willed and foolish. It was only when I came to France this year, met Georges, and experienced the irrational, undeniable impulsiveness of my own sexual desire that the importance of birth control hit home for me. But abortion! That's too much for me to take in right now. For now, I put these ponderings on the back burner as life speeds on.

◆

We spend the day in Bavaria touring Mad King Ludwig's Neuschwanstein Castle, the one that looks like the castle in Disneyland. The guide tells us Walt Disney actually used Neuschwanstein as his model. We also have a look at Linderhof Palace, the smallest of three palaces Ludwig built, and the only one he lived to see completed. At Linderhof, we tour the Hall of Mirrors, a drawing room where Ludwig, who slept in the daytime and stayed awake at night, could sit in his niche, reading by candlelight amid parallel mirrors that reflected the flames a thousand times in a seemingly endless avenue of light. We see the table with the lapis-lazuli top, the carpet made of ostrich plumes, the ivory candelabra, lapis mantelpieces, gilded bronze ornaments. In the dining room, we see the disappearing dumb waiter with its table set for Ludwig and his imaginary dining companions—people he admired and wanted to spend time with, for example, Louis XV, Madame de Pompadour, Marie Antoinette.

We visit Mad Ludwig's bedchamber—bed positioned on steps in an alcove barricaded by a gilded balustrade that made his sleeping quarters look like an altar glorifying the king as he slept all day beneath the halo of a candelabra bearing 108 candles. We traverse the elaborate gardens surrounded by a breathtaking natural alpine landscape and end our tour at the artificial Venus Grotto, modeled after a scene from Wagner's *Tannhäuser*. This is where Ludwig had himself rowed over the lake in his golden swan boat. Using twenty-four dynamos, the grotto could be illuminated for Ludwig with changing colors. By the time our tour has ended, my head is reeling with the grotesqueness of the mad king's obsessions and the decadence of his willful, wasteful dissipation of resources. And yet, he's bequeathed to us a certain obscene splendor.

～～～

That evening, at a beer hall in Munich, I sit with my American companions at a long table among a crowd of tourists, singing, swaying, lifting mugs of thick frothy beer. My new Chicago feminist friend with the sausage tits tells me about a Women's Camp, held on an island called Femø in Denmark. The Danish Women's Movement, she tells me, founded the camp in 1970. And just last year, 1973, they launched an International Week on Femø, a week that's set aside to welcome women from all over the world.

Sausage Tits, aka Maggie, pulls out a pocket calendar, points to days she's circled in red ink. I chide myself for calling this woman names, realizing I'm a bit jealous of her sizable breasts and her obvious satisfaction with her body. "This year International Week runs from the last Saturday in July through the first Saturday in August," she says. "Women will be coming by bus from Copenhagen, then taking the ferry from Kragenæs to Femø. A camp shuttle service will be stationed at the Femø harbor to pick up new arrivals and their luggage, and take them to the camp. Some women are gonna want to walk to the campground, get a first look at the island—which, by the way, is beautiful, I'm told! There's a sandy beach with a meadow that runs along the sea. All kinds of grasses and flowers. Plenty of shallow water for wading and splashing." Maggie laughs one of her loud, low-pitched guffaws and merrily slaps me on the back.

"You should come, little Country Girl! Be part of the International Women's Rights Movement. Pitch your own tent or stay in one of the communal sleeping tents. It'll be a week you'll never forget. Sure, you'll be asked to take on some of the communal tasks like cooking and dishwashing, but it's all done in a spirit of mutual caring and respect. Workshops and talks will fill your hours. Laughter and storytelling and song. Sports and games. Cloud watching by day and stargazing at night. The lapping of waves. Beach life.

"Midweek there's usually a party night in the common tent. Women-centered fun, performances, live music! Ample time for chats, deep conversations. And at week's end there'll be a common meeting for summing up thoughts and feelings. For sharing experiences. You can even become an activist, take a role in organizing future activities. On Saturday you will clean up, pack up, and prepare for the journey back home. Oh, Lissa, you really should come! Join us. Join the movement. Be a feminist."

I travel on with the three American women to Berlin. Here we encounter heavy, incessant rain, And I'm without a rain cape! My American comrades had the good sense to pack waterproof ponchos. Will I ever learn to take care of myself? I follow along, like a forlorn puppy, drenched to the skin, muddling my way through the downpours.

When sunny skies do finally return to us, we have reached the Berlin train station, and I am bidding goodbye to these latest friends. Pale, redheaded Ohio, who throughout our voyage tended to fade, complacent, into the woodwork, leaves first. She's returning home to her fiancé, Dwayne, who's waiting to start a family with her in Youngstown. She smiles, waves politely, well prepared, it seems, to slip back, quietly, into her conventional American lifestyle.

"Goodbye, Lissa! See you at Femø!" Sausage Breasts calls out to me, waving broadly as if she's sending semaphore signals, and dashes off to catch her train for Amsterdam.

"Yes, yes! I really want to do that." But my words are hesitant, trail off at the end, subsumed by the parting din. I have never thought of myself as a feminist, and I'm not sure yet what that actually entails. Feminist. That identifier is intriguing, but also vaguely threatening to my past sense of self as Daddy's little girl.

I spend another half hour or so waiting at the station with the humanist middle school teacher, who is short and pleasant and determinedly optimistic. A fellow Marylander. "My apartment is not so far from where you live, Lissa," she says. "We should get together once we're both back home."

"Yes. Let's get together. We should definitely get together this fall," I say. She lives in Columbia, a planned community, newly developed, just about forty-five minutes from my farmhouse. Then the humanist takes a train to Italy, to visit relatives in Sicily, and I voyage on alone.

CHAPTER TWENTY-EIGHT

❧

Wiener Walzer

"Vienna lulls me, swathes me in a silken chrysalis of old-world gentility, and conveys an overwhelming sense of righteousness, insisting that this is how all civilized people should behave."
—*Lissa's notebook*

I TAKE THE WIENER WALZER, the night train east to Austria's capital city, fall into a heavy sleep, and don't wake until it's morning and the train is pulling into a station called Wien, Vienna. Here I fall in love again, this time with the "City of Music," the "City of Dreams," its wide gracious avenues and boulevards, its parks, its music, its bands playing in gazebos.

I board a city bus to the edge of town in search of the local youth hostel. The gentlemanly conductor wears a formal uniform. At each stop he gallantly escorts any passenger who is old or feeble down the aisle as they deboard the bus. No one on the bus seems rushed or impatient at these delays. This is so unlike the No. 8 bus trips I used to take downtown to Baltimore, where everyone was rude and rushed and angry. At the end of the line, the conductor gently takes my elbow and escorts me to the exit.

When I ask him, "How do I get to the youth hostel?" he

actually steps down off the bus with me, points along the wide tree-lined cityscape, patiently explains—in lovely English and in great detail—how to walk to my destination. Vienna lulls me, swathes me in a silken chrysalis of old-world gentility, and conveys an overwhelming sense of righteousness, insisting that this is how all civilized people should behave. But I also find myself chafing against a quaint acceptance of this facade. I find it difficult to trust or accept these appearances at face value. Didn't some of these same genteel citizens collaborate with Hitler not so many years ago?

But then I visit Schönbrunn Palace and fall under Vienna's spell all over again. I sign up for the palace tour and am assigned to a small group of English-speaking tourists. We are met by a slim young woman with short black hair. Brisk, energetic, and eager, she greets us with a crisp accent and leads us to a suite of rooms. "Welcome to the home of the Empress Elisabeth, nicknamed Sisi. Her subjects called her their beloved Fairy Queen, the Most Beautiful Woman Alive. Her chestnut hair was extraordinarily long and thick. She was the love of Emperor Franz Joseph's life. These are Sisi's private rooms. These are her flying rings that dangle here, empty now. They testify to Sisi's gymnastic prowess. And her riding rings, which you will see later, speak of her equestrian skills. Sisi reigned here during those final shining years of Hapsburg rule, a time when art and culture flourished under royal patronage."

Our guide walks us through the halls of the imperial palace. "Let me transport you back to a majestic time and place where gifted artists thrive, where Gustav Klimt paints murals, Johann Strauss II composes waltzes for Emperor Franz Joseph and his Empress, and where Franz Liszt is moved to tears at his first glimpse of Sisi's phenomenal beauty. Let these palace walls speak to you. Hear the echoes of Richard Wagner's epic *Ring Cycle* opera. For a moment, if you will, savor this world, for it is magical." The guide's voice grows wistful. "But, also, it is unsustainable, and soon it will come tumbling down."

The guide waves vaguely at a spot beyond the palace walls. "Keep in mind that these are dynamic times in Europe. The modern world is rapidly approaching. Even while Sisi's court thrives, a young Sigmund Freud has set up a clinical practice not far from here and begins to examine his patients' behavior, probing the human psyche, and positing theories that pave the way for a whole new school of medical thought.

"In 1898, Sisi is killed by an anarchist and the nineteenth century draws to a tragic close. In 1914, Archduke Franz Ferdinand, Franz Joseph's nephew and heir to the throne, is assassinated. The Austro-Hungarian Empire is propelled headlong into a disastrous world war. And by 1918, when this First World War ends, the notion of imperial infallibility has been irreparably damaged, and the once-mighty Hapsburg monarchy collapses."

I leave Schönbrunn Palace contemplating changes and transitions. I replay Austria's history and imagine the nineteenth century waltzing through its years, moving to the beat of Strauss's "Acceleration Waltz." At first the dancers relax, step gracefully, and turn slowly with great dignity. The waltz continues, as expected, but it picks up its pace so that the dancers must exert themselves, move their feet more quickly, and swirl through their turns with more abandon. As the nineteenth century nears its end, the waltz becomes more frantic and intense. Then, unavoidably, the century changes. The twentieth century rushes in and waltzers must struggle to keep their balance. Some dancers will continue, but some will collapse on the dance floor, and some will abandon the dance completely. But the waltz must go on.

I, too, must move on, head back to Paris and begin the next lap of my journey. I anticipate a shift coming, new situations to deal with, and the need to make important decisions about my future.

On the train ride from Vienna to Paris, I ponder the weeks of incessant voyage, of transitioning rapidly from country to country, of breathing in the rarefied atmosphere of travel. Enduring repeated adjustments in culture—shifts in language, currency, geography. Relocating every few days, catching yet another train, deboarding in a new city, desperate to find a safe place to spend the night—often a youth hostel at the far end of town, probably overcrowded, bunk beds, little privacy, possibly only cold water for washing in a communal shower—or maybe just a bracing splash of water, on face and arms, from the basin of a courtyard fountain. Early morning forced checkout. Nowhere to check your bags for the day. So, you carry your bags with you. The nagging daily search for food—at inexpensive restaurants, local groceries, or snack kiosks. Daunting logistics intensify survival instincts, induce an adrenaline-heightened state. Yet part of me rejoices in these insecurities, this risk-taking behavior that makes me feel more alive than ever before.

I fear this heady condition will fade, a half-remembered dream, when I am back home. If and when I resume my former lifestyle, will I fail to perceive its dullness, will my newly awakened senses be slowly, inexorably supplanted by the ingrained sights and sounds of my home country? I don't want to lose whatever expanded awareness I may have attained. But I sense the ephemeral nature of this new knowledge. It covers me like one of Daddy's veneers—exquisite, but because so thinly applied to the surface, it is delicate, fragile, easily fissured by conventional, everyday wear and tear.

CHAPTER TWENTY-NINE

꒰ ꒱

Solitary Sojourn in Paris

"This home-away-from-home for the Lost Generation of Anglo-American writers in Paris still beckons and I must go!" —Lissa's notebook

A S I RIDE THE WIENER WALZER BACK to Paris my thoughts shift to Spence, and I realize the date of his scheduled arrival in Europe is fast approaching. Soon it will be time to meet Spence at Orly. I pull out a copy of *Europe on $5 and $10 a Day*, which I just purchased at the Vienna train station. With this guide in hand, I feel I've officially joined a league of summer adventurers who have gained entrance to no-frills, self-guided tours in the land of European ancestors, "the old country." The book steers me to the Left Bank in Paris, to a neighborhood where students congregate and can find inexpensive fixed-price menus inscribed in chalk on the *ardoise*, the slate. Here the day's specials are prominently displayed on the sidewalk or on a wall outside the entrance to the restaurant. And although these menus provide pre-set and limited choices, they include two or more courses. Enough, or nearly enough, food to satisfy the gnawing, cavernous stomach of a young traveler who carries a slim wallet.

Bearing my big leather shoulder bag, I stride along boulevard Saint-Michel in search of lodging. I plunge into the first hotel that catches my eye, pass through a door guarded by an elaborately uniformed doorman who seems intensely alert to the faded jeans and hiking shoes I wear. Several impeccably dressed young gentlemen stand at attention behind the front desk.

The lead gentleman accosts me with a wry smile, cunning like the malicious fox I encountered years ago in a childhood fairytale. "I think you must be in the wrong place. Do you have a reservation? I doubt that you could afford it here." His companions behind the desk size me up and laugh.

This lead deskman quotes the nightly rate. I nod—a big, long, up and down, ridiculous nod—and mumble in French something like, "I suppose not," and make a hasty, though bumbling exit, my big awkward American elbow grazing a gold button on the doorman's double-breasted jacket. I keep my eyes riveted on the rich colors of the hotel carpeting to avoid seeing the look on his distinguished face.

I end up at a relatively cheap hotel that's listed in my *Europe on $5 and $10*, and from then on consult this guide regularly before approaching any place of dining or lodging.

Spence is scheduled to arrive tomorrow. So, I've booked a room with twin beds to accommodate the two of us. To fill the time while waiting, I make a special visit to the Shakespeare and Company bookstore. It's a magical-sounding place I read about in Hemingway's *A Moveable Feast*. I read that book last summer, just months before leaving home to begin my student year in France. But how many lives have I lived since then? I don't feel like the same naïve schoolgirl I was back then. But the image of that bookstore—that celebrated mecca for young, aspiring expatriate writers, the likes of Hemingway, F. Scott Fitzgerald, Ezra Pound, and Gertrude Stein—remains vivid in my imagination. James Joyce apparently used this shop as his office. This home-away-from-home for the Lost Generation of Anglo-American writers in Paris still beckons and I must go!

But, as I'm learning, all objects, no matter how cherished, are subject to dissolution. When I check around, I find that the original Shakespeare and Company that Hemingway was referring to, the one at 12 rue de l'Odéon, no longer exists. According to the tourist brochures, the original S and Co closed in 1940 when the Nazis occupied Paris and never opened again. In 1951, a new bookstore named Le Mistral opened at 37 rue de la Bûcherie, and subsequently, in 1964, adopted the name Shakespeare and Company in the same spirit and with the blessing of S and Co's original founder. This new S and Co continued the vision of bookstore as combination bookseller/lending library, a place where authors and poets can gather, give readings, even eat and spend the night if need be. This spirit of continuity, this literary phoenix rising from the ashes of war comforts me.

It is to this second coming, so to speak, that I make my way on the Paris metro on an exceptionally sultry July morning. This new S and Co, the brochure tells me, has hosted a newer generation of expatriates, the Beat Generation writers, Allen Ginsberg and William S. Burrough, for example. Other well-known authors have visited, including Richard Wright, Henry Miller, Anaïs Nin, and James Baldwin. So much literary talent!

According to my guidebook, the building that houses S and Co dates back to the early seventeenth century. It was once a monastery. Looking for something sequestered and austere, I'm taken aback when, from blocks away, I spot the brightly painted storefront, its flagrant green-framed doors, the nameplate announcing "Shakespeare and Company" in bold lettering splayed obstinately against a bold backing of bright yellow paint. A jumble of books, new and used, appears to have spilled from the store onto benches and bookracks arranged on the pavement out front. I cross the green threshold to find a vast army of books of all shapes and sizes, perched on shelves from floor to ceiling.

At this time of day, the shop is relatively empty. The interior, dark and cool, exudes an eclectic blend of smells—herbs and spices and sweat and alcohol, tinged with faded perfumes and exotic incense, all this mixed in with dust from old book pages, disintegrating. A wobbly-looking staircase leads to a second floor.

Just a clerk or two mind the store, no one famous, or at least not famous yet. *Tant pis.* Too bad! But to bring myself writer's luck and make the visit more meaningful, I crane my neck in awe and run my fingertips along the spines of a multitude of books conjuring the ghosts of all the once-banned, now-dead S and Co writers who must surely haunt this musty oasis for the literati. I mouthe a silent prayer that one day—against all odds—I will return as a member of the newest generation of American writers, a published author, invited to give a reading here from my very own book. And with that dream still on my lips, I exit the shop at 37 rue de la Bûcherie into sweltering Paris heat. My guidebook tells me this is Kilometer Zero; at this point all French roads begin.

Strolling through the timeworn neighborhood, I traverse a bewildering maze of streets. Before long, I find myself haplessly and happily lost, a perpetual wanderer who's found her home in the heart of Left Bank bohemia, a stone's throw from the Seine, Notre Dame, and Île de la Cité. Late in the afternoon, over-whelmed, exhausted by the heady *mélange* of sights and sounds and smells of Paris, I take refuge on a wicker lawn chair some-where in the heart of this great throbbing city, in front of one or another iconic tourist site—the famous buildings and monu-ments all a blur by now.

The bells of a nearby cathedral chime the hour; it's four o'clock, and by now I'm in the seventh arrondissement—this much I know—not far from Les Invalides where I've just made a quick visit to stand for a beat of time on a balcony under the magnif-icent baroque dome and peer down in awe at Napoleon's tomb. A majestic-looking display, stone upon stone. An enormous purplish-red sarcophagus, resting on a green base, atop a black slab, aggrandizes the memory of the great historical figure. Yet, concealed deep inside is history's irony. For at the core of this massive pile of rocks lie the diminutive remains of another notoriously short and ultimately defeated man.

Now, I sit at an outdoor café where clinking glassware mingles with zealous conversation only to be muffled by the frenetic rush of Paris traffic. I sit very still. I am trying to collect my thoughts and picture what it will be like seeing Spence again, coming face to face with my past after all that has changed in me. I'm wondering how to explain to him that I may be staying on in France and he may be going home alone.

To get back to my hotel, I take the metro. It's crowded and I wind up standing in the aisle, holding on to the handrail, striving not to topple over. I'm feeling like a captive sardine, pressed tightly between sweaty bodies. Not a lot of deodorant used here. At some point, I become aware of an insistent prodding behind me and turn to face a young brown-skinned workman who's got his fist jammed into my butt. Experienced now and travel wary, I prod back at him with a string of crude invectives. "*Qu'est-ce que tu fais, sale cochon? Sors ta main de mon fils!*" What are you doing, you filthy pig? Get your hand out of my ass!

CHAPTER THIRTY

Travels with Spence

"Now begins another round of frenzied travel. I feel myself seizing the day, each day." —Lissa's notebook

N EXT MORNING EARLY, I'm at Orly, standing in the arrival
area among an expectant throng of family and friends,
along with professional welcomers who grip sign boards
that identify specific travelers. Each one of us is eagerly awaiting
someone on this flight. We seem to wait forever. But then an
agitated buzzing, palpable as the trilling of a surging horde of
insects, moves though the group. Barely audible at first, indistinct
murmuring. But this curious human whirring increases rapidly
and crescendos into a medley of shouted greetings as passengers
begin to emerge.

I spot Spence at a distance across the debarkation lounge,
awkwardly wielding a large piece of luggage. He's confused, startled. His eyes dart about seeking something familiar to latch onto.
My heart goes out to him. I wave and call out, "Spence, Spence!"
But he doesn't seem able to zero in on my voice amid the bedlam
of airport noises—salutations, boarding announcements, quick

footsteps coming and going along floor tiles, clicking, echoing around us in all directions.

It's not until I jump up and down—to the point of actually receiving quick stares from the surrounding greeters—that his eyes lock on mine and he makes a beeline in my direction, encumbered by the unwieldy suitcase. When he gets close enough, I rush up to him, give him a big hug. Looking up from the hug, I notice how pale his face is, practically gray. His pupils seem dilated. His gait is a bit unsteady as I guide him toward the exit, and I wonder how many drinks he's had on the plane. It occurs to me, for the first time, that he is terrified, that here in Europe my big brother is the vulnerable one.

Spence is obviously disoriented and completely wiped out. So, we go back to our room at the hotel where he can rest. I introduce him to the woman who works behind the front desk. I think she's the owner's wife.

I tell her this is my brother, Spence, who's visiting France for the first time. The woman smiles. She's plump, friendly, welcoming. Not what I've come to expect in Paris.

"*Mais il peut parler français.*" But he can speak French, I add, wanting to encourage Spence to come out of his shell. He did take several years of French in high school.

"*Ah. Bonjour Monsieur Spence.*"

But Spence just stares back at her. "*Vous ne devez pas être timide monsieur.*" You mustn't be shy, monsieur, she says, and gives Spence a motherly, encouraging smile.

Spence remains frozen, looking miserable and intimidated. I realize I've made a big mistake, pushing him forward like this. Especially now when he's wrung out from his trip, jet-lagged and still trying to acclimate.

"*Merci madame,*" I say, and proceed to get him registered. I take the room key she proffers, and steer Spence and his ungainly suitcase toward the elevator.

While Spence naps, I run out to a bar nearby, pick up a couple of sandwiches and some bottled drinking water. Next morning,

I order room service for the two of us, a continental breakfast—coffee, juice, croissants. I'm eager to chat with Spence and catch up. But he still looks groggy. I keep quiet, give him some space, and allow him to adjust to the time difference.

⌇

Now begins another round of frenzied travel. I feel myself seizing the day, each day. So much to see in Paris, so little time! We spend the better part of an exhausting day at the Louvre, taking in as many exhibits as our overloaded senses will allow. Then, fortunately, we stumble upon the nearby Jardin des Tuileries, stroll through, and find a spot where we can relax in chairs beside a large basin. Here we watch children launch toy sailboats across the shallow water and Spence begins to relax a bit. I find myself soothed by the children's laughter and the pulsing of a single fountain at the center of the pool.

We opt out of ascending the Eiffel Tower—too expensive. With just one day left before heading on to other countries, I ask the hotel owner's wife if she would recommend that we spend it at Versailles. "Ah," she rolls her eyes and gives a sly grin. "So much history and gilt there. And so much decadence, too," she tells us. Her description turns me off. Enough of that, I think. I'm longing for something restorative.

So, instead, we take a long metro ride, then walk toward the Paris Zoo where a big artificial rock is visible from far away. This, we learn, is *le Grand Rocher*, The Big Rock, which rises more than two hundred feet above an extensive park, the Bois de Vincennes. The grounds are spacious. Here, instead of imprisoning animals in undersized cages behind heavy metal bars, the designers have created a more natural habitat. Antelope imported from African savannahs and rocky hills have space here in their new home to run, leap, climb, and lift their antlers under open sky, separated from us humans by a deep ravine. Tropical birds fly about in a greenhouse that simulates their rainforest home. We see all kinds of animals: giraffes, ostriches, lions, and on and on, including exotic breeds and species threatened with extinction. This zoo impresses me. It leaves me with a good feeling about how the animals are cared for.

Spence still doesn't say much, which is not unusual. He's more of a pacer and a thinker than a talker. But he's more relaxed now. He seems to be enjoying himself—more comfortable with animals than with people. As we follow the zoo's pathways, Spence strides along, humming the tune of an old nursery rhyme about going to the animal fair. From time to time Spence erupts with snatches of lyrics, " . . . big baboon by the light of the moon, . . . combing his auburn hair, . . . funniest was the monk . . . sat on the elephant's trunk . . . elephant sneezed . . . fell on his knees . . . end of the monk, the monk, the monk."

Next day, we voyage on to Amsterdam where we pay our respects to Vincent at the Van Gogh Museum. At the end of the day, I realize that, somehow, I've lost the palette knife I've been carrying with me all over Europe. But rather than embrace the bitterness of loss or theft, I choose to believe that I dropped the knife off at the museum where Vincent himself has reclaimed it.

As we leave Amsterdam, we stop in at a bookstore and Spence discovers Tolkien's *The Lord of the Rings*. For the remainder of the trip, he spends most of his time hunkered down, engrossed in Middle Earth—its fanciful inhabitants and their apocalyptic exploits. I wind up going out alone one night to see *The Exorcist*. The depiction of evil overcoming innocence makes me feel jumpy for the rest of the night.

The movie ends, the audience spills out, *en masse*, senses heightened and on high alert, into the bright lights and throbbing nightlife of the city. At first, enfolded in this pulsing aggregation of human flesh, I feel myself warmed, carried along the sidewalk. But as the crowd moves away from the movie house, it disperses gradually. Suddenly, I find myself walking alone through a darkened neighborhood at the far edge of town toward the third-floor room we've rented in a family home. Spence waits for me alone in this room, immersed in Tolkien's fabulous realm.

Along the way, I pass a creepy boarded fence where untrimmed dark branches protrude across the narrow walkway like demonic claws. They poke through the wall's warped and weathered slats, and scrape at my face. I quicken my pace to a trot, then find myself running the final block, scrambling up the narrow back staircase, pounding on the door. No response. I panic, wrench at the doorknob, feel it turning beneath my hand. Spence has neglected to lock up. As I burst into the room, gasping for breath, Spence looks up from his book, seeming only mildly surprised, and blithely returns to Middle Earth.

~~~

Next, it's on to Copenhagen. On the way in the train, I check my calendar, remind myself that, per Maggie, this year's International Week for women at Femø runs from the last Saturday in July through the first Saturday in August. Wow! It's coming up soon. At the end of this week! Spence is still engrossed in *The Lord of the Rings*. So, maybe I can take a chance, duck out for a few days, spend some time on an island, communing with nature and liberated women. Might get to see Maggie again. She said she'd be there.

I run the idea past Spence, but he barely listens. He's far away, still escaping into Tolkien's fantasy. We are settled into a nice hotel in a quiet section of Copenhagen. And for the first time in our European travels, Spence seems comfortable. No language issues. The staff all speak perfect English. And I know he will eat well while I'm away. Each morning an elaborate Scandinavian breakfast board, a smorgasbord, is laid out in the dining room. Hotel guests help themselves to a variety of extremely healthy foods, an abundance of local specialties—a spread of dried and smoked fish, cheeses, flatbreads, and thick slices of the traditional Danish rye bread, Rugbrød, which is bursting with nutrients—whole grains, seeds, nuts. Also, there's ham, liver pâté, tomato, bell pepper. And tea. And, of course, plenty of hot coffee to drink.

Throwing caution to the wind, I secure our hotel room through August 10—the women's camp on Femø closes on August 3—so that gives me plenty of time to get back before Spence has to deal with traveling again. To Spence, I say, "I'll meet you back here no later than August 5. That's five days before we have to check out." He grunts and turns a page in the hefty Tolkien novel.

To myself I say, *yes, Lissa, you owe this to yourself.* This is probably the only chance you'll ever have to spend time at a place like Femø. I give myself permission to pursue my own fantasy and book a seat on a bus to Kragenæs where I'm supposed to catch the afternoon ferry for Femø.

After a very long drive, the bus driver—a sturdy, middle-aged fellow, who looks typically Scandinavian to me with his trimmed beard and fisherman's cap—announces my stop, "Kragenæs!" I look around me. I'm the last person on the bus. I look out the bus window at the terrain outside. No one out there. The landscape is rugged, remote. And it's getting dark. I remember the long ride I used to take as a small child, in the back of our Oldsmobile, out from Baltimore, way out to my grandparents' farmhouse in the northern county. I remember thinking that the farmhouse—now my brother's and my farmhouse—was "at the far end of nowhere." But now the trip to this out-of-the-way—and perhaps fabricated—island in Denmark truly feels like an even farther end of nowhere.

The driver peers back at me in the rearview mirror, calls out again, "Last stop!"

Where are all the other international women who are supposed to be taking this bus from Copenhagen? And why am I here so late. I was supposed to catch a ferry that leaves here at 1:25 p.m. But it's much later than that now.

"Can I catch a ferry here for Femø? I'm here for the international women's camp."

"The afternoon ferry left already."

"Were any international women on it?"

"Can't say, miss."

"Will I be able to get out to Femø tonight?"

"One more ferry this evening. Leaves for Femø in about an hour."

"Is International Week for women being held on the island this week?"

"Can't say, miss. Always something going on out there. Ferry launch is just over there." He points to a pier about a hundred feet away. I can hear insect noises and water lapping. I begin to step down off the bus, but stop to ask the driver, "When is the next bus?"

"This is the last one today," he tells me. Dark thoughts arise. I picture myself waiting alone here in the dark on this remote foreign shore, waiting for a last ferryboat that may never come. I see myself stranded out here, passing the night alone, prey to unseen insects until the next bus arrives at some time tomorrow to take me back to the capital. Doubts fill my mind and drain me of every ounce of plucky courage I summoned to get this far. And so, I relinquish my Danish fairytale, retreat back onto the bus, and ride back to Copenhagen.

When I let myself back into the hotel room, Spence looks up from his reading, and although he doesn't say it, I can tell he's relieved to see me back again so soon. He's eager to talk to me about Middle Earth and the hobbits who live there, insists on reading a passage out loud to me about the wizard Gandalf, and I begin to understand how traumatic this jaunt around Europe must be for my reclusive, introverted brother. From this point on, I pay closer attention to Spence's sensitivities and vow, during this travel time, to assume the role of protective sibling, the role he's always taken on for me.

We visit the places he's talked about since he was little and became enraptured with Norse mythology and folklore. At the harbor, we pay our respects to Hans Christian Andersen's Little Mermaid. In honor of *Hamlet*, Spence's favorite Shakespeare play, we spend a spooky hour at Elsinore. Here, we come upon a long wood trestle table. On the table, a banquet waits, a dozen places set, a feast recently served, still cooling, apparently awaiting the imminent arrival of royal guests. Or perhaps signaling the guests' hasty desertion of their meal. We leave not knowing.

That evening, back at our hotel in Copenhagen, we catch the news on international television, see clips of Richard Nixon giving a nationwide address on August 8. He announces his resignation from the office of President of the United States effective noon the next day. In my heart, I cheer.

Next day we go to Carlsberg Brewery and sample Elephant beer. We spend a day at Tivoli Gardens, ride the Ferris wheel in a passenger car that looks like a parachute. I can't get enough of the ice cream—large warm waffle cones filled with vanilla ice cream, topped with strawberry jam and a fat, creamy chocolate-covered marshmallow cookie! It's called the Amerikaner. I've never tasted anything like it in America. But it does remind me of the chocolate-dipped vanilla ice cream Daddy used to buy me at Timonium State Fair when I was little. I'm enchanted by the evening of fireworks at Tivoli. It's a magical place.

We go to a Danish circus, see amazing acrobats and unusual clowns who are much more nuanced than our American Bozo; these Danish clowns are more like our Emmett Kelly. He's always been my favorite clown. The circus in Copenhagen is housed inside a large permanent building—not at all like the itinerant circuses our parents took us to as children—Ringling Brothers, Barnum and Bailey.

Each year these American circuses would arrive in Baltimore, in warm weather, with much fanfare, to be laid out in temporary tents with a three-ring main attraction under the Big Top. In anticipation, Spence would pedal his tricycle, as fast as he could, up Franklintown Road, down Harlem Avenue, around the block with me standing on the step behind his seat, holding on for dear life, both of us chanting at the tops of our lungs, "We're going to the circus! We're going to the circus!"

Traveling alone with Spence, my only sibling, is nothing new.

We have been paired since childhood. In the early years, our mother dressed us in matching outfits that seemed to dissolve our two-year age difference. People often assumed we were twins.

Spence and I share a lifetime of memories. We went everywhere together. From kindergarten through high school, I tagged along behind him to the same schools. We attended the same Sunday School. We stayed alone together in the old farmhouse through Daddy's final days and nights. As brother and sister, we shared meals together and tried to cope. We did our best to care for our father as he lay dying in the bedroom upstairs. We are like Saint-Exupéry's little prince and fox. For, after all, we have formed a unique bond, a special relationship unlike any other in the world. We need each other.

CHAPTER THIRTY-ONE

Decision Point in Clermont

"Here again in Jardin Lecoq, this perpetual garden." —Lissa's notebook

M Y TRAVELS IN EUROPE with Spence draw to a close on the long, uncomfortable train ride from Copenhagen back to Paris. Soon we will be flying home, my year abroad drawn to a close. My desire to be an author quickens and intensifies as I sense each mile of track passing beneath my feet. Spence retreats back into *The Lord of the Rings*, and remains absorbed there for most of the trip. To soothe the tiresome hours on the train, I take out my notebook and begin, as Spence says, to "scribble a story": *Travel Tale: A Train Ride to Paris. In Europe one takes trains . . .*

We spend the night at a modest hotel in Paris, then catch an early train to Clermont so I can pick up the things I've left behind. With Spence, I take a cab to Trudy's old apartment building. Many rooms are shuttered—most locals take their annual vacations in July and August. And as expected, Trudy and her family have gone back home. We climb the worn stairs. I reclaim my suitcase from the musty closet and take Spence to Jardin Lecoq to grab a bite to eat.

Here I am again with the ducks, a swan, the buoyant umbrellas, replaying a familiar scene in Clermont, another day in a series of life's circles, looping incessantly back and around, back and around. Here again in Jardin Lecoq, this perpetual garden. This time around I'm sharing a table—not just with memories of the Brits and Ghislaine and the ghost of Junjei—but also with my brother.

Spence sits across from me on the refreshment pavilion's outdoor balcony, at one of the small round tables. Although his presence is very real, he seems almost ephemeral. I must grasp him in conjunction with real objects. So, I order Pschitt! and Orangina. As we sip French soft drinks from tall glasses, a puzzled expression emerges on his face along with the beginnings of a grin at the odd-sounding names of these foreign beverages I have ordered for him to taste.

Here in the garden, Spence's face seems discolored, strained, bizarrely distorted and fragmented—like a Picasso cubist portrait—beneath the rippling orange and cream stripes of the table's umbrella. Spence looks so fragile, sitting here, staring out across the pond. He carries a sadness that reminds me of Junjei.

As the minutes pass, I seem to hear familiar voices coming from across the pond: our mother saying from her sickbed, "Lissa, always take care of your daddy and your brother"; our father imploring us to unite in an unbreakable bond, "Now that your mother's gone, we have to stick together, the three of us, like the Three Musketeers, 'All for one, one for all.'"

Does Spence hear these voices? Or, does Spence hear different words coming from our father, repeating his persistent demand, "Always take care of your sister, Spence. She's just a little girl."

Suddenly, the decision point is upon me—do I tell Spence I plan to stay on here in Clermont for another year, as *assistante d'anglais*? Or, do I trot back home with him to the farmhouse and finish up my bachelor's degree at my American university?

Spence continues to stare across the pond. The water is a dull gray today, agitated by intermittent jags of wind, mottled beneath moving clouds. Three ducks paddle around. Silly. Going nowhere. A single white swan glides by, unperturbed, at peace with it all.

I study Spence's face. He has sacrificed so much for me. Instead of going to college in New Mexico and following his dream to become an astronomer, he stayed at home to support me. He lost Jill, in part because he was so wrapped up in my needs. He's been left alone, poring over endless computer printouts, holding down a steady job at the bank so he could fund my year abroad. He believed in me and gave me wings to fly, even as he stayed behind in the farmhouse. I remember him saying, as he sent me off for France, "If somebody's going to do something important, then maybe it should be you."

And in that moment, the decision comes to me as clearly as if that magnificent swan had spoken it to me. Spence is not able to speak for himself, but he really needs me. Both our parents want us to take care of each other. I must not break the bond. I must not stay for another year in Clermont. Not now. I will not abandon my brother to his loneliness as I abandoned Junjei!

While still at the small round table, I tear a page from my notepad, scribble a letter for Mme Arlette, informing her, with my sincere regrets, that I will not be able to accept the position of *assistante d'anglais* at *lycée Jeanne d'Arc*. Not at the present time. I fold the notepaper, walk with Spence to her apartment, drop my letter through her mail slot, knowing that she is away on vacation now. This decision seems, somehow, monumental. I feel as if a door is closing heavily against my face.

❧

That evening Spence and I fly home from Orly. When we near JFK airport, thunderstorms cause turbulence. The plane drops, jarring dinner trays, spilling drinks. As we make our way to the gate to wait for our flight to Baltimore, I spot rows of New York City phone books suspended from metal brackets along the walls.

"Wait a minute, Spence. I want to look up Jill's phone number. We have time. She told me I should look her up if I was ever in town."

I dash over to the rank of telephone directories. Spence hasn't come with me. I can see him, waiting, planted next to a water fountain, out of the way of bustling travelers, his arms folded tight as if to defend against any invasion of his privacy. He watches me, resuming the role Daddy assigned him so many years ago—sister's protector. I can tell he's not pleased with my decision to look up his former fiancée, but he gives in to me, indulging the little sister who always got her way with Daddy.

But all those massive phone books, the tiny print, so many names in varying configurations, enumerated to infinity, it seems. I can't find her. So, I go back to Spence, follow him to our gate for the connecting flight to Baltimore. We are back in the US, and I let him take charge.

CHAPTER THIRTY-TWO

丷 ⸒

Home Again

"I hear my father's voice, disapproving, 'Travel has changed you, Lissa. The world has stolen your innocence. Where is my little girl? Have you left her wandering, lost on some foreign soil?'" —Lissa's notebook

WHEN WE RETURN HOME FROM THE AIRPORT and pull up the gravel driveway, the old farmhouse looms eerily, its off-white shingles stark under a dim moon; its many windows stare blankly out at me. What have I come back to?

Spence parks the rental car, carries in bags, goes off to bed, and I am left alone, wide awake, to wander about the house. I meander from room to room as if in a dream, a ghost returned, compelled to roam its once-familiar surroundings, opening doors, inspecting closets, sizing up provisions in the pantry, staring at the fresh supply of unopened cleaning products Spence has lined up along the bottom shelf. I take in small details, noticing and cataloging old furnishings and belongings that once I scarcely noticed. But now these previously unassuming possessions confront me like abandoned friends, insulted.

In the wee hours, I mount the narrow farmhouse staircase, enter my bedroom for the first time since last October when I left for France. But before I allow myself to collapse on my childhood bed, I check out the oak desk that Daddy made for me when I was in elementary school. I open the various drawers, looking for nothing in particular, just trying to refresh my memory. I lift the desktop and rummage through the spacious deep storage compartment Daddy built inside. Here, I find stacks of old correspondence and pads of paper, report cards, high school notebooks, and a familiar old elementary-school composition notebook. I open the notebook's black-and-white marbled cover, page through to find the unfinished book about Spence's moon rocket project I began to write all those years ago, printing it in pencil, drawing crude illustrations with my crayons. The story ends abruptly at Chapter Three, with Spence peering out the round window of his pointy-tipped homemade spaceship as it blasts off into space on a trail of flame and smoke. I promise myself I'll go through all this stuff more carefully someday.

Then I pull out each of the two long side drawers. The one on the left has an assortment of pens and rulers, an old combination lock I used for my high school gym locker. The contents of the long drawer on the right alarm me. The drawer is stuffed with the dried brown seedpods that spin down each fall like miniature helicopters from the two big front-yard Norway maples. A nest, made perhaps by chipmunks? I pull out the drawer full-length and poke around. The nest seems empty now. But how did chipmunks get into my bedroom to build it?

I dump the drawer's contents into the wastebasket, and there, among the dried seedpods, I spy an antique golden treasure! It's the 14-karat gold wristwatch Daddy gave me when I was just a little girl and the bracelet was way too loose, even at its smallest adjustment. It was his mother's watch Daddy told me and said, "Always take good care of this watch, Lissa, and it will always take care of you." Now when I put it on, the watchband fits me perfectly. When I wind it, it still runs and somehow it feels right for me to start wearing it again. Funny, I traveled all over Europe without a timepiece, yet now I feel the need to don a watch, and a nostalgic antique one at that!

~ ~ ~

The next day, Saturday, I walk around outside, taking stock of our yards and outbuildings. The barn still stands, but it's careening, the north wall buckling. The hayloft looms dark above the opening of the old garage. The shed roof has a big hole in it. The corn crib is half filled with molding corn husks, animal droppings, and God knows what else. The crib's door is dangling by one rusty hinge.

At the back of the house, Daddy's woodworking shop remains locked, the windowpanes riddled and shattered by shots from a BB gun. My brother thinks they were made by a neighbor's boy. Random mischief or maybe target practice executed when my brother was away at work or sequestered inside the farmhouse, at his work table in the dining/living room, huddled over his stacks of computer printouts, oblivious to the outside world.

My Aunt Essie still lives in the house next door, and I walk over for a visit. I pass the old grape arbor—now overgrown, collapsing in on itself—and remember watching my father there in his last years, climbing up the frame to reach the upper vines, agile as a wizened old monkey in search of a healthy meal. "Just getting myself a belly full of grapes," he would call out to me. He didn't bother to wash them; they weren't sprayed with any pesticide. He plucked them off the thick twisted vines, stuffed the fruit directly into his mouth, spat out the heavy seeds and thick skins. Those grapes had coarse skins, a deep bluish-purple. Concord grapes. My grandmother, Magda, cultivated them more than forty years ago for her jellies.

I follow the footpath. Still visible, though barely, it runs from our house to Aunt Essie's. My feet—bare in summer, booted in winter—etched this path over the course of countless childhood visits to my aunt.

As always, Aunt Essie's house is unlocked. And, as always, I give a loud rap on the side door and enter, calling out just as my mother did, "Hello! Anybody home?" Then I walk on in, following the direction of my aunt's voice.

Today, Aunt Essie is sitting in the living room, watching TV. "I come bearing gifts from my travels in Germany," I say, and present her with a Bavarian woodcarving of a miniature squirrel and a pair of garish quilted potholders that say "München." She delights in these trinkets as I knew she would.

"Can't have too many potholders," says Essie, the inveterate cook. "And I just love this little squirrel. Reminds me of one of Grandpap's woodcarvings. I have just the spot for it here in my curio cabinet." My mother's and Essie's side of the family descend primarily from German stock, some Prussian, some Bavarian. Some of the Bavarian relatives were woodcutters and cabinetmakers.

Aunt Essie invites me to come back to church with her on Sundays, but I plead too much school work is coming up. "Well, how about this coming Saturday? It's my sixty-fifth birthday. The church ladies, bless them, will be holding a celebration her me. I'd love for you to be there."

It's late afternoon by the time I get home and try to pick up with my usual weekend activities—scrubbing the bathroom, dusting, vacuuming, catching up on dishes and laundry, ironing Spence's shirts for the coming week.

~~~

The next morning dawns, a golden August Sunday. So, I decide to take a walk. I head toward Aunt Essie's place, then continue on "just down the road apiece," as country folks say, to a long and rutted, unpaved driveway. Growing up, Spence and I called this Zora Clay's Lane. It leads off the main road, starting out flat and curved. Then, gradually, it descends down a series of gentle slopes through wide fields, and dead ends at a barn with a silo that rises like a rustic watchtower less than 50 feet away from a solid-looking brick farmhouse, the Clay family home. A nondescript gray-shingled tenant residence cowers behind the landowner's house, humbly resigned to its rightful position. The home and outbuildings are sheltered like precious possessions, cupped in the palm of a small grassy valley where they are fringed by trees and safeguarded from foul weather.

The sturdy brick farmhouse was built about a decade and a half ago by the Clays' only son, Cory. Designed to be compact and efficient, it still strikes the eye as relatively modern. Most of the farmhouses in our neighborhood were built before the second world war. They look old now. But the house that Cory built resembles the homes in the newer suburban housing projects that began to crop up around here in the 1950s.

That's when white families, eager to take flight from Baltimore City, began buying up acres of rustic farmland—left and right, cheap—from struggling farmers. Back then, and still now, we white folks always seem to be afraid, always trying to escape from something. Where does this fear of desegregation come from? Is it some kind of misplaced generational guilt that's bred right into us?

Mine was one of those "white flight" families. We lived in a section of West Baltimore that was becoming more and more integrated, and my father harbored an old man's fears for the safety of his young children and the value of his row house property. So, when my grandparents passed in the mid-1950s and my mother, Jimmie, inherited her parents' chicken farm, we seized upon the opportunity, sold the house on Franklintown Road, and moved out to our own twelve acres in the country.

It wasn't until much later, in college, that I began to learn just how Jim Crow laws and lingering racist policies and attitudes had stacked the deck—continue to stack the deck—against our darker brothers and sisters. I was late to learn how "redlining" persists among lending institutions, restricting home ownership and ensuring that certain city neighborhoods remain all-white.

I'm not sure who owns the farm now. Zora and her husband, old man Clay, have both passed away. I know they had a daughter. Maybe she inherited the place. Their son, Cory, of course, is no longer in the picture. How many years is it now since, goaded into bankruptcy by his puerile wife, Fay, he came home one night and put a bullet through his head?

As I stroll, I'm comforted to see that Mr. Clay's fields are still being tended. Recently mowed, strewn with bales of hay, the acreage rolls gently alongside the dirt and stone driveway. Patches of straw, fallen in clumps from the harvester, lie abandoned here, forming patches across the driveway that cushion my footsteps as I walk down Zora Clay's Lane.

The sun is bright today. It warms the earth, and as the straw beneath my feet dries, it releases a delicate sweetness that mingles with a cloying sugary smell. It's an unpleasant odor that rises from a mound of fresh cow manure, recently dumped here to ferment at one side of the lane. The manure proofs like a pungent yeast in the warm, moist air, transforming itself into a dark fertile paste that farm hands will spread—like a stinking chocolate frosting—across these fields in the next planting season. As I walk, my senses confirm for me that I have returned, that I am—for better or worse—home again.

CHAPTER THIRTY-THREE

Voices from the Past

"I try to continue on my journey, but voices from the past pursue me, confront me." —Lissa's notebook

LATE ON SUNDAY AFTERNOON, I plow through the huge pile of mail Spence has stacked for me on the dining/living room table. At the top of the stack, I find a battered envelope. My address is scrawled on the front in a childishly cramped and slanting handwriting. There's no return address on the envelope. So, curious, I tear it open right away, scan the crooked lettering that spills across and down the front and back of a single sheet of lined notebook paper torn from a spiral binding. The sender's return address appears crammed in at the very bottom of the letter, apparently as an afterthought.

It's from Wanda, a little friend I met during my 1965 experience as a volunteer camp counselor. I was Wanda's counselor at West River Camp as part of Operation Open Air, a program sponsored by the Methodist church. The goal was to give underprivileged inner-city kids a respite from Baltimore's crime-ridden neighborhoods, expose them to a week-long camping experience in a more natural environment. Wanda was nine years old that summer. That was a little more than nine years ago.

She must be a young woman now. But in this letter, Wanda still addresses me as "Teacher." It's what she always called me at camp even though my other girls called me Miss Lissa. But Wanda would always call out, excitedly, at times almost frantically, "Teachah! Teachah!"

Hello, Teacher!

I been missing you something awful. Found your address in an old shoebox full of stuff I got at camp and stuck under my bed long time ago. That old shoebox has been moving with me every house I go to. Got your address stuffed in my wallet along with my bus pass and other important stuff. God knows why. For old time sake? For good luck?

You remember I used to talk about my little brother, Bobby? Well, he dropped out of high school and really messed up. Got himself locked up over at Jessup. He's the baby there. Gets raped in the butt all the time by the older prisoners. So bad he gotta wear a tampon.

You are my hero, Teacher. Always have been, always will be. Few years back saw your pitcher in the Sunpapers. Pitcher of you with your crown on when you won that beauty contest. Cut it out of the paper. Got that in my wallet, too. Pulled it out the other day. For some reason. Got to thinking about you. Thought you might still be at that same old address. Thought I might as well take a chance and write you.

Got me a job now, waitressing at Thompson's Sea Girt House out on York Road in Govans. Got to take the bus a ways to get out there. But tips are pretty good. Saving up. Gonna buy me a car someday.

Anyways, got to thinking about you lately. Thought maybe you might remember me. Maybe we could meet up one day at the restaurant. I'd make sure I got to wait your table. I'd give you the best service. Got good seafood. Crab imperial. Steaks. Lots of other stuff, too. Fried chicken.

Well, maybe someday you could come there. Just in case, here's my address. Might just see you again.

You never know.

Your friend always, Wanda

Wanda's missive seems to race down the page. The closing lines are compressed and smaller, squeezed in at the bottom as though they must all fit on a single sheet of paper. I feel shaken by this sudden communication. This young friend's voice after so many years of silence, so many changes, overwhelms me. Her letter is touchingly open, unpretentious. It tugs at my heart, draws me into the past. This letter was postmarked several months ago. So, it demands my immediate attention.

～

Near the bottom of the stack of mail, I find a letter from Paloma, my best friend in high school. It's mailed from Calgary, Canada, postmarked December 1973, telling me she's six months pregnant, heading back to Charlottesville, and would love to see me sometime.

That evening, I give her a call. She picks up right away, and I'm startled to hear again the closeness of that familiar voice after so much time has passed. But we seem to pick up right where we left off—almost.

"Hello?"

"Hi, Paloma."

"Lissa!" She recognizes my voice right away. "Wow! Long time, no hear. So, how are you? Whatcha been up to?"

We catch up on all the major life events—her events more than mine. I'm at a loss to sum up all that's happened to me since we last saw each other. I haven't processed it yet myself.

Paloma's divorced now, living in Charlottesville again with her mom and five-month-old son, Joplin, named in honor and memory of Janis. Seems Paloma and Gary moved back to Charlottesville from Canada when Joplin was born. Soon after, Gary got a local redneck girl named Sheryl pregnant. He and Sheryl live with their new baby girl in a trailer park somewhere between Crozet and Waynesboro. I'm on the phone with Paloma for more than three hours. Before hanging up, I promise to come down for a visit soon.

It's after midnight when I mount the old staircase, sit at my desk in the old familiar bedroom, pull out a sheet of personal stationery from the supply that remains in its original box, and compose a quick response to Wanda on the fancy notepaper. The paper is pale blue, gray-flecked with deckle edges. Daddy let me select it myself from the supply catalog.

"Dear Wanda," I write beneath a delicately monogrammed LMP, my initials. Daddy printed these on his small hand press, using a custom-made cut he special-ordered from the Kelsey printing company in Meriden, Connecticut. "So glad to hear from you," I continue. "Please call me and we'll get together." I close the letter with my phone number, then fold the notepaper, put it in a matching envelope for mailing.

~~~

On the last day of August, a Saturday, I attend a luncheon in the Fellowship Hall at our church. It's a celebration of my Aunt Essie—past-President of the Women's Society, perennial participant in every Bible study offered, former Sunday School teacher, current Secretary for the Church Council, all-around church leader and pillar of our little Methodist congregation—on the occasion of her sixty-fifth birthday.

Our church ladies show their love and deep affection with their cooking. So, in honor of Essie, the ladies drape the long serving table with a starched white linen cloth and load it with homemade goodies. They set out casseroles representing every food group, plus salads, bread in all forms—loaves and muffins and rolls and biscuits—and an assortment of homemade desserts. All the ladies' specialties are featured—pies, cakes, cookies, brownies. They lay out heavy silverware—forks, knives, spoons—polished and lined up in rows, ready for service, beside stacks of fine chinaware bowls and plates.

Featured on a round side table, a cut-glass punchbowl—accompanied by a silver dipper and circled by matching cut-glass cups—makes a delightful vessel for displaying a creamy concoction of fruit juices, ginger ale, and frothy orange sorbet. Beside the punch bowl, a frosted layer cake—decorated with dainty pink-and-green rosebuds blossoming on a field of beige sour-cream frosting and inscribed with Essie's full name in deep pink—stands proudly by, waiting for the guest of honor to slice it.

Essie arrives, fresh from a morning at the Grangerville beauty parlor, hair freshly "done," permed into tight bluish-silver curls.

As Essie's niece, I sit close by her at the family table, up front beneath the large wooden cross on the brick wall that separates the Fellowship Hall from the sanctuary. I'm halfway through my first plate of food, when a young man—tall, dark, slightly hunched—approaches Aunt Essie and introduces his young family, a wife and three little daughters. I wonder who this strange guy is. I don't think I know him . . . but he looks vaguely familiar. Maybe a distant cousin? I have lots of cousins I've never met.

Then he speaks, "Miz Essie! How are you? It's been a while." He wrings Aunt Essie's hand. That unforgettable bass voice cuts through me, deep and raw. It's Lonny!

Lonny looks my way a couple of times. But if he recognizes me, he never lets on. Could it be he doesn't know who I am? After all, I'm almost twenty-four now; I must look a lot different from that scrawny seven-year-old cowering in the corner of the hayloft, tightening herself, refusing him entry.

And really, I don't want him to identify me. So, I don't speak. Instead, I fade as much as possible into the family grouping— among Essie's nieces and nephews and cousins—at my end of the table, feeling the heavy presence of the cross on the wall above me. But I am curious about this man whose actions affected me so strongly, filled me with unconscionable shame and inexplicable guilt for so many years.

I strain my ears to listen in whenever he speaks, trying to gain some understanding of what makes this "bad boy" tick after all these years. As it turns out, these days Lonny lives an exemplary life. He has a house over in the next county, works as a truck driver for a local stone quarry. Says he saw an announcement on his church's bulletin board about the party for Aunt Essie. Thinks of Essie as a saintly woman, like a mother to him, who saved his skin by taking him in all those years ago. He's married now, he says, to a good woman. This woman has saved him, he says. And under her influence, he's become a born-again Christian.

"God is good!" says Aunt Essie, lowering her eyes and speaking in her most sanctimonious voice.

"May the Lord be praised!" says Lonny's wife.

"Praised!" echoes Lonny's oldest daughter between bites of cake. A chilling thought comes to me: this little girl, this daughter, looks to be just about seven years old right now—the same age I was when Lonny molested me in the hayloft of the old barn.

~

In the evening, just as Spence and I are sitting down to supper, the wall phone jangles, startles me with its loud ring. Though this phone is newer—a rotary version of the black dial-less party-line telephone we had when I was growing up—it's still the only phone in the house and hangs here in the same location, just outside the kitchen, in the hallway on the wall under the second-floor staircase. The ring is so unexpected—we don't get many phone calls here—I jump up from the kitchen table to answer, wondering who it might be.

"Hello, Lissa! How are you?"

At first, I can't place the voice. It's familiar, lightly accented, foreign. . . .

"It's Latif, *Amérique*. I'm in New York. You remember me?"

That name! *Amérique*! It summons up memories I seem to have set aside during my travels. Older friendships discarded, buried under so many new adventures, so many new faces. But the calling of that nickname, *Amérique*, retrieves, like the urgent shriek of a lifeguard's whistle, faded scenes from Clermont. A back table in a student café bobs to the surface, and with it a circle of Arab faces, my friends—overshadowed by that one elusive lover's face.

That face—Georges's compellingly handsome face—remains silent, forever an enigma for me.

One by one, I imagine the others greeting me—Mohammed, Ibrahim, Yusuf, Paul, and last of all Latif, the quiet, serious one with the gentle manner. I do remember him . . . yes. Yes, on my last visit to the café, Latif told me he had a cousin in New York. That he would someday visit him there. Latif told me he was studying English. That he longed to come to America. I remember now . . . I jotted down my address and home phone number for him. Said, yes, he could contact me. . . .

I grip the phone's receiver, tuning in to what Latif is saying. "I am so excited, Lissa, to be finally in America. My cousin has found work for me here. For now, I mop floors at night, and for now, I am content. Soon great things will happen for me. This is a great country, you have, *Amérique*, and I am happy here. So happy!"

I hardly know what to say to Latif. In France, he was one friend among many. But here, he seems like someone I scarcely know. Here his foreignness overwhelms me. I glance over at Spence, looking for a referential anchor, struggling like a drowning woman, desperate to touch the sandy bottom of the ocean floor, anxious to find some stable footing in this crashing wave of culture shock that threatens to drown me.

After what seems like a long moment, I manage to stay afloat by grasping a snippet of polite conversation, like a fragment of buoyant driftwood. "Latif, it's . . . it's so good to hear your voice," I finally say, hoping my voice doesn't betray my insincerity, doesn't reveal my discomfort. I look again over at Spence, but find no reassurance there.

Latif speaks again, and like a naïve child, seems unable to contain his excitement. "Maybe we can meet in New York one day. It's a very great city, this New York City. So fast, so very busy. I love New York! New York, New York. This is one Big Apple!"

What's wrong with me, anyway? Why wouldn't I meet up with Latif in New York City? It might be fun.

But I wind up going for the safe response, and end the call with the noncommittal response, "Yes, Latif, let's meet up someday. You have my number. You take care of yourself now. Bye-bye." With that I return the phone receiver gently to its cradle and beat a cowardly retreat, back to my American comfort zone. I sigh and reflect. Who am I now, anyway?

CHAPTER THIRTY-FOUR

❧ ❧

The Balance Sheet

"And what is the balance sheet of your scholastic year in France?"
—Dr. Albert

I RETURN TO CAMPUS for the first time in early September, just after Labor Day, driving a brand-new tan Ford Pinto my brother has just bought me. In response to my effusive "thank yous," Spence produces a lopsided smile and one of his noncommittal grunts. "I don't need you pestering me to drive you places all the time."

The only empty parking space I can find is at the far end of the overflow lot at the campus's western rim. From there, I trek over to the Student Union, and follow the signs to an expansive lobby set up with rows of long tables, manned by staff members, to accommodate today's registration activities.

Pleased with the courses I've signed up for this first semester of my senior year, I make a quick stop at the bookstore to pick up some of the books on the professors' reading lists. As I check out, I glance up at the clock on the wall. It's nearly noon. I walk, quickly as always, taking long and purposeful strides, and head up the hill, making a beeline for McCullough Hall. I pass gaggles of students—decidedly American students—who mill about, congregate, sprawl on the grassy bank, or seat themselves on wood and concrete outdoor benches. From heavy plastic bags or canvas sacks embellished with the college logo, these eager students pull, like magic rabbits from hats, hefty textbooks newly purchased at the student bookstore. To me these American kids look fresh-faced and hopelessly naïve. Sheep in a bucolic pasture.

A gently sloping, picture-perfect emerald-green lawn defines the space between Cullough and the campus library. And although, no doubt, it's been chemically treated, professionally graded and groomed to present an aesthetically pleasing, albeit false, image on recruitment brochures, I prefer the lumpy ground on my own few acres. My country yard may be riddled with ant-hills and molehills and rabbit dens, dappled in uneven shades of faded green and wilted brown, sprinkled with wily weeds, with clover and chicory and vagrant dandelions, scarred with bare patches of earth between farmhouse, woodworking shop, and barn—but that property is genuine. It belongs to me, and I can call it home if I want to.

Here, in this section of campus, a grid of sidewalks carves the expanse of unnatural green into orderly thirds. Concrete walk-ways lead to each of three main buildings—the massive library at the top of the hill, a gray concrete science building that rises solidly, matter-of-factly against a wooded backdrop on the southern rise, and a pale tan limestone building at the bottom of the hill-side. At the center of this vista, a fountain pulses eager throbs of water. The basin's wide-lipped cement rim forms a circular bench where students settle to exchange animated greetings, catching up with each other after a summer's absence, chatting about anticipated courses and instructors, laying plans for weekend dorm parties and on-campus student activities. As a commuter, I remain an outsider to all of this. So, for now, I can only eavesdrop and imagine.

I take the path downhill to a three-storey limestone building that squats, bland and insignificant, at the base of the hill. This is McCullough Hall where the humanities struggle—in the shifting sands of academia—to retain a modest footprint on campus. What has for generations been a small state teacher's college is morphing into a newly expanded and modernized corporate business model. Rumor has it that, striving to expand its scope and increase its financial base, the college is moving toward officially becoming a university and developing a more competitive football team.

Once inside McCullough, I head for the third floor where, not so long ago, lessons in Latin and Greek and Pedagogy were conveyed—with great solemnity and authority—to future generations of public schoolteachers. These time-honored disciplines have given way to newer branches of learning. Third-floor McCullough is now home to the Modern Languages Department. And I'm here today to schedule a meeting with Dr. Albert so he can assess the results of my junior year abroad in France.

⁂

The secretary, distracted by multiple other duties, pencils me in for this Friday. On my way out, I pass the open doorway of the Dr. Albert's office, gaze inside. The room is empty, desk chair by the window unoccupied, walls heavy with the scent of his cigarette smoke. Gauloises.

I head back down the stairs, musing about Dr. Albert, wondering how he looks these days, how I will feel about my former crush who, in my mind, stood me up last winter when he rescinded our Paris rendezvous. I'm pondering what I'll say to him at this first meeting after a year away when, suddenly, here he is! Coming up the stairs toward me.

"*Tiens!*" I say, and realize I have addressed him using the second-person familiar. I've inadvertently *tutoyered* him, calling out "Hey!" as if he were a close friend—not a respected professor. What is that look he gives me? Is it surprised? Disapproving? Amused?

Embarrassed, I hurry on to tell him, in the best French I can muster, that I've signed up for his Twentieth Century French Novel seminar. He smiles, touches two fingers to the outside of his right eyebrow in an odd, military-style salute. I rush past him and exit the building. Once outside I pause, taking a desperate gulp of fresh air.

On Friday, I sit uneasily in the chair beside Dr. Albert's desk. The forever-present student chair, tacitly designated for formal student-teacher consultations, is pulled up close beside the professor's standard-issue metal desk.

We go over the courses I completed at the French university. I show him my second degree in French letters. The diploma is a bit crumpled from being tucked away inside my suitcase, and its assessment is a mediocre "*passable.*" Acceptable. Merely acceptable. And no third-level diploma. I try to explain, justify to Dr. Albert the context of my year.

"*J'ai voyagé avec un homme qui travaille pour la Chambre de Commerce.*" I traveled with a man who works for the Chamber of Commerce, I tell my professor, and watch his face for a reaction to this plain and graceless explanation of why I didn't attend classes in the second part of the school year. Dr. Albert, worldly Parisian that he is, appears to suppress a canny expression, an assumption of inevitable hanky-panky in such a situation. But he doesn't comment. He gives me all As and Bs and awards me with a generous helping of credits toward my French major. I thank him, trying to justify my derelict behavior, saying traveling was a good opportunity to learn firsthand about the local French culture. "*C'était une bonne occasion d'en apprendre davantage sur la culture français locale.*" Dr. Albert raises no objection or argument. I am mildly surprised and greatly relieved.

As I stand to leave the meeting, Dr. Albert asks, "*Et quel est le bilan de votre année scolaire en France?*" And what is the balance sheet of your scholastic year in France?

"*Je n'ai pas encore fait le bilan,*" I respond. I haven't taken stock yet.

Dr. Albert escorts me to his office door, shakes my hand, and gives what I would like to perceive as a gentle and approving smile. "And so, what do your parents think of your accomplishments?" he adds.

I give him a rueful look and say, "*Je n'ai pas de parents. Mais heureusement, j'ai toujours la ferme.*" I don't have any parents. But fortunately, I still have the farm.

"*Ah, bon, Mlle Power.* Go home then. To your farm."

CHAPTER THIRTY-FIVE

\/ /

An Interloper and a Mentor Appear

"Ah, Lissa, you are the most un-clichéd person I have ever met."
— *Dr. Paddy O'Hara, Chairthing*

I HEAD BACK HOME right after my meeting with Dr. Albert. It's still fairly early on Friday afternoon. Spence doesn't usually roll up the driveway until six p.m. or later on weekdays. So, I'm surprised to see a sporty blue convertible parked behind the house, right next to my brother's fiery orange-red Opal GT two-seater. Inside the house, I find a strange woman, a sassy-looking bleached-blonde, cuddling with Spence on the sofa in the dining/living room. Spence is startled. He seems uncomfortable having the two of us in the same room.

Reluctantly, he introduces me. "This is Laurie. She's one of the programmers I'm training at work . . . at the bank."

"So, you must be Spence's sister, Lissa. Nice to meet 'cha." She flashes me a quick smile, extends her hand. At a loss for words, I stare at this unsuitable woman in my house and limply return her handshake. Before long, Laurie scurries out and zooms off in her hot little sports car.

After that, even when I don't see Laurie, I find evidence of her visits in the house's only bathroom—empty contraceptive packaging and used plastic contraceptive foam inserters discarded in the small plastic trash bin beside the toilet.

Apparently shattered when his fiancée, Jill, broke up with him right before I left for France, and feeling alone and deserted in the old farmhouse, Spence hooked up with Laurie. I remember Jill mentioning her to me once, how Laurie—even though she was married—was infatuated with my brilliant brother, the newly discovered prodigy at the bank, math whiz, golden boy, discovered by an employee aptitude test, identified and trained by the bank's senior programmers, elevated swiftly from lowly coin room clerk to computer operator, then junior programmer and trainer on the rise.

So apparently, while I was in France intent on losing my virginity, Laurie began cheating on her husband, came calling on my brother, and established regular visits to his bedroom at the farmhouse.

It's hard for me to picture them here in Spence's childhood bedroom. My brother and this flagrantly modern blonde engaging in unorthodox coupling within these old familiar walls. It violates the innocence of a cherished setting. It's difficult for me to imagine the naked humping that's happening here. Even harder for me to accept it. How can an act so foreign be played out in a setting so familiar without altering the very essence of that venue?

Also, I wonder what's in it for her. Why would this sexy, worldly blonde want to shut herself off with my brother in his stark little boyhood bedroom. It's weird! After all, this is the room where Spence has spent his nights since the summer before his ninth birthday when we moved out to the farm. Maybe it's all a kinky rural adventure for her.

Yet here they are screwing amid the same faded and stained wallpaper—in the same narrow single bed with its cheap metal frame, on the same lumpy mattress that Spence and I jumped up and down on until we shook the chandelier below and Daddy came up to yell at us, near the same clothes trunk where Spence once held me captive as a child, in plain view of the same knotty pine desk Daddy made for Spence, beside the same battered maple chest of drawers that once held Spence's worn-out dungarees and stretched-out polo shirts full of holes that Spence gnawed in them, within reach of one of the only two undersized clothes closets fitted into these crudely built farmhouse walls.

But now that I'm back home, my brother seems uncomfortable continuing with this socially questionable relationship. Or maybe he just picks up on my own discomfort. Anyway, not long after I first meet her, Spence breaks off with Laurie.

Now, as the days pass, my brother depends on me more and more. He seems happy to have me back, cooking and cleaning, ironing his shirts, doing all the chores I did for him during those growing-up years after our mother, Jimmie, died. He seems to expect and need to return to all the familiar ways where he can abide in sibling comfort and security. And I find myself returning there, too. Regressing. Shrinking back into my former cloistered self.

౿

It's the final year in my bachelor's degree program. So, in addition to Dr. Albert's Twentieth Century French Novel seminar, I've signed up for several courses to round out my English major—Shakespeare as a major figure, a Structure of the English Language course that's required for English majors, and, on a whim, a poetry writing seminar, which Paddy O'Hara is introducing this year as an expansion of the Creative Writing curriculum he has so lovingly nurtured for the past several years.

Dr. O'Hara, or simply "Paddy," as he likes to be called, has been an inspiration to me. I took his Fiction Writing workshop the year before leaving for my junior year abroad in France. Paddy invariably found value in my short stories. He found the strengths in my stories and praised them, enthusiastically, in front of the class. His praise validated my childhood dream of being a great writer and storyteller, kindled a notion I was secretly harboring. Soon, I was seized with a frighteningly powerful desire to become a great American writer, expatriate if need be.

So now, just before classes resume, I meet with Paddy O'Hara in his office suite at the southern end of the second-floor hallway, in the American Literature wing of the English Department. A handwritten sign hangs thumbtacked to his office door. "Chairthing," penned in red Magic Marker, facetiously undercuts the more formal title "Chairman" that's displayed on the bronze doorplate. This is classic whimsical Dr. O'Hara.

Petite, rhythmic, Irish Paddy O'Hara. I am convinced he is indeed a magical leprechaun. With a sweeping wave of his arm and a court jester's capricious bow, the "Chairthing" ushers me into his office suite, seats me, then takes his seat across from me at a wide impressive-looking desk—a desk warranted by a department chair. He seems to observe me for a long moment, then asks, "So Lissa, what's it like for you, coming home after your year's sojourn in France. Are you in culture shock?"

"Culture shock? I'm in constant culture shock. Have been all my life." Paddy's question has me asking myself what it is about American culture that strikes me now? Why do the American students here seem so excessively boisterous, self-assured, unaware? Or is the difference in me? Am I now more mature, sophisticated, more worldly than before? Or is that just my own wishful thinking?

Paddy watches me, and his eyes sparkle in amusement. An impish grin breaks across this face. A mischievous wee man, dredged up from ancient Celtic legend. A few minutes in, and I begin to recall just how much I've always liked him.

"Ah, Lissa, you are the most un-clichéd person I have ever met." He winks, then goes all serious and gives me another penetrating look. He lights a cigarette, squints at me through a haze of smoke, and says, "I'd love to see what you're writing these days." And once again, my heart opens to him, this dear professor who praised my early scribblings. It was his enthusiasm that landed my best short story on page one, the featured work, of the college literary magazine. Paddy is, for me, that treasured mentor, the one who comes along—if luck or fate would have it—at just the right moment in a young person's life. It was Paddy who, in those ragged days just as my father's life was fading, validated my passion to become a great writer at the very moment my cocooned life was poised to open. It was Paddy who told me I had a gift for writing fiction.

And so, for today's meeting, I've taken the liberty of bringing along the first story I wrote in France, "Arabian Night–Fall 1973." Late last night in my bedroom, I went searching for the portable typewriter Daddy bought me years ago after I graduated from high school. I'm not much of a typist. Didn't take typing in high school. Learned to type from a correspondence course. Anyway, I find the typewriter tucked into a corner beside my dresser, and slowly, making lots of mistakes that I type x's over and retype, I produce a messy, but legible copy of the original, the handwritten version I penned last October in my dorm room on those strange French notebook pages that look like graph paper.

But I fear Paddy won't like my story. It's bolder than anything I've ever written. So, I wait until the very end of our meeting, and then just thrust it across the desk at him, and scurry off like a cowardly mouse before he has a chance to look at it.

CHAPTER THIRTY-SIX

Moving On, Along
History's Slant Rhyme

"As life moves on, memory fades and deconstructs. Recollections of what has happened return filtered, distilled, abrogated, distorted, and embellished." —Lissa's notebook

AND SO, THE WHEEL OF LIFE continues to turn. Even as one cycle ends and the next begins, some conditions persist causing history to echo forward, to repeat itself. History rhymes, but it is a slant rhyme—slightly altered—as the next phase spins out. When on September 8, 1974, President Ford pardons Richard Nixon, some critics accuse the new President of making a "corrupt bargain." But for me, the Watergate Scandal succumbs with a whimper, deflates for now, recedes into the background as my undergrad senior year slips quietly into place.

In the old farmhouse kitchen, I flip the wall calendar forward—September, October, November, December—naïvely unaware of events to come. Just four months from now a new year will begin. The old Regulator clock still hangs over Daddy's chair at the round wooden table where as a small girl I used to sit on his lap to say grace. I have replaced the white oilcloth table cover with a red gingham cloth. But on the wall, the clock remains. When I returned from France, I found the clock's pendulum stopped. Out of duty, I reset the clock, rewound it, and with a touch of my fingers, set the brass pendulum swinging. Now I wind the clock faithfully every week so that time resumes with Daddy's Regulator marking out the hours.

As it turns out, Paddy O'Hara is struck by "Arabian Night–Fall 1973." "It's polished. Mature. Provocative," Paddy tells me. "Like something you'd see published in *Esquire* magazine!" Paddy's excited response validates my writing. His praise for my work gives me the impetus to apply for a graduate degree in imaginative writing, an MFA.

And soon after, on an otherwise routine school day, I walk the second-floor hallway of McCullough Hall, from the English Department's British to its American wing, and notice a flyer, thumbtacked to the Departmental bulletin board, advertising a short fiction contest to be judged in coming weeks.

The idea of a writing contest sets me scribbling, and I come up with a trilogy of short pieces that I think may fill the bill. I'm embarrassed by the rawness of my anecdotes, drawn from very personal experiences growing up. They dig deep. But by weaving the personal into the fictional, these nascent stories make it possible for me to release into the world those feelings my shame has kept buried for so long. The power of writing! How magical it is when naked facts, forbidden actualities that must remain hidden, can be freed, released as words on paper, spilling onto a yellow legal pad, creating images, describing scenes, embodying the voices of characters who can speak my truth for me.

As hours pass and days unfold, I revisit, again and again, Dr. Albert's question to me: "And what is the balance sheet of your scholastic year in France?"

As I take an accounting of this past year, I discover that submitting the base metals of my human nature to the intense heat of experience has resulted in permanent change. I see experience as a form of alchemy, a purification process. In separating gold from dross, it results in gain as well as loss. I attempt to weigh the gains against the losses.

As a writer, I find myself relying more on words than on numbers to gauge the balance. I spell out the pluses and the minuses. The pluses: I have spread awkward wings, dipped a toe into foreign waters, looked deep into eyes watching mine from faces of many colors, cultures, and countries. I have endeavored to overcome my prejudices, my social as well as my physical inhibitions. I have conversed in limited French. Sought to parse out hidden meanings cloaked in foreign tongues. Experienced the heart-thumping exhilaration of international travel. Attempted to open my mind to new perspectives.

I've seen so many facets of the human condition on display. The authentic ones: Beatrix and Danny, comfortable in their own skins. The pretenders: Dorothy, a bundle of inhibitions posturing, pretending; Parapluie, ashamed and hiding.

So many mentors and role models along the way. So many of them are strong women. Beatrix making her merry way through life. Mme Arlette opening the minds of young girls. Trudy launching her engaged American self. Clare, an intrepid bundle of energy, seeking adventure, charging boldly onto life's battlefield, ready to compete, to take on any challenge. Serena, free spirit, seeker of truth. Maggie, feminist, daring to be liberated.

And the men? In my innocence and ignorance, I have fabricated so many complex configurations of manhood. Danny, unashamedly working class, as kind as he is rough and tumble. Dr. Albert, my French professor, conjured as an idealized romantic figure. Georges, my dark mysterious love object. Junjei, sensitive gay poet. Mohammed, the wise prophet, sufferer, and visionary.

So many missed opportunities. Being governess for the children of the mayor of Boudes and his wife. Assuming the role of full-time, paid *assistante d'anglais* in Clermont. Exposing myself to another year or more abroad. Exploring feminism at Femø.

But so many risks actually taken. Spurred on by Clare's daring, I voyaged up a French mountain's arduous flank to learn to ski, only to tumble right back down again. Embarrassed. My short-comings revealed to all the world. With Georges, I exposed my body to new sensations and opened my heart, attempting to savor the headiness of sexual desire, the forbidden mingling of white flesh with brown. In tasting of the apple of wisdom, I forfeited my virginity and was forced to swallow the bitterness that comes when desire is misplaced, misguided, unrequited, and ultimately unfulfilled.

I sacrificed innocence for knowledge. Knowledge of so-called deviant human behaviors that, at first, with Parapluie, seemed wrong, crude, unnatural to me. With Junjei, these same behaviors came filtered through the beauty, tenderness, and sensitivity of a soul blessed with that very otherness. A soul I loved. A soul I lost.

And so, what do I conclude? By returning to Spence, my funder and protector, who seals himself into his own secret universe, have I resigned myself to living a constricted life? Have I resumed a life of bad faith, financially dependent on my brother, shirking my own responsibility for myself?

No! After all of this, despite the setbacks and missteps along the way, despite the successes and failures, the ups and downs, the bumpiness of the road, I believe I am moving toward a life that is potentially—even inexplicably—good, fulfilling, ripe with promise. I vow to continue my explorations, to voyage on, sending out ripples, in ever-widening circles, to mingle with other ripples coming to me from across endless oceans.

However, life goes on, and its daily rhythms interrupt my philosophical deliberations. Dutifully, I attend classes and try to focus on completing my bachelor's degree. As the weeks pass, my attention is diverted by a classmate, a fellow English major who begins to follow me everywhere. His bizarre behavior fascinates me. I learn he is a chess master. He has a brilliant mind that challenges mine. I can feel his complicated personality enmeshing me. His name is Misha. But that's another story.

Acknowledgments

I would like to thank:

Dede Cummings, who welcomed me into the Green Writers Press (GWP) family five years ago, who continues to believe in my writing, and has used her artistic talents to enhance my book with an intriguing cover and elegant design. Dede and GWP have turned my dream of *A Lissa Power Series* into a reality.

Robin MacArthur, who reviewed an early draft of this novel, gave valuable structural advice, and appreciated the protagonist and her story.

Maria Tane and Livia Cohen, two vibrant young GWP editors who provided a thoughtful review, insights, and guidance.

My son, Alex, who read early chapters and never failed to cheer me on along the way.

And as always, my husband, Jack, whose love and support are beyond description.

About the Author

CHRISTINE DAVIS MERRIMAN is a Maryland-based author, a ripening Baby Boomer whose auto-fiction re-counts and re-examines what it has been like, from the inside-out, growing up and living through the second half of the twentieth century and beyond. As a counter-point to reports and commentary from news media and historians, she captures one woman's unique perspec-tive of an era that carries great impact even as it draws to a close. As a former program coordinator/writer for a Johns Hopkins maternal and child health affiliate, Christine traveled extensively in the developing world. She lives with her husband, Jack, in a 1930 farmhouse.

Printed in the USA
CPSIA information can be obtained
at www.ICGtesting.com
JSHW021531011023
49138JS00003B/12